AIF

THE HOUSE OF A HUNDRED *WHISPERS*

BY GRAHAM MASTERTON

The House of a Hundred Whispers

Ghost Virus

THE KATIE MAGUIRE SERIES

White Bones

Broken Angels

Red Light

Taken for Dead

Blood Sisters

Buried

Living Death

Dead Girls Dancing

Dead Men Whistling

Begging to Die

The Last Drop of Blood

THE BEATRICE SCARLET SERIES

Scarlet Widow

The Coven

Graham MASTERTON

THE HOUSE
OF A
HUNDRED
WHISPERS

HEAD
of ZEUS

9 7 5 3 1 2 4 6 8

A catalogue record for this book is available from
the British Library.

ISBN (HB): 9781789544244
ISBN (XTPB): 9781789544251
ISBN (E): 9781789544237

Typeset by Siliconchips Services Ltd UK

Printed and bound in Great Britain by
CPI Group (UK) Ltd, Croydon CR0 4YY

MIX
Paper from
responsible sources
FSC
www.fsc.org   FSC® C020471

Head of Zeus Ltd
First Floor East
5–8 Hardwick Street
London ECIR 4RG

WWW.HEADOFZEUS.COM

For Dawn G Harris, for her sparkling creativity

For Piotr Pocztarek, for my brilliant Polish website

For Hubert Pstrągowski, with all best wishes for a
wonderful life

As he reached the top of the staircase, Herbert heard a door opening. He paused, one hand on the newel post, listening intently. The full moon was shining so brightly through the diamond-patterned windows that there had been no need for him to switch on the landing light.

'Who's there?' he demanded. He was trying to sound authoritative, but he could feel his heart beating against his ribcage and he was breathing hard. After forty-two years he had become inured to the musty old-oak aroma of Allhallows Hall, but he could smell it strongly now, almost as if the house were sweating with anticipation.

He heard a creak of floorboards behind him and he turned around, but there was nobody there, only the dark oil portraits of the Wilmington family that hung around the landing, staring back at him balefully through four hundred years of walnut-coloured varnish.

He hadn't intended to come back into the house, not after dark. Whenever the moon was full, he left Allhallows Hall for three days and went to stay at the Marine Hotel in Paignton. This time, though, he had forgotten to take his accounts book, and he was already two weeks late in filing his annual tax return.

He waited a full minute longer. The only sound was the wind whistling sadly down the chimneys, but he had been living on Dartmoor for so long that he was used to that constant wind, too, and he no longer found it eerie.

'Oh, well,' he said. 'Whoever you are, you miserable reprobate, enjoy your weekend.'

With that, he took the first step downstairs. As he did so, though, he heard footsteps running towards him. Before he could turn around again, he was hit on the bald spot on the back of his head with what felt like a hammer. He pitched forward and tumbled down the first flight of stairs, his arms and legs flailing and his accounts book flying, so that he was surrounded by a shower of bills and receipts and train tickets.

He collided with the panelling halfway down the stairs, striking the left side of his forehead against the skirting board, and jarring his shoulder. Stunned, disorientated, he tried to climb up onto his hands and knees, but he lost his balance and tilted sideways down the second flight of stairs. He fell head over heels, so that he felt and heard his spine crack. When he reached the hallway, he lay with his cheek against the threadbare Agra rug, staring at a faded yellow lotus flower. His heart bumped slower and slower.

Footsteps came slowly down the stairs from the landing, and Herbert's receipts and invoices were kicked aside like dead leaves. A figure appeared at the top of the second flight, silhouetted against the windows. If Herbert's neck hadn't been broken, and he had been able to look up, he would have recognised this figure by his hair, shaved up at the sides and then gelled up into a point like a shiny shark's fin.

The figure stood looking down at Herbert for over a minute, as if he were reluctant to go down to the hallway to check his pulse, but still wanted to be sure that he was never going to get up again.

After a while, though, he climbed back upstairs. If Herbert had still been conscious, he would have heard the squeaking of floorboards as he crossed the landing, and then the soft faraway click as he closed the bedroom door.

2

Rob was sitting in front of his computer, frowning in concentration, when the phone started to warble.

'Vicky!' he called out. 'Can you answer that?'

'I'm right in the middle of grilling Timmy's sausages!'

'And I'm right in the middle of a whiteboard animation! I can't leave it, even for a second!'

Vicky didn't answer, but the phone went on warbling and warbling, and eventually Rob heard her leave the kitchen and walk through to the hallway. She picked up the phone and he could just about make out her saying, 'Really? I see.' After that there was a long pause, and then she said, 'Yes. All right. I'll tell him.'

'Mummy!' wailed Timmy. 'I'm *hungry*!'

'I won't be a moment, Timmy,' said Vicky. She came into the dining room, which Rob was using as his studio. Rob didn't look at her because he was drawing a woman walking a dog down a tree-lined street.

'Who was that?' he asked her. Then, 'Damn.' He had lost his concentration and smudged the dog's tail.

'Margaret Walsh, from Makepeace and Trott.'

'That's my dad's solicitors. What did she want? *Damn!*'

'Your dad's dead.'

Rob kept on staring at the screen for a few moments. Then he sat back and turned around and said, 'He's dead?'

'He was booked into the Marine Hotel in Paignton, that's what she said, but he didn't show up. The hotel rang him but he didn't answer, neither his landline nor his mobile. In the end they called the prison, but the prison couldn't get in touch with him either, so they sent two officers round to his house. His car was still outside in the driveway and his front door was open. They found him lying at the bottom of the stairs.'

Rob turned back to his computer and switched it off. He would have to go back to the beginning with that animation, but he felt too numb to continue.

He had often wondered how he would react when his father died. Sometimes he thought that he would be relieved, even elated. Herbert Russell had been selfish and short-tempered, and a harsh disciplinarian. To give him his due, he had occasionally been capable of unexpected acts of generosity – giving out hampers to his wardens at Christmas or donating money to local charities. But Rob had always suspected that he had been trying to convince both his family and his prison staff that his bullying was beneficial for them, and that one day they would thank him for it. Either that, or he had been trying to make sure he didn't compromise his chances of being admitted to heaven.

'Where is he now, did she tell you?'

'They took him to Derriford Hospital in Plymouth for a post-mortem – what with his death being unexplained and everything. And the police are looking into it. They think he might have been attacked by somebody breaking into the house.'

'Really? He had more than his fair share of enemies, too. Well, you would do, wouldn't you, if you were a prisoner governor. Especially a prison governor like him.'

Vicky came up to him and stroked his wavy brown hair. 'You're not upset, are you? Not just a little bit? He *was* your father.'

Rob reached up and took hold of her hand. 'The only thing that upsets me is remembering how miserable he used to make my mum. And we'll have to have a funeral. And that means getting together with Martin and Katharine, God help us, and Grace. Well, I don't mind Grace, so long as she doesn't bring along that ghastly Portia.'

He stared at his blank computer screen. He could see his ghost reflected in it, and he looked so much more like his late mother than his father. It had been his thirty-ninth birthday only a week ago, but he could have passed for ten years younger. Vicky had once said she had fallen for him because he resembled Lord Byron, with his dark curls and his slightly hooded eyes. For his part, Rob had fallen for Vicky's soulful violet irises and her pale dreamy face and her braided blonde hair, and he had loved the way she wafted around in flowing ankle-length dresses like a Pre-Raphaelite artist's model, although there was nothing soulful or wafty about her personality.

'Did Margaret Walsh tell you if he wanted to be buried or cremated?'

'No.'

'In that case I'll have to wait, won't I?'

'Wait for what?'

'Wait to find out if I can dance a jig on his grave or if I have to flush his ashes down the toilet.'

'You're not that vengeful, Rob, and you know it.'

'Actually, you're right. I'm not. If there was one thing I learned from Dad, it was how to be kind. One smile is more effective than a thousand shouts.'

'*Mummy!*' called Timmy.

3

It was foggy when they arrived in Sampford Spiney, that chilly white Dartmoor fog that can take until midday to clear. Even then it can still be seen clinging in the hollows and over the leats, the narrow channels that were dug across the moor to bring water to forges and farms and houses like Allhallows Hall.

'This place never ceases to give me the creeps,' said Vicky, as the square tower of St Mary's church came into view behind the trees. 'There's never anybody around, and it's so *grey*.'

They had driven for the past five miles along a single-track road with high granite walls on either side, which always made Rob feel claustrophobic. His claustrophobia was only compounded as he turned into the gateway of Allhallows Hall, and there was the manor house in which he had been brought up. After he had left home to go to Worthing College of Art he had never returned, except two years ago to visit his mother when she was dying of cancer. His father had rarely been there when he had visited, and even when he was he had shown little interest in Rob's life or his career.

'It gives *you* the creeps?' he said. And then, 'Thanks, Martin, I love you too.'

His brother Martin's bronze Range Rover was parked diagonally across the narrow drive, so that he had to park his own Honda close to the wall, giving him barely enough space to open his door. He turned around to see if Timmy had woken up yet. Timmy had been sleeping in his car seat all the way from Exeter.

'Timmy? Timmy, we're here!'

Timmy opened his eyes, yawned, and then peered out of the window with a frown. 'Oh... it's Grandpa's house! I thought you said he was dead!'

'He is. But we had to come here to decide what we're going to do with his house.'

'We're not going to live here, are we?'

'No,' put in Vicky, before Rob could answer. 'Definitely not.'

'Well, we'll see,' said Rob.

'What do you mean, "we'll see"? If you think I'm going to live way out here in the middle of nowhere at all, surrounded by a whole lot of bleating sheep, then you are sorely mistaken.'

They climbed out of their car. The fog made Allhallows Hall look even more forbidding than it usually did. A stone arch led from the driveway into a paved courtyard. In the centre of the courtyard stood a fountain with a headless cherub perched on top of it, coated in thick black moss, and the walls all around were lined by rectangular lead planters, every one of which was thick with dead grass and decaying weeds.

'I thought he had gardeners,' said Vicky.

'When he was governor he could get prisoners to do it for him, and he didn't have to pay them. When he retired, he just let it all go to pot.'

The main house had been built in 1567, out of local granite with a slate roof, and it was overgrown with rusty-coloured ivy. Two large granite barns had been added in the seventeenth and nineteenth centuries, which made the courtyard feel even more enclosed. Rob looked up at the window that had once been his bedroom, and it looked smaller and darker and more secretive than he remembered. He used to have nightmares that there was another boy, sleeping under his bed, and he wondered if *that* boy was still there.

'I'm *thirsty*,' said Timmy.

'Timmy, for God's sake, you're always something! If you're not thirsty you're hungry and if you're not hungry you're tired and if you're not tired you're bored.'

'Oh, leave the poor boy alone,' said Vicky. 'It's all right, darling, we'll find you something in a minute. Your grandpa must have left something in the house that you can drink.'

'Apart from Scotch?' said Rob. 'I very much doubt it.'

As they approached the porch, the oak front door opened and Martin appeared, with his wife, Katharine, close behind him.

'Aha! You remembered where the old house was, then!' he said, in his usual trumpeting voice.

Martin was at least three inches taller than Rob, and bulkier, with curly hair that was prematurely grey for a man of forty-four. His cheeks were already rough and red, like Herbert's had been, and his eyes were the same pale citrine colour. He was wearing a maroon cable-knit sweater, which gave him the appearance of a city dweller who assumed that this was what country people usually wore.

Katharine was skinny and petite, with a bleached-blonde angular bob, permanently narrowed eyes, and a sharply pointed nose. She could have been quite pretty if she didn't always look so sour, with her lips tightly pursed. She was wearing a beige Burberry cardigan, which Vicky guessed must have cost at least seven hundred pounds.

'No, I'd totally forgotten where it was,' said Rob. 'That's what satnav's for, isn't it? So that you don't have to remember where you spent your unhappy childhood.'

He was quite aware that Martin was making a sarcastic comment about the fact that he hadn't been down to Sampford Spiney to see their father since their mother's funeral.

Martin came out and gave him a clumsy hug. He smelled of bitter woodsmoke and some expensive aftershave.

'How's it going in the arty-farty business? Making any money yet?'

'Oh... a few bob here and there. I'm doing some animation for Aardman and some dancing leprechauns for Tourism Ireland. How's life in the City?'

'I could say obscenely profitable, but that would be an understatement.'

Katharine and Vicky had exchanged no more than tight, polite smiles. Vicky said, 'Shall we go inside? It's freezing out here and Timmy's thirsty.'

'By all means, come on in. I've just lit the fire in the drawing room. Dad's solicitor should be here in a half hour or so, what's-her-name. And Gracey said she'd be here about eleven. She's catching a taxi from Tiverton.'

They entered the hallway. Its walls were panelled in oak so dark it was almost chocolate-coloured, and its granite floor was covered by the faded red Agra rug that Herbert Russell had been staring at when his heart stopped beating.

Martin turned around at the bottom of the stairs and said, 'They found him right here, apparently. His skull was bashed in, although they don't yet know how that happened. Could have been a burglar, or perhaps he smashed his head on the banisters as he fell downstairs.'

'*Martin*,' Vicky scolded him. 'Not in front of Timmy.'

'Oh, I'm sure Timmy's heard worse than that, haven't you, Timmy? Play Fortnite, do you?'

'Martin, he's only five. We're still on Super Mario.'

Martin led them into the drawing room. It had always been gloomy in here, because the diamond-leaded windows were small for a room this size. Most of the furniture was Jacobean, upholstered in brocade, with barley-twist legs, although a wing chair with a worn leather cushion stood close to the fireplace, and this was where their father always used to sit – 'Herbert's throne', their mother, Florence, used to call it. The fireplace itself was huge, like a granite bridge, with a cast-iron basket that was big enough to roast a hog. Martin had stacked three large ash logs into it, and the kindling underneath them was crackling sharply.

Rob looked around. The same paintings still hung on

the walls – dreary landscapes with overcast skies, mostly of Dartmoor and the Walkham Valley. One of these paintings Rob had always found deeply unsettling. In the middle of a dark grove of trees twenty or thirty figures were gathered, all wearing white robes with pointed hoods, as if they had assembled for some pagan mass, and were waiting for Satan to put in an appearance.

'Let's see if there's anything to drink in the kitchen,' said Vicky, and took Timmy out through the door on the right-hand side of the fireplace. Martin, meanwhile, sat down in Herbert's throne, briskly chafing his hands together, while Katharine perched herself like a kestrel on the arm of the throne beside him.

Rob remained standing on the other side of the fireplace, staring unfocused at the logs as they started to smoulder. He had promised himself that he wouldn't allow Martin to irritate him, but it wasn't easy. Everything Martin said and did got on his nerves – even the way he crossed his legs to expose his yellow socks.

'Bit early for a drink,' said Martin. 'But later on we could shoot down to The Royal Oak at Meavy, if you fancy it.'

'Let's get this house business over first, shall we? How much do you think Allhallows is worth now?'

'Oh… not a lot more than one and a half million, I'd say. Dad couldn't get planning permission for the upper field, could he, and let's face it – this is the arse end of the back of beyond. That's assuming we put it on the market, of course.'

'Why wouldn't we?'

'For a start, one of us might want to live here.'

'Well, Vicky and I certainly don't. Don't tell me that you and Katharine do. You couldn't possibly commute to the City from here, and Petulia's still at school at Tormead, isn't she?'

'Gracey might want to. Who knows?'

'Why would Gracey want to live in an eight-bedroom house with three and a half acres of land to take care of? It's not even as if she and that Portia will ever have any children.'

'They might adopt. Plenty of gay couples do.'

'Get real, Martin. They're going to adopt seven children? Besides, I can't see Portia leaving her job, whatever it is. Gender equality führer for Islington Council, something like that.'

'Well, yes, but it seems a pity to sell it. Historic houses like this are always a good investment. We could let it out, couldn't we?'

'I suppose so. But it would probably cost more to keep it up than we could charge in rent. And we'd have to install smoke alarms and fire doors and God knows what. And I can't think who on earth would want to rent it.'

Vicky came back into the drawing room.

'I found Timmy some tonic water in the fridge. Now he's gone exploring.'

'Martin doesn't think Allhallows is worth more than one-point-five million,' said Rob.

'Only as little as that? Oh, well, I suppose you can't complain. You'll all get five hundred thousand each.'

'Now, hold on,' said Martin. 'We haven't seen Dad's will yet.'

'Surely he's divided his assets equally among the three of you.'

'We don't know yet, do we? Gracey was always the apple of his eye.'

Rob was about to say that, yes, Herbert had doted on Grace; but at the same he had made it no secret that he had favoured Martin over Rob. Maybe it was because Martin had inherited his bullish looks, and had chosen to pursue what he considered to be a 'pragmatic' career in finance. He had shown little or no appreciation of art and had dismissed Rob's paintings and drawings as 'daubs and doodles'. 'Even Van Gogh was poverty-stricken, while he was alive.'

Then again, Herbert's preference for Martin could be connected to a blazing argument that Rob had once overheard from his bedroom window when he was about thirteen years old. His father had shouted at his mother, 'Of course he's nothing like me! And we both know why *that* is!'

He had never dared to ask his mother what his father might have meant.

4

Grace and Portia arrived shortly after eleven. Martin opened the front door for them and helped them to carry in their overnight case, and then he ushered them into the drawing room. Rob immediately had the impression that the two of them had been arguing. Portia was usually holding Grace's hand or wrapping her arm around her waist and giving her affectionate but also proprietorial squeezes – *I love her, and she belongs to me.*

'Good trip?' asked Katharine, still perched on the arm of Herbert's throne.

'Bloody awful, as a matter of fact,' said Portia. 'Some idiot had decided to throw himself in front of a train at Tisbury, and that held us up for over an hour. I honestly don't know why they don't build a special branch line for people to commit suicide, so they don't inconvenience the rest of us.'

'Dad's solicitor will be here in a minute,' said Martin. 'I asked her about funeral arrangements but she said they won't be releasing his body until they've completed the post-mortem, and that's going to take at least another three or four days.'

'I suppose we could hold the funeral service here, at St Mary's,' said Grace. 'I know Dad wasn't religious, but it's close to the prison, isn't it, if any of his old wardens want to pay their respects.'

'Not religious?' said Rob. 'Pff! That's the understatement of the century. The only god he worshipped was himself.'

'I don't know,' said Martin. 'The last time I came down, he seemed to be quite worried about something. He asked me if I thought he'd led a good life.'

'Oh, you mean he was worried that he might go to hell. He gave me that impression, too, once or twice.'

'Any chance of a cup of tea?' asked Grace.

Vicky went up to Grace and gave her a hug and a kiss on the cheek. 'Of course, Grace. How are you? We haven't seen you since that Leonardo exhibition.'

'We've been busy decorating our new flat,' said Portia sharply. 'We've made a start but we still have so much to do.'

In other words, thought Vicky, *don't expect to see us for quite some time in the future, either.*

Like Rob, Grace strongly resembled her mother, but she had more of her father in her than Rob. She was tall and full-figured in her olive faux-fur-collared anorak, with coppery hair and green feline eyes and a squarish chin. Vicky could picture her leading an army of Scottish rebels over the border, wearing an impressive iron breastplate and waving a claymore. In reality, though, she was gentle and softly spoken and shy.

Portia was wearing a brown leather biker jacket and tight black leggings and brown leather boots. She was pretty and slim, with large hazel eyes and a little turned-up nose and short black razor-cut hair. There was no question who was the dominant partner in their relationship. Rob and Vicky knew from experience that if they wanted to invite Grace and Portia to visit them, or even to find out what either of them wanted for Christmas, they had to ask Portia.

'I'll help you,' said Grace, as Vicky went back towards the kitchen. 'Does anybody else want tea?'

Before she had reached the door to the kitchen, it suddenly burst open, and Timmy came out. He stopped and looked at them all in bewilderment.

'What's up, Timmy?' asked Rob. 'You look like you've seen a ghost.'

'Who's that upstairs?'

'There's nobody upstairs, darling,' said Vicky. 'We're the only people here.'

'There had jolly well better *not* be anybody upstairs,' put in Martin, rising from his throne. 'The last thing we want is squatters.'

'You saw somebody?' said Rob. 'What did they look like?'

'I didn't see them. Only heard them.'

'Oh yes? And where were they?'

'In one of the rooms, right down at the end, by the coloured window.'

Martin turned around and said to the rest of them, loudly, 'He must mean the stained-glass window,' as if none of them could guess.

'I was looking through the different-coloured glass, so

that the garden went red, and then it went blue, and then it went yellow.'

'And that's when you heard them? How did you know it was more than one? What – were they talking?'

Timmy nodded. Rob had rarely seen him look so serious, with his wide eyes and that little sprig of hair sticking up at the back of his head.

'Did you hear what they were saying?'

Timmy said, 'No. I couldn't. I pressed my ear up against the door, but they were whispering.'

Martin turned to Rob. 'Right! I think we'd better take a shufti, don't you, Rob. Can't have uninvited guests!'

Rob and Martin climbed the stairs to the first-floor landing. Rob hadn't been up here since the day he left for art college, and he had forgotten how low the ceilings were, and how the floorboards creaked, and how strongly the corridors smelled of oak and wood polish and dried-out horse-hair plaster.

Two corridors led off from the landing: one directly ahead of them, with three bedroom doors on the left-hand side and the large stained-glass window at the end. The other led off to the right, with another five bedroom doors and a door at the end to the bathroom.

'I still find it hard to believe that we'll never see Dad again,' said Rob, pausing at the top of the stairs. 'I keep thinking that at any minute I'm going to hear him shouting up at us to stop making so much bloody noise up here.'

'I think a lot of people misjudged him,' said Martin.

'He meant well. He didn't have such an easy childhood himself.'

'Just because he didn't have an easy childhood himself didn't mean that he had to take it out on us. Or Mum, God bless her.'

'Well, let's go and see if we've got any unwelcome visitors, shall we?'

They walked along the corridor towards the stained-glass window, and Martin opened each of the first two bedroom doors. They had dark oak dados all around them, and stained-glass windows, too, although these were much smaller and glazed with diamond patterns in red and yellow and green. Ventilation and a little more illumination came from skylights in their sloping ceilings; both were streaked grey with lichen and bird droppings.

There was nobody in either bedroom, only antique beds with faded cotton quilts, and bedside tables with dusty lamps on them.

'*Shh*,' said Martin, cupping his hand to his ear. 'Do you hear any whispering?'

They waited in silence, their faces lit up by the harlequin patterns of coloured light shining through the stained glass.

The window depicted Walkham Valley under a dark-blue sky, with a leat running through it. Beside the leat, with his back turned and his arms spread wide, was an impossibly tall man wearing a long black cloak with a high collar turned up. All around him, bristling black hounds were standing in a circle on their hind legs, their fangs bared and their red tongues hanging out.

According to the previous owner of Allhallows Hall,

the man in the black cloak was Old Dewer, which was the Dartmoor name for the Devil. The story went that on certain nights of the year, Old Dewer would mount a huge black horse and take his pack of ferocious hounds out hunting across the moor, searching for young women who hadn't been able to reach home before it grew dark.

Whether it was true or not, the window had apparently been installed to make Old Dewer believe that he was respected by the owners of this house, and so that he wouldn't come snuffling around it looking for souls to steal, especially the souls of their daughters.

'I'll bet you it was the wind that Timmy heard,' said Martin. 'Or maybe the plumbing. The front and the back doors were both locked when we got here, and the burglar alarm was still on. I can't see how anybody could have got in.'

'Martin, there's no wind. And the plumbing has never sounded like whispering. It sounds more like somebody slaughtering a pig.'

Martin opened the last door. There was no bed in here, only an assortment of half a dozen spare chairs, some of them stacked on top of each other, and a wine table crowded with tarnished brass candlesticks and inkwells, all of which were draped with dusty spiderwebs.

Under the window there was an oak window seat, with a hinged lid covered in cracked green leather. Rob went over and lifted the lid. It was full of nothing but legal documents, all rolled up and tied around with faded red ribbons.

'See? Nobody here. And it doesn't look as if Dad's been in here for years.'

'Oh, well. Maybe Timmy imagined it. He does have quite an imagination. He won a prize at school for a story he wrote about a bad egg that fell in love with a bullying centipede.'

'Takes after his father then. Always making things up.'

Martin closed the door. But as soon as they started to walk back along the corridor, Rob heard what sounded like a man's voice, talking in an urgent whisper.

'Stop, Martin! No, *stop*! Can you hear that?'

Martin stopped, and listened.

'No. What?'

'It was definitely somebody whispering.'

Martin waited a few moments longer, but then he said, 'No. I can't hear anything.'

'Really. I'm sure it was somebody whispering.'

'Did you hear what they said?'

'No. They weren't speaking loud enough. But they sounded – I don't know – *panicky*.'

'Oh, come on, Rob. I think you and Timmy have both caught a dose of Allhallows-itis. You remember that old woman who used to live across at Wormold's Farm? She used to tell us this house could drive anybody who lived in it "maze as a brush".'

'You mean old Mrs Damerell. She was a couple of sausage rolls short of a picnic herself.'

Downstairs, they heard knocking at the front door.

'Come on,' said Martin. 'That'll be Dad's solicitor. Let's go down and find out who's inherited what.'

Rob followed him downstairs. 'Knowing my luck, it'll be the headless cherub.'

5

When they came downstairs, they found that the drawing room was hazy with acrid smoke. The logs in the fire were well alight now, but it looked as if the chimney was blocked. Katharine was flapping her hand in front of her face and Timmy was coughing.

'God, that's Dad all over,' said Rob. 'Too tight to have the chimneys swept.'

'I can't *breathe*!' Timmy squeaked.

'Open the windows, will you, Rob,' said Martin. 'I'll go and let Ms What's-her-name in.'

The smoke was billowing out of the fireplace, thicker and thicker. Rob managed to force all the windows open, even though some of them were jammed with decades of rust and dirt, and he had to shake them several times before they gave way.

'We'll meet in the library!' Martin called out.

'Let me put this bloody fire out first!' Rob called back.

He went through to the kitchen. The last time it had been modernised was in 1911, and it still had a monstrous black iron range and reddish marble worktops and high copper taps over the sink. Long-handled ladles and whisks and spatulas were hanging in a row from the ceiling, all tangled together with cobwebs.

Rob found a grimy white plastic bowl in the bottom of the sink and poured water into it. The taps juddered and knocked because there was air trapped in the pipes, and as usual the plumbing started to groan like an animal in pain. Once the bowl was full, he carried it into the drawing room and tipped it slowly over the fire. The logs sizzled and poured out smoke and when Rob breathed in he felt that he was going to choke, but at last the fire was out. With all the windows open, a chilly draught gradually cleared all of the haze away in a series of shudders, although the drawing room still smelled strongly of charred wood.

Rob dropped the plastic bowl back into the sink and then went through to the library, which was on the left-hand side of the hallway. It was less than half the size of the drawing room, with bookshelves on two sides and a small stone fireplace. The window overlooked what had once been the walled kitchen garden, but which was now a jungle of dead thistles and drooping grass.

Margaret Walsh was already sitting at the oak writing table in the middle of the library, with a leather-bound folder in front of her. She was a sturdy, big-bosomed woman in a red tweed suit with red and white feathers in her trilby hat. She looked as if she had dressed to go out on the moor, shooting grouse.

Grace and Portia were sitting on the two-seat leather sofa next to the fireplace, holding hands, so whatever they had been arguing about, they seemed to have made up.

Vicky sat in an upright chair by the window, while Rob and Martin remained standing. Vicky had buttoned up Timmy's yellow jacket again and sent him out to play, and Rob could see him in the kitchen garden, swishing a stick from side to side to knock the heads off dead thistles.

'Well, you're all here, good,' said Margaret Walsh, and opened up the folder. 'Before I go into detail, I have to tell you that your father changed his will two and a half years ago, and changed it quite radically.'

'Don't tell me he left everything to the dogs' home,' said Rob.

'No, not exactly. He had twenty-eight thousand pounds left in his Barclay's Bank deposit account, but an overdraft of three thousand seven hundred in his current account at Lloyd's. He also had considerable debts. He owed approximately thirteen thousand to HMRC, six thousand three hundred to Ladbrokes the bookmakers and four thousand two hundred and fifty to Paddy Power.'

Martin had been counting in his head. 'You must be joking. That leaves only seven hundred and fifty pounds. Two hundred and fifty each. You can't even buy lunch at The Ivy for that.'

'The very last time I saw him, he swore *blind* to me that he'd given up gambling,' said Grace. Portia gave her a quick sympathetic hug.

'You still have the house to share between you, don't you?' said Katharine. 'If you can find the right buyer, you may be able to sell it for quite a bit more than a million and a half.'

'Well, not exactly, I'm afraid,' said Margaret Walsh,

turning over a page in her folder. 'Originally, Allhallows Hall was going to be divided equally between the three of you – Martin, Rob and Grace. But when Mr Russell altered his will, he specified that after his death it should be held in trust.'

'Held in *trust*?' Martin retorted. 'Held in trust by whom? And how long for?'

'Held in trust equally by the three of you for thirteen years. During this time you will be equally responsible for its maintenance, repair, council tax and utility bills and so forth. Should any of you pass away before the thirteen years is up, the surviving trustees will continue to bear the costs until the trust comes to an end.'

'But what happens when the trust comes to an end?' asked Rob. 'Can we sell the house then?'

'When the trust closes, the freehold of the house passes to your son, Timothy, who by then will have reached eighteen years old.'

'To *Timmy*?' Martin demanded, almost shouting. 'What about me? What about my daughter Petulia? And what about Grace, come to that?'

'I'm sorry, Mr Russell,' said Margaret Walsh. 'That is what your father stipulated in his will, and I've already drafted the trust instrument.'

'But this is *absurd*,' Martin protested. 'Why should we be expected to cover all of the expense of keeping the house up when we're going to get no benefit out of it? And why in God's name did Dad decide that he was giving it to Timmy and not share it out between all of us?'

'I'm sorry, Mr Russell, but that's what it says in his will.

The only circumstance in which the title to the freehold would be shared between you is if Timothy were to pass away before his eighteenth birthday.'

'Fat chance of that happening. Not unless we club together and buy him a car when he's old enough to drive and send him off to Postbridge.'

'Oh, *Martin*,' said Grace. She knew he was referring to the local story about the Hairy Hands – a ghostly force that was supposed to seize control of drivers' steering wheels as they sped through Postbridge, which was only thirteen miles away. It was said to cause them to veer wildly off the road, crash into a wall, and die.

'I don't care,' Martin told her. 'Dad always told me that when he died he was going to bequeath Allhallows equally between me and Rob and Gracey. In fact, he even confirmed it to me in a letter, and I believe I still have that letter somewhere. If I can find it I'm going to contest this will, and even if I can't find it I'm going to contest it.'

'It does seem a bit odd, I'll admit,' said Rob.

'A bit *odd*? What do you mean, a bit odd? It's bloody ridiculous. If you ask me, Dad was losing his marbles. I mean – did he tell you *why* he wanted to change his will? Did he appear *compos mentis*? I can't understand it. He never even seemed to like Timmy very much. In fact, he always seemed to regard him as nothing but a flaming nuisance.'

Outside, Rob could see that it was starting to rain, and that the wind had started to rise. He went over and opened the window and called out to Timmy to come inside. Timmy threw his stick away and came stamping his way back up the weedy garden path.

'What about the contents?' asked Grace. 'The paintings, and the furniture? And there's at least two antique dinner services and two canteens of solid silver cutlery.'

'Yes,' put in Martin. 'The paintings alone are worth a fair bit. That one with all the people in hoods – it's not signed but it's supposed to be a Northcote. If it is, it's worth thousands. Tens of thousands, even.'

'Your father specifically says that all the contents of the house should be kept intact, and that nothing should be separately sold off.'

'What about renting? That would help to cover the cost of its council tax and its upkeep.'

'As trustees, any of you are free to live here, or use it as a holiday home. But under the terms of the trust you are not permitted to rent it to anybody outside the family. Your father was adamant about that.'

They heard the kitchen door bang as Timmy came in. 'That does it,' said Martin. 'I'm definitely going to talk to my solicitor about this. *And* I'm going to talk to Dad's doctor. I'm sure he must have been going doolally.'

'I can't comment on that,' said Margaret Walsh. 'When your father changed his will, his affairs were being handled by Walter Besley, our senior partner, but he's retired now. I took over his affairs only nine months ago.'

'In that case I'll go and talk to him, too. Dad *must* have been losing it. I mean, honestly, this will makes no sense at all. I'm certainly not going to pay for the upkeep of a property I'm never going to own.'

'Well, even though I'm Timmy's father, I have to confess that I agree with you,' said Rob. 'I'm not ashamed to admit that I could use the money right now, even if it's only a third of the selling price. And, like you say, there's the contents. The paintings and so forth. And even the furniture must be worth a fair amount. They're all genuine antiques.'

Margaret Walsh said, 'I've brought a copy of the will for each of you. Once you've had the chance to read it through I'll apply for probate, identify your father's assets and sort out any liabilities and inheritance tax and whatnot. Let me know in due course if you decide to contest the will, but of course it could be a very long-drawn-out procedure. And expensive, too.'

'I'm beginning to wonder why we bothered to come,' said Martin. 'Do you know what time we had to set out this morning? Twenty past five.'

Rob said, 'Listen... why don't we all go down to The Royal Oak, like you suggested, and talk this over somewhere warm and comfortable?'

Margaret Walsh handed out copies of Herbert Russell's will, and then they all left the library. Rob went into the drawing room to close all the windows and to see if Timmy was there, but there was no sign of him. He went into the kitchen, but Timmy wasn't there, either.

'Timmy!' he called out, going back into the hallway. 'Timmy, we're going out now for something to drink and something to eat!'

There was no answer, so Rob went to the bottom of the stairs and called out again. 'Timmy! We're all going out now! Come on down!'

He waited, and then he turned to the rest of the family, who were all putting their coats on.

GRAHAM MASTERTON

'He didn't go back out again, did he?'

'I didn't hear him,' said Grace.

Rob went back into the library and looked out into the kitchen garden. Timmy's stick was still lying on the path, but there was no Timmy.

'He must be upstairs. He's probably shut himself in one of the bedrooms and he just can't hear me.'

Rob climbed the stairs to the landing. Even up here, it still smelled of woodsmoke. He opened the doors to the three bedrooms that led to the stained-glass window, but Timmy wasn't in any of them.

'Timmy!' he shouted. 'Come on, Tim-tim, this isn't funny! We're going out!'

He went along the corridor to the bathroom, opening one door after another, and leaving them open. He even looked under the beds, and he couldn't help thinking about the sniggering boy that he had always imagined was hiding under his own bed. He went into the bathroom, too, with its huge antiquated bathtub, on lion's-claw feet. It was chilly in there. The rain was pattering against the frosted-glass window, and a tap was dripping, but those were the only sounds, and Timmy wasn't there.

Rob went back and searched each of the eight bedrooms again, opening up the tall oak wardrobes and even pulling out the drawers from the tallboy dressers. Some drawers were filled with sweaters and socks and wrinkled underwear. Some were empty. But Timmy was hiding in none of them.

'Any luck, Rob?' Martin called out, from the hallway.

Rob went to the top of the staircase, the same place

where Herbert had been standing when he was struck on the back of the head.

'No,' he said, his throat clogged so that he spoke in not much more than a whisper. Then, louder, so that Martin could hear him, 'No! I can't think where he's gone!'

6

They went outside into the fine grey drizzle.

Margaret Walsh said, 'I'm sorry... I'd help you look for him, but I have to meet a client in Plymouth at half past one.'

'That's okay, he'll be around somewhere,' said Vicky. 'He's probably hiding in one of the barns to scare us. He's always been a mischief.'

Rob crossed the courtyard to the smaller barn. The wide oak door was fastened with a rusty padlock, and the only windows in it were four narrow slits that were at least five metres high. Timmy loved Spiderman but there was no way he could have climbed all the way up that sheer granite wall.

'Timmy!' Rob called out again. 'Tim-tim, this isn't funny any more! Come on out!'

He went across to the larger barn. Although the door had no padlock on it, its hinges had collapsed years ago, so that it had dropped down to the ground and couldn't be shifted except with enormous effort. However, there was a narrow triangular gap in between the side of the door and the doorpost, and it was just possible that Timmy could have squeezed through it.

'Give me a hand here, Martin,' said Rob. The two of them rammed their shoulders against the door and kicked it, and at last they managed to force it half-open. It was dark inside, because the only two windows had been covered, for some reason, with hessian sacking. The whole barn smelled of mouldering hay.

'Timmy, are you in here? Come on out, if you are. You're not in trouble, son, just come out.'

Rob took out his phone and switched on the flashlight. He shone the beam from one side of the barn to the other, but apart from the dank heaps of hay, all he could see was a stack of plastic milk crates full of empty whisky bottles, a few gardening tools and the skeleton of an old Scott motorcycle.

'No, not in here. He must be hiding in the garden somewhere. Maybe the garden shed.'

They left the barn and walked around the side of the house. The shed was at the end of the kitchen garden, but, like the smaller barn, its door was padlocked. Rob peered in through the dusty window, but he could see only spades and forks and shelves with tins of weedkiller.

'So where the hell *is* he?' said Martin. It was beginning to rain harder now, and he turned up the collar of his coat. 'Don't tell me he's run off into the field.'

Vicky joined them. 'Rob – I'm really worried now. I know he's a little devil, but this is not like him at all. He would have jumped out and said "boo!" by now.'

They went through the gate of the kitchen garden and into the field. From the back of the house the field rose steeply uphill and on a clear day the sinister granite peak of Pew Tor could be seen over the hedgerows. When he and Florence had first moved to Allhallows Hall, Herbert Russell had arranged with a local farmer for sheep to graze in this field, but some kind of obscure argument had blown up between him and the farmer and now it was nothing but overgrown grass and Japanese knotweed and brambles.

Rob had never found out what the argument was, but knowing his father it was probably something petty. Perhaps he had imagined that the sheep were looking at him disrespectfully.

'No... I can't see Timmy anywhere here,' said Martin, shielding his eyes with his hand. 'He couldn't have gone all that far, could he, and he's wearing that bright yellow jacket.'

'But that's the thing,' said Vicky. 'He took his jacket off when he came inside, and left it in the hallway. He's out here in all this rain with nothing but his jumper.'

'I think we should search the house one more time,' said Rob. 'There's so many nooks and crannies. He's probably hiding in the larder or one of the cupboards in the library and giggling his head off because we can't find him.'

They went back into the house, wiping their muddy shoes on the front doormat.

'Timmy!' Rob shouted, and Vicky echoed, 'Timmy! Come on out! You won't have ice cream with your lunch if you don't come on out!'

They waited for a few moments, but there was utter

silence. The longcase clock in the hallway had probably wound down days ago, because they couldn't hear the endless weary ticking that had been an integral part of their lives at Allhallows Hall.

'*Timmy! Can you hear us?*' Rob bellowed, cupping his hands around his mouth. '*Timmy!*' There was still no answer.

'Well, let's go through the house, top to bottom,' said Martin. 'If you girls search the downstairs, Rob and I will take the upstairs again. We'd better go up into the attic, too, Rob, although I can't see how Timmy could have managed to climb up there, not without the ladder.'

'Oh God,' said Vicky, taking hold of Rob's hand. She had tears on her eyelashes. 'Please don't let anything terrible have happened to him.'

They separated, with Vicky and Katharine going back into the library and Grace and Portia making their way round to the kitchen.

In the kitchen, Grace opened the doors of the range and peered into the ovens. She remembered Herbert threatening to roast her brothers alive if they misbehaved, and she wondered if Rob had told Timmy about it. But the ovens were cold and empty and crusted with years of burnt-on food. Grace doubted if their father had cooked anything since their mother had died.

Portia was looking in the larder. The middle shelf was crowded with glass jars of herbs and spices – coriander and chives and cayenne pepper. She picked one up and read the label. 'Best before 09/08/07.' Then she picked up a half-empty bottle of Heinz tomato ketchup. 'Best before

17/11/09. Wow. It's like *everything's* antique in this house, Gracey. Even the food.'

They opened every cupboard in the kitchen, even the eye-level cupboards around the walls, which were stacked with dinner plates and mugs. A narrow scullery led off the kitchen, its granite floor heaped with Herbert Russell's muddy old walking boots. There was a small space under the sink, covered by a soiled green seersucker curtain. Grace tugged it back but there was nothing behind it except for a sink plunger and a bottle of Harpic drain cleaner.

'If you ask me, your little nephew's taken himself off for a walk somewhere,' said Portia.

'In this weather?'

'I climbed out of my bedroom window once in the middle of the night and went for a walk in a thunderstorm. Barefoot, and wearing nothing but pyjamas. I was only about seven. I was soaking, but I loved it.'

'But that's just like you. Timmy's naughty sometimes, but he's not bonkers.'

Portia narrowed her eyes in mock annoyance. 'Who are *you* calling bonkers? After what you did with that courgette?'

'I was drunk. I can't even remember.'

'Maybe *you* can't, darling, but I'll never forget it for as long as I live.'

In the library, Vicky and Katharine opened all the cupboards under the bookshelves. Most of them were filled with old copies of the *Prison Service Journal*, as well as photograph albums with mock-crocodile covers and accounts books bulging with receipts. In one of the cupboards, Vicky found a black-and-white photograph of Rob's mother in a silver frame, face down. The glass was smashed, so that it looked as if she were staring out from behind a spiderweb.

Katharine pulled out some of the books on the shelves to check behind them. 'Perhaps there's a secret compartment. You see them in some of those spy films, don't you?'

'I can't really see Timmy having the strength to pull out a whole bookcase, Katharine.'

'You never know. There might be a secret mechanism.'

'Even if there was, how would Timmy have found out about it?'

'All right. There's no need to get tetchy.'

'I'm not being tetchy, Katharine. My son's disappeared and I'm going out of my mind with worry.'

'Oh, come on, Vicky. He'll be all right. If he's not hiding in the house, he's probably gone off exploring.'

'There's nothing to explore around here. Only the church, and the graveyard.'

'You know what kids are like. They find everything fascinating.'

'Well, yes. But not in this weather.'

Upstairs, Rob and Martin had checked every bedroom again, just in case Timmy had been hiding under a quilt or behind a door and they had somehow managed to miss him. Then they dragged out the heavy old wooden stepladder and positioned it under the trapdoor in the corridor ceiling that gave access to the attic.

'There's no way he could have got himself up there,'

said Rob. 'What did he do – fly? And then shut the door behind him?'

'Of course he couldn't,' Martin agreed. 'But you know what they say about leaving no stone unturned. You wouldn't want to go up there in ten years' time and find his skeleton.'

'Martin, for Christ's sake.'

'I know. Sorry. But you know what I'm trying to say. Better to be sure now than sorry later.'

Rob climbed up the stepladder first. One of the cords that held its legs together had frayed and broken, and the stepladder swayed and creaked with every step. He pushed up the trapdoor so that it fell sideways with a clatter, and immediately he smelled stale air and mould. He took out his phone and switched on the flashlight, pointing it left and right.

'What's it like up there?' asked Martin.

'Musty. I doubt if anyone's been up here in years.'

Rob heaved himself up through the trapdoor and stood up. The attic floor was completely boarded over, and the rafters had been covered with plasterboard, stained with brown patches of damp. There was a light switch on the joist next to the trapdoor, and he turned on the two naked bulbs that hung from the ceiling. Martin pulled himself up after him, grunting with effort.

'God almighty. I haven't been up here since I was about twelve.'

At one end of the attic stood the rusty iron water tank and all the noisy ancient plumbing, groaning and shuddering as usual. But at the opposite end Rob was surprised to see at least a dozen suitcases, chaotically heaped up one on top of the other, as well as three or four khaki haversacks and two bulging duffel bags.

'What the hell is that lot?' asked Martin. 'I don't remember seeing them before. All that used to be up here was our old toys and Gracey's cot.'

Rob went over to the pile of suitcases. Some of them were leather and looked expensive, even though they were scratched and battered. All of them carried luggage labels around their handles, and he turned one over and read it.

Ronald May, HMP Dartmoor, Tavistock Road, Princetown, Yelverton PL20 6RR.

He picked up another label. This one carried the name *Mohammed Baqri*. The next belonged to *Thomas Friend*. Yet another belonged to *Lukasz Sokolowski*.

'These are all prisoners' belongings. What are they doing up here in Dad's attic?'

He picked up one of the suitcases, laid it down on the attic floor and clicked open the catches. When he lifted the lid, he found that it was filled with neatly folded clothes: a navy-blue jacket, at least five shirts of different colours, socks and underpants. There was even a black leather washbag, with a razor and a toothbrush and a Gillette stick deodorant inside it.

He opened up another suitcase, and another. They were all filled with men's clothes. One of them had two pairs of good-quality leather shoes in it, wrapped in tissue paper.

'I don't get this at all. It looks like these prisoners were all packed up to go away somewhere. But if they didn't go away, where did they go? Back to the prison? But if that's where they went, why did they leave their suitcases here?'

'We can easily check with the prison,' said Martin. 'If they *did* go back, maybe some of them are still banged up there, and they can throw some light on why Dad kept their stuff.'

Rob looked around. 'Meanwhile, there's no sign of Timmy up here. We need to go back down and start searching around the village. I only hope he hasn't gone anywhere near the well.'

'That's covered over, isn't it?'

'Yes, but he was really fascinated by it, the last time we brought him down here, just before Mum died. He'd been reading some fairy tale and he kept asking if trolls lived down there.'

7

They buttoned up their raincoats and lifted the three large umbrellas out of the elephant's-foot umbrella stand by the front door. The smoke had cleared out of the drawing room now so that Rob could close all the windows, but the house was so cold that they were stamping their feet and rubbing their hands together to keep warm.

'First priority after we find Timmy is to call a chimney sweep,' said Martin. 'And maybe go into Yelverton and buy ourselves a couple of electric heaters.'

They left the house, opening up their umbrellas, and walked along the driveway to the steep winding road that led up to St Mary's church and the village. The wind had risen and it was drizzling almost horizontally now. Vicky's umbrella was blown inside out with a loud clap.

'I'm trying to think like Timmy,' said Rob, as he helped her to bend the spokes back again. 'He might have gone to the well, but then again he might have gone to the churchyard. You remember how interested he was in some of the statues, and the carvings on the gravestones. You know what boys of that age are like – full of morbid curiosity.'

'I'm praying that you're right, Rob. But I still think he would rather have stayed indoors, playing Angry Birds on your phone.'

'Look – if he's not in the village, I'll call the police. It starts getting dark by four, so we need to find him before then.'

They reached the intersection of three narrow lanes and the triangular green in between them. Four large houses stood on one side of the green, and two on another, and that constituted the 'village'. The houses looked empty. Their front gardens were overgrown, their fences were broken, and their walls were streaked with damp. The well stood in the centre of the green, with a mossy tiled roof. Its borehole had been covered over years ago with a heavy oak lid, although an old wooden pail still rested on top of it, with a rope attached to its handle.

'He couldn't have fallen down there,' said Rob. 'He wouldn't have been strong enough to pick up that lid, for starters, and even if he had, he couldn't have put that bucket back on top of it, could he?' He didn't allow himself to think that some abductor might have dropped Timmy down the well, and replaced the pail afterwards. That was Grimms' fairy-tale stuff.

'All the same,' said Martin. He rolled the pail off to one side, and then he heaved the lid up high enough for them to be able to peer down inside the shaft. Rob shone his flashlight down it, but all they could see was the mass of tangled roots that had grown between the brickwork, and the glint of water, at least twenty metres below. The air smelled like bad breath. But there were no trolls, and no Timmy.

Martin lowered the lid. 'Right, then. The churchyard.'

The six of them crossed the green and went through the lychgate that led into the churchyard. The church itself was built of granite, with a tall square tower at its western end, dappled with grey and orange lichen. The graveyard sloped steeply downhill, with twenty or thirty gravestones leaning at various awkward angles, as well as two grand Victorian mausoleums closer to the church, one of them for several members of the Wilmington family.

Apart from the pattering of the rain on their umbrellas, the churchyard was silent. Rob hesitated for a moment, and then shouted out, 'Timmy! Timmy! Can you hear me, Timmy?'

His voice sounded strangely flat, and there was no echo. Neither was there any reply.

Vicky said, 'We'll go and look inside the church.'

Together, she and Katharine walked along the path that led to the church doorway, followed by Grace and Portia. The crunching of their shoes on the gravel was curiously muffled. Meanwhile, Rob and Martin made their way between the graves. Rob had a chilling premonition of finding Timmy lying between the kerbstones in front of one of the graves, white-faced, his jumper soaking wet, his hands laced together.

Martin stopped and read out the inscription on one of the memorials. '*Lieutenant William Staines, 1817. Resurgant.* What do you think that means?'

'*Resurgant*? That means "I shall rise again",' said Rob.

'Oh. I was never any good at Latin, not like you. So you're going to rise again, are you, Lieutenant Staines? I won't hold my breath.'

He moved along to the next memorial. '*Elizabeth Chase, 1864. In Coelo Quies.*'

Rob stopped beside him. 'Roughly translated, that means "Peace in Heaven".'

'She'll be lucky. What with all those angels sitting on clouds and strumming away at their harps.'

Vicky and Katharine came back out of the church. Vicky shook her head. 'We looked everywhere,' she called out. 'Even the toilet in the vestry.'

The graves along the second row were obviously much older – some so old that their inscriptions had been either weathered away or completely obscured by lichen. But at the end of the row there was a larger headstone with an inscription that was still mostly readable.

'*Matthew Carver*, can't read the date, but it looks like sixteen-something. *Stat adhuc tempus.* That's something about time, isn't it?'

'What?' said Rob. He was growing increasingly stressed, his eyes darting all around the graveyard for any sign of Timmy.

'*Tempus.* That's something about time, isn't it? Like *tempus fugit.*'

Rob turned around and frowned at the headstone. '"Time stands still", that's what it means.'

Vicky and the other three women, meanwhile, had been looking into the two mausoleums and searching the weedy overgrown area at the back of the church. As Rob and Martin reached the end of the third row of gravestones, Vicky came back up the path in tears, and Rob went across to hug her.

'Oh God,' she wept. 'Where is he? Please don't let him be hurt.'

'Come on, darling, he'll be all right. He's just wandered off somewhere and got himself lost. He's definitely not here, though. I'm going to call the police.'

He took out his phone and dialled 999, and the emergency operator answered immediately.

'Our five-year-old son's gone missing around Sampford Spiney. We've been searching for over an hour but we still can't find him. We're getting seriously worried.'

'Hold on a moment, sir, and I'll put you through to Crownhill police station.'

As he waited to be connected, Rob looked down to the lower end of the graveyard, where the granite wall was overshadowed by oak trees. At first he couldn't be sure, but when he lifted his hand to shield his eyes from the drizzle, he thought he could make out a figure standing there, wearing a grey overcoat and a trilby hat with a wide drooping brim, similar to the hat their father used to wear when he let his two Staffordshire bull terriers, Max and Bullet, out of their kennels and took them walking on the moors. He was about to point out the figure to Martin when a voice said, 'Crownhill police, how can I help you?'

Quickly, trying not to sound panicky, he told the duty sergeant that Timmy had disappeared and that they had searched for him everywhere they could think of, without success. Next to him, Vicky kept her hand pressed over her mouth to stop herself from sobbing out loud.

When he looked down to the end of the graveyard again, the figure had gone. Maybe his stress had led him to imagine it. The wind was blowing the trees so that every now and then a gap appeared between them that resembled a human shape.

'The police should be here in less than twenty minutes,' he announced. 'We'd better get back to the house to meet them.'

8

The rain had cleared away by the time the police arrived at Allhallows Hall, although a blustery wind was still blowing and a silvery sun kept playing hide-and-seek behind the clouds.

Two squad cars were parked in the driveway, as well as a van with three officers in dark-blue overalls and a dog handler with an Alsatian.

'Well, you've come out in force,' said Martin, as he opened the front door for them.

'Sergeant Billings,' said the leading officer, in a strong Devon brogue. He was stocky and short, with a buzz cut that was going grey at the sides, and a broken nose like a jug handle. 'When a young person goes missing, the sooner we start looking for them the better. 'Specially this time of year, when it gets dark so early.'

'Come in,' said Rob. 'It's our son, Timmy, who's missing. He's only five but he's quite grown-up and independent for his age.'

'We've searched the whole damned house from top to bottom, *and* the church,' put in Martin. 'We've even looked down the well, God help us. And my good lady and I were supposed to be heading back to London by three.'

'Has he ever gone missing before? Did you have an argument with him, or tell him off for something?'

Rob shook his head. 'Never, and no. We don't have to read him the riot act very often, but when we do, usually he sulks and shuts himself in his bedroom and plays video games. But that never lasts for long. He's not the kind of kid who bears grudges, especially when it's teatime and there's beans on toast.'

'Do you have a picture of him?'

Rob dug his wallet out of the back pocket of his jeans and took out the latest photograph, which he had taken when they were on holiday in Portugal.

'Thanks. And do you have an item of his clothing for the dog to take a sniff at?'

'Here,' said Vicky, picking up Timmy's yellow jacket from the back of the chair in the hallway.

Sergeant Billings turned around and called out, 'Jones! Do you want to fetch Axel in here?'

A lanky ginger-haired dog handler came across the courtyard with his Alsatian. At first the dog was eagerly trotting forward with his tongue hanging out like a pink silk cravat, but as it neared the front door it slowed down, and when it reached the first step of the porch it stopped. Its ears and its tail stood up erect and its fur bristled as if it had been electrocuted.

'Axel! Come on, boy!' snapped its handler, tugging at his lead. He managed to drag the dog a few more inches forward, but almost immediately the dog scrabbled its claws on the granite steps and pulled back again.

'Axel! What the flaming Nora's the matter with you? Come on, boy! *Now!*'

'Get your skates on, Derek!' called Sergeant Billings. 'We haven't got all day! We've got a little lad to find before it gets dark!'

Axel's handler pulled at the dog's lead again and again, but it still refused to move.

'It's no use, sarge! He won't budge! Something's spooked him!'

'What?'

'Something's frightened him. I don't know what. He's never done this to me before.'

'Can't you give him a dog biscuit or something?'

'He's scared shitless, sarge. A dog biscuit's not going to make any difference.'

Sergeant Billings turned back to Vicky. 'Well, I don't know. For some reason the dog doesn't want to come into the house. If you can hand me that jacket, I'll take it outside and see if he'll sniff at it there.'

Vicky gave him Timmy's jacket and he took it over to the dog handler, who had retreated with his dog now to stand beside the headless cherub. The dog handler bunched it up and held it under the dog's nose.

'Okay,' said the dog handler. 'He's got that now.'

'Take a look around the garden first,' Sergeant Billings told him. 'Meantime, we'll give the house another search.'

'I can tell you, sergeant, we went over it with a fine-tooth comb,' said Martin. 'The boy's not in there. We even looked up in the attic, just to make sure, even though there's no way he could have climbed up there.'

'Is there a cellar?'

'There is, but for some reason it's been bricked up. It was bricked up before we came to live here.'

'Very good, sir. I appreciate that you've gone through the house already, but we have to make a thorough search ourselves so we can record that we've carried it out. And – no offence – we can sometimes spot something that a civilian might have overlooked.'

'All right, then, fine. Go ahead.'

The police officers trooped into the house, and once they were gathered in the hallway Sergeant Billings split them up and sent them off to different rooms.

'If he's not here on the property, sir, he'll have left his scent outside, and Axel will pick it up, I can assure you of that. He's the best tracking dog we've got, by far.'

'It's been raining buckets, though,' said Martin. 'Won't that have washed any scent away?'

'Not so much that Axel can't follow it. I've even known him follow a trail when there's snow a foot deep.'

The family waited in the drawing room while the police searched the house. Because it was so cold they all kept their coats on, although Vicky couldn't stop herself from shivering. They hardly spoke, but sat and listened to the heavy footsteps above them as the officers went into each of the eight bedrooms. Through the latticed window they could see the dog handler circling around the garden, with Axel sniffing the pathways and the grass borders.

The dog handler disappeared from sight, but after a few minutes they heard him calling out to Sergeant Billings from outside the open front door. Sergeant Billings went to see what he wanted, and they heard them talking together in the porch. Eventually he came back into the drawing room, holding up a polythene evidence bag. Inside it, they could see a claw hammer with a wooden handle. The hammerhead was tarnished almost black and frayed string was tied around its handle.

'Axel just sniffed this out. Apparently it was wedged down the side of the retaining wall by one of the flower beds, so it's hardly surprising that it wasn't discovered when we searched the place before – you know, after Mr Russell was found fatally injured.'

'What does that have to do with finding Timmy?' asked Rob.

'Well, nothing, sir. But it might throw some light on what happened to Mr Russell. I've seen the preliminary report from the forensic pathologist, and she suggested that he was probably struck on the back of his head with a blunt instrument of some kind. He had a circular indentation in the parietal bone, which would suggest it was a hammer. So we'll be taking this away with us to run some tests on it. You never know.'

'But what about Timmy? Wasn't there any trace of him?'

'Sorry, sir – no. But Constable Jones hasn't taken Axel the full circuit around the house yet. Don't you worry. Like I said before, if anybody can track where your little lad's strayed off to, he can.'

'You really think that hammer could have been used to murder our father?' said Martin.

'It's not for me to say, sir. But a fingerprint and DNA test should tell us, one way or another. I don't know the full facts of the case, but I do know that there were no signs of any intruder… no sign of forced entry and no footprints. So this might give us an idea what actually occurred. On the other hand, maybe it won't. Maybe it's been lying in that flower bed since your father fell downstairs.'

Sergeant Billings hesitated, suddenly realising what he had said. 'Sorry. My apologies. Bad choice of words there. What I meant was, maybe it's been there for donkey's years.'

One after the other, the police officers who were searching the house returned to the hallway to report that they had looked everywhere without finding any sign of Timmy. A few minutes afterwards, the dog handler called out to Sergeant Billings again, and Sergeant Billings went outside to talk to him. He came back with a serious face to say that Axel had picked up Timmy's scent from the time when he had been knocking the heads off thistles in the kitchen garden, but nowhere else. If he had left Allhallows Hall and wandered off, he would have left a trail that Axel could follow, but there was none.

'What if somebody picked him up and carried him away?' said Vicky. 'He wouldn't have left a trail then, would he?'

Rob said, 'He came back into the house, darling, and

closed the kitchen door behind him. We heard him. He took off his jacket and hung it on the chair. How could anybody have got into the house and carried him off, without us hearing them? And surely Timmy would have shouted out.'

'You say you heard him closing the kitchen door when he came in,' said Sergeant Billings. 'But did you hear him go out again?'

'No,' said Rob. 'Not that we were really listening out for it. We just assumed that he'd gone into the drawing room to play one of his games on my phone.'

'Still, it's pretty clear that he's not in the house, so he must be outside somewhere. There must be a reason why Axel couldn't pick up his scent. Maybe you're right, sir, and the rain did wash it away.'

'So what can we do now?' asked Vicky. 'Can we get a search party together?'

'Me and these officers will divide up the immediate area between us and conduct a systematic search. If that doesn't bear fruit then, yes, I'll call for extra officers from Crownhill and we'll extend the search area more widely. I might well call for another GP dog, too. It's going to get dark in a couple of hours and it looks like it'll rain again, so we'd better get a move on.'

'We'll come out and search, too,' said Rob. 'Just tell us where you want us to look.'

They all went outside, except for Vicky, who stayed in the house in case Timmy came back. As they trudged up the driveway, Rob could hear Portia arguing with Grace, telling her that she *knew* how much she cared about her missing nephew, but if they stayed here much longer they would miss the last train back to London.

Grace's reply was unusually brave. 'What if we leave and they find him drowned in a leat or fallen down a quarry? What do you think I'm going to feel like then?'

Portia didn't answer that, but snapped open her umbrella because the rain was starting again, big heavy droplets that pattered into the gravel like a dog trotting quickly to catch up with them.

They split up and searched until it grew dark and the rain became so heavy that the leats started to overflow and water ran across the fields. Rob walked along the narrow hedge-lined lane towards Horrabridge for over an hour, calling out Timmy's name again and again.

When he reached Walkhampton church, Sergeant Billings rang him and advised him to go back to Allhallows Hall. It was pointless him continuing in total darkness. He would call Dartmoor Search and Rescue at Tavistock, a team of more than thirty volunteers with years of experience in finding people who were lost and injured on the moors. They would immediately send out a team experienced in night searching, but if they hadn't found Timmy before it started to grow light tomorrow, they would call in more volunteers and fan out over a wide area all around Sampford Spiney.

'Let's hope your lad's come to no harm and that he's found himself somewhere to shelter.'

They all returned to the house, soaked and exhausted.

Vicky had lit the range in the kitchen and left the oven doors open so that it was warm. She had also phoned Mac Vac, the local chimney sweeping service, and they had promised to come around early in the morning and clear out all of the blocked-up flues.

'I don't know why you bothered, quite honestly,' said Katharine. 'It's not as though any of us are going to be living here.'

'It's still up to us to look after it, Katharine,' Vicky told her. 'And Rob and I are going to be staying here until we find Timmy.'

Sergeant Billings said, 'I'll see you tomorrow, around seven. Give us a call immediately, won't you, if the little fellow shows up.'

Once he had gone, Martin stood in front of the range warming his hands. 'Well, we'll have to stay here, too, at least for tonight. I'm too knackered to drive all the way home, especially in this weather. What shall we do about eating?'

'The fridge has been cleared out,' said Vicky. 'But I looked and there's still food in the freezer. I'm not at all hungry myself, but even if I was, I don't think I'd fancy eating my late father-in-law's steak and kidney pie.'

'I'll tell you what,' said Martin. 'I'll call The Rock pub in Yelverton and see if they'll do us a takeaway. Their steaks and their pies are terrific. When they're ready I can whizz over and collect them.'

He looked up The Rock's menu online, and they all chose what they wanted to eat. Grace asked for a chicken salad bowl but Portia was vegan, and so she opted for the butternut squash risotto. Rob went for the fisherman's pie. Vicky insisted that she didn't feel like anything to eat, but he knew she might be tempted to share it with him. Martin ordered the Devonshire rump steak, cooked rare. Katharine wanted nothing more than crushed avocado on toast, with a hen's egg.

They didn't need to order any drinks. Sixteen dusty bottles of Jail Ale were stored in the bottom of the pantry, as well as seven assorted bottles of red and white wine and a half-empty bottle of Jameson's whiskey.

It was past eight o'clock by the time Martin returned from Yelverton with their food. While they were waiting, Vicky had gone upstairs to choose which bedroom she and Rob were going to sleep in, and make up the bed, although Rob guessed that she was also looking yet again for any sign of Timmy, even though she must have known it was fruitless.

They ate their supper in the kitchen, hardly saying a word to each other. They were all tired and depressed, and they all felt that the legacy of Allhallows Hall was weighing down on them like some grim unwanted responsibility from which they would never be free. Rob thought it was like having to look after an elderly relative with dementia, who neither recognised them nor appreciated the care that they gave him. Herbert Russell had dominated them when he was alive and he was still dominating them, even now that he was dead.

'What if we *can't* find him?' said Martin, cutting into his steak so that the diluted blood ran across his plate.

'Don't even think that, Martin,' Rob snapped at him. 'Of course we're going to find him.'

'Well, yes, sure. Of course we are. But I was only wondering what the situation would be, you know, as far as the house is concerned.'

'Martin, I don't give a flying fuck about the house. Our five-year-old son is lost out there somewhere on Dartmoor in the pouring rain and right now that's all that matters. I don't care if the house collapses around our ears. In fact, I hope it does. It's like Dad personified.'

Martin said nothing, but pushed another piece of steak into his mouth and shrugged. Rob was almost tempted to say, 'You're like Dad personified, too. All you ever care about is you.'

9

Rob had wound up the longcase clock in the hallway, so that as they lay in bed he heard it strike two.

'Are you still awake?' he asked Vicky.

'I can't sleep. I can't even close my eyes. I won't be able to sleep until we've found Timmy.'

'Listen, try to have a nap at least. You're going to be exhausted otherwise. Timmy may be naughty sometimes, but he's not stupid. He's bound to have found himself somewhere to shelter. My guess is that he got himself lost and some passing motorist has picked him up and taken him home for the night until they can find out where he came from.'

'They would have called the police, wouldn't they?'

'I don't know, darling. I'm just hoping for the best.'

They lay for a while without speaking. The rain was still pattering against the window and they could hear it pouring into the downpipes with a sound like a choking child. They had chosen the second largest bedroom, at the end of the corridor next to the bathroom. Martin and Katharine had taken the master bedroom opposite, while

Grace and Portia were sleeping in the bedroom at the top of the stairs that used to be Rob's room. Grace and Portia had to share a single bed, but they said that they liked to sleep snuggled up closely together.

Rob wondered if they would have the same feeling that a strange boy was hiding underneath their bed, listening to them breathe. He shivered, because the room was so cold and the patchwork quilt that covered them was damp, and smelled damp.

The clock chimed half past two. Gradually, the rain eased off, and the moon began to shine intermittently through the gap in the curtains.

It was then that Rob heard whispering. He wasn't sure at first if Vicky had fallen asleep at last and was whispering to herself. But when he lifted his head up from the pillow, he realised that somebody was whispering in the corridor right outside their bedroom door. He strained hard to hear what they were saying, because they sounded hurried and anxious, like the whisperer that he was sure he had heard in the room next to the stained-glass window.

He didn't think it was Grace or Portia, because the whispering was low-pitched and slightly hoarse, like a man. Maybe it was Martin. But if it was Martin, what was he doing out of bed at this time of the night, and who was he whispering to? Rob sat up, so that he could hear more clearly.

Vicky turned over and said, 'What's the matter?'

'Can you hear that?'

'What?'

'That whispering.'

Vicky listened for a moment and then she sat up, too. 'Yes, I can. Who is it?'

The whispering went on and on, and the whisperer sounded more and more desperate with every passing second. Then they heard another whisperer, who sounded threatening, as if they were warning the first whisperer to keep quiet, or else.

'It's Martin, it has to be,' said Rob. 'Martin and Katharine, having one of their barneys.' He reached over and switched on the bedside lamp, which flickered and crackled before it popped on fully. He swung his legs off the bed and padded across the room, dressed only in his shirt and sweater and socks. He pressed his ear against the door, trying to make out what the whisperers were saying, but their voices were still indistinct, and so he opened it.

The corridor was dark, but not so dark that he could see there was nobody there. The whispering abruptly stopped.

'Rob? Who is it?'

Rob leaned out of the doorway and looked along the corridor as far as the landing. The moonlight brightened for a moment, and then dulled again.

'It's nobody.'

'What do you mean, it's nobody? Somebody was whispering, even if it wasn't Martin and Katharine.'

'I know it sounded like it. But it couldn't have been.'

Rob closed the door and turned around. 'It must have been a draught. Or maybe the plumbing.'

'No, it wasn't. It was *whispering*. Whoever it was must

have heard you opening the door and made themselves scarce.'

'They couldn't have. I would have seen them. I would have heard their footsteps, too. The floorboards are much too creaky.'

'Perhaps they've hidden themselves in the bathroom.'

'Oh, and I wouldn't have heard them close the bathroom door?'

'You could at least go and check.'

Rob blew out his cheeks in exasperation. 'All right, if it makes you happy. But I swear to God there's nobody there. You know what this house is like, full of all kinds of weird noises. It could have been mice, running along behind the skirting boards.'

'Rob – mice don't whisper. Not like that. That was definitely two people, having an argument. You know it was.'

Rob opened the door again and went along to the bathroom. It was chilly inside, with only the sound of the bath tap dripping. He tugged the light cord, and looked around, but there was nobody there. His dead father's toothbrush was still on the shelf above the basin, its bristles splayed. Too parsimonious to buy himself a new one.

He went back to the bedroom. 'Even if there was somebody there, darling, they're not there now. All we can do is try to get some rest. They'll start searching again as soon as it gets light.'

Vicky punched her pillow and lay her head back on it. 'I wish we'd never come. I hate this house. I hate Dartmoor.

I just want Timmy back safe and well so that we can go home and never ever come back.'

About twenty minutes before dawn, Grace came tapping at their door, carrying two mugs of tea, and half a packet of Hobnobs in her cardigan pocket.

'We thought you ought to have something inside you, even if you're not hungry. Did you sleep at all?'

'I think I might have dozed off a couple of times,' said Vicky. 'How about you?'

'On and off. Don't tell her I told you, whatever you do, but Portia kept snoring. And I'm sure I could hear some people whispering outside our door. I didn't want to get up and see who it was because I didn't want to wake Portia, and it stopped after a while anyway.'

'We heard the same,' Vicky told her. 'Rob took a look outside but there was nobody there.'

'You always thought Allhallows was haunted, didn't you, Rob? You used to think there was a boy just like you lying under your bed.'

'Did I tell you about that? I don't remember telling *anybody*.'

'Yes, you did. You always used to kneel down and look under your bed before you got into it. You did it every night and one night I asked you why.'

'Anyway, Grace, thanks so much for the tea,' said Vicky.

'That's all right. If you want a top-up, or anything more to eat, we're down in the kitchen. I expect the police will be here soon.'

Almost as if it had heard her, Rob's phone rang. He picked it up and it was Sergeant Billings.

'We'll be with you in about half an hour, sir. We've got a couple of dozen volunteers from Dartmoor Search and Rescue to help us and if necessary they should be able to muster some more later.'

'That's brilliant. Thank you, sergeant.'

'We'll find your little lad. The weather forecast looks fine. It's not going to rain, any road, so that should help.'

Vicky was sitting up in bed, holding her mug of tea in both hands. She looked white and exhausted, and her eyes were filled with tears. Rob went and sat down beside her and put his arm around her shoulders.

'They're sending out a search and rescue team. And I'm going to pray.'

'Who to? You don't believe in God.'

'I've just been converted. At least until we find Timmy.'

10

An orange sun was rising dimly through the fog as the Dartmoor Search and Rescue teams arrived in the driveway in two Land Rovers. There were fifteen volunteers altogether, including a dog handler, all wearing crimson parkas. They varied in age from teenagers to pensioners, serious but friendly, mostly men but with two women among them, and their team leader came up to Rob and Vicky to introduce himself. He was in his mid-forties, with a weather-beaten face and pale-blue eyes that seemed to be focused on some distant tor. He spoke with a strong Devon accent.

'Everybody you see here is trained and experienced in searching for missing people,' he said. 'And we have all the equipment – radios, GPS. And first aid, if it's needed, which we sincerely hope we won't. You have a picture of your boy we could take a look at? Sergeant Billings says he's five.'

Rob handed him his photograph and the team leader handed it around.

'His name's Timmy. He's wearing an oatmeal-coloured jumper and brown corduroy trousers.'

'What's his personality? Quiet, is he, or a bit of an angletwitch?'

'Oh, quiet, most of the time. But he's like all kids. He has his foot-stamping moments.'

'I get you. And have you something that Barney could have a smell of?'

Vicky was already holding Timmy's yellow jacket over her arm. She gave it to the team leader and he beckoned the dog handler to come over. Barney was a black-and-white border collie and his amber eyes had the most riveting stare that Rob had ever seen on a dog. He took a deep and enthusiastic sniff at Timmy's jacket, a connoisseur of what tragedy smelled like.

'We'll start from the house here, since this is where your son went missing from,' said the team leader. 'If Barney can pick up his scent, all well and good. If not, we'll be spreading out all around Sampford Spiney. Our volunteers here have a brilliant understanding of all the terrain around here, and they know the most likely paths that he might have taken. We can't do an aerial search just yet because of the fog, but if it clears before we've located him, we could consider it.'

'He's been out all night,' said Vicky. 'He's going to be frightened and soaking wet and very miserable.'

'Of course,' the team leader told her, laying his hand on her shoulder and giving her a reassuring smile. 'But in all the seven years since I've been a member, we've never yet failed to track down a single missing person. We'll find your boy, don't you fret.'

★

After twenty minutes, the dog handler came back to the team leader to say that he had circled all around the house and had only picked up Timmy's scent in the kitchen garden, just like the police dog handler. There was no trace of him leading away from the house.

'Well, no worries, sometimes the dogs find it hard to follow a scent in wet weather, and this driveway is all shingle, which doesn't help. We'll just have to get out there onto the moor and carry out a systematic search on foot. He's only five, so his little legs couldn't have taken him that far – not in the dark.'

Rob and Martin and Grace each joined one of the three search and rescue teams. Vicky and Katharine would stay in the house in case Timmy returned, and to wait for the chimney sweep. Portia had volunteered to borrow Rob's car to drive into Tavistock and buy food and wine and two electric fan heaters, as well as a fresh inhaler for Grace's asthma. The dampness in the house had made Grace short of breath, but she was determined to stay here until Timmy was found. 'Portia – he's my little nephew, and I'm never going to have a child of my own, am I?'

'There's always IVF,' Portia had retorted, but almost immediately she said, 'Sorry – *sorry*.' Yesterday she had made no secret of her impatience to return to London, but whatever argument they had settled between them, it was apparent that she had made some concession to Grace. She had made no mention of it this morning, and on the whole she was being much more conciliatory.

As the day went on, the fog thickened, rather than clearing, and the search parties looked like ghostly shadows as they walked down the lanes and crossed over the fields and climbed up the steep granite tors. They called out 'Timmy!' over and over, and then they would stop for a few moments and listen, but there was no response before darkness began to creep over the moors.

They combed woods and hedgerows and ditches. They followed the Grimstone and Sortridge leat all the way up to the Windy Post Cross, peering into the running water to make sure that Timmy's drowned body wasn't trapped below the surface.

They looked as far as Merrivale in the north, and Whitchurch to the west, and even as far as the Burrator reservoir to the south. They talked to the few local people they came across out on the moor, and knocked on several doors to ask if anybody had seen a small boy wandering out on his own, but nobody had. Rob was beginning to wonder if some passing motorist might have come across Timmy, picked him up and driven him away. For what purpose, he dreaded to think.

Eventually, at about half past five, they returned cold and weary to Allhallows Hall. Although they had given up for the day, the search would continue throughout the night, with replacement teams who specialised in looking for missing people in the dark. The search area would be widened, too.

The chimney sweeps had visited that morning and cleared out the flues in the drawing room, the kitchen and the library, and Vicky had lit fires in all of them. For the first time since they had arrived yesterday, the house felt welcoming and warm.

Rob collapsed into Herbert's throne by the fire. He had wanted to go back out onto the moors after a short rest, but when he was climbing over a pile of rocks under Pew Tor he had twisted his ankle and it was starting to throb. He switched on the West Country news on television and silently prayed that there would be no items about a five-year-old boy found dead around Sampford Spiney.

Vicky brought him a bottle of Jail Ale and stood beside him, looking bereft.

'What if they never find him? What then?'

'They will, darling. We can't give up hope.'

'Tell me this is all a bad dream. Tell me we never came here.'

Rob tried to stand up but winced and sat back down again. Vicky knelt down beside his chair and rested her head in his lap. He stroked her hair, but that was all the comfort he could give her.

Martin, meanwhile, had gone through to the library to see if he could find any notebooks or diaries that might throw some light on why their father had been killed. The police had taken all the invoices and receipts that had been scattered on the stairs when Herbert Russell was found dead, as well as his laptop, and had yet to return them. When Martin had been helping to search the house for Timmy, however, he had lifted the lid on the window seat and found six or seven dog-eared *Racing Post* diaries, as well as other books. Now he lifted them all out and set them down on the writing table, and he saw that they were Herbert's accounts books for the nine previous tax years.

He sat down and began to leaf through them – the diaries first and then the accounts. The diaries had no day-to-day accounts of Herbert's life. They were crammed with nothing but notes about race meetings and odds and horses that he must have fancied.

It made him feel strangely abandoned to see his father's idiosyncratic handwriting again, with its thick upright strokes and its heavily crossed 't's. His father had always made him feel valued, much more than Rob or Grace, and had constantly promised him that he would be someone special when he grew up – someone who took no nonsense from anybody. He had lost count of the number of times his father had said to him, 'Remember – no matter how much anyone disagrees with you – *you're* always right and *they're* always wrong. Full stop.'

Most of the entries in his accounts books were mundane. Travel expenses. TV licence. Car maintenance. Firewood from Liz's Logs in Yelverton. But then some of the credits were more mystifying. PP £11,230. L/b £3,226. And then some much larger credits. JD 1729515 £128,000. BdF 2367838 £347,500.

When Martin added up all of these obscure credits, he reckoned that in those nine years Herbert Russell had been given over £7.5 million, and that was on top of his prison governor's salary. But apart from their initials and their reference numbers, there were no further details of who the donors were, or why they had given him so much money.

Martin jotted down the figures on a torn-off sheet of paper and then went through to the drawing room.

'Rob? I don't know where that Margaret Walsh got her financial statements from, but according to Dad's own account books, we should all be reasonably rich.'

'Spag bol all right?' called Grace, from the kitchen.

'Yes, Gracey. Wonderful,' Rob called back, and then frowned at Martin's piece of paper. 'Blimey. Do we know who gave him all this money? Are these individual people, or companies?'

'I haven't the faintest. That's all he's written down. Look at this one – KW 2703145 £545,000. Who would have given him more than half a million? I mean, what for? And what did he do with it? Did he spend it? Did he invest it? Did he bury it in the garden in a pickle jar?'

'He didn't keep a diary, did he?'

'There's racing diaries, with all the gee-gees he bet on, but that's all. I don't ever remember him keeping one, and there was no sign of one in the library, or in his bedroom.'

'I thought he had accountants to do his tax returns. Maybe they would know.'

'I think he used to, but from the look of his books he was doing them himself for the past nine years at least.'

'Perhaps he has another bank account – one that he never told Margaret Walsh about.'

'In which case we bloody well need to find it,' said Martin. 'There's no way in the world I'm going to let seven and a half million go unclaimed. That's two and a half million each. I know it's not the National Lottery, but you and I could buy ourselves much bigger houses, and Grace could buy her first house, couldn't she?'

'Right at this moment, Martin, I'm not interested in whether I could buy a bigger house or not.'

'Well, no, sorry, Rob, of course not. But I'll get to work on it. And if they don't find Timmy tonight, I'll be out there again tomorrow, looking for him. I promise you.'

'Thanks, Martin,' Rob told him. One of the logs in the grate lurched and dropped downwards, and a shower of sparks flew up the chimney. For a split second, they looked like a glittering, demonic face.

11

They ate their supper in the kitchen, in silence – too tired and too depressed to think of anything to say. Rob had cautioned Martin not to tell Vicky or Grace about the £7.5 million that he had discovered in Herbert Russell's accounts. There was no way of knowing if it actually existed anywhere, or if Herbert had borrowed it and paid it all back, and apart from that Vicky could think about nothing but Timmy, and she would only find it insensitive if he started talking about some illusory inheritance.

As for Grace, she never liked to speak about their father much, for some reason. She always gave a little shudder when they mentioned his name, as if they were talking about some food that she couldn't stand, like pickled herring. She had made it clear that she had only come to Allhallows Hall because Portia had insisted that she should lay claim to what was hers – and would be *theirs*, when they had legally married.

Just after half past ten, a short, broad-shouldered man with scruffy blond hair knocked at the door. He was wearing a crimson anorak and he introduced himself as one of the team leaders from Dartmoor Search and Rescue. He told them that his name was John Kipling – 'no relation to Rudyard, unfortunately'. He and his volunteers would be searching the moor until six tomorrow morning, and unless they had found Timmy earlier, he would call again then.

They all sat in the drawing room to finish their drinks, watching the fire die down. They had the television switched on, but muted, in case any news item came up about Timmy; but there was little hope of that. Martin went outside for a cigarette and when he came back, still wearing a cloak of cold air and the smell of tobacco, he rubbed his hands together and said, 'I don't know about you, but I'm for bed.'

Rob fell asleep almost at once. Vicky stayed awake, reading a book she had found in the library called *The Legends of Dartmoor*.

The book described the demon dogs that were said to roam the moor in packs, and the ghosts of wife-murderers, and how the Devil had demolished a local church spire with bolts of lightning. But it wasn't all about frightening apparitions. The chapter that had caught Vicky's attention told of friendly piskies who are supposed to flit around the tors at night, and who will guide any ramblers who find themselves lost – although they will do the opposite to anybody who upsets them, and deliberately lead them miles out of their way. The people of Dartmoor still call it being 'pisky-led'.

'The piskies are appreciated, most of all, for the care they take of little children who have gone astray, drying

their tears and taking their hands and showing them the way back to their anxious mothers.'

When she read that, Vicky closed the book, her mouth tightly puckered to prevent herself from sobbing out loud. She didn't want to wake Rob. She knew how exhausted he was, and how much his ankle hurt. He had taken two paracetamol before going to bed.

She switched off her bedside lamp, snuggled down and pulled up the quilt to cover her shoulders. Out here on the moor, at night, the darkness was total, so they had left a light on in the hallway downstairs, in case any of them needed to get up to visit the bathroom. All she could hear was Rob's steady breathing, the weary ticking of the longcase clock, and the soft, sibilant sound of the wind outside, like an old man whistling between his teeth.

She tried to imagine where Timmy was now, and how he was keeping himself warm and dry. He had always liked to put up makeshift shelters at the end of the garden, under the hedge. It was usually one of Rob's raincoats draped over a framework of sticks and the handles of his wheelbarrow. He would sit there, cross-legged, while it was raining, singing songs he had made up himself, like 'The Sheep Goes Beep'. She desperately hoped he had managed to build himself some kind of shelter out on the moors, although by now he must be weak with hunger, and thirsty, too, unless he had drunk water from a leat.

Dear God in heaven, she prayed, under her breath. *Please protect my Timmy wherever he is, and bring him back to us safe and unharmed.*

Her eyes closed and she was almost asleep when she

thought she could faintly hear a child crying. She opened her eyes and listened. A whole minute went by without her hearing it again. Rob stirred and made a wuffling noise, but then he continued to breathe normally. No – she must have been thinking so intently about Timmy that she had dreamed it as she was dropping off. She closed her eyes again. She had never felt so tired in her entire life. She couldn't imagine the grief of losing a child forever. The funeral. The small white coffin.

Then she heard the child crying again. It was so muffled and indistinct that she couldn't be entirely sure it wasn't a fox yelping somewhere outside, or one of the bedroom doors creaking in the draught. Dartmoor was the highest upland in the country, so it was almost always windy. She sat up, holding her breath. Another minute went by. Then – yes, she heard it again. What if it was Timmy, and he was stuck somewhere in the house in some cupboard or chimney or cranny where they hadn't been able to find him?

She folded back the quilt and climbed out of bed, trying to disturb Rob as little as possible. She tiptoed to the bedroom door and eased it open. The corridor outside was dark, except for the faint glow of light from the lamp in the hallway, which was enough for Vicky to see that there was nobody out there.

She waited, and then she heard it again. It sounded as if it were coming from the side corridor that led to the stained-glass window of Old Dewer. She crept along to the landing, stopped, and listened again. It was not crying so much as a repetitive and hopeless plea for help, in the same way that children in hospital call out endlessly for their mummies, even though they know it might be hours before they come to visit them. But it was definitely a child, and not a fox, or an owl. She couldn't be sure that it was Timmy, but what other children had come to Allhallows Hall lately?

Holding her breath again, she made her way down the corridor to the stained-glass window. In the dark, the design on the window appeared to have subtly altered, as if the hounds were cowering down low, and Old Dewer himself was looking at her over his shoulder with one gleaming eye. Outside, it was still pitch black and there was no light shining through the coloured glass, so that it was difficult to tell for sure.

Although it sounded so faint and faraway, the child's voice seemed to be coming from the end bedroom, the one in which Rob and Martin had found nothing but six spare chairs and a wine table crowded with cobwebby candlesticks. She opened the door and strained her eyes to see if there was anybody inside, but it was too dark, and so she reached around for the light switch.

'Timmy? Are you in there?' she called out, but quietly.

She waited, but there was no answer, and the crying had stopped.

'Timmy?'

She took a step into the bedroom, but as she did so she heard a soft rushing noise, like the wind rising, and the wine table rocked as if somebody had knocked into it. Three of the candlesticks toppled over and dropped onto the carpet, and then Vicky gasped in shock as what felt like two invisible hands were shoved into her chest to push her violently backwards into the corridor. She lost her balance and her shoulder struck the mahogany dado behind her before she sprawled onto the floor.

She looked up to see who had pushed her, but instantly the light in the bedroom was switched off and the door slammed shut.

She climbed to her feet and stood in front of the door, trembling and rubbing her shoulder. She was convinced that it had been a man who had knocked over the candlesticks and pushed her, but how could she not have seen him?

Vicky stayed where she was for a few seconds, listening for the child, but all she could hear now was the wind, and the first few patters of rain against the stained-glass window. She didn't dare to open the bedroom door again. Her shoulder was aching and she felt as if her breasts were bruised.

She walked back quickly to her own bedroom, switched on Rob's bedside lamp and sat down on the bed next to him. She shook his arm and said, 'Rob – Rob – wake up! Please, Rob, wake up!'

Rob stirred and opened his eyes. 'What is it? What's going on?' Then he propped himself up on his elbow and said, 'Have they found Timmy?'

'No. But I heard a child crying and I thought it might be Timmy, so I went to take a look.'

Rob now saw how shaken she was. He sat up and put his arms around her and said, 'What? What happened?'

'I thought the child was crying in that end bedroom, so

77

I went in and somebody pushed me out and slammed the door shut.'

'What? Who?'

'I don't know who.'

'Well, what did they look like?'

'That's the whole point. They didn't look like anything. It felt like a man, but he was invisible.'

Rob stroked her back. 'When you say "invisible"…'

'*I couldn't see him, Rob! He pushed me so hard that I fell over but there was nobody there!*'

Rob climbed out of bed, wincing as he put weight on his twisted ankle. He picked up his tweed jacket from the back of the bedroom chair and quickly tugged it on.

'Right,' he said. 'Let's go and take a look. If this *is* somebody playing some kind of stupid prank—!'

He limped along to the landing, with Vicky following close behind him. He turned down the corridor that led towards the stained-glass window and went up to the bedroom door.

'You're sure you heard the child crying from in here?'

'It was very faint. But I think so. I don't know where else it could have been coming from.'

'Well, like I told you, I heard whispering coming from this bedroom myself. Martin said I was imagining it.'

'I wasn't imagining somebody pushing me out of the room and switching off the light and slamming the door in my face.'

'All right. Let's find out who it was.'

Rob opened the door and switched on the light. There

was nobody in there. He stepped inside and cautiously looked around. Vicky stayed by the door.

'No... nobody here,' said Rob. He circled all the way round the room, waving his arms from side to side. 'Can't see them, and I can't *feel* them, either, even if they're invisible.'

'The candlesticks,' said Vicky.

'What about them?'

'Some of them fell on the floor, but whoever it was has picked them up and put them back on the table.'

Rob lifted one of them up. 'Yes... these three don't have any cobwebs on them. But you don't have to worry, darling. I believe you. Something really weird is going on in this house and we need to find out what it is.'

He paused, and looked around the bedroom again, wondering if there was something he had missed.

Then he said, 'Do you know, I have a gut feeling that somebody may be doing all this spooky stuff on purpose... the whispering and everything. Maybe it's somebody who doesn't want us to inherit it and they're trying to frighten us off by making us think that it's haunted.'

The longcase clock in the hallway struck a dolorous three. Vicky said, 'Listen... there's nothing else we can do tonight. The search and rescue people will be back here at six. Let's try and get some rest before then.'

She paused, still rubbing her shoulder, and then she said, 'I think you could be right about somebody playing tricks on us. I don't believe in ghosts. Especially ghosts that can push you over.'

12

They were both still awake when they heard a Land Rover crunching to a halt in the driveway, and its door being slammed, and after a few seconds there was a knock at the door.

Rob looked at his watch. Twenty-five minutes to six. The search and rescue team was early.

He hurried down the stairs, with Vicky following close behind him. When he opened the front door he saw that it was only John Kipling, in his crimson anorak and a black knitted bobble hat. Behind him, it was still raining, although softly and quietly.

'No luck?' asked Rob.

John shook his head. 'I'm sorry. We searched nearly eight hundred hectares. All we found was a broken-down Toyota and a dead sheep.'

'Why don't you come inside and have something hot to drink?' said Vicky. She looked over his shoulder towards the Land Rover in the driveway. 'Are you alone or is there anybody with you?'

'No, I'm alone. And a hot cup of tea would go down a treat.'

He stepped into the hallway and pulled off his bobble hat. Although he must have been forty-five or older, he looked as fit as a much younger man. He had high cheekbones and a snub nose that made him look Swedish or Polish. His accent, though, was pure Devon.

He sat down and eased off his wellington boots. 'There's a hole in my sock but my feet don't smell.'

'After what you've been doing all night, smelly feet would be forgiven, don't you worry about that.'

Vicky went through to the kitchen to make John a mug of tea while Rob led him into the drawing room and switched on the lights. The fire had burned down to a heap of grey ashes, but Rob set about shovelling them out and lighting a fresh fire with crumpled-up pages of the *Tiverton Gazette* that he had found in the scullery, and ash twigs.

'Always comes out on Tuesday, the *Tiverton Gazette*,' said John. 'Unusual day for a weekly paper to be published, but it coincides with market day, when there's more people in town to buy it. It's been going since 1858, believe it or not. The fellow who started it was only twenty-two, but he died three years later.'

'Well, you know your local history,' said Rob, striking a match.

'I do, as a matter of fact. I've lived here all my life and it's a fascinating part of the world. There are so many legends and fairy stories about it – spooks and demons and witches. That's natural, I suppose, considering the landscape. You can go out on a foggy morning and imagine that you're the only human being in the world, but you can hear weird animal noises quite close by and see shadows flitting around, behind the fog.'

'What do you think our hopes are of finding Timmy?' Rob asked him.

'Like I said before, we've never failed to find a missing person yet. Not if they're out on the moor. But it could be that your lad's wandered off somewhere else, or that somebody's seen him walking along the road on his own and picked him up.'

'That's what I was thinking. But surely if somebody had picked him up, they would have taken him to the nearest police station.'

'Perhaps they have, but then maybe your boy wasn't able to tell them where you are. But there's no point in speculating, Mr Russell. That's one thing I always tell my team before we start searching. You can predict from experience which way your missing person is most likely to have strayed off to, but sometimes you find them in the most unlikely places. Last month we were looking for a woman rambler who was trying to find her way back to Langstone Manor caravan park. Eventually we found her stuck down a crevice in the rocks at Pew Tor, miles out of her way.'

'Maybe she was pisky-led,' said Vicky, as she came in from the kitchen with three mugs of tea on a tray.

'Oh, you know about the piskies?' said John.

'I was reading about them last night in a book about Dartmoor. I was trying to see if it had any clues to where Timmy might have gone.'

'The king of the piskies is supposed to live under Pew

Tor. But in all my years I've never caught sight of him. Nor any other pisky, for that matter.'

At that moment Martin came in, puffy-eyed and unshaved. He was wrapped in Herbert's brown check dressing gown and was still wearing his yellow socks.

'I didn't realise it was six o'clock already. God, I feel rough. Any news?'

Rob shook his head. 'John and his team have been searching all night but there's still no sign of him.'

'I'll be checking in with Sergeant Billings in a minute,' said John. 'Since we haven't been able to find Timmy, he'll be putting out a bulletin on the local television news and Twitter.'

He blew on his tea to cool it, and took two or three sips. Then he said, 'I know this might sound more than a bit condescending, but you have made a thorough search of the house?'

'Of course we have,' Martin retorted. 'And the police have, too. What – do you think he might be hiding under one of the beds and we haven't noticed?'

'Sorry – I didn't mean to imply that you haven't searched properly. But these houses have all kinds of funny little alcoves and recesses that you wouldn't find in a modern house. That's because they were built without plans, and sometimes the upstairs rooms didn't quite fit with the load-bearing walls, and so there'd be a niche left over, which was plastered over.'

'If it was plastered over, how could anybody get into it?'

'I don't know. But I do know that this house has a priest's hole, or priest's hide, as they're sometimes known.'

'I've heard of those,' said Vicky. 'Those were secret rooms, weren't they, where Catholic priests used to be hidden during the Reformation, so that the priest hunters couldn't find them.'

'That's right,' said John. 'The Wilmingtons, who built this house, were Catholics, and when they were approached by a priest to give him shelter, they asked a fellow called Nicholas Owen to construct a priest hole for them. Nicholas Owen was a Jesuit lay brother. He was also an incredible craftsman. He'd already made priest holes in at least five country houses. In Harvington Hall, in Worcestershire, he made at least seven, and there could be more in the same house that nobody has been able to find because he concealed them so brilliantly.'

'We never knew there was a priest hole here, at Allhallows Hall,' said Martin. 'Surely it would have been mentioned in the title deeds, or the property information form, or whatever.'

'I only found out about it three or so years ago when I was researching the Wilmington family,' said John. 'The existence of a priest hole would only have been known to the owner of the house and Nicholas Owen himself. And when I say they were brilliantly concealed... some of them were quite amazing. He would build them under staircases, and over fireplaces, and behind panelling. Even down drains. He was caught eventually, and tortured, and executed, but he was canonised and became the patron saint of escapologists and illusionists.'

'Did your research give you any idea where in the house this priest hole is?' Rob asked him.

'No... only that there must have been one, because the priest hunters came here looking for a Catholic priest. Apparently they were acting on a tip they'd been given by a local villager from Yelverton, who bore some kind of a grudge against the Wilmingtons. They searched the house without finding him.'

'So how did they know that there *was* a priest hole?' asked Martin.

'Ah – they'd got wise to their existence by then, and how difficult they were to discover. They went away, but the same afternoon without any warning they came back, and by that time the priest had come out of his hole and they caught him on the road to Yelverton. He was tortured to make him renounce his Catholic faith and pledge allegiance to the Church of England, but he refused and they hanged him.

'The Wilmingtons could have been in serious trouble, too, but they denied knowing the priest. Even though it was almost certain that they must have been hiding him somewhere in Allhallows Hall, the priest hunters still couldn't find a priest hole, and so they had no evidence to charge them with.'

By now, both Grace and Portia had appeared, wearing thick sweaters and jeans – Grace in pink and Portia in purple. Rob introduced them to John Kipling and quickly explained what he had just told them.

'If there is a priest hole, we weren't able to find it, either,' said Portia. Her studded denim jacket made her look even more boyish. 'And anyway, if *we* weren't able to find it, how could Timmy have found it? And even if he had, surely he would have come out of it by now.'

'He could be stuck inside it and he *can't* get out,' said Grace.

'But he'd be starving hungry by now. He'd be shouting out and banging on the walls, wouldn't he?'

Vicky was about to tell them about the childish cries that she had heard coming from the end bedroom, and the way she had been violently knocked over when she went to investigate, but Rob squeezed her hand and gave her a concentrated stare that cautioned her to stay silent. In the unlikely event that either Martin or Grace had somehow arranged for all this whispering and crying, he didn't want them to know that they had heard it, and that it had disturbed them – although he still couldn't understand how Vicky had been pushed.

'How do you go about finding priest holes?' asked Rob. 'I mean, if you take a look around the house, John, do you think that *you* might be able to work out where it is?'

'I could try,' John told him. 'I've seen two of them already – one at Grimstone Hall and the other in a house in Tavistock. The one at Grimstone Hall was under the staircase and the priest had to pull out the riser from one of the stairs and slide himself sideways into the chamber that Nicholas Owen had built underneath. At Tavistock, a section of the wall over the fireplace was hinged upwards, and the priest's hole was a narrow space behind the chimney. But, like I said, Nicholas Owen was such an expert craftsman that they're very hard to find.'

'And what if you can't find one here at Allhallows Hall?' asked Martin, with a slightly aggressive tone in his voice. 'What then?'

'Then we don't give up. We bring in one of our sniffer dogs and if our sniffer dog can't find it then one of our team works for a company that insulates cavity walls. He can drill a neat hole in any wall that he thinks might have a priest hole behind it, and take a look behind it with a borescope.'

'Very well,' said Martin. 'But let's start with the dog first, shall we, before we start turning the house into a sieve?'

13

After he had finished his mug of tea, John Kipling stood up, peeled off his crimson anorak, and started his search of the house. He went around the ground floor first, rapping with his knuckles on the dark oak panelling to see if it sounded hollow anywhere. Then he measured the walls in each room to compare them with the walls of the rooms next to it, to see if there was any disparity.

Outside, the rain had eased off, and three fresh search and rescue teams had spread out over the moors in their continuing effort to find Timmy. Grace and Portia went out to help them, although Rob had to stay behind because his ankle was still swollen and he could only hobble on it, and Martin had to catch up with more than twenty urgent business calls.

While John slowly tapped his way from the kitchen to the library, Rob and Vicky sat in the drawing room watching the television. The local BBC News had already shown a picture of Timmy, with an urgent request for anybody who had seen him or who had any information about his whereabouts to get in touch with the police at Crownhill. An appeal had also been posted on Twitter.

'Do you think I should tell John about that child I heard crying and my getting pushed over?' asked Vicky. 'Perhaps we should tell him about all that whispering, too. He seems to know all the Dartmoor myths and legends.'

'Let's hold off until he's finished on the ground floor,' said Rob. 'We don't want him heading straight upstairs until he's made a thorough search down here. This priest hole could be anywhere and we don't want him to miss it.'

'But we *both* heard something strange up in that end bedroom. I heard that child and you heard those people whispering.'

'We don't know if those noises came from a priest hole, do we? And if there *is* a priest hole and Timmy somehow managed to get himself stuck inside it... well, maybe he's too weak to call out any more. Or... I don't know.'

'Or what? You think he could be dead?'

'Vicks... I didn't say that. To be honest with you, I don't believe that he's here in the house at all. But we have to think of every place that he might have found himself and everything that might have happened to him.'

John came into the drawing room, running his hand through his bristly blond hair. He looked tired.

'There's no sign of a priest hole down here. I'll be taking a look upstairs now, if that's okay.'

'We'll go up with you. We didn't tell you before, but we've been hearing some odd noises and we think they come from one of the bedrooms.'

'Odd noises such as what?'

'Like a child calling out, and people whispering. But very faintly, so we couldn't quite tell for certain if that's what they really were, or if it was the wind, or the plumbing, or some fox outside on the moor making a mating call.'

John frowned, and then he said, 'Okay. Perhaps you'd better show me this bedroom. I mean, I know where they are, most of the priest holes around the country, but there's no record of anybody ever hearing voices out of them. Not even at Grimstone Hall and that's supposed to be haunted by at least three ghosts.'

They went upstairs, with Rob grabbing at the banister rail so that he wouldn't put too much pressure on his ankle.

'I've always wanted to take a look around Allhallows Hall,' said John. 'It has a fair old history, I can tell you. I'm only sorry that I've had to come here under such unhappy circumstances.'

Vicky led him along the corridor to the stained-glass window of Old Dewer. John stopped and stared at it, and he was obviously fascinated.

'The Devil,' said Rob. 'One of the previous owners of this house had this window installed to keep him away.'

'Understandable,' said John. 'There's still a few folks believe that Old Dewer goes out hunting in the middle of the night. It's unbaptised babies he's looking for. Chrisemores they call them, round here. Anybody else he chases to the top of the Dewerstone so that they fall over the edge, plunge down into the River Plym and die.'

'Yes. That's what we were told when we first came to live here. As if this house isn't creepy enough without stories like that.'

Rob opened the bedroom door. Nothing had changed

since he had last looked around it. Here they were, exactly as before: the odd collection of spare chairs and the cobwebby candlesticks. None of them had been moved.

John stepped into the middle of the bedroom, turned around and sniffed. 'Bit fusty,' he said. 'I can smell something but I'm not sure what it is.'

Rob sniffed too. 'I can't smell anything, but then Allhallows Hall has always smelled fusty. I suppose I'm used to it.'

'No, there's something else. It's really familiar but I can't put my finger on it. Cinnamon? Oranges?'

Vicky sniffed, and frowned, and said, 'I can smell it, too. Maybe it's just the leather seats of those two chairs.'

Rob shook his head. 'I still can't smell it. But then I can never smell toast burning, either.'

John paced the length of the bedroom, toe to heel, to measure it, just as the priest hunters used to. 'Just over twelve feet, I'd say. Let me go next door and see what that room comes out at.'

He left the bedroom and came back a few seconds later. 'It's about the same. I thought there might be a hidden compartment at the end of this room, but it doesn't look like it.'

John went slowly around the room, tapping on each panel of the dark oak dado and shifting the stacked-up chairs beside the window so that he could reach the dado there. When he had gone all the way around, he came up to Rob and Vicky and said, 'I don't know. I couldn't hear any cavities. But that Nicholas Owen was such an ingenious bugger he might have worked out a way of muffling the sound. My friend the cavity wall contractor could find out for certain with a borescope.'

Vicky looked around and shuddered. 'There's definitely something weird about this room, even if it doesn't have a priest's hole. I didn't just fall over so *something* must be hiding here. I was pushed really hard.' With that, she pulled down the neck of her sweater to show John the crimson bruise on her shoulder.

'You're right,' said John. 'I don't reckon a ghost could have done that.'

They left the end bedroom and John looked into the other seven bedrooms, rapping at the dados and pacing out their dimensions. Rob knocked at the door of the master bedroom because Katharine was still in there.

'Katharine? Are you decent?'

'Of course I'm decent. What do you want?'

'John from the search and rescue needs to take a look around your room. He's looking for hidden hidey-holes.'

'All right. If he must.'

They went in. Katharine was sitting at the dressing table, brushing her hair. Rob had never seen her without make-up before and was surprised that she looked much younger than forty-two. It could have been the dim light in the bedroom, or the fact that he could see only her face in the mirror. Maybe the mirror was the opposite of the portrait of Dorian Gray – your reflection always stayed young while you grew older.

'We think there must be a priest hole somewhere in the house,' Rob told her. 'John here knows all the local history and everything points to the possibility that the Wilmingtons had one built in.'

'Well, you're welcome to look. But surely your dad would have known about it, wouldn't he?'

'Not necessarily,' said John. 'Their existence was always kept a very close secret. The punishment for hiding a priest could be severe. You could forfeit your house and be sent to prison and tortured on the rack or even hanged.'

Katharine said nothing to that, but went on brushing her hair, although harder this time, as if it had done something to annoy her. John went around the bedroom, knocking at the dado panels. The tester bed was still unmade, so he lifted the pillows away and took a close look at the carved wooden bedhead, which was elaborately decorated with fruit and flowers. He tried sliding it from side to side, and then tugging at it, to see if he could dislodge it. If it could be removed, it would certainly have opened up a wide enough space for a priest to squeeze himself through.

He tugged at it again and again, but eventually he put back the pillows and shook his head. 'Solid elm. Only a bedhead. Pity. Would have been quite ingenious, wouldn't it?'

He paced the length of the bedroom to measure it. 'Thirteen feet, the same as the room next door. There's no priest hole in here, either.' Turning to Katharine, he said, 'Thank you… sorry if we disturbed you.'

Katharine shrugged. 'Personally, I think you're wasting your time searching the house. Timmy's probably miles away by now.'

'Oh, we're still combing the moors. And if we haven't found him by lunchtime we'll have at least two dozen more volunteers out this afternoon, before it starts getting dimpsey.'

Katharine said nothing, but put down her hairbrush and leaned forward to stare at her reflection in close-up.

When John had finished checking all the bedrooms, he took a look in the bathroom. When Allhallows Hall was built, long before hot running water and flushing toilets, this would have simply been another bedroom, so it was possible that there might have been a priest hole built into one of the walls. But after tapping and measuring yet again – even climbing into the bath so he could knock on the wall behind it – he had to admit that he was unable to find one.

'Perhaps the priest that was caught here had simply been hiding in a wardrobe or under one of the beds,' Rob suggested. 'I used to have nightmares about somebody hiding under my bed… maybe that was why.'

As they made their way back towards the landing, John looked up at the trapdoor in the ceiling.

'Is it easy to get up into the attic?'

'Reasonably,' said Rob, opening the nearest bedroom door and showing him the old wooden stepladder that was leaning against the wall. 'But Martin and I went up there yesterday and we couldn't see anywhere that Timmy could have hidden. There's nothing but the water tank and a whole pile of old suitcases.'

'All the same,' John told him. 'And I'll want to search *that* bedroom, too.'

Rob dragged the stepladder out into the corridor and opened it up. 'Just be careful... I'll hold on to it because the cord's broken and we don't want it doing the splits when you get to the top.'

John warily mounted the stepladder, which creaked ominously with every step that he took. He lifted the trapdoor, reached around and switched on the lights. Then he heaved himself right up into the attic, and disappeared.

Rob and Vicky waited in the corridor as they heard him walking from one side of the attic to the other.

'Anything?' called Rob, after a while.

'No... nowhere to hide a priest. And no sign of your little lad... not unless he's hiding under all these clothes.'

'What clothes?'

'All these clothes that are strewn all over the place. You said there were suitcases up here, didn't you? They're wide open, all of them. The whole attic looks like an H-bomb's been dropped on a charity shop.'

'You're joking,' said Rob. He beckoned to Vicky and said, 'Can you hold the stepladder steady for me? I have to see this.'

He climbed up until he was high enough to see inside the attic. Carefully turning around, he saw John standing beside a knee-deep heap of sweaters, jackets, shirts, trousers and underwear, as well as washbags and books and several pairs of men's brogues. All of the suitcases he had seen when he had climbed up here with Martin were lying around, and as John had said, all of them were gaping wide open. Somehow, somebody had managed to gain access to the attic without being seen or heard by any one of them, open up all the suitcases and tip out their contents onto the boarded floor.

'I'm stunned,' said Rob. 'I'm totally baffled. I mean, this is seriously creepy. None of these cases was open when we saw them yesterday. I can't understand how anybody could possibly have got up here to do this. Or *why*.'

'Whoever it was, it could be that they were looking for something.'

'That's more than likely, although I still can't work out how they got up here without us being aware of it. But we'll never know what it was they were looking for, will we? If they found it they'll have taken it away, and even if they couldn't find it, because it wasn't here, we *still* shan't know what it was.'

John bent down and lifted up the label that was tied to one of the suitcase handles.

'*A. Mallett. HMP Dartmoor*.'

'Yes... they're all prisoners' suitcases, although I have no idea why my dad had them all stored up here in his attic.'

'Now that somebody's been rifling through them, I think we need to tell Sergeant Billings. Just like you say, we can't guess what they were looking for and whether they found it or not. Could have been anything, couldn't it? A gun? Drugs? Uncut diamonds? Some incriminating piece of evidence?'

He stood up straight again, taking a last look around the attic. 'Whoever it was, they weren't hiding in a priest hole up here, because there isn't one.'

★

They climbed back down the stepladder.

'What is it?' asked Vicky. 'You look like you've seen a ghost.'

'I think I'd feel better if I had seen a ghost,' said Rob. 'At least that would have been some explanation.'

He told her about the open suitcases, and how their contents had been scattered around the attic floor.

'John thinks we ought to tell the police about it, and of course I will. I still can't understand what all those prisoners' belongings were doing up in the attic anyway.'

'You don't think your father could have—?'

'Stolen them? No. Why would he? It's not as though there's anything valuable in them – not as far as we know, anyway. Only clothes and toiletries and shoes – the sort of things you pack when you're going away for a holiday or a business trip.'

They walked back to the landing.

'I'm going to call Sergeant Billings now,' said Rob, but before he could start back downstairs, John caught hold of his sleeve and said, 'Wait a moment, Mr Russell.'

'What is it?'

John pointed to the small latticed window on the left side of the landing.

'Look how far away that window is, compared to the stained-glass windows in the first two bedrooms. Hold on, let me measure it.'

He walked heel-to-toe towards the window and then

turned around. 'Twenty feet. More than seven feet longer than the distance from the doors to the windows in the bedrooms.'

'I never noticed that before. But it doesn't make any sense, does it? Those two bedrooms both have windows that look out over the garden. If you go down to the garden you can look up and you can see them. Both stained glass.'

'Can you open them?'

'No, but they both let daylight in.'

John knocked on the wall. He pressed his ear to the plaster and knocked again, harder this time.

'I'm not sure, but I think there could be a cavity behind here.'

'Okay... but how would anybody manage to hide themselves in it? There's no door.'

'Let's check the bedrooms again. I was only tapping at the dado last time, to see if it sounded hollow, which it didn't. But maybe the panelling can be opened up somehow. If there's a cavity there, there must be some kind of access to it.'

They went back to the first and second bedrooms. John switched on the bedside lamps, as well as taking out his own pocket flashlight. He inspected the dado panelling inch by inch, occasionally tugging at the beading in between the panels to see if it came loose, and trying to slide the dado rails right and left.

'Nothing that I can see so far,' he said, as they stepped back out into the corridor. 'But I have the strongest feeling that there's a recess behind there.'

'I don't see how there can be,' said Rob. 'Those are outside walls.'

'But there's a seven-foot discrepancy between the length of the landing and the length of all three bedrooms.'

'It could be just an optical illusion. I mean, the whole house is wonky. They didn't build them with plans in those days.'

'A few inches out of line, yes, I can go along with that. But seven feet?'

Rob could only shrug in resignation. He was at a loss to explain how the landing could be so much longer than the bedrooms beside it, but the bedrooms had windows in them, so there was no possibility that there was any kind of priest's hole behind their end walls.

John went back into the third bedroom. Again, he went all the way around the dado, tapping and tugging and sliding.

'This is driving me insane,' he said, when he had finished.

Vicky had been looking around, too. She lifted the lid of the window seat, even though she knew that Rob and Martin had already looked inside. She leaned over and picked up some of the rolled-up bundles of legal documents. Underneath them she found a white pennant with a red cross on it, frail with age, like the pennant carried by *Agnus Dei*, the Lamb of God. When she lifted that up, she uncovered even more rolled-up documents, but she could also see something metallic glinting right at the bottom of the chest. She cleared aside more rolls of paper and saw that it was a mottled brass crucifix, a little less than a foot long, with an irritated-looking Jesus nailed onto it.

'Anything interesting?' asked Rob, peering over her shoulder.

'No… just a lot of old deeds and wills by the look of it. And this.'

She tried to pick up the crucifix, but the foot of the cross was hinged to the floor, and she could only swing it upright. It swung up quite easily, as if it had been oiled.

'This is peculiar, Rob – look,' said Vicky. She folded the crucifix back down flat, and then swung it up again so that he could see.

'Wow. I wonder why on earth it's stuck to the floor like that.'

He was interrupted by a sharp scraping sound, followed by a series of plaintive creaks. He turned around to see that the three central panels of the dado at the end of the bedroom were slowly opening up, like the lower half of a stable door. Behind them was another room, dimly illuminated with reddish light.

John had been texting on his phone, but he stopped, too, with his finger poised over the keys.

'Well, bugger me,' he said. 'That Nicholas Owen. Even more cleverer than I thought he was.'

He dropped his phone back into his pocket and went over to the window seat.

'Do you know what? This crucifix isn't a crucifix at all. It's a handle. It's probably attached to a lever, and when you lift it up, it must activate some arrangement of strings and pulleys and weights under the floorboards, and the dado opens up. There's a similar set-up at one of the priest holes in Tavistock – a warming pan hanging on the kitchen wall. You tilt the warming-pan handle to one side and a door opens up in the brickwork beside it. It's cunning, but not quite as cunning as this.'

'You mean to say this crucifix has been lying here for four hundred years and nobody has found out what it's for?'

'The likelihood is that the Wilmingtons knew exactly what it was for. But Allhallows Hall was passed down from one generation of Wilmingtons to the next. Your father was the first to own it who wasn't a Wilmington.'

Vicky took hold of Rob's hand and squeezed it tight. 'Do you think there's anybody in there? You don't think that—' She didn't say, 'Timmy's in there, unconscious or dead?'

'One way to find out,' said John. He went to the end of the room and crouched down by the opening in the dado. 'Anybody in there?' he called out. Then, even louder, 'Is there anybody in there because if there is you'd best be coming on out as quick as you like!'

He waited, but there was no answer. He looked back at Rob and Vicky, and then, with his head down and his knees bent, he shuffled inside. When he stood up straight, they could see him only from the waist down.

'Everything okay?' Rob asked him.

'Gobsmacking. That's all I can say. You both need to come in here and see this. You won't believe your eyes.'

14

Rob and Vicky crouched down to enter the room and then stood up. The room had roughly plastered walls and the floorboards were covered in coarse brown horsehair matting that felt as if it were two or three inches deep. The air was stale, but the faint hint of cinnamon and oranges was slightly more distinct, so that even Rob could smell it.

At the far end of the room lay a heap of dirty wool blankets, as if several people had been sleeping there, but the room was empty. There was no sign of Timmy, and no sign of whoever or *whatever* might have pushed Vicky out of the bedroom. But it was the windows that caught their attention most of all. On the left-hand side of the room were the two stained-glass windows at the ends of the first and second bedrooms, with their multicoloured diamond patterns. On the right-hand side were two identical stained-glass windows, which must have been the ones that overlooked the garden. From the outside of the house, nobody would have realised that they weren't the same windows.

'So this is the priest's hole that the Wilmingtons had built,' said John. 'It's extraordinary those priest hunters never found it. I mean, they were pretty canny. Pursuivants they were called, and they were former spies and mercenaries. They could make themselves a fair amount of bounty if they caught a priest.'

'We were certainly never aware that this room was here,' said Rob. 'I can't believe the size of it.'

'Yes – it's much larger than most priest's holes, but that's the trick, in a way. All three bedrooms along this corridor are the same length. You can imagine the priest hunters rushing upstairs to see if they could catch a priest up here, and measuring the bedrooms. They obviously overlooked to compare the length of the bedrooms with the width of the landing.'

'We only ever used the first two bedrooms for visitors, and the end bedroom we never used at all, except for storing stuff. I lifted up that window seat once but when I saw that it was stuffed full of old papers I didn't bother to look any further.'

'Your father must have bothered to look, some time after you left home. If not your father, somebody did. I wonder if he found this room but never told anybody about it.'

'I don't see why he wouldn't. But then he was such a grumpy bastard. He wouldn't tell you what day of the week it was if he could help it.'

'*Rob*,' Vicky chided him.

'I know. I shouldn't speak ill of him now he's dead. I just hope they have spy cameras in hell so that he can hear what we've been saying about him.'

John stamped two or three times on the floor. 'Nicholas

Owen would have laid down all this horsehair so that nobody downstairs could hear the priest walking about. And there's an extra layer of plaster on the walls, by the look of it.'

He paused for a few moments, his eyes half-closed, as if he were listening. Then he said, 'Do you feel something in here? There's that cinnamony smell... but something more than that.'

Vicky closed her eyes, too. After a while she said, 'I'm not sure. Rob? Can you feel anything?'

'Like what?'

'Like... I don't know. It's almost as if there's somebody else in here with us, but we can't see them, and they're holding their breath, too, so that we can't hear them, either.'

'That's exactly what I feel,' said John. He went over to the heap of blankets and lifted up two or three of them to look underneath, but there was nothing there.

Rob closed his eyes. He listened hard, but all he could hear was the faraway sound of a tractor puttering its way up the lane towards Wormold's Farm.

'No,' he said, but as he opened his eyes he felt somebody brush against his left shoulder, only lightly, as if they were squeezing past him to get off a bus. He clapped his hand against his arm and turned around, but there was nobody there.

'What?' said Vicky.

'I thought – I thought somebody touched me. That's what it felt like, anyway.'

'It might have been. It could have been. Somebody pushed me over, Rob, and I couldn't see them, either.'

John looked serious. 'It's not a joke, this. I think there's something real queer about this room. I don't believe in ghosts. Not the sort that go around in white sheets going "*wooo!*" Not that sort, anyway. But I do believe we all have spirits and who's to say that those spirits don't outlive us when we're gone?'

'You may be right and you may be wrong, but we've found the priest hole and Timmy's not in it. So what are we going to do now?'

'We'll carry on searching over the moors, of course. And the cops'll be doing everything they can... putting out appeals on the telly and the radio, asking people for dashcam footage, knocking on doors.'

Vicky circled around the room, reaching out and gently touching the walls and the stained-glass windows as if she could pick up clues about Timmy's whereabouts. Her eyes were filling up with tears again, and when she spoke her voice was tight with pain. 'I don't know, Rob. I know it's not logical. But I have such a strong feeling that Timmy's still here somewhere – here in the house.'

'Vicks, darling, we've looked everywhere. He just isn't.'

'But I feel that he *is*! I don't know why, but I do!'

John glanced at Rob as if he were seeking his approval, and then he turned back to Vicky. 'If you feel that, then I don't think there's any harm in my calling on Ada Grey.'

'Who's Ada Grey?'

'Oh, she's well known around here. She lives in a cottage

up at Rundlestone. Well, there's only two cottages at Rundlestone and she lives in one of them. She does all that occult stuff. You know, tarot cards and all that. But some people say that she can talk to people who have passed over. If there's spirits in this house, and they know where your little lad is, she's about the only person I know who's got any chance of getting it out of them.'

'She's a medium?'

'She doesn't call herself that. She calls herself a charmer.'

'All right, then, if you really feel that she might be able to help. I'm like you, and I have to admit that I've never believed in that kind of thing – not ghosts. But something pushed my wife over, and I definitely felt as if somebody brushed up against me, and even if it wasn't spirits I'd like to know just what the hell is going on here.'

At that moment there was a loud knocking at the front door, which made Vicky clap her hand over her heart.

15

Rob opened the front door to find Sergeant Billings standing in the porch, as well as a tall man in a brown trilby hat and a long brown raincoat.

'This is Detective Inspector Holley, from Plymouth CID,' said Sergeant Billings. 'He'd like to have a word, if he may. Not about your Timmy, I'm afraid to say. We're still out looking.'

'Of course, come in.'

DI Holley stepped into the hallway and looked around it, this way and that, like a prospective buyer. He had a large bony nose like a hawk and glittery, close-set eyes. Even though Rob didn't have the keenest sense of smell, he could tell that DI Holley was a smoker.

'And you're Mr *Robert* Russell, I presume?' he asked Rob.

'That's right, and this is my wife, Victoria.'

DI Holley gave Vicky a peremptory nod, as if he had been asked to put a price on a Dartmoor pony but really couldn't be bothered.

'Could you call Martin, please, Vicky?' Rob asked her, and Vicky went through to the library, where Martin was still hunched over his laptop, making Skype calls to his investors.

Rob led DI Holley and Sergeant Billings through to the drawing room and they all sat down. The wind had changed direction so that the fire was sulky and subdued and kept puffing out little clouds of fine white ash.

Martin came in, looking irritated. 'Yes?' he said. 'Is this about Dad?'

'Detective Inspector Holley,' said DI Holley. 'And you're Mr Martin Russell?'

'Yes.'

'This is indeed regarding your late father, Mr Herbert Russell. Earlier this morning I received the final results of the autopsy that was carried out to ascertain the cause of his death. There is no question at all that he was struck a severe blow on the back of his head by a hammer. This fractured his skull and caused a fatal cerebral haemorrhage.'

'I see,' said Martin, although he still didn't sit down. 'We thought it was something like that.'

'As you're aware, a hammer was located in the back garden of this house and forensic tests have shown beyond doubt that it was indeed the same hammer that was used to kill your father.'

Rob said, 'My God. Do you have any idea yet who might have killed him?'

'We're working on several theories, Mr Russell. The front door of the house was open when your father was found. His car was unlocked and there was an overnight bag in the boot, and we know that he was booked in to stay for three nights at the Marine Hotel in Paignton.'

'Yes. He did that every month, without fail, although we never knew why.'

'It's possible that he could have been about to leave but returned to collect the accounts book and receipts that were found scattered on the staircase, as if he had dropped it. An intruder could have followed him into the house and attacked him. If he was attacked in the hall, however, it's hard to understand how he could have dropped the accounts halfway up the stairs.'

'Yes. I see the problem.'

'In my opinion, Mr Russell, it's far more likely that his assailant was already on the premises and attacked him at the *top* of the stairs, after which he fell down and dropped his accounts during his descent.'

'I see what you're getting at, yes. Do you have any idea who that might have been?'

'He was governor of Dartmoor Prison for nineteen years. I imagine there are quite a few former lags who might bear a grudge against him, for one reason or another. We'll be visiting the prison and going through their records to see who the most likely suspects might be. Perhaps it was somebody he shut up in solitary confinement, something like that. If it *was* a former lag, though, it's questionable that your father would have invited him into the house voluntarily. And our examination of the doors and windows on the premises showed no indication of a break-in.'

'So where do you go from here?' asked Martin.

'Don't take this the wrong way, but a considerable percentage of homicides are committed by relatives. As a formality, we're going to ask both of you and your sister to take DNA and fingerprint tests. Only to eliminate you, and so as not to confuse any other tests that we might be carrying out.'

'Rather pointless, don't you think?' said Martin. 'None of us were anywhere near here when Dad met his Maker.'

'It's only a formality,' said DI Holley. 'But we have to make sure that we've covered every possibility. Even the remotest possibility.'

'I understand,' Rob told him. 'I've no objection to that.'

'A forensic team will be here shortly to carry that out. Meanwhile, do you have any questions you want to ask me? Or has any further information occurred to you that might conceivably be of use to us in this investigation?'

'I was going to call you about this anyway,' said Rob. 'When we were searching the house we found a number of suitcases in the attic, maybe as many as a dozen, all of them packed full of clothes. Every one of them was tagged with a label with the name of a Dartmoor prisoner on it.'

'Really?' said DI Holley, and then he turned around to Sergeant Billings. 'Your officers searched the house, too, didn't they, sergeant? Didn't *they* see these suitcases?'

'We didn't check the attic, sir, on account of there was no way that a five-year-old boy could have climbed up there and shut the trapdoor after him. Not without leaving the stepladder under it, anyway.'

'Fair enough,' said DI Holley, and turned back to Rob. 'But – Mr Russell – do you have any idea *why* your father would have been storing all those prisoners' suitcases?'

'No idea at all, I'm afraid. They weren't up there when my brother and sister and I were living here. But there's something more. We looked up in the attic again today with Mr Kipling here because he was trying to find a priest's hole.'

'Really? I've heard of those. You think there's one here?'

'There *is* one here, and we've found it,' said John. 'It's the largest I've ever come across. Just over six metres by two, behind three of the upstairs bedrooms. Very cunningly done, too, with duplicate stained-glass windows.'

'Oh, you've found it?' said Martin. 'Well, thanks for telling me.'

'Martin – we were still up there when DI Holley here knocked at the door.'

'Nobody in it, though, I presume?' asked DI Holley.

John looked across at Rob as if to say, *Let's not tell him about the priest hole's spooky atmosphere. Not just yet, anyway. He'll probably think we've got a screw loose.*

Rob looked at Vicky and he could see that she had got the message, too.

'No, nobody in it,' he said. 'But when we went up in the attic, we found that all the prisoners' suitcases had been opened and the clothes inside them had been tossed around all over the place.'

'And you've no idea who might have done it?'

'Absolutely no idea at all. Totally baffled. We haven't seen or heard anybody breaking in, and we can't understand how they could have got up into the attic or why they should have emptied all those suitcases out. They might have been looking for something, but of course we don't know what.'

DI Holley said nothing for a few moments, frowning as

if he wished that Rob hadn't told him about the suitcases, because it further complicated the mysteries of Herbert Russell's murder and why Timmy had disappeared.

At last he said, 'You didn't disturb any of the clothing? Good. When forensics come up here I'll ask them to examine it. And you say that all the suitcases are labelled with the names of Dartmoor inmates?'

'We assume that's what they are. They're all addressed Dartmoor Prison.'

'Okay then. We'll make a list of the names and when we visit the prison we'll see if we can match them. Perhaps that might even give us a lead to whoever it was who assaulted your father. Meanwhile, do you want to show me the attic? And while we're up there, you might let me take a look at this priest's hole that you've found.'

'Yes, of course.'

They all stood up. John said, 'Listen – if you've no further need of me, I have one or two errands to run and things to do at home. I can come back later, though. About fiveish? Depending on – you know.'

Rob gave him the thumbs up. He knew that when John came back, he would be bringing with him Ada Grey, the self-styled 'charmer'.

Martin said, 'I wouldn't mind seeing this priest's hole too. You know – seeing as how I *do* have an interest in this property, no matter how tenuous.'

Rob was about to tell him not to be so shirty, but he decided against it, not in front of two police officers. He didn't want DI Holley to suspect that there was any resentment between them about the inheritance of Allhallows Hall. People had been murdered for far less.

Martin and DI Holley had much the same reaction to the priest's hole. They were both deeply impressed by the mechanics that opened up the hidden panel in the dado, and by the way in which the stained-glass windows had been placed to conceal the room's existence. But neither of them could see that it was any more than an historical curiosity. It was empty, and there was no indication that it had been occupied recently, even if the crucifix lever lifted so easily, as if it had been lubricated not too long ago. DI Holley bent over the window seat and sniffed it and said, 'WD-40.' If he picked up the scent of cinnamon and orange, he didn't mention it.

Four forensics experts turned up two hours later and Rob helped them to climb up into the attic to examine the suitcases and the scattered clothes. They were still up there three hours later, clumping about and taking pictures.

With the help of two more uniformed officers, they removed all the clothing and the suitcases from the attic, carried them downstairs and loaded them into a police van. Then they took fingerprints and DNA swabs from Rob and Martin, as well as Vicky and Katharine, although Katharine made it clear that she thought it was preposterous. 'Can you *seriously* see me driving two hundred miles down here to hit my father-in-law over the head with a hammer? I ask you!'

Before the forensic officers left, Grace and Portia returned from searching the moors with the DSR team, and they were able to give their fingerprints and DNA samples too. Portia didn't mind. She thought it was quite erotic that she should be suspected of being a murderer so that her lover could inherit her father's sixteenth-century mansion.

16

It was nearly seven o'clock by the time John Kipling arrived at the house with Ada Grey.

Martin had taken Katharine to Taylors restaurant in Tavistock because she had told him that she was becoming increasingly stressed and claustrophobic in Allhallows Hall and needed an evening away to calm herself down. Grace and Portia were snuggled up together on the sofa in the drawing room, watching a film about a domineering male lawyer being prosecuted for sexual harassment. They were murmuring together and kissing occasionally and sharing a bedraggled spliff.

Rob had imagined that Ada Grey would be middle-aged, if not elderly, with her hair fixed up in a fraying grey bun and a shapeless ankle-length dress and about a dozen silver chains and pendants around her neck. He had guessed right about the silver chains and pendants, but that was all. Ada Grey couldn't have been more than thirty-two or thirty-three years old. She was tall, with glossy black hair that was cut straight across her forehead in a severe fringe but then spread wide over her shoulders like a cape. She had dark-blue feline eyes, a short straight nose and full sensual lips, which looked as if she had just finished blowing somebody a parting kiss.

Underneath her long black overcoat she was wearing a short grey velvet dress and shiny black leather boots. She had very large breasts, so that all her chains and pendants and magical talismans were arranged across them like a display on a jeweller's tray. She smelled strongly of some floral perfume.

'This is Ada,' said John. 'She says she can't wait to see this priest's hole that we've found.'

'I'm Rob,' said Rob. 'And this is my wife, Vicky. Thanks for coming. We could do with somebody who knows about ghosts and spirits and stuff like that. This house is beginning to give us the heebie-jeebies.'

'You've heard things?' asked Ada. 'Seen things, have you? Felt things?'

'Yes and no. *Heard* things and *felt* things but not actually seen anything. Come on in and we'll show you the priest's hole and tell you all about it. Here – let me take your coat.'

Rob lifted Ada's coat off her shoulders and as he did so Vicky raised her eyebrows as if to tell him, *Just watch it, Russell, with this bosomy witch. I've got my eye on you.*

'John tells me you call yourself a charmer,' said Rob, as he led them all upstairs. His ankle was still tender so he had to bite his lip and cling on to the banister rail.

'I'm a witch, really, but most folks have totally the wrong idea about witches,' said Ada. She had a soft Devon accent, slow and breathy. Rob almost felt as if she were breathing in his ear. 'What I do mostly is tell fortunes and talk to hunky punks.'

'Hunky punks?' asked Vicky, as they reached the top of the stairs. 'What are hunky punks when they're at home?'

'That's what we call fairies, or piskies. But also the spirits of folks what's passed over to the Otherland. Children, mostly, who went before they ever had the chance to be baptised.'

'And you can really talk to them?'

'Of course. Anybody can. Folks still say that their late loved ones are looking down on them from heaven, but these days hardly any of them really believe that's true. And they're right. Because you don't go to heaven when you pass over – or hell, for that matter. You go to the Otherland, that's all.'

'And where is it, this "Otherland"?'

'It's *here*, close by. Only it's not here. It's like Alice, stepping through the mirror. It's like seeing your reflection in the window, standing in your garden late at night, except that's all you are, just a reflection, and there's no you standing in the room looking out. Not any more.'

'I think you're giving me the creeps already,' said Vicky. 'In this end room – right here – I felt somebody pushing me. In fact, they pushed me right over so that I banged my shoulder. I felt them but I couldn't see anybody.'

Ada had been staring at the stained-glass window of Old Dewer, but when Vicky told her that she turned and looked into the bedroom.

'Somebody actually pushed you? But what? They was *invisible*?'

'I felt somebody brushing up against me too,' said Rob.

'Again, there was nobody there. Nobody that I could see, anyway.'

Ada seemed puzzled. 'That doesn't sound like nobody from the Otherland. I've never known one act aggressive. Mostly they're sad. They tell you how much they miss the folks they loved and the life they used to enjoy. When you hear them talking, it's more like voices whispering inside your head, and if you see them, which isn't often, they're almost transparent. I've felt two or three of them touch me, but it's not much more than stroking your hair or kissing your cheek. None of them never pushed me, nor hurt me. Nothing like that, never.'

'Anyway, come and see this priest's hole for yourself,' said Rob. He led Ada into the bedroom and opened up the window seat.

'See this crucifix? Well, watch.'

He swung up the crucifix and the panel in the dado creaked open.

'Golly... that's gurt amazing,' said Ada, shaking her head.

John said, 'I'll tell you – I could hardly credit it when it first opened up. I've seen some incredible priest's holes built by Nicholas Owen, but this one really takes the cake. Come and have a look inside.'

They all ducked down under the dado rail and then stood up inside the room. Ada slowly padded around the thick horsehair carpet, stopping now and again to close her eyes and take deep breaths.

'There's someone here,' she said, after a while.

'What do you mean? A spirit?'

'Oh, there's spirits everywhere around Sampford Spiney. Spirits and piskies. There's a famous poem about it.

'For mebbe 'tis a lonesome road
Or heather blooth, or peaty ling
Or nobbut just a rainy combe
The spell that meks 'ee tek an' sing
An' this I knaw, the li'l tods
Be ever callin' silver faint
Thar be piskies up to Dartymoor
An' tidden gude yew zay there bain't.'

'You're not trying to say that there's piskies in here.'

'No, not piskies,' said Ada. 'But there's somebody here. In fact, there could be two or three somebodies. I can feel them. Possibly more. And I can smell at least one of them.'

'We could smell something, too,' John told her. 'Sort of like cinnamon, and maybe oranges. Is that what you're getting?'

'I think... I think it's a toilet water,' said Ada. She breathed in again, and held her breath for at least ten seconds. Then she breathed out again and said, 'No... it's an aftershave, and I think I know which one. My father used to wear it. Old Spice.'

'Old Spice?' asked Rob. 'Are you serious? There's a spirit in here and he's wearing Old Spice?'

'What's so unbelievable about that?'

'I don't know. It's so naff.'

'Would you have believed it more if it had been Dolce and Gabbana? Spirits often carry their smell with them to the Otherland. And it's not only Old Spice in here. There's other smells. But what's most interesting is that none of them are *dead* smells.'

'I don't get you.'

'Spirits who get into contact with me from the Otherland mostly don't smell of nothing at all. Usually they're too faint and distant and all I can hear is their voices, right inside the back of my brain. Now and then, though, they're closer than that, especially the ones who have only just passed over. I can see their outlines sometimes, *shimmering*, and I can smell embalming fluid, or smoke. Rotten flesh, sometimes. That's what I mean by dead smells.'

'But these aren't dead smells?'

Ada closed her eyes again and breathed in. 'No. And that's what makes it so strange. There are definitely presences in this room... multiple presences. But I wouldn't call them spirits.'

'What are they then?' asked Vicky. 'Ghosts?'

'No, they're not ghosts neither. Ghosts are supposed to be the souls of dead people who come back to haunt us because they still had unfinished business when they died, or because they want to get their own back on folks who have done them wrong. But there's no such thing as ghosts like that.'

'So what are these – *presences*?' Rob asked her. 'We've heard people whispering at night, outside our bedroom door. Could that have been them?'

'I don't know, shag, to be honest with you. I'll have to do some reading about this, and then come back and do a few tests. I have some suspicions, but I don't want to start meddling until I know for certain what it is I'm up against. If there's a presence here that has the strength to push you over, even though you can't see it, then – well, I think we need to be wary.'

Rob said, 'Just a minute, Ada. If I'm understanding you correctly, you're saying that these presences aren't dead people? They're not spirits and they're not ghosts. So does that mean they're alive? How can they be alive and we can't see them?'

'That's why I need to do some looking into it,' said Ada. 'There's a wizard I know in Monkscross, Francis Coade. He doesn't call himself a wizard the same like I don't call myself a witch. A *gleaner*, that's how he describes himself, because most of his time he picks up the spiritual bits and pieces that people have left behind them when they cross over unexpected. You know, just like farmers used to let poor folks pick up the bits and pieces in the fields after a harvest was over. He knows more about this kind of thing than I do – folks appearing to be dead but not dead. Gone but not gone, if you follow me.'

'I can't say that I do. But, please, by all means get in touch with this wizard – this "gleaner". Because Vicky thinks she heard a child crying, as well as whispers, and if there's any chance that was Timmy—'

'Of course,' said Ada, tilting her head sympathetically and giving him a little smile. 'I'll try to get over to see Francis in the morning. Once I've talked to him, and set up one or two experiments, I promise I'll be back to you dreckly.'

★

After John and Ada had left, Rob and Vicky went into the drawing room. There was still a faint smell of weed but the logs in the fire were blazing strongly and had carried most of it up the chimney. Rob could hardly complain: he had smoked joints regularly when he was at Worthing art school and at one time he and his friends had solemnly lowered more than thirty deckchairs into the boating pool, chanting all the while, in the belief that they were carrying out a solemn religious ceremony.

'That was a rather gorgeous-looking witch,' said Portia.

'She calls herself a charmer, rather than a witch,' Rob told her.

'I don't blame her,' said Portia. 'She *is* a charmer.'

Grace gave her arm a petulant slap, but Portia blew her a kiss. 'Don't worry, Gracey,' she said, and sang, '*Nothing compares to you!*'

'What did she say, anyway?' asked Grace. 'Did she think that priest's hole is haunted?'

'Not exactly haunted, but she said that she can feel something there. Presences, that's what she called them. She doesn't think they're ghosts, or spirits, or anything like that. She's not at all sure what they are. She's going to do some research and talk to some fellow she knows in Monkscross who's a wizard.'

'Oh my God. This gets more unbelievable by the minute.'

There was a knock at the door and Vicky went to answer it. It was a woman member of the search and rescue team. Apart from her crimson anorak she was wearing a bulbous grey bobble hat and huge grey knitted gloves that looked like characters from *Sesame Street*.

Rob came into the hallway to join them.

'There's still no sign of your Timmy, I'm afraid,' the woman told them. 'We've had over a hundred and fifty volunteers out this afternoon, plus three dogs. The dogs are usually brilliant at picking up trails, even in bad weather, but there's nary a trace. We'll still be searching tonight, and again tomorrow, but we have to be realistic. Wherever he is, we don't think he's out on the moor.'

'Thank you,' said Rob. 'I can't tell you how much we appreciate everything that you've been doing. You've been extraordinary.'

The woman lifted one of her gloves and looked at it as if it were a faceless puppet. 'We always say that God created the moor for its beauty and its wildlife, but He also created it to test how much we care for our fellow human beings.'

17

That night, the wind began to rise again, until it was whistling and shrieking through every gap in the window frames and moaning down the chimneys like a choir at a funeral.

Rob and Vicky were both worn out, so they went to bed at ten-thirty and Vicky took a Unisom to see if she could manage to get some sleep. Rob wished he could have taken one too, but he wanted to stay alert in case there was any more whispering. He had not only closed the panel in the dado but also locked the bedroom door. If there really were any presences in the priest's hole, dead or living, they would have to knock it down to get out.

Grace and Portia went to bed soon after them, both slightly stoned. They knew that with Timmy still missing this wasn't a time to be giggling, but they couldn't help themselves. Rob could hear them stifling their laughter as they crept along the corridor to their bedroom. He forgave them. Even at its most tragic, he thought, life never stops being ludicrous. He couldn't stop thinking about some sinister presence that smelled of that most dated of aftershaves, Old Spice.

'Did you believe that witch?' Vicky murmured, with her back turned to him.

'You mean, do I believe that there are some kind of living people in that priest's hole? People we can't see?'

'*I* believed her. I'm sure that I can feel them. And *smell* them.'

'I don't know. She could be right, but even if she is, I wonder if these "presences" have any connection to Timmy disappearing? I'm beginning to think more and more that somebody's picked him up and driven off with him. I mean, they can't find him on the moor and the dogs can't pick up a scent. He's not here in the house and he couldn't have *flown* away, could he? He's not a pisky.'

Vicky was silent for a long time, and then she said emphatically, 'I'm sure he's not dead.'

Rob didn't answer. He had a catch in his throat and he didn't want to sound as if he were losing hope.

Vicky turned over and laid her hand on his. '*You* don't think that he's dead, do you? We'd know, wouldn't we, if he was dead? I think we'd feel it.'

Rob nodded, and then shook his head, but he still couldn't draw in enough air to speak.

They heard the front door slam. Martin and Katharine were back from Tavistock. Martin called out, 'Hello? Hello? Anyone at home?' and then Rob heard him stumble against the chair in the hallway. He was obviously drunk.

For a minute or two, Martin and Katharine banged around downstairs. Martin went into the kitchen and Katharine snapped, 'What are you doing in there? For God's sake, Martin, you don't need any more to drink!'

Rob couldn't hear Martin's reply, but then Katharine demanded, 'Come to bed! God, you made such a fool of yourself! They'll never let us back into Taylors again, ever! Come to bed!'

Katharine's voice rose as shrill as an opera singer's falsetto, and she sounded almost as drunk as Martin.

Martin came out of the kitchen and said something to Katharine. Rob couldn't make out what it was, but it sounded like a string of expletives.

Eventually, after almost ten minutes of arguing and pacing around, Katharine clawed her way unsteadily upstairs and tottered along the corridor to the master bedroom, bumping into the panelling all the way along. She closed the door very quietly behind her, but Rob heard a crash from inside the bedroom that sounded as if she had knocked over a bedside lamp.

He waited, listening hard, but he didn't hear Martin follow her up to bed. Vicky was asleep now, and breathing evenly, although every now and then her lips moved as if she were talking to somebody in a dream. He was finding it hard to keep his own eyes open, and he lay back on the pillows and switched off the lamp.

'Dear God,' he said quietly. 'Please keep Timmy safe, wherever he is. And please let us find him tomorrow. I know I didn't believe in you before, God, but I promise you that I believe in you now.'

He was woken up by whispering outside their bedroom door. Sharp, persistent whispering, as if the whisperer were anxious or afraid. He groped his hand across to his bedside table and picked up his watch. The luminous dial told him that it was 2:37.

The whispering went on and on, and after a few minutes the first whisperer was joined by another, and then another. Rob lifted his head up from the pillow and strained his ears, but he was unable to make out what they were all saying.

He didn't want to switch on his lamp in case he woke Vicky, but the darkness inside the bedroom was total. There was no light shining under the door so the corridor must be in total darkness, too. Even if anybody was out there, would he be able to see them? If they were anything like the presence that had pushed Vicky over, or the one he had felt brushing up against him in the priest's hole, they would be invisible.

He took several deep breaths. Then he eased himself out of bed and shuffled as quietly as he could towards the door, his hands held out in front of him like a blind man.

The whispering persisted, and it sounded increasingly urgent. He reached the door and pressed his ear against it. It was still difficult to make out what the whisperers were saying, but he thought he caught one of them hissing, '*It's no use! You know it's no use! Not before then! And what's going to happen, once we get out? Have you thought about that?*'

Another whisperer replied, and even though Rob couldn't hear what he said, it sounded angry and dismissive.

Right, he thought. I'm going to open the door and confront them, even if I can't see them. I want to know who they are and what they want – 'presences' or not. And most of all I want to know if they're hiding Timmy, or at least if they have any idea where he is.

He put his hand on the cold brass door handle, but before he could open it he heard another whisperer, and he froze. He felt as if a thousand chilly woodlice had been poured down his back, inside his shirt. *This* whisperer was inside the bedroom with him, and so close that he could feel his breath against his cheek.

'*If I was you, mate, I'd keep meself to meself, and leave our business to us. You with me?*'

The voice was harsh, with an East London accent, and there was no mistaking that this was a warning. Rob felt as if he were being threatened from beyond the grave by one of the Kray brothers. He was so frightened that he couldn't move, but stood with his shoulder against the door, still holding on to the ice-cold handle, staring wide-eyed into the blackness for any faint flicker of light that would show him who had entered the room and was now standing so close to him. And *how* had this man entered the room? He hadn't come through the door or climbed in through the window. He couldn't have walked through the wall.

'Who are you?' he said, quite loudly.

There was no answer, but he could still feel that breath against his face.

'I said, who are you? What are you doing in this house? You're trespassing, do you know that?'

After a long pause, the whisperer said, '*Trespassing? You can't trespass if you don't have no choice. And you*

*know what it says in the Lord's Prayer. Forgive them nasty
bastards what trespasses against us.'*

Vicky stirred and mumbled, 'Rob? Rob, what's going on?'

Rob yanked down the door handle and tried to pull
the door open, but he felt somebody throw their whole
body weight against it, and it slammed shut again. He
was thrown violently backwards, losing his balance and
toppling sideways over the end of the bed and onto the
floor. He tried to get up, but then he was kicked in the hip
by what felt like a leather boot, and then a second time,
even harder, just below his kneecap.

'*Rob!*' screamed Vicky, and switched on her lamp.

Rob rolled over and managed to climb up onto his
hands and knees, like a beaten dog. But when he lifted up
his head and looked around, there was nobody else in the
room – nobody that he could see, anyway. He listened, and
the whispering had stopped.

Vicky was sitting up in bed, looking terrified.

'Rob, what's happened? What on earth are you doing
on the floor? Are you all right?'

Rob climbed to his feet. He limped over to the door,
opened it, and looked out into the corridor. By the light
from Vicky's bedside lamp he could see that there was
nobody there.

He closed the door and went back to sit down on the
edge of the bed. 'I'm okay, darling. But you know how
somebody pushed you over? That just happened to me.
And I was kicked, too. Look.'

He lifted up his knee and it was already red and starting
to swell up.

Vicky pulled back the covers and came across the bed to sit beside him.

'I heard whispering,' he said. 'Right outside the door, at least three people whispering by the sound of it. When I went to see who it was, somebody came right here into the room and wouldn't let me open the door. Then he pushed me over and kicked me.'

'I don't understand. He actually came into the room? How?'

'Don't ask me. I can't think how the hell he got in and after he'd kicked me I can't think how the hell he got out.' He looked around the bedroom, holding his knee and wincing. 'He could still be in here, for all we know. He could be standing right here in front of us.'

'Oh, don't say that, please! Whatever it is in this house, Rob – whether it's ghosts or spirits or demons or God knows what – we need to get out.'

'But how can we, if there's any possibility that Timmy's still here? Supposing he's here and he can see us and hear us but we just go and leave him behind?'

'We could go and stay at one of the local hotels and come back and search for him during the day. All this whispering, it's much too scary. And now we've both been pushed and you've been kicked. Supposing it doesn't stop there? What if they throw us down the stairs? What if they strangle us when we're asleep, or cut our throats? What if it was one of them who murdered your father and they come and hit us with a hammer?'

'It's scary, Vicks, I agree with you. I mean, it's more than scary. But there has to be an explanation. Even Ada doesn't believe in ghosts and she's a witch. She's coming back in the morning to do some tests to try and find out what these presences actually are. I think we should wait and see what results she comes up with before we decide what to do next.'

'Rob, I can't get over you sometimes. You're so bloody – pragmatic. You've just been pushed and kicked by some invisible person who couldn't possibly have got into the room, and you're still saying that there has to be an explanation.'

'Our only son has disappeared, Vicks! There has to be some explanation for that! If he's disappeared the same way that these – *presences* – have disappeared – we need to find out how they do it.'

Vicky closed her eyes and lowered her head. 'You're right. I don't want you to be right, that's all. This house terrifies me and it confuses me and I wish we'd never come back here. I wish I'd never even heard of Allhallows Hall. All I want is to hold Timmy in my arms again.'

Rob held her close and hugged her and kissed her hair. Then he said, 'Listen... I'm just going to do a quick tour of the house. I don't think I'll find anything, but I won't be able to go back to bed until I do.'

'Oh, God. Do you have to? Supposing he's out there, waiting for you?'

'Well, this time I'll be ready for him. Or *it*. Or whatever the hell he is.'

'All right. But shout out if anything happens, and I'll wake up Martin.'

'I think Martin could still be downstairs. I didn't hear him come up to bed. Mind you, I did drop off for a bit.

Maybe he came up later. But he sounded like he was pissed as a newt, didn't he?'

'I know. And so aggressive.' She paused, and took hold of his hand. 'Sometimes I find it really hard to believe that you and he are brothers.'

Rob tugged his jeans back on and pushed his bare feet into his tan leather shoes, although he didn't bother to tie up the laces. He went out into the corridor and switched on the light. As he had expected, there was nobody there. Nobody visible, anyway.

He walked along to the landing, where he stopped and listened. No whispering. Only the thin persistent whistling of the wind, and the faint rattling of a door somewhere downstairs, and the low sad moaning of the chimneys. He went along to the end bedroom door, next to the stained-glass window. He tried the handle, just to make sure that it was still locked.

It was so dark outside that he could hardly see the figure of Old Dewer in his black cloak, with his back turned. But he couldn't help thinking of the words the presence that had somehow entered their bedroom had whispered to him. '*Trespassing? You can't trespass if you don't have no choice.*'

What had he meant by that? That he couldn't leave Allhallows Hall, even if he wanted to? That he was trapped here? That was what it had sounded like.

He walked back to the landing and paused for a few seconds at the top of the stairs, listening. He thought he had caught the sound of somebody whispering down in the hallway, but it could have been the wind, which seemed to have changed direction. The flap of the letterbox in the front door had started to clap, intermittently, as if there was somebody outside in the porch who wanted to be let in. Somebody old and tired, who barely had the strength to knock.

Rob went downstairs and switched on the light in the hallway. Katharine's boots were lying where she had tugged them off, and her coat was slung awkwardly over the back of the chair. The letterbox clapped again, twice, but Rob resisted the temptation to go and open the front door to see if there was anybody there. All reason told him that it was only the wind.

He went into the drawing room. Fine white ash from the fire had blown across the hearthrug, but the fire itself had died out. Martin's navy-blue overcoat was spread out on the sofa as if he had been lying on it, its blue satin lining creased, but there was no sign of Martin. He must have sobered up enough to stagger up the stairs and go to bed.

Rob looked into the kitchen and the scullery and then he went through to the library. He even checked the downstairs lavatory, with its high old-fashioned cistern and its framed postcards by the saucy seaside artist Donald McGill. Herbert Russell had collected these postcards for years, and found them hilarious. Hardly anything else made him laugh so much, except seeing other people accidentally spill their drink into their lap, or stumble over and hurt themselves, or scald their hands under a boiling hot tap.

Before he went back upstairs, Rob went over to the

bricked-up door to the cellar, which was next to the door to the library. The oak door frame was still there, but the bricks had been plastered over and papered and painted. From the state of the plaster, this had clearly been done a long time ago, maybe more than a century, but there was no record in the deeds or local history as to exactly when, or why.

Rob stood in front of it for a while, although he didn't really know what he was expecting to see, or to hear. He even pressed his ear to the plaster, in case there was whispering on the other side, but there was nothing. Since the cellar was sealed up, nobody could have come out of it, or gone back in; but then nobody could have entered their bedroom through a closed door, either.

He switched off the lights and went back upstairs. As he climbed in next to her, Vicky said, 'Anything?'

'No. And Martin must have managed to get himself to bed.'

'Maybe there's something in this house that makes us hallucinate. My grandmother was almost blind by the time she was eighty, but she used to see people and animals who weren't there. She saw a clown's head in her bathroom basin once. Charles Bonnet syndrome, that's what they call it.'

'But that's only seeing things, isn't it? It's because you're nearly blind. She never *heard* anything, did she? She didn't get pushed over and kicked?'

'No, I don't think so. If she did, she didn't tell me about it. But I'm only trying to be like you, Rob. I'm only trying to think of some rational explanation. Even if there isn't one.'

18

Rob tried to keep his eyes open, but after about half an hour he fell deeply asleep. He dreamed that he was outside on the moor, completely naked, with an icy wind slicing against his skin, stiffening his nipples and shrinking his scrotum and bringing him up in goose pimples. He was desperate to find his way back to the house before anybody saw him like this, and he was cursing his own stupidity at having forgotten to put on any clothes before he came out.

He had reached the front driveway and he could feel the sharp gravel underneath the soles of his feet. But then he heard Timmy calling out to him, from somewhere far beyond the Grimstone and Sortridge leat. He stopped, and listened, and it was definitely Timmy. He didn't know if he ought to go into the house and quickly get dressed, or run out into the wind to rescue Timmy, still naked.

'*Timmy!*' he shouted. '*Hold on! Daddy's coming!*'

He hurried back to the house and was relieved to find that the front door was unlocked. As he entered the hallway, he could hear a phone ringing. It sounded as if it were coming from the drawing room. He wondered if he ought to find it and answer it, but then it stopped. He was about to climb the stairs when it started ringing again.

He sat up in bed. For a moment, he couldn't think where he was. But it must be morning. He could see a wan grey light between the curtains, and when he turned over and picked up his watch he saw that it was 8:17. And that phone was still ringing, although it was very faint.

He recognised the ringtone: it was that irritating up-and-down plinking 'waves', which meant that it was Martin's phone. But why didn't he answer it?

The ringing stopped. Rob rubbed his face with his hands and yawned and swung his legs out of bed. Vicky stirred and murmured, and he stayed still for a few moments in case he woke her up. She needed all the sleep she could get.

He quietly got dressed. If they needed to stay here at Allhallows Hall for yet another night, they would have to drive over to Tavistock sometime today and buy themselves some fresh clothes. There was the Farley Menswear shop and Brigid Foley, the women's boutique. They had washed and tumble-dried their underwear and socks yesterday evening, but this was the third day that Rob had been wearing the same plaid shirt. At least his father had left some spare razor blades in the bathroom. He would have found it too eerie to shave with the same blade his father had used on the day he had been murdered.

He went to the bathroom. It was unrelentingly chilly in there, and the taps dripped, and when he pulled the chain the plumbing let out its usual groaning, like a slaughtered pig.

As he came out, he met Grace, all wrapped up in their mother's pink candlewick dressing gown.

'My God,' he said. 'Where did you find that?'

'It was hanging behind our bedroom door. Dad must have missed it when he got rid of her clothes.'

'He didn't only get rid of her clothes, did he? He got rid of everything that belonged to her. Her sewing basket, her music box, all of her books. All those things you would have thought he might have kept, you know, for sentimental value. It only occurred to me yesterday that there isn't a single picture of her anywhere.'

'Dad didn't have a sentimental bone in his body, Rob. You know that. Except for himself, of course. The only person that Herbert Russell felt sentimental about was Herbert Russell.'

'How did you sleep?'

'On and off. I heard Martin and Katharine come in, and I heard you going downstairs.'

Rob paused. Grace's auburn hair was tousled and her green eyes were puffy, but this morning she looked so much like their mother, rather than their father, and it wasn't only the dressing gown that gave her that appearance. Rob guessed that it was coming to Allhallows Hall and realising she would never see her father here again, ever. She was free of him.

'You didn't hear any of that whispering again, did you?'

Grace shook her head. 'Our window was rattling all night because of the wind, and apart from that, Portia snores like somebody sawing up logs. But for goodness' sake don't tell her I told you. Anyway, I must go to the loo.'

As Grace closed the bathroom door, Rob heard Martin's phone again. The ringing wasn't coming from the master bedroom, but from somewhere downstairs. He hurried down to the hallway, and it was then that he realised it was coming from the drawing room. He went in, lifted Martin's overcoat up from the sofa and found the phone in his side pocket, still ringing.

He took it out and said, 'Hello?'

'Oh, hi, Martin! For a minute there I thought you weren't going to pick up. It's Ted, about that Regis investment.'

'Sorry, but this isn't Martin. This is his brother. Martin's tied up at the moment. I'll have to ask him to call you back.'

'I see. Okey-dokey. But can you ask him to make it asap? I've had a tip-off about Regis but once it goes public the price is going to go up like a fucking rocket.'

'I'll go and tell him right away.'

'Thanks. There's a good chap.'

Rob went back upstairs. He knocked at the master bedroom door and called out, 'Martin? Martin, there's a phone call for you. Business.'

He waited, but there was no answer, so he knocked again.

'Martin? There's someone called Ted on the phone for you, about some investment. He says it's urgent.'

There was still no response, so Rob opened the bedroom door and cautiously looked inside. It was dark, because the heavy velour curtains were still drawn, and there was a strong smell of stale alcohol and cheesy sick. When he opened the door wider, Rob saw the lamp lying on the floor where Katharine must have knocked it off the bedside table. Katharine herself was lying on her side on top of the patchwork quilt, fully dressed, her skirt hitched up at the back. For a moment Rob had the terrible thought that she might have choked on her own vomit, but as he came around the bed he heard her breathing, even though she sounded clogged up. She had brought up sticky yellowish lumps all over her pillow, which he guessed was half-digested homity pie.

She was alive, but she was lying there alone. There was no sign of Martin, not even when Rob lifted up the overhanging quilt and looked under the bed. He and Katharine had been arguing when they came in, so he had probably decided to sleep in another bedroom.

Rob left Katharine asleep and closed the door quietly behind him. He went into all of the other bedrooms, except for the bedroom that Grace and Portia were sharing. Martin was in none of them, not even in either of the two bedrooms with the stained-glass windows. The door to the end bedroom, next to the Old Dewer window, was still locked. The key was on the outside, so Martin couldn't have gone to sleep in there, quite apart from the fact that it had no bed.

So where the hell is he? He wasn't anywhere downstairs, because I checked every room last night, even the toilet. Don't tell me he went back out. It was pitch dark last night and cold enough to freeze the balls off the proverbial brass monkey, and he had left his overcoat in the drawing room. Apart from that, Martin never goes anywhere without his phone. Ever.

All the same, Rob looked into the drawing room again, and the library, and the kitchen. He even opened the larder door, though he knew that was ridiculous.

When he was sure that Martin was in none of the rooms downstairs, he shrugged on his coat and opened the front door. Ragged grey clouds were hurrying across the sky like Old Dewer's hounds, and there was still a biting breeze blowing. He prayed to his new-found God that he wouldn't find Martin lying in the garden somewhere, dead of hypothermia.

He crossed the courtyard to the larger of the two granite barns, wrenched the door open and went inside. The smell of damp hay seemed to be stronger than ever.

'Martin? Mart? You're not in here, are you?'

He circled around the barn, kicking at one of the heaps of hay to make sure Martin hadn't covered himself with it to keep warm. He didn't think it at all likely that Martin had come in here to spend the night, no matter how fiercely he had argued with Katharine. Martin relished his comfort too much, just like their father. Besides, he would have been too drunk to lift up the half-collapsed door.

He went into the smaller barn, but there was no sign of Martin in there, either. Then he walked around the back of the house, and into the kitchen garden. It was starting to rain again, and the weedy vegetable beds looked more dismal and neglected than ever.

Back in the house, he found Portia in the kitchen, in a mustard-coloured sweater and tight denim jeans. She had lit the fire under the range and was boiling the electric kettle.

'What were you doing outside, Rob?'

'I've been looking for Martin. He seems to have gone missing, like Timmy.'

'You're kidding me.'

'No. I heard him come back from Tavistock last night and he sounded like he'd had a few. He didn't go up to bed and I thought he was kipping down on the sofa in the drawing room. But when I came down this morning he wasn't there and I can't find him anywhere.'

'Huh! Perhaps he thought he'd had enough of this house and decided to leave. I don't mean this personally, but I've had quite enough of it myself. It's the spookiest house I've ever slept in, bar none.'

'Oh, come on. His Range Rover's still in the driveway, and there's no way he would have left on foot.'

'He's not hiding in that priest's hole, is he?'

'The door's locked and the key's on the outside, so he couldn't be in there.'

The kettle started to whistle, and Portia poured boiling water into the coffee percolator. 'Would you like a coffee? You look frozen.'

'Thanks. Yes.' He watched her taking three mugs down from the kitchen cabinet. Then he said, 'You don't have to stay here, you know. There's scores of police and volunteers out looking for Timmy and they keep showing pictures of him on the news. I don't know what else we can do.'

'Grace wants to stay to support you and Vicky. And if that's what Grace wants, that's what I want. I know I'm a bit of a bossy-boots sometimes, but you have to be when everybody at school calls you lezzy or dyke and your parents disown you because they wanted you to marry some drippy estate agent called Malcolm.'

Rob couldn't help smiling.

Portia said, 'Grace loves you, you know. She says you always stood up for her when she was little and your father shouted at her for being clumsy, and then when she was older and he began to suspect that she was attracted to girls more than boys. She loves you, and she loves Vicky and Timmy just as much, and she's not going to let you down. And I love her more than I can tell you, so as long as she wants to stay, I'll stay, too.'

Katharine came into the kitchen. Her face was white and her eyes were bloodshot and she had put on her red roll-neck sweater backwards, so the collar came right up under her chin.

'Oh my God,' she said. 'Jack Ratt scrumpy. Never again. I feel like I've been sat on by a horse.'

'Katharine—' Rob began.

'Is that coffee? I'd love some. But I think I'd better drink some water first. I've been sick, and I'm so dehydrated.'

Portia poured Katharine a large glass of water, which she drank in huge gulps, her eyes swivelling around, as if she had been crawling for five days across the Sahara. When she had finished, Rob said, 'Did Martin give you any idea where he might be going off to?'

Katharine wiped her mouth with the back of her hand and stared at him, baffled.

'What do you mean? He slept here downstairs, didn't he? We had a row. I can't even remember what it was about.

But he didn't come up to bed. At home he usually sleeps in his study if we've had an argument about something or other.'

'He didn't sleep downstairs, Katharine. I don't know where he slept. I've looked all around the house for him, and outside, too. I can't find him. He's disappeared.'

'*What?* Martin isn't the kind of man who disappears. Well, not without a reason. And not for long, anyway, although sometimes I wish he would.'

Rob showed her Martin's phone. 'Wherever he's gone, he's left his phone behind, and that's not like him at all. He had a call this morning from somebody called Ted wanting to talk to him urgently about business.'

Katharine suppressed a hiccup, and held on to the kitchen counter to steady herself. 'You say you've looked everywhere?'

'All around the house. Every bedroom, and I've even checked the barns. He's not here, Katharine, and he can't have driven off anywhere because your Range Rover is still here.'

Katharine scraped out a wooden chair and sat down. 'Oh, he's sulking, that's all. He'll be back. He always has to be the centre of attention, and at the moment it's all about your Timmy. And he's very angry about this house, too, and your father's will. Not just angry. He's seething about it. And I mean *seething*. Being the oldest, he always thought the house would come to him.'

'Has he done this kind of thing before?'

'Once or twice. Usually after he's been drinking. We

were on holiday in France once and he disappeared for two whole days. When he turned up again, he expected *me* to apologise.'

'Well, if that's the case, I'm not going to report him missing just yet. The police don't normally log an adult as missing for at least twenty-four hours, not unless there's special circumstances. But if he's not back by the end of the day, I'll call that Sergeant Billings.'

Katharine stood up. 'I'll be back for my coffee in a minute. I have to change the bed and I think I might need to be sick again.'

When she had left the kitchen, Rob shook his head and said, 'Martin can be such a dick sometimes. I only hope he hasn't done anything stupid, like got his foot wedged in some crevice up on Pew Tor, or fallen into the Grimstone leat and drowned himself.'

19

At nine o'clock, John Kipling knocked at the door to report that last night's specialist team of volunteers had still found no trace of Timmy. During the daylight hours today they would widen their search area as far as Willsworthy and Wistman's Wood, both about eight miles away, but if they couldn't find him by the time it grew dark, they would have to consider calling off the full-scale search.

'It's the dogs that make me think he's not in the area any more,' John told them. 'They haven't picked up so much as a sniff of him. But we'll extend the search for as far as a five-year-old could feasibly walk, and a bit further.'

'I'm afraid to tell you that we have another missing person,' said Rob. 'My brother, Martin. He came home from Tavistock last night a little the worse for wear, but we haven't seen him since.'

'We're not panicking yet,' put in Katharine, her voice sharp and steady like a schoolmistress. 'He's pulled this kind of trick before. But your people might keep an eye open for a rather bedraggled middle-aged man. They'll be able to recognise him because he'll be wearing a navy-blue blazer with gold buttons and he'll look as if he's suffering from a crashing hangover. If they do come across him, they might be so good as to suggest that he returns here to Allhallows Hall as soon as he finds it convenient.'

John looked at Rob as if to say, *Gosh, she's angry with him, isn't she? If and when he eventually turns up, I'll bet he's in for the roasting of a lifetime.*

As he turned to go, he snapped his fingers and said, 'Nearly forgot to tell you. Ada called me first thing this morning. She's dropping over to Monkscross to see Frank Coade around ten, so she reckons she'll be here around half past eleven. She would have called you but she forgot to make a note of your number.'

'Okay, fine.'

'And – Rob – please don't give up hope of us finding your Timmy. Children don't just vanish off the face of the Earth. The rector and his partner are going to be joining us today so maybe we'll have some divine assistance.'

Rob was about to say that he didn't believe in God, but then he remembered that he did, at least for the time being. But if Timmy were never to be found, he knew that he would instantly go back to being a committed atheist. No God of any denomination would allow a dear little boy like Timmy to be lost to his parents forever.

Ada arrived at noon. It was lashing down with rain, but strangely the sun had come out from behind the clouds so that the courtyard and the garden were dazzling. She was wearing a black boat-neck sweater today and very tight black jeans, and she was accompanied by an elderly man in a hooded khaki raincoat. When he stepped into the porch and took his raincoat off, and shook it, Rob saw that he looked almost saintly, like medieval paintings of Joseph the stepfather of Jesus. His white beard was neatly trimmed, and although his crown was bald and mottled, he had two wings of long white hair. His eyes were bright, but the irises were so pale they were almost colourless, giving him the appearance of being blind, although he clearly wasn't, and didn't even need to wear glasses.

He was wearing a three-piece suit in purplish herringbone tweed, with padded shoulders and wide lapels, which suggested it must be at least twenty-five years old.

'Rob – Vicky – this is Francis Coade I was telling you about – the gleaner. I hope you don't mind but after I described your priest's hole to him he was itching to come and see it for himself.'

Francis Coade held out his hand and said, 'How do you do,' in a thin, raspy voice, with an accent that sounded more Cornish than Devon. 'I gather your priest's hide is really quite something.'

'Well, it's pretty big, as priest's holes go,' Rob told him. 'When you consider how long we've lived in this house, I really don't know how we failed to realise it was there. But it's disguised really cleverly. The windows on the inside are identical to the windows on the outside, so that you wouldn't immediately guess there was another room in between them.'

He led the way upstairs. As he followed close behind him, Francis said, 'I've seen many a priest's hide around this part of the world, a dozen at least, because of course St Mary's church was Catholic when it was built – around 1250, long before the Reformation. Most if not all of those hides were constructed by Nicholas Owen.'

'John Kipling thinks he built this one, too. It's so well hidden that we only found it by accident.'

'It's interesting that it's so large. Nicholas Owen's closets tended to be tiny. Stifling, some of them, so that the priests who were hiding inside them would sometimes suffocate. He made two at Stoke Climsland House and they were concealed inside the pillars in the entrance hall. There was only enough room inside each pillar for a priest to stand up straight, with his arms by his sides, and he may have had to stay shut up inside it for hours – if not days. Nothing to eat, nothing to drink, and nowhere to relieve himself.'

Rob unlocked the end bedroom and opened the door. Before he went in, Francis stared at the stained-glass window and said, 'My God. Who has a window with the Devil in it? And his pack of Whist Hounds, too.'

'Whist Hounds?' Vicky asked him.

'"Whist" means weird, or eerie,' said Ada. 'Anything that gives you the willies.'

'It was the Whist Hounds that gave Conan Doyle his inspiration for that Sherlock Holmes story, *The Hound of the Baskervilles*,' added Francis. 'Old Dewer's pack, though – they were supposed to be fifty times more ferocious than that. So the legend goes, they used to rush around the villages all about Dartmoor, sniffing out unbaptised babies, dragging them out of their cribs and tearing their lungs out so that they could never breathe a word of devotion to God.'

'Timmy's been christened,' said Vicky. She realised as soon as she said it how fatuous that sounded, because the Whist Hounds weren't real, but Rob put his arm around her shoulders and gave her a comforting hug. He understood that Timmy being baptised had given her one less threat to worry about, even if that threat was supernatural dogs.

They went into the bedroom. Francis looked around it, breathing deeply, his blind-looking eyes flicking from the ceiling to the floor to the wine table with all its cobwebby candlesticks.

'I can distinctly smell something. Something *tangy*.'

'We could, too. We reckon it smells like that aftershave, Old Spice.'

'I can *feel* something, too. Some kind of atmospheric disturbance. It's hard to put my finger on it. It's not like the usual resonance you can feel in a house that's supposed to be haunted.'

'When I was in there, I was sure I could feel someone brushing past me.'

'Hmm,' said Francis. He looked around some more, and then he said, 'The hide's behind that panelling, I presume?'

'Yes,' said Rob, and lifted the window seat. 'And this is how it opens.'

Francis leaned over so that he could watch Rob lifting up the crucifix. The dado creaked back, revealing the hidden room behind it. Because the sun was shining so brightly through the stained-glass windows, the horsehair floor was dappled with red and green and yellow diamond patterns.

'That's an ingenious bit of engineering, that,' said Francis. 'But I doubt if it was made by Nicholas Owen.'

'Really? Why's that?'

'Nicholas Owen may well have built a priest's hide here, but like I say, his hides tended to be tiny, and very cramped.'

He bent down under the dado rail and stuck his head into the hidden room.

'It's an amazing piece of *trompe l'oeil*, I have to admit. But apart from its size, there's this crucifix. Nicholas Owen would never have risked installing a lever in the shape of a crucifix. Those priest hunters weren't only searching for priests. They were searching for any kind of paraphernalia to prove that people were holding the Roman Catholic Mass illegally – such as statues of the Virgin Mary, or rosaries, or crucifixes like this one.

'They were relentless. That's because they were awarded a generous bounty for every priest they winkled out and every Catholic worshipper they discovered. Even a share of their property.'

He crouched down under the dado rail and entered the hidden room. Ada and Vicky and Rob followed him, although Katharine held back.

'This is too scary for me. I'm going back downstairs. I don't know. Perhaps Martin will come back in a minute.'

Once inside the hidden room, Francis looked around intently – up at the ceiling, down at the floor, out of the windows. He ran his fingertips all the way along the walls and then he lowered himself down on one knee and rubbed the horsehair matting between his fingers.

'What do you think, Frankie?' said Ada. 'There's some presence here, isn't there? Or even *presences*, plural. I'm sure I can sense them even now. And I don't feel as if they're at all friendly. It's almost like this room itself resents us being here.'

Francis stood up straight again, letting the stray horsehairs drift from between his fingertips.

'Do any of you have a match on you?'

'A match? No,' said Vicky. 'But there's a box in the kitchen. I'll fetch them for you.'

While they waited, Ada lifted up her shoulder bag and said, 'This is my conjure-bag. I've brought two tests with me. A mirror test, and a powder test.'

'Why don't you try them now?' Francis suggested. 'I have my suspicions about this room, but at least your tests might be able to give us some idea of what these atmospheric disturbances actually are.'

Ada took an oval hand mirror out of her bag. Its brass handle was cast in the shape of a fairy and its frame was formed by her wings curling up behind her. She didn't look like a good fairy, though. She had narrow, catlike eyes and a gleefully malevolent grin.

The mirror itself was polished and highly reflective, but it wasn't glass. Instead, it was totally black.

'This is a scrying mirror,' said Ada. 'It's made of obsidian, from Mexico. Obsidian allows you to see through it into the Otherland. I often use it to find out if there's a spirit still wandering around somebody's house.'

'I remember you showed me that before, over at the Channings' place,' said Francis. 'We didn't see anything in it, though, did we?'

'That's because Mary Channing wasn't being haunted. She was suffering from early-onset dementia, and you can't see that in a scrying mirror. But I think there's much more chance of seeing something in here.'

She held up the mirror and started to walk slowly around the room, angling it repeatedly from side to side.

'Nothing so far,' she said, as she passed the outside windows.

Rob was tempted to say, *If they're invisible, these presences, they're going to be just as invisible in a mirror as they are in real life*. But even if they couldn't be seen, both he and Vicky had experienced how violent they could be, and how solid they felt, and if there was the slightest chance of discovering what they were, he was prepared to go along with it.

Once Ada had completed a circuit of the room she stopped still, lowering the mirror and closing her eyes. She started to murmur something under her breath, although Rob couldn't clearly make out what it was. He thought he caught words that sounded like *Evokare lemures de mortuis*, but that was all.

She was silent for a few more seconds. Then, abruptly, she lifted up the mirror so that she could look over her shoulder.

'*I see them!*' she screamed. '*I see them!*'

At that instant, with a sharp crack, the obsidian in the mirror exploded, and splinters of glittering black were scattered onto the horsehair floor. Ada flung away the broken mirror as if it were red-hot and turned to Francis, her eyes wide. She pointed towards the far corner of the room, so terrified that she opened and closed her mouth several times before she could speak.

'They're *there*, Frankie! I saw three or four of them at least! Jesus Christ, they're actually there!'

Francis gripped her arm and said, 'Come on, steady. What do they look like?'

'I don't know! I don't know! I only caught a glimpse of them before the mirror broke! They were all shadowy – but they looked like men – men, three or four men!'

'Maybe we should get out of here,' said Rob.

'No, no—' said Francis. 'We need to find out who they are. They haven't done anything to harm us, have they?'

'Oh, not much. They've only pushed me and Vicky over and kicked me in the leg. Who knows what else they're capable of? The one who kicked me told me that I needed to mind my own business, if I knew what was good for me.'

'Rob – I have a strong suspicion about what's going on here. If I'm right, this could be the answer to where your son has disappeared to.'

'So what is it, this strong suspicion?' Rob asked him. He couldn't take his eyes off the corner of the room where Ada had said that she had seen three or four men. He couldn't make out anybody there at all, not even the faintest wavering in the air. He couldn't even see the impressions of any feet in the horsehair matting.

'Let me test it out first,' said Francis. 'Ah, look – here's your good wife now, with the matches.'

Vicky came into the room and immediately realised that something had happened.

'What's wrong? You haven't felt any more of those presences, have you?'

'Ada's seen them,' said Rob. 'She had this special mirror that lets you see spirits and she saw some standing in the corner over there.'

'Oh my God, you're joking. They're not still there, are they?'

'That is what we are going to try to find out,' said Francis. He held out his hand and she passed him the box of matches. 'I don't know whether this will prove my suspicion, but if it does, it will go a long way to explaining what has been going on here at Allhallows Hall. If I'm mistaken – well, we'll have to try some more tests, such as Ada's powder test, although I am not at all sure that will tell us anything we don't already know.'

He took out one of the matches and struck it. It was a long kitchen match, which Herbert Russell had used to light the range. When it was burning, he wedged the end of it into a narrow split in the oak of the nearest windowsill, so that it stood upright.

'Right, now let's all get out of here,' he said.

'That's a bit dangerous, isn't it, leaving that there?' asked Rob, nodding towards the match.

'Not if I'm right about this room. Come along, let's get out as quick as we can – chop-chop!'

They all crouched down under the dado rail and went back into the bedroom, closing the panelling to seal the room behind them. Francis took a pocket watch out of his waistcoat and held it up.

'Let's give it five minutes,' he said. 'That should prove it beyond any question.'

'Either that or the house will start to burn down.'

'Trust me.'

Rob said nothing, but thought, *How am I going to explain this to the insurance company if the house does burn down?* 'Oh – I allowed a wizard to stick a lighted match in a wooden windowsill in a room carpeted with dry horsehair.' 'And why did you do that, Mr Russell?' 'What do you think? We were trying to find out if there were any ghosts in there, of course.'

Vicky said, 'These presences, Ada. Did they look human?'

'As far as I could tell. I only saw them for a split second before my scrying mirror broke. They looked like ordinary men, though. No horns or wings or anything like that.'

'Three minutes,' said Francis.

'Are you going to tell us what we're waiting for?' Rob asked him.

'If I'm wrong about this room, it won't matter.'

'But if you're right?'

'Then I'm not at all sure what we're going to do. I've heard about these rooms but I've never actually come across one before. Not in the flesh, so to speak.'

'But what? Are they evil, these rooms? Are they dangerous? Are we going to need an exorcist?'

Francis gave a shake of his head that was almost imperceptible, and the faintest of smiles. 'You only need exorcists when a person or a house is possessed by Satan or one of the seventy-two demons listed in the *Lesser Key of Solomon*.'

'But you don't think that's what we have here?'

'No, because Satan doesn't exist and neither do any of

his demons. The only evil in this world is in the minds of men. And women, of course. I don't want you accusing me of sexism.'

He lifted up his pocket watch again. 'There... five minutes. That should do it. Let's all go back in.'

Francis ducked under the dado rail first and the rest of them followed. The sun had gone behind the clouds now, and the room had become colourless and gloomy. When they stood up straight, though, they saw that the match stuck into the windowsill was still alight, and that it hadn't burned down even a fraction since Francis had wedged it there.

Rob went over to examine it closely. It continued to burn, but it still stayed the same length.

'This is a conjuring trick, right? You rubbed some grease on it, or something like that, so that it burns like a candle.'

'I did nothing to it. And it isn't a trick. What you're seeing is a natural phenomenon.'

'Matches that last forever? I never heard of those before.'

Francis looked around the room again. His expression was different now, more wary than it had been before. He leaned forward slightly and stared with his eyes narrowed at the corner where Ada said she had seen the presences.

'Ada, do you want to try your powder test?'

'They're there, aren't they?' Ada asked him.

'I don't know. They may have left when they saw me lighting the match. I have no idea if they're restricted to this room only, or if they're free to roam around other rooms, too. Judging by what happened to Rob and Vicky here, they can wander about the whole house.'

'All right. But let's hope it doesn't annoy them, this powder test, and they decide to attack us.'

Ada reached into her conjure-bag and took out a hexagonal green glass bottle with a silver cap.

'This is battlefield dust,' she explained. 'It was originally used by bereaved relatives who had lost a soldier in battle but the body had never been found. They would go to the battlefield long after it was all over and collect any bones they could dig up from where their loved one was thought to have fallen – or as near as they could tell from what their surviving comrades had told them. Then they would take these bones home and grind them into powder, rather like they do in crematoriums.'

'So what would they do with this powder? Bury it? Scatter it?'

'No, no. They would blow it up into the air in the rooms that their loved one used to frequent, usually their bedrooms. They hoped that if he was still haunting the house where he used to live, the powder would settle on his ghost. In that way they would at least be able to see his outline.'

'But we're not related to these presences, are we?'

'That doesn't matter. Battlefield dust works for all spirits, not only relatives. I've used it myself twice now and seen the outline of two people who were long dead. One was a grandmother in Cadover Bridge. I distinctly saw her sitting in front of her fire in her parlour, and as far as I could make out she was knitting. The other was a young farmer in Bellever, who had been run over by his father's tractor. I saw him in his bedroom sitting on his bed, and even though I couldn't hear him, his shoulders were shaking like he was crying.'

She unscrewed the cap of the green glass bottle and held it up. 'This particular dust is supposed to have come from the Battle of Leipzig in 1813. I bought it three years ago when I went to a spiritualists' fair in Germany. It's supposed to have enormous spiritual potency, because over ninety thousand soldiers died in that battle, and hundreds of their bodies were never recovered. There were so many skeletons left on the battlefield that more than fifteen years after it was over, tons of bones were collected up and shipped to Scotland for fertiliser. However—'

She stopped, and glanced uneasily over to the far corner of the room.

'I don't know. Even if these presences are still there, Frankie, I'm not at all sure now that I really want to see them.'

'Ada, we have to. Most of all we need to know if they have anything at all to do with Rob and Vicky's little boy disappearing. And even if they don't, we can't just leave them trapped in this house forever. They need to be laid to rest, and when you've carried out this test I'll tell you why.'

'All right, then. But don't give me a hard time if I scream. Talking to spirits in the Otherland, that's one thing. They're never threatening. Almost every one of them is sad to have died, and some of them are not even aware that they have.'

She padded her way cautiously down to the far end of the room until she was facing the corner where she had seen the figures in her scrying mirror. She stood there for over half a minute, her back turned, not moving, not speaking. Eventually she looked over her shoulder for reassurance from Francis.

'Go on, love, you can do it,' he urged her. 'We're here. We'll protect you.'

'I don't know. I was much more confident about this before I actually saw them. I mean, I've seen spirits before – but these didn't look the same as spirits.'

'It's up to you, Ada. But Rob and Vicky here, they're counting on you. People like us who have the gift of communicating with the spirit world – we have a duty to share that gift, don't you think so, no matter how much of a risk it might be? You wouldn't refuse to help a blind man across the road, now would you, just because you were scared you might get run over by a truck?'

From the look on Ada's face, it was plain that she wasn't entirely sure what Francis was talking about, but all the same she turned back and faced the corner again. She held out her left hand and carefully tipped the green glass bottle until her palm was heaped up with pale grey powder.

In a high, piercing voice, she sang out, '*Poudre, poudre, envole-toi, montre-moi les visages que je cherche aujourd'hui!*'

She sang that three times, and then she bent her head forward and carefully puffed on the powder in her hand until it flew up and filled the air above her in a fine cloud.

Nothing happened at first. But as the powder slowly began to sink down from the ceiling, it appeared to be settling on something the shape of a man's head – and after that another, and another, and yet another. Then it settled on their shoulders, and their backs, and on their arms, and they could gradually discern that there were four men standing in the corner, even though they were nothing more than shadowy outlines formed of dust.

'Christ almighty,' said Francis, under his breath. 'I've seen some weird things, I can tell you, but this—'

'Ada – do they know that we can see them?' Rob called out.

'I can't tell. Their faces aren't clear enough.'

'Do you think they might be able to hear us? Can you ask them questions?'

'I'll try.'

'Can you ask them if they know where Timmy is?'

Vicky was clinging on to the sleeve of his jacket. 'Rob – they won't know his name, will they? Just ask them if they've seen a small boy. Oh God, I've never been so frightened in my life. Supposing they do know where he is? What then?'

The four men were still only dimly visible, despite all the fine grey powder that had drifted down onto their heads and their shoulders. All the same, Rob could see that at least two of them looked broad-shouldered and bulky. One of them had his hair brushed up in a point, while another had curls. The other two looked as if they were bald or at least shaven-headed.

'Can you hear me?' Ada called out to them. 'Turn around and look at me if you can hear me.'

Three of the four men slowly turned to face her. Rob could make out their foreheads and their cheekbones and the tips of their noses, where the dust had fallen, but that was all. Their eyes were empty. He could see the wall behind them through their eye sockets.

'We haven't come to disturb you,' said Ada, her voice rising up a pitch. 'We're looking for a lost boy, that's all. Five years old. We think he may be somewhere hidden in this house, but we can't think where.'

The men looked at each other, although with every move they made more of the powder fell off them onto the horsehair matting, and it was increasingly difficult to see them distinctly. They started to whisper – the same conspiratorial whispering that Rob and Vicky had heard in the corridor outside their bedroom. It sounded almost like a chant.

'What are they saying, Ada? Do they have any idea where Timmy is?'

'I can't hear, Rob. I'm just hoping they'll – *aah!* Let go! I said, let go of me!'

'Ada? What are they doing?'

'They're pulling my arms! I said, stop it! Let go of me! *Let go!*'

Both Rob and Francis immediately hurried towards her. Even though the four men had all but vanished, Ada was jerking and kicking and thrashing her arms, and it was clear that they were dragging her further down the room towards the end wall. They were kicking up the horsehair matting all around her, and Rob could hear them grunting and swearing to each other in tense, hissing whispers.

He reached Ada and seized her shoulders. He couldn't

believe how violently she was flinging herself around, as if she were dancing to some frantic disco music. He tried to wrench her towards him, but then he was punched, hard, on the side of his head, an inch above his left ear. He had never been hit so hard in his life, and he pitched backwards, stunned, his brain singing, and collapsed onto his back on the floor.

He managed to sit up, even though he was so disorientated and his vision was blurry. Almost at once, with a loud thud, Francis dropped onto his hands and knees close beside him, shaking his head like a dog that had been swimming in a lake.

Ada screamed, and her scream was so high-pitched that it was almost beyond the range of human hearing. Rob blinked and tried to focus on her. He could see that she was kicking and frantically flailing her arms, but she wasn't strong enough to resist the four men who were pulling her away. By now they had shaken off all the battlefield powder, and so they were invisible again, but he could still hear them sharply whispering to each other.

Pull her – pull her, for Christ's sake! Pull the bitch harder!

Rob managed to heave himself up on one knee, gripping the nearest windowsill to give himself support, but it was then that he saw Ada rammed up against the end wall, still furiously struggling to get herself free.

Yet she wasn't just rammed up against the wall. She began to disappear *into* it – swallowed up by the plaster as if she were being dragged behind a thick white curtain. It happened in seconds. Rob saw her right arm waving in a last desperate appeal to be saved, and then she was gone.

There was nothing he could do but stand and stare at the wall in disbelief. Francis stood up, too, and said, 'My God. I was right. But I never thought – oh, my God. I never realised *that* could happen.'

Without a word, Rob went back and ducked under the dado rail. He crossed the end bedroom, knocking over two or three candlesticks with a brassy clatter, and then he ran along the corridor to the landing, so that he could look at the other side of the wall through which Ada had disappeared.

There was nobody there. The house was silent. He listened, but he couldn't even hear any whispering. He walked back and rejoined Vicky and Francis. Vicky was pale with shock, and she caught hold of his arm.

'I can't believe it,' she said. 'How could she go through the wall like that? You don't think she's dead, do you? You don't think they've killed her?'

'No,' said Francis. 'I don't think they've killed her. I think they've done something worse than that.'

20

'Do you think we should call the police?' asked Vicky. 'I don't know,' said Francis. 'I really don't know. What are we going to say to them, if we do? From what Ada told me, the police are already beginning to wonder if you're all a bit doolally. And even if they *do* believe us, what can they do about it? What's happened to Ada isn't criminal, it's metaphysical.'

'But where has she gone?'

'It's this room,' said Francis.

He went up to the end wall and pressed his hand flat against it.

'It's solid, see? Perfectly solid. But only in *this* time.'

'What do you mean, "in this time"?' Vicky asked him.

'I don't have conclusive proof, but I don't think that this is a priest's hide at all. Well, it might have been, to start with. In fact, it's quite likely that it was. These duplicate stained-glass windows – they could well have been fitted by Nicholas Owen. They're just the kind of optical illusion that he excelled at.'

He looked around the room, thoughtfully rubbing his bruised right elbow.

'Like I said before, though, Nicholas Owen would never have used a crucifix as a switch to open the dado. Far too risky. That would have been fixed in much later – I'd guess even centuries later – and probably the whole pulley mechanism was installed then, too. Before that, who knows? To get into this room originally, the priest might have had to lift the floorboards in the bedroom and slide underneath the floor. That was a typical Nicholas Owen trick.'

'So if this room isn't a priest's hole or hide or whatever you want to call it, what is it?'

'To my mind, this match proves it. Look, it's still burning. I believe that this is what in the sixteenth century they used to call a "witching room". I've read quite a bit about them. There are all kinds of different names for them in different cultures. The Scandinavians used to call them "frozen rooms". In Slovenian, I think they're called something like "ageless chambers". In Greece, "*chronovóres táfoi*", which roughly means "tombs that eat time".

'From what I've read, an alchemist will have mixed various elements into the plaster so that after the plaster dried the room was kept suspended in time. If you entered the room and somebody recited a particular incantation, that incantation would trigger a metaphysical reaction from the walls, and you would become trapped in the moment that it was spoken to you, forever. You would never age from that moment. Your physical body would remain in that exact second, like an insect in amber, while the rest of the world carries on. The room itself is timeless. That's why that match will burn and burn but will never go out, ever. We could come back here in twenty years' time and it will still be there, burning.'

'So those men who took Ada – those presences – what are they? If they're stuck in the moment when they first came into this room – how can they walk about the house? How can they walk through walls, and pull Ada through a wall?'

'It's not *them* you saw, Rob. It's their energy. They're still here, in this room. Or somewhere in this house, anyway.'

'I don't understand. Where?'

'Let me put it simply. Supposing on Monday you're standing on a street corner by a letterbox. If I go to that same street corner on Tuesday you won't appear to be there, will you? But supposing *you're* still stuck in Monday. Time will have moved on but your physical existence won't have moved on with it. You'll still be there.'

'But those presences? Those men we saw?'

'They're what people mistakenly call our souls, or our spirits. We all have an incredible amount of electrical energy that makes up our physical being and our personality. That energy can leave our bodies, usually when we're asleep, and roam around. That's why we dream. Occasionally somebody's energy can become visible, or partially visible, and that's what we call ghosts, although ghosts are never the energy of dead people. When you die, your energy dies with you.

'Those men we saw just now when Ada threw that powder over them... yes, I suppose you could call them ghosts, but they're not dead yet. They're still here, in this house, in what you might call suspended animation.

In the same way as I described you still standing by the letterbox, the only reason we can't see them or feel them is that they're not here *now*, not in today. They're all still back in the very hour – the very minute – the very *second* when they were first trapped here. For all we know, some of them could have been here for a hundred years, maybe even more.'

'But Ada says she sees the spirits of dead people, doesn't she?' said Vicky.

'What Ada sees is the resonance that people sometimes leave behind after their death, especially in the walls of the houses in which they used to live. She calls it the Otherland, although I like to think of it as more of a spiritual echo. It fades, eventually, this resonance, like all echoes fade. There is no afterlife. No heaven, no hell – even though all the atoms that once made us what we were will go on milling around the universe for all eternity. Matter can neither be created nor destroyed.'

'Do you think that these presences could have taken Timmy, too?' asked Rob. 'I mean – is it possible that Timmy could be stuck right here in this room, except we can't see him because he's still back in Wednesday afternoon, when he disappeared?'

'I don't know, Rob. I simply don't know. This is the first witching room I've ever found myself in. As I say, I've read a fair amount about them. It was when I was studying to be a gleaner and I found a translation of an essay written by Nicolaus Copernicus after he studied medicine under Girolamo Fracastoro in Padua. Its title in Latin is *Stat Adhuc Tempus*, or *Time Stands Still*. Just as Copernicus theorised that the Earth goes round the Sun instead of the other way around, he suggested that certain combinations of chemicals could stop people growing old so quickly or even stop time in its tracks.

'But, honestly, I need to find out so much more. I have no idea how these witching rooms were made, or who made them, or exactly what for. I have no idea what chemicals were mixed into the plaster or what incantation has to be spoken to suspend a person for ever in the moment when they first entered. Without being flippant, I suppose it's a bit like those incantations to raise a specific demon, such as Asmodeus or Barbatos, or like saying "Alexa" and immediately hearing the tune you want.'

'I can't believe this,' said Vicky. 'This is completely doing my head in. But I saw those men and I heard them whispering and I saw Ada go right through that wall. We have to do something, don't we? That's Timmy gone and Martin gone and now Ada gone. Who's going to be next?'

'We'll have to tell the police,' said Rob. 'After a while somebody's going to come looking for Ada, aren't they? Does she have family around here? Or a boyfriend?'

'She did have a boyfriend. Bill or Will, I think his name was. But I think they split up two or three months ago and he went back to wherever he came from. Australia, as far as I remember. And I think she has a brother in Plymouth.'

'Well, let's look around the house first. If she disappeared into one wall, maybe she's reappeared out of another. Or maybe there's some trace of where those men have taken her.'

They looked around the room one more time. Rob went

across to the window and blew on the match, which was still burning. He blew again, harder, but it didn't even flicker. Francis picked it up and took it out of the room with them, and once they were back in the bedroom he nipped it out between finger and thumb.

'*Stat adhuc tempus*,' he said, 'but *nihil durat in aeternum*. Time may stand still, but nothing lasts forever.'

They found Katharine in the kitchen. She was sitting at the table staring into space. She had a mug of tea cupped between her hands, which she had obviously forgotten about because the teabag was still floating in it and it had steeped to the colour of mahogany.

She looked up when Rob and Vicky and Francis came in.

'Has something happened? I thought I heard that Ada shouting.' She paused, and blinked, and then she said, 'Is Ada not with you? Has she gone?'

Vicky pulled out a chair and sat down beside her. 'Ada's been – well, there's only one way of putting it. There were men in that room. It looked as if there were four of them. But they were like ghosts.'

'Ghosts? Are you serious?'

'Ada threw some of this special powder in the air and it fell on them and we could see them. But then they grabbed hold of her and they—' Vicky stopped. She couldn't bring herself to say it.

'They what? They *what*?'

'They pulled her into the wall and she vanished,' said Francis, in his throaty voice.

Katharine looked at him with her eyes narrowed as if he were totally deranged.

'Is this a joke?'

'I know it sounds absurd, but that's what happened. It's that room. It has what you could call a particular charisma. If you enter it and certain words are spoken, you become trapped in time. You don't die, but you disappear, because you're no longer in the same time as all the rest of us. The train pulls away but you're left behind on the platform, so to speak.'

Katharine turned to Vicky.

'Do you believe this?'

Vicky nodded. 'Yes, Katharine, I do. Francis is going to do some more research into it, but at the moment we can't think of any other explanation. We all saw those men, and when Rob and Francis tried to stop them pulling Ada away, they knocked both of them down onto the floor. And we all saw poor Ada disappear into that wall. One second she was there, the next she was gone.'

Katharine frowned. 'You don't think – you don't think the same thing could have happened to Martin, do you? I know he's gone off in a huff before, but apart from leaving his phone behind he hasn't made any attempt to get in touch. He hasn't even rung me from some pub to tell me what a bitch he thinks I am. And Timmy. You don't think these men could have pulled Timmy into a wall, do you? Perhaps that's why we can't find him.'

She hesitated, and then she said, 'No – no – it's all too ridiculous. It's like some fairy story. Are you absolutely sure that's what you saw? It wasn't some trick of the light, something like that?'

'Katharine, she disappeared into the wall,' said Rob. 'We're going to search the house again. I was wondering if there might be some cavities behind the walls, and she's trapped in there. It could be that Timmy's trapped in there, too. I know it all sounds like madness, but they have to be somewhere, even if Timmy's still stuck in Wednesday and Ada's stuck in – well, five minutes ago.'

Katharine looked at her mug of tea, and then she stood up, walked over to the sink, and tipped it down the drain.

'I'll help you look. We need to find out what's going on in this house for good and all. And I need to find out where Martin's disappeared to, just like you need to find Timmy.'

They searched the house again, room by room, as thoroughly as they had searched it twice already. They looked in the wardrobes and under the beds and tapped on the walls. Rob climbed back up into the attic and Francis went back into the witching room.

'Nothing there?' Rob asked him.

'Nothing visible. But there's no question that feeling's still there. That tension. That *frisson*. Otherwise – no.'

They went back down to the drawing room. The fire had burned right down to the grate, so Rob jabbed the glowing ashes with the poker and stacked three fresh logs on top.

Vicky said, 'You're right, Rob, we'll have to call the police, even if they do think we've all gone barmy.'

She turned to Francis, who was still ruefully massaging his elbow. 'I know you're going to try and find out how that witching room works, Francis, but three people have disappeared now and how are we going to explain it? If we don't tell the police, they're going to start suspecting that we've got something to hide, aren't they – that *we* made them disappear. You remember that case of those two young girls who were murdered in Soham, what were their names? And before the police realised it was him who had killed them, that Ian Huntley went out and helped to look for them.'

'I don't think that the police have a better chance of finding them than we do,' said Francis. 'In fact, I don't think they've got a hope in hell, to be honest with you. My bicycle was stolen last month and they never caught the fellow who took it, even though I had him on CCTV. But I'm inclined to agree with you. It *would* look suspicious if we didn't report them missing. The difference between us and Ian Huntley is that we didn't have anything to do with their disappearance, so we don't have anything to worry about. Hopefully, anyway.'

21

They were still talking when there was a loud postman's knock at the front door.

'Grace and Portia,' said Rob. 'I'll get it.'

When he opened the door, he found Grace and Portia standing in the porch in their muddy wellingtons, looking exhausted, but standing close behind them was DI Holley, as well as another detective in a raincoat, and two uniformed officers.

'Mr Russell?' said DI Holley. 'All right if we come in?'

'What's wrong? You haven't found Timmy, have you?'

'Still no sign of him yet, Mr Russell, I'm sorry to say. But we need to ask you a few questions about another matter.'

'Really? What other matter?'

'If we can come inside and you can find us somewhere to talk in private.'

'Yes, of course. Come on in. Are you all right, Grace? You look knackered.'

Grace was wiping her nose on a crumpled tissue. 'Oh, God. I don't know how many hills we've climbed up and down. And it's *freezing* out there. I'm just about ready to drop.'

'Thanks, anyway. You too, Portia. Thanks. Why don't you two go into the drawing room and get yourselves warm?'

'We will, yes. Just let us pull these boots off.'

Rob said, 'Come into the library, detective inspector. We won't be disturbed in there.'

He led the way into the library and DI Holley and the other detective followed him, while the two uniformed officers remained in the hallway.

'This is Detective Constable Cutland, by the way,' said DI Holley. Rob gave him a nod. He thought he looked more like a local farmhand than a detective. He had jet-black short-cropped hair, bulging eyes and a chin as deeply cleft as a stag's hoof. He also smelled faintly of stale sweat.

Rob closed the door and the three of them sat down around the library table.

'Is your brother here?' asked DI Holley. 'You might want him to sit in while we talk to you.'

'Martin? No, he's not here just at the moment. But what's this all about?'

'I need the answer to one or two questions, Mr Russell, but if you lead me to believe that you're being evasive or non-cooperative then I may be forced to give you a formal caution.'

'Why? What am I supposed to have done?'

'Can you account for your whereabouts between the twenty-eighth and the twenty-ninth of last month?'

'The twenty-ninth? That was the day my father was found dead, wasn't it?'

'Yes. And I'm asking you if you can tell me where you were on that day, as well as the day before it.'

'Where do you think I was? At home, in Hersham. Number fifteen, Larkwood Close. I'm an animator and I work at home. I was finishing off a commission for Lancaster Home Insurance.'

'Have you any way of verifying that?'

'You can check my phone. You can check my PC. You can ask my next-door neighbour, Nigel Pardoe. I met him in the local shop when I went to buy a paper that morning. Simpler still – why not go through to the drawing room and ask my wife?'

'It's more than likely that we'll be taking you up on all of those suggestions, Mr Russell. You see, the thing is that we've had the preliminary results back from the DNA samples that we took from you and your other family members.'

'And?'

'Our forensic examiners found numerous fingerprints on the handle of the hammer that was discovered by our GP dog in the garden here on these premises. Unfortunately they were too smudged to be able to make a positive identification. However they *were* able to collect a DNA sample, and it turned out that it's an exact match for *your* DNA.'

'*What?* That's impossible.'

'No question about it. It's a ninety-eight-point-nine per cent match. And our forensic experts in Exeter have now conclusively established that it was that very hammer that was used to strike Mr Herbert Russell a single blow on the back of his head, resulting in a fatal brain haemorrhage.'

'This is insane. I didn't even know of that hammer's existence until your police dog found it, and I certainly never touched it. Quite apart from the fact that I was two hundred miles away when my father was killed.'

'Nevertheless, Mr Russell, the preliminary DNA test does appear to show beyond any reasonable doubt that it was you who was the last person to be holding that hammer.'

'Wait a minute… surely my brother and sister have the same DNA? Although I'm not suggesting that either of them killed our father.'

'Your sister wouldn't have the same DNA – no,' put in DC Cutland. He may have looked like a farmhand, but the way he spoke was dry and technical, with little licks of his lips and sideways rolls of his bulging eyes in between sentences. 'Humans have twenty-three pairs of chromosomes and when you compare the first twenty-two pairs you can't tell the difference between males and females. But when it comes to the twenty-third pair, the sex chromosomes, males have an X and a Y chromosome, but females have two X chromosomes and no Y. And as far as your brother is concerned – well, we're still waiting on a final report from the lab, but their initial analysis showed that you and your brother don't share identical genomes.'

'Meaning what, exactly?'

'In your case, you both had the same mother, apparently, but not the same father.'

Rob stared at him. Suddenly he was thirteen again, hearing his father shouting at his mother outside his bedroom window. '*Of course he's nothing like me! And we both know why* that *is!*'

DI Holley cocked his head to one side, in that hawklike way of his.

'I'm sorry, Mr Russell. Did you not know that?'

'No. I mean, yes. Of course I did. It's just never been tested before. You've thrown me, I'm afraid. I never expected—'

'You never expected what?'

'This – this accusation that I killed my father. Of course I didn't kill him. As I've told you, I wasn't anywhere near here when he was attacked. I never laid a finger on that hammer. And in any case, why would I kill him?'

'There's this house to be inherited after his demise.'

'Oh, come on. You don't seriously think I'd murder my own father for this dump? A grade-one listed building like this is more trouble than it's worth. In any case, his solicitor has told us that it's not going to be passed directly to any of us – neither to me nor to Martin nor to Grace. It's going to be held in trust for our son, Timmy.'

'Your son, Timmy, who is sadly still missing.'

Rob was growing angry, as well as confused. His father might have been accusing his mother that night of conceiving him during an adulterous affair, but he had never heard either of them mention it again. Over the years he had grown to accept that his father must have simply been having one of his rages, which were frequent, and boiling, and usually bizarre. When she was only eleven, he had shouted at Grace for waiting by the gate for the postman, so that she could 'snog' him. The postman had been about fifty years old, with hair like a scrubbing brush and no front teeth.

Yet this DNA test seemed to have proved that Herbert Russell had been right, and that he *was* his mother's love child, by another man. He suddenly felt as if he shouldn't even be sitting in this house, answering questions about a father that he certainly hadn't killed. A father who wasn't even his real father. He suddenly felt like a stranger.

'What are you trying to suggest about Timmy? That I murdered *him*, too, so that I could have the house to myself?'

'Children have been done away with for far lesser reasons than that, Mr Russell, and I speak from experience.'

'That's an outrageous thing to say to me. Who's your superintendent? I'm going to make a complaint.'

DI Holley appeared to be unruffled by this. He rubbed his hands together as if he were Pontius Pilate absolving himself of all legal responsibility.

'As DC Cutland here has told you, we're still waiting for a confirmatory autosomal test on your DNA, Mr Russell. We expect to receive that later today or tomorrow. Until then I won't be taking this investigation any further.'

'Oh, I see. You're not going to arrest me? Not yet, anyhow?'

'No. But I'm requiring you to remain here in this house and not attempt to evade any further questioning.'

'In other words, you're telling me not to do a runner?'

'If you want to put it that way, Mr Russell. Also, I would recommend if you have a legal representative to contact him or her without delay.'

Rob sat back with his hands flat on the table and stared at the two detectives in disbelief.

'Do you honestly, seriously think that I drove all the way down here from Hersham one night so that I could hit my father over the head with a rusty old hammer? Or should I say stepfather?'

DI Holley gave him a one-shouldered shrug. 'If I've

learned only one thing from my twenty-year career in the force, it's that "impossible" is only a word.'

Rob saw the officers out and then went into the drawing room.

'My God, you look serious,' said Vicky. 'What was all that about? You told them about Ada and Martin?'

Rob shook his head. 'No. I'm under enough suspicion as it is. I didn't want them to start thinking that I did for Ada and Martin as well as Dad. They even hinted that I might have killed Timmy so that I could inherit the house.'

'That's ridiculous. But what do you mean, "as well as Dad"? They don't suspect that you had anything to do with him being murdered, do they? They can't!'

'They can and they do. They've proved that hammer they found in the flower bed was used to kill him, and they've found my DNA on the handle.'

'How on *earth* could they have done that?' said Grace. 'They showed it to us in a plastic bag and you never touched it.'

Francis said, 'Conceivably you held it years ago when you lived here, and that's where your DNA came from. But I don't think that's likely. DNA that could be a million years old has been found in fossilised insects, but it breaks down quite quickly if it's exposed to sunlight or water. Even if your DNA *was* still on it, whoever used it to kill your father might have worn rubber gloves.'

'Well, they seem to be pretty sure about it. They're doing

some extra tests to make certain, but they've told me not to leave here until they do.'

'We weren't going to go, anyway, were we?' said Vicky. 'Not until we've found Timmy, and Ada. And Martin's showed up.'

Rob went to stand in front of the fire. His mind was churning over and over. If only his mother were still alive, and he could ask her outright. Who was it, Mum? Why didn't you ever tell me? If Herbert Russell wasn't my father, why did I have to come down here to Allhallows Hall and lose our Timmy? Who's that whispering? What in the name of the bloody imaginary God that I don't believe in am I doing here?

Vicky came up to him and laid her hand softly on his shoulder. She had that concerned, searching look in her eyes, and he knew why. She could tell that he was holding something back.

'Yes,' he said, even though she hadn't said a word. 'But not here. Later.'

Portia stood up. 'I think we could all do with some lunch, don't you? Pizza, anybody? And I don't know about anybody else, but I could do with a drink. Francis?'

The longcase clock chimed and Francis looked at his watch. 'I'd love to, but the best thing I can do is go back home now and see if I can dig up more about witching rooms. I'll call John Kipling, too, and tell him about Ada. It could be that he has some ideas about what might have happened to her – how she could have disappeared into the wall like that. I don't think there's anybody in the country who knows as much about priest's holes and secret hideaways as he does.'

22

Ada opened her eyes. She felt as if she had just woken up from a deep and wine-saturated sleep, and at first she couldn't focus. She was sitting upright on the floor of a dimly lit room, her back against the wall, and she could hear rain stippling the window close beside her. Her spine ached and her right shoulder felt sore.

Gradually, the room began to take shape. It was the witching room, with its stained-glass windows and its thick brown horsehair matting. The same room from which she had been dragged through the wall. Yet here she was, back again. And as she turned to look around, she could see that she wasn't alone.

Halfway down the room, seven men were sitting or standing. One of them had flowing white shoulder-length hair and a sallow face and he was bony as a clothes horse beneath a black ankle-length cassock. A heavy silver crucifix was hanging on a chain around his neck. The man standing next to him was broad-shouldered and russet-bearded, with a countryman's rugged features, and he was wearing a long brown doublet and knee breeches, as if he were rehearsing for a seventeenth-century play. The others were all scruffily dressed in grey or blue sweatshirts and tracksuit pants or jeans. Three of them were bald. Two had short tousled hair. One had the sides of his head shaved but his black hair greased up into a shark's fin.

One of the bald men realised that Ada had opened her eyes and nudged the man standing next to him. ''Ere, look, she's come to,' he whispered, in an East End accent.

They all turned to look at her, and then the bony priest walked across and crouched down next to her. He was handsome in a sad-looking way, with a long nose and large dark eyes like an abandoned mongrel. Ada could smell stale incense on his cassock, and when he leaned close to her and whispered, she could smell his bad breath, too. His lips were crusted with cold sores.

'I hope you forgive us for taking you,' he told her. He was whispering so softly that she had to read his lips to understand everything he was saying to her. 'We had no choice, I'm afraid, because we have to protect ourselves.'

Ada was so frightened that she was finding it difficult to breathe. The priest reached out and laid his hand on hers, and his long, thin fingers were so cold that she felt as if strips of raw fish had been draped across her knuckles.

'Our incarceration here is not of our doing,' the priest whispered. 'We cannot be blamed for our predicament. But we have the right to save ourselves from oblivion. Oblivion, you see, is our only alternative.'

'Who are you?' Ada asked him. '*What* are you?'

The priest pressed his fingertip against his scabby lips. 'Shh, my dear, some of us are still in the land of nod.' He pointed down to the heap of dirty blankets at the end of the room. Out from under the blankets a man's hand was protruding, like a dead crab.

'I'll talk as loud as I like, thank you! In fact, I'm going to shout out for help.'

'It will be futile, I'm afraid. The pilgrims won't hear you.'

'Pilgrims? What are you talking about? What pilgrims? All I want to know is who you are and how you managed to get me in here. And *why*.'

'The pilgrims are those outside this chamber – those who are free to continue their journey through one year after another until they finally reach the end of their days. Unlike us.'

He gave her a small, regretful smile.

'My name is Thomas. I have been here the longest. I was alone for so long that I believed I would remain alone for all eternity. But eventually my companions appeared. Bartram first. Then – after many more tiresome years had rolled past us – all of these others. And here we are. Exactly where we were, going nowhere.'

The other six men had now crossed the room and were gathered in a semicircle with their arms folded, staring down at her. Apart from the bearded man in his knee breeches, Ada had rarely seen such hard-looking characters since her brother had taken her down to visit his body-building gym. Their necks were thickly corded and their biceps bulged, so they had obviously been taking steroids and regularly working out. The man with the shark's-fin hair had a snake tattoo on his neck that curled up to his left ear.

'Blimey, you're a gift from God and no fucking mistake,' he said, grinning at her. 'What's your name, love? Mine's Ron but you can call me Jaws. Everybody else does.'

Ada said nothing, but drew up her knees and squeezed her thighs defensively together, making herself as small as she could.

'So what was you and them two geezers and that other bint all doing in here? You was trying to catch a sneaky butcher's at us in that mirror thing, wasn't you? Don't say you wasn't. And then chucking all that fucking dust all over us. What was that all about?'

Ada still said nothing, but Thomas leaned close to her again. 'I quite understand your reticence, my dear, but I think you fail to understand the transformation that you have undergone. Most of all, its *permanence*.'

'What are you talking about? What transformation? All I know is that one second you were all dragging me down the room and the next I hit the wall and then I woke up here. What time is it?'

'Time is no longer of any consequence. Not for any of us here in this chamber, and that includes you.'

Jaws hunkered down close beside her, so that she could strongly smell his Old Spice aftershave. He was handsome in a dark, untrustworthy way, with a permanent look of self-satisfaction, as if he knew something that nobody else could guess at, but was never going to say what it was.

He cupped one hand over Ada's left knee and said, 'Let's put it this way, darlin.' There's no point in you asking what the time is, because it's the same time as when we pulled you through the wall and always will be. You want to know what the time is? Look at your watch.'

'Take your hand off me,' Ada told him.

He grinned again, and said, 'Make me.'

'The police are coming back here soon. I can have you arrested for indecent assault. Not to mention threatening behaviour.'

'No you can't, love. Look at your watch. You're still stuck in that second when we fetched you in here but those coppers are hours ahead of you already. Tomorrow they'll be a day ahead of you and next week they'll be a week ahead of you. Then they'll retire and then they'll die and you'll still be here. There's no way they can come back in time to find you and there's no way you can go forward in time to whinge that I've been touching you up. Which I'm not, am I? Only being friendly.'

Ada looked at Thomas for support and for some kind of rational explanation, but all Thomas could do was give her a beatific smile.

'I don't believe you,' she said. She lifted up her right hand and squeezed her wrist between the fingers of her left. 'There – look! I'm solid. I can feel myself. I'm not stuck in time. I'm real. Now, whoever you are, if you'll just take your hand off me and get back out of my way, I'm leaving.'

'Look at your fucking watch,' said Jaws.

'I don't have to look at my watch. Maybe my watch has stopped. I'm getting out of here and that's all there is to it.'

Jaws lifted his hand from her knee and stood up, still giving her that knowing, secretive look.

'Go ahead, love. Try. I've done a whole lot of things in

my life that I'm less than proud of, but if there's one thing I'm not, it's a pork pie merchant.'

The seven men all stood back and watched Ada as she climbed to her feet. She went over to the panel in the dado that had opened to let her in, along with Francis and Rob and Vicky. It was closed now, and there seemed to be no lever on this side to open it. No crucifix, nor any other kind of switch.

She ran her hands under the dado rail to see if she could feel a gap where she could get a grip on it and pull it open, but it was seamless.

'See?' said Jaws, making no attempt to hide his satisfaction. 'You're trapped, love, same as we are. Rats in a trap, all of us – you included.'

Ada slapped on the wall hard, first with her right hand and then with both hands.

'Frankie!' she shouted, at the top of her voice. 'Frankie, I'm stuck in the priest's hide! I can't open the panel! Can you hear me, Frankie? Frankie – get me out of here!'

She stopped, and listened, to hear if she had any response. Jaws watched her, still smiling.

'Go on,' he said. 'They can't hear you. I told you to look at your watch, didn't I? That's when you were here. They can't hear something that's happened in the past.'

'You're not making any sense,' Ada snapped at him. 'I'm banging the wall, aren't I, and I'm doing that now. And if *you* hadn't been here at the same time that I was here, how did you manage to pull me out of here, and knock my friends over?'

She clenched her fists and started thumping the wall again and again, as hard as she could.

'Frankie!' she screamed. 'Frankie, I'm stuck in the priest's hide! Get me out of here! Frankie! Rob! *Get me out of here!*'

She waited almost half a minute, but there was still no answer from the other side. Ada started to knock on the wall again and call out miserably, 'Frankie – Frankie, *please!*' but then she stopped and started to cry.

Thomas came up to her, put his arm around her shoulders and gently pulled her away from the wall.

'It's of no avail, my dear,' he whispered. 'You will have to accept your destiny. All any of us can do is make the best of our lives in this room, and in this house.'

'You shouldn't have come looking for us, love,' said Jaws. 'That was your mistake. You and your mirror and your magic dust. You should have left well enough alone, do you know what I mean?'

The russet-bearded man in the long brown jacket came up to Ada, too. She smeared the tears out of her eyes with the sleeve of her sweater and looked up at him. Close up, she could see that he had a deep diagonal scar across his forehead and his left cheek, as if he had been cut by a sword, and that his left eye was milky white and blind.

'Our lives as pilgrims have been stolen from us,' he whispered. 'But we have to safeguard the lives that we still have left to us, if only to outlast the rest of humankind.'

He had a strong, slurred accent that sounded more French than West Country, and every word ended in a strange airy whistle, so that Ada could barely understand what he was saying.

'When all the other men and women who have walked on this Earth are rotting in their graves – when the sun dims and winks out for the final time – when total darkness and icy cold swallow everything – we shall still be here, we few, to greet that darkness and that cold, and beyond. We shall be here for eternity, so that we can see what God has planned for the universe after the disastrous failure of humanity.'

Ada took a deep breath to steady herself, and then she said, 'I'm not interested in eternity, whoever you are. I just want to get out of here. Now, tell me how I can do that.'

'You can't,' Jaws whispered. 'Don't you understand what we've been telling you, me and Father Thomas here? He's stuck back in sixteen-something or other. Bartram here, he's stuck back in seventeen thirty-five.'

'May the ninth, seventeen thirty-five, at one minute past nine in the evening, to be precise,' Bartram put in. 'The clock had just finished chiming.'

'Me... five to five on Sunday, June the tenth, nineteen-seventy-nine,' Jaws went on. 'The day after Derby Day. Back then I didn't have a fucking clue what *that* was all about, but it didn't take me too long to work it out, did it, not after Billy here got pulled in, too. Fucking Russell had lost a packet betting on the wrong horse. What a muggins I was. And there was me thinking I was the sharpest chisel in the box.'

Ada said, 'I can't stay here forever. I *can't*.'

'As I told you, my dear, none of us has a choice,' said

Thomas. 'We cannot take our own lives. We cannot cut our wrists because our circulation stopped at the moment of our entry and we would not bleed. We cannot starve ourselves because we never need to eat, or to drink for that matter. We can breathe, yes, and we can talk, but every breath we take is the last breath we took when we were trapped, breathed over and over again, *ad infinitum.*'

'Recycling, you might call it,' grinned Jaws.

'Wait a minute,' Ada protested. 'You keep saying you're trapped in this room, but you're not, are you? That family who've been staying here... they've heard you walking about the house. They haven't been able to see you, but they've felt you... You pushed that woman when she came looking for you, and you pushed that man over, too – and kicked him.'

'That didn't happen.'

'Yes, it did. I've even seen their bruises.'

'No, love, that didn't happen. That was all a dream.'

23

Rob and Vicky had been planning to go out in their car that afternoon and drive around the Tamar Valley, or even to the south as far as Plymouth – way beyond the area that was being covered by the search and rescue teams. They were hoping that by some chance Timmy had been picked up by a stranger and then abandoned miles away.

They knew that it was a remote chance, millions to one, but it would have been better than sitting in Allhallows Hall listening to the rain clattering outside in the courtyard and watching the logs lurching in the drawing-room grate.

Now that Rob had been ordered by DI Holley to stay in the house, they had to give up on that plan. Grace and Portia made some sandwiches with Sharpham Rustic cheese and they all sat around the fire, drinking Herbert Russell's Jail Ale out of the bottles and saying very little.

Katharine was still feeling hungover and tired, so she took herself upstairs to bed. There had still been no word from Martin, and they agreed that if they hadn't heard from him by the time it started to grow dark, they would report him missing.

Rob sat on Herbert's throne, prodding at his phone to see if he had any messages and to catch up on the latest news on the Devon Live website. A teenage girl had been found naked and dead in the River Tavy, under Harford Bridge. It was not yet known if she had been sexually assaulted, but a pentagram had been carved into her back with a knife.

Vicky was sitting on the floor next to him. She poked at the fire and then she looked up at him and said, 'Perhaps we should take another look in the witching room. I still can't believe how Ada disappeared into the wall like that.'

'You think she might have come back? If she has, she would have shouted out to us, wouldn't she?'

'I don't know. If she went through the wall one way, maybe it's possible that she's been able to come back through it the other way. But maybe after doing that she's too weak to shout out.'

'Ten out of ten for imagination, darling.'

'Are you joking? After those ghostly men we saw, pulling Ada through the wall, and all that whispering, and both of us being pushed and kicked by people we couldn't even see? For God's sake, Rob, who needs to have an imagination?'

'All right. You win. Let's go and look. But I don't think we're going to find that it's any different.'

Grace said, 'I'll come with you. Portia?'

Portia was sitting on the sofa with her feet up, playing a game on her phone.

'No, thanks. You go. I'm trying to de-spook myself.'

They climbed the stairs and walked along the corridor to the end bedroom. Grace said, 'This witching room...

there's no danger that *we* could be pulled into the wall, is there?'

'We're only going to take a quick look, just to make sure that Ada hasn't managed to come back,' Rob told her. 'Those men we saw when she threw that dust all over them... I think they grabbed her because she upset them. They were only whispering, but they sounded furious, didn't they?'

He lifted the lid of the window seat, reached down inside and pulled up the crucifix. For some reason it was stiffer than it had been before, and the dado opened more slowly, with an anguished creak that sounded like a grieving grandmother, and a dry clanking of cogs.

They bent down and went inside. The room appeared to be empty. There was no sign of Ada, nor anybody else who was visible.

Grace inhaled and said, 'Yes... you're right... it's Old Spice, isn't it? That's *so* creepy! I can really smell it. Ooh. Can we go now?'

'Wait a second,' said Vicky. 'What's happened to those blankets? They were all piled up before, weren't they? Now they're all folded back.'

'Yes, but Ada was kicking them about like mad when she was trying to stop herself from being pulled through the wall.'

'I know. But after she disappeared they were still lying in a heap. It was almost like there was somebody hiding underneath them.'

'John looked. There wasn't.'

'Can we go now?' Grace repeated. 'I'm sure I felt somebody breathing against the back of my neck.'

'Hold on,' said Rob. 'I'll take another look.' He went down to the end of the room, picked up the blankets one after the other and shook them. They were heavy and damp and dirty and woven out of coarse unwashed wool. Gingerly, he lifted up the corner of one of the blankets and held it under his nose. It had the lard-like reek of sheep's grease but also the musky odour of stale human sweat.

Grace, by now, had already crouched down so that she could back out into the bedroom.

'Go on, Gracey,' said Rob. 'But I'm taking one of these blankets with me. It smells like somebody's been sleeping in them. I'll ask Sergeant Billings if he can get one of his police dogs to sniff it.'

'What good will that do?'

'I'm not sure. But maybe they can identify whose scent it is, and where in the house we can find them, even if they *are* invisible.'

Katharine had drawn the curtains so that the master bedroom was dark, taken off her skirt and climbed under the heavy embroidered quilt. She thought she could still faintly smell cheesy vomit on the pillows, but she had changed the sheets and the pillowcases and she guessed that it was just her guilty imagination.

She had tried to appear nonchalant about Martin's disappearance in front of the others, even cynical. There were many times during the course of their marriage when it had taken only the slightest of provocations for him to lose his temper and storm off for hours or even days. But she had learned that he had inherited these bursts of rage from his father, both genetically and from the way that Herbert had brought him up. He may have appeared to be domineering and full of himself, but she had come to realise that his anger was set off by frustration and a lack of belief in his own self-worth, and an irrational feeling that everybody was demeaning him behind his back.

She knew that he loved her, and even more than that, how much he depended on her. He would never have been such a success in the City without her business and social contacts, and because she had pushed him to go for some highly risky investments. He was terrified of bankruptcy, because he had seen how much his father's life had been blighted by debt, even if he had never guessed the scale of it.

She loved him, too, although sometimes she never fully understood why. She used to see him staring out of the window and wonder what was going on inside his mind, and if she would ever be able to find out. She had given up asking him what he was thinking about, because he always said, 'Oh. Nothing much.'

She closed her eyes. She felt hungry but her tongue felt as if it were coated with fine sand and she didn't think she would be able to swallow anything.

She was starting to slide into darkness when she felt fingers gently touching her hair, and a voice whispered, '*Kathy?*'

For a second she thought she was dreaming, but then the voice whispered, 'Kathy? Are you asleep?' and she jerked her head up off the pillow. It had sounded like Martin, but there was nobody there.

She sat up, her eyes flicking from one side of the master bedroom to the other. It was still raining and the water that was gurgling in the gutter outside the window sounded like a child choking.

'Kathy, it's me. I know you can't see me, but I'm here.'

'Martin? Am I dreaming this? Where are you?'

'You're not dreaming it, Kathy. I'm still here in the house.'

'Where? I don't understand. We looked everywhere for you.'

There was a long silence, and then it sounded as if Martin had crossed the room and was standing next to the door. 'I have to be careful. I don't want the others to hear me. I don't know how many of them are sleeping.'

'What others? What are you talking about? How can I hear you but not see you?'

'Kathy, you have to find a way to get me out of here. That witch-woman that Rob was talking about. Maybe she knows how.'

'Martin, if it's really you, you're doing my head in. How can I find a way to get you out of here if you're not here?'

'I *am* here. I'm shut up in that priest's hole, along with the rest of them. You have to get me out, Kathy, or else I'll never get out. And I mean *never*. I'm begging you.'

'Martin, this is scaring me to death.'

'*Shhh!*'

Katharine was about to ask Martin how he had become trapped when she heard whispering outside in the corridor. Sharp, persistent whispering, between at least three or four people. She sat up in bed and drew back the quilt as quietly as she could. The whispering went on and on, and it sounded like an argument.

'*So where is he?*'

'*How should I know? I'm not his keeper.*'

'*You could have fucking waited. Both of you.*'

'*Stop fretting, will you? It's the first of the fulness tomorrow. If we don't find him tonight we'll find him then.*'

The whispering continued, although the whisperers must have been walking away along the corridor because Katharine could no longer distinguish what they were saying. Eventually their voices faded altogether, and apart from the rain and the sibilant whistling of the wind down the chimneys, Allhallows Hall was quiet again.

'Martin?' said Katharine. She began to wonder if she was asleep and having a nightmare, although she could feel the bobbly stitching on the quilt and the lumpy mattress that she was sitting on, and she could make out the looming mahogany wardrobe and the outline of the door. She hesitated to reach over and switch on the bedside lamp in case she saw that Martin really wasn't there, or in case he suddenly appeared. She didn't know which would frighten her more.

'Martin? Say something.'

There was no answer. She waited a little longer and then she clicked on the lamp. Even if Martin had been nothing more than a watery outline, she couldn't see him.

She said, 'Martin? Are you still there?' but he didn't reply. Suddenly she felt deeply cold, all the way down her spine, and she started to shiver. She tried to say 'Martin' again, but her teeth were chattering and she couldn't even pronounce his name.

After a minute she stood up, went to the window and drew the curtains. Outside, over the moor, the sky was beginning to clear. She went back to the bed and sat down again, still shivering. She had never felt so helpless in her life.

24

Rob called Sergeant Billings at Crownhill police station, but was told that he wouldn't be back for at least an hour because he was attending a serious car accident on the A388 at Polborder. He had only just put down his phone, though, when there was a brisk knock at the door. Vicky went to answer it and found John Kipling standing outside, brushing the rain off his crimson anorak.

'John, come in,' said Rob. 'Has Francis been in touch?'

John entered the hallway and prised off his wellingtons. It had stopped raining now, and three DSR volunteers were standing outside in the courtyard having a smoke. A black-and-white border collie in a waterproof dog parka was sitting patiently beside them, its tongue lolling out, next to the headless cherub.

'Yes...' said John. 'I was halfway up the side of Cox Tor when he called me. I don't know what to think. I gather there's been no sign of her?'

'No. We've searched the house all over again, every nook and cranny, believe me, but she's totally vanished. And I'm supposing that there's no trace of Timmy, either.'

'Sorry, no. We've had three drones circling all around

for most of the morning, but nothing. Only a few stray sheep.'

He paused, and then he said, 'Francis told me all about that hammer that was used to kill your dad – how the police found your DNA on it and everything. I mean, how weird is that?'

He paused again. 'Have you told them about Ada yet? I think I'm still in shock about that.'

'Not yet, but we'll have to. And about my brother, Martin, too, if he doesn't show up. Listen – you know those blankets that were lying on the floor in the "witching room" or whatever you want to call it. It looked as if somebody had disturbed them, so I've brought one down. I was going to ask Sergeant Billings to send a police dog up here to see if it could pick up a scent from it, but since you've got one of your search dogs here already – maybe he could have a sniff.'

'Well, yes. Sure. Why not?'

John was about to call to his companions in the courtyard when Katharine appeared halfway down the stairs. Her blonde hair was sticking up as if it had been lifted by static electricity and her face was as pale as oatmeal.

'Katharine! What's wrong?' asked Vicky, going over to the foot of the stairs. 'You haven't been sick again, have you?'

Katharine came slowly down the last remaining stairs. 'It's Martin. He came into the bedroom and he whispered to me, but he wasn't there.'

'What? Come and sit down. I'm sorry, but you look terrible.'

They went into the drawing room. Grace and Portia stood up so that Katharine could sit down on the sofa. She was shaking uncontrollably and Vicky sat beside her and took hold of her hands.

'My God, Katharine, you're *freezing*! Rob – would you fetch her coat for her?'

Katharine looked at her in desperation. 'I was nearly asleep and then I felt him touch me. He said that he was trapped in that priest's hole and he didn't know how to get out. He pleaded with me to help him. I don't understand how he could have been trapped in that priest's hole but yet he was whispering to me in the bedroom at the same time. I thought for a moment that I must be having a bad dream or going mad. But Vicky, I *felt* him, and I *heard* him, I swear it. I heard him as clear as anything! And then I heard more of them whispering outside the door, and it sounded as if they were looking for him.'

Rob came back in with Katharine's overcoat and draped it around her shoulders. She clutched it tightly around her, still shaking as if she had Parkinson's.

Vicky looked up to Rob. 'Martin's still here in the house, Rob. I know it's crazy, but he must be. And if *he's* still here, what are the chances that Timmy's still here, too, *and* Ada?'

John said, 'After what Francis was telling me, I believe now that there's a very good chance of that. And I'm not saying that because I believe in half the stories that folks around here tell about hobgoblins and piskies and ghosts and Old Dewer. I'm saying that because the DSR have never conducted a search as thorough and as wide-ranging as the one we've been carrying out for your Timmy and never found not the slightest trace at all. We always find something – a footprint, or a fragment of wool that's got snagged on a brimmel. But this time, nothing at all. Even supposing somebody drove right past the front of the house here and collected him, the dogs didn't pick up even the faintest scent going out from here to the road.'

'But – Jesus – we couldn't have gone through the house more thoroughly if we'd demolished it stone by stone,' said Rob. 'What I can't work out is how these people can be here and yet not here. Francis said they might be nothing but energy. All right, supposing they are, how do we find them and how do we get them back to reality? That's if it's even possible to get them back.'

John raised both eyebrows. 'Right now, your guess is as good as mine. And Francis didn't seem to have too much of a clue either. But there are so many stories about Nicholas Owen and the priest's holes he built. There are still at least a dozen of them that have been written about in the histories of the various houses where he fitted them, but which nobody has ever been able to find.

'What I'm asking myself now is: *why* can nobody find them? Is it because his carpentry was so clever, or did he discover some way of installing them in what you might call a different dimension? You know, like a sort of a parallel universe. That's what Francis was trying to explain to me, more or less, although he was pretty sure that the priest's hole in this house might have been changed into a witching room later on, by somebody else.'

'Yes, he told us that Nicholas Owen would never have

used a crucifix,' said Rob. 'He reckoned that whoever did it mixed some kind of strange chemicals into the plaster, so that if somebody went into the room and they said this special incantation, that person would get stuck in time for ever. It sounds bonkers, doesn't it? I mean, it sounds utterly and completely bonkers. If Timmy and Ada and Martin weren't missing and if Vicky and me hadn't felt and heard those whispering people for ourselves, I think we'd turn ourselves in to the local mental hospital and beg to be sectioned. Katharine, too, after what she's just been through.'

'Let's make a start, anyway,' said John. 'I'll have Bazza bring his dog in, and he can have a good snuffle at that blanket.'

He went back to the front door and Rob followed him. The volunteers out in the courtyard were flicking their cigarette ends away and they looked as if they were getting ready to leave.

John called out, 'Bazza? Do you want fetch Pluto into the house here for a moment?'

'Okay – but I warn you, John, his paws are proper gacky!'

'Don't worry about that,' said Rob. 'This is a lot more important than a few muddy footprints.'

'So long as you're not bothered.'

Bazza looped Pluto's lead twice more around his fist and started to walk the collie towards the house. He had only gone three or four steps, though, before Pluto stopped, and went completely rigid, his legs as stiff as pokers.

'Come on, Ploots, what's got into you, ya mackerel?'

Bazza tugged at Pluto's lead again and again, and whistled, and clucked, and snapped, 'Come on, will ya?' but the collie refused to budge. When Bazza began to drag him across the courtyard, he started to bark, not just angrily, but hysterically, almost as if he were screaming, and wouldn't stop.

'What the devil's got into him, Bazza?' called John.

'I don't have a notion. He's never behaved this way before. Normally, like, he's not scared off by nothing! You could drive a tractor straight at him and he wouldn't flinch an inch!'

'Look, there must be something about this house that gives dogs the willies,' said Rob. 'There was a police dog here the other day and he wouldn't come near it either. Perhaps it has a smell to it that puts them off, even though humans can't smell it. I'll bring the blanket out and he can have a sniff of it outside.'

He went back inside and returned with the blanket over his arm, which he carried over to Bazza and Pluto. The other two volunteers were watching, half in interest and half in amusement.

'You've lost control of him there, Baz! Just like your missus!'

'You shut your cakehole!' Bazza retorted, although Pluto was barking so furiously now and straining on his lead so hard that he was having trouble keeping his balance. 'For Christ's *sake*, Ploots, you gurt gawk! Hold still, will you?'

Rob patiently waited, but it was obvious that Pluto wasn't going to calm down.

'It's no use,' John told him. 'Whatever's got into Pluto

there, it's spookified him good and proper. Bazza – why don't you take the poor fellow away before he barks his head off?'

Bazza took Pluto off down the shingle driveway, although it was Pluto who was doing all the pulling, as if he couldn't put enough distance between himself and Allhallows Hall. When he reached the road he stopped barking, but he turned his head around to look back at the house and Rob could see that his eyes were bulging as if he had been seriously frightened.

Rob and John went back inside. Rob dropped the blanket down behind the elephant's-foot umbrella stand and sniffed his fingers. 'I don't know about this blanket. I can smell grease and dried sweat, but nothing else. Obviously poor old Pluto picked up some smell that really scared him.'

He looked around the hallway and said, 'This house only smells musty to me, but for some reason dogs hate it.'

'Yes, but a dog's sense of smell is forty times keener than ours, isn't it?' said John. 'And they've done some recent tests that show that when dogs pick up a scent, they can actually create a mental picture of it. Like a ball, or a toy, or even a lost child. Whatever it is that scares them about this house, they can actually *see* it.'

'It's a pity they can't talk. Then they could tell us what it is.'

Vicky was waiting for Rob by the fire. Katharine was still hunched up on the sofa, bundled up in her coat, and Grace had made her a mug of tea to warm her up. Portia was standing in front of the painting of the pagan mass, with its gathering of hooded figures. She was studying it with such concentration that Rob could have imagined she was trying to pick out the face of somebody she knew.

'What happened?' asked Vicky. 'I heard barking.'

'Barking!' said Rob. 'I think that just about sums up the whole of these past few days.'

He clamped his hand over his mouth for a moment, and squeezed his eyes tight shut to hold back the tears. When he took his hand away, he said miserably, 'All I want is Timmy back, safe and sound. That's all I want. And I want to know that Martin's safe too. But how do people bear it when they lose their children? How do they bear it? How can you keep on going into the future when you've left your child in the past?'

Vicky came up to him and put her arms around him, and Grace came up and embraced him, too. John could only stand there, looking grave, while they hugged each and wept.

Portia turned round from the painting and said, 'Just look at this picture. It's like everything that's been happening in this house. If you ask me, it's all the Devil's work.'

25

Ada felt overwhelmingly tired, and she would have done anything to lie on her side on the horsehair matting and close her eyes for an hour or two. But she stayed sitting upright. She was all too aware of the men gathered at the far end of the room, and how they were glancing in her direction from time to time as if they were checking that she was still awake.

She had read dozens of books by mediums who had made believable claims that they had encountered spirits and departed souls. Even more convincingly, she had seen and felt for herself the resonance of more than thirty people who had left this world and gone to the Otherland. She had never agreed with Francis that their resonance was nothing more than an emotional echo of the life they had recently left, and that it would eventually fade altogether, in the same way that an echo eventually dies.

She had seen the spirits of at least three people who had been deceased for more than five years. The most memorable had been a widow standing on the beach at Heybrook Bay, waiting for a drowned husband who would never return to her. This widow had been visible only intermittently, nothing more than a darker shadow that flickered in the persistent sea breeze, her scarf flapping behind her, but Ada had been able to see her twice. Once, she was sure she had heard her calling out her husband's name.

Because of this and all her other experiences as a 'charmer', Ada was convinced that the men who were gathered in this witching room were not spirits, or ghosts, or phantoms, or however dead souls were usually labelled – they were all still alive. Spellbound, but alive.

In spite of that, their movements appeared to Ada to be narrowly constrained by the spell they were under. 'Spell' sounded like something out of a fairy story, but it was the best description of it that she could think of, since it meant both a state of enchantment and an indeterminate period of time.

She guessed that the men were visible at certain times – visible to her, at least, like they were now, and each other – even if nobody else who came into the witching room could see them. While they were visible, it seemed as if they had no choice but to stay penned up in here. At other times, though, they seemed to be able to roam invisibly around the house in some form or another, whispering, angry, frustrated, and even capable of hitting and pushing the people who were staying there.

She wondered if they were angry and frustrated not only because they were trapped in time, but because they were trapped in Allhallows Hall, too. They might be able to wander around the house, but if they couldn't take their physical bodies with them they wouldn't be able to leave it.

She tilted her head tiredly back against the wall. She had been friends with Francis for at least five years, and she knew how knowledgeable he was when it came to spells and necromancy, as well as physics. She prayed that he was doing everything he could to devise a way to release her from this temporal suspension, and out of this stuffy, airless, horsehair-smelling room.

Behind the stained-glass windows, the light was beginning to fade. The thought of the night approaching filled her with dread. What was it going to be like in total darkness, with all of these men? To begin with, she had counted only seven or eight, but now she could see that there were more, at least eleven, and more seemed to be appearing all the time. They seemed to rise up off the floor, as if from nowhere, and their whispered conversation grew louder and more insistent.

'*You must – we must – there must be a way—*'

'*Now that he's gone – I wish that I could go out and spit on his grave—*'

'*No, they'll cremate him – ashes to ashes – mistrust to dust—*'

Ada closed her eyes for a few moments. When she opened them again she found Jaws crouching down close beside her, his face half in shadow now, but enough for her to see that he was smiling with that enigmatic, self-satisfied smile.

'You trying to doze off there, love? You'll be lucky. It's not bedtime yet and it never will be.'

'No. Just thinking, that's all. What do *you* want?'

'Nothing in particular. Just felt like being friendly, that's all.'

'Sorry, I'm not in the mood. Why don't you crocky down somewhere else and be friendly?'

'Hah! You're a right local girl, aren't you? Talk like fucking pirates, you lot. *Oooh* this and *aaarrh* that. But there's no point in you being all shirty. You're going to need a mate, I'll tell you that for nothing. It's going to be dark before you know it and some of these blokes have been shut up here since the fucking millennium.'

'I told you to go away. I'm not interested in you being my "mate", thank you very much, and I can take care of myself.'

'Oh, you think so? Couldn't stop us from chanting you, could you? Even with your friends there.'

'What do you mean, "chanting"?'

Jaws pressed his fingertips to his forehead as if he were trying to remember something that had slipped his mind, but then she realised that he must be visualising the moment when he himself had been trapped in this room. For him, that must have happened only a split second ago, and yet it was years ago, too. The day after Derby Day, nineteen seventy-nine.

'The chanting is the words that freeze you. Don't ask me who made them up or what half of them mean. We all know them now because we've heard them so often we could Wallace and Gromit. In any case, I went down to old Russarse's library one fulness and took a shufti through his book of mumbo-jumbo for myself.'

He didn't explain himself any further but continued to

stare at Ada as if he could see right through her eyes and into her head. It made her feel so uncomfortable, almost as if he were sliding his hand into her jeans, and so she turned away and looked towards the other end of the room, where the opening dado was – the door to reality that she was powerless to open.

'You're cream-crackered, aren't you, love?' Jaws asked her, after a while.

She kept her head turned away. 'Leave me alone, will you? Whatever you've got to say to me, I'm not interested and I don't want to hear it.'

Instead of standing up and leaving her, Jaws shuffled himself even closer. Every breath she took in was pungent with his Old Spice aftershave.

'What you can't work out is, how can you be cream-crackered when it's still exactly the same time as it was when you first come in here? I saw you looking at your watch. What about Father Thomas, how can *he* be tired when as far as he's concerned he's still back in sixteen-hundred-and-whenever-it-was? Father Thomas hasn't aged a second, let alone three and a half fucking centuries.'

'I'm not listening to you so you might as well shut your teeth.'

Jaws ignored her, and again he cupped his hand over her knee to get her attention.

'We never need no sleep, not us, not in the way we used to sleep before we was banged up in here. We just don't need it. But our heads get worn out from thinking, do you know what I mean? Your brain can't go on like a fucking washing machine, turning over the same thing again and again and again. You'd go mum and dad if it did. So now and then we have to have a bit of a lie-down and we call that having a "weary".'

Ada turned back to look at him. She couldn't decide from his expression if he was being genuinely helpful or lascivious. He slowly raised his hand off her knee, but he didn't take his eyes off her and he didn't blink.

'How long for?' she asked him.

'How long do we have a weary for? It all depends, love. It depends on how long we've been in here and what kind of a state we're in – you know, up here.' He tapped his forehead. 'Some of these blokes, they're right nutters. Others, it's hard to tell. They keep themselves to themselves and you can never work out what's going on inside of their heads. See that bloke next to the wall there – the one with the glasses and that long grey shirt untucked? Professor Corkscrew they call him, and believe me you don't want to know why. But I don't think I've heard him say more than ten words the whole time he's been here, and two of them was "eff off".'

'How many men are here altogether? Do you know?'

'Seventeen, love. I've been here long enough to know them all, even though you never see them all at once, simultaneous-like, on account of them all having a weary at different times. But give yourself a year or two, and you'll get to know them all, too. That bloke with the droopy moustache, that's Wellie. You want to stay well away from Wellie, he's a fucking headcase. It's a good thing there's no kettles in here. That was Wellie's favourite trick, in the nick if you crossed him. Boil a kettle of water, mix it up with sugar, and pour it all over your bonce. But – you know – even the nuttiest of nutters have hearts.'

'What does that mean?'

'What do you think? It means they have wives and girlfriends – or boyfriends, some of them. They have mums and dads and kids of their own. But they ain't going to see none of them again, never. Once old Russell was brown bread, at least we was able to go up into the attic and go through our suitcases. All of us had family photos in our luggage, and personal letters, and now we've got them back. Mind you, I'm not sure if it doesn't stick the knife in even harder, having all those photos of somebody you ain't never going to be able to put your arms round again and reading the letters they've sent you over and over until you know every fucking word of them off by heart.'

'Aren't there any women here?'

'No, love. Only you. That's why I said you should have left well enough alone.'

It had grown so dark now that Ada could barely see him – only the glitter of his eyes. The only light was a faint red-and-green glow behind the stained-glass window at the end of the second bedroom. The door must have been left open, and the landing light was shining along the corridor.

Jaws stood up. 'You want my advice, love? Take each day as it comes, because you've got more days coming to you than you can ever count. You'll never get any older, so you might as well try to get wiser. I never pretended to be the nicest bloke in the world, and who knows, I might be tempted to take advantage of you, too, because you're a looker, no mistake about that. But I'm here if you need me.'

Ada sat there in the darkness, breathing her last breath over and over again.

'So why do they call you Jaws?' she asked him, and she realised that she was whispering, too.

'Lots of reasons. One of them is, I don't never bite off more than what I can chew.'

'Is that all?'

'Another one is, my bite is a whole lot worse than my bark.'

He went back to join the rest of the men, who were whispering together in the far corner. She strained her ears to hear if they were whispering about her, but their voices were too sibilant and soft. They sounded like a troop of sad children traipsing their way slowly through heaps of autumn leaves. *Whisper, whisper, whisper.*

The red-and-green light in the stained-glass bedroom window was suddenly extinguished, so somebody must have closed the door – somebody in that other world from which she had now been cut off. Now she understood how people must feel in that very last moment of brain-consciousness, when they die.

She started to recite some of the Dartmoor poems she knew. If she kept her thoughts varied, and interesting, maybe she wouldn't succumb to this so-called weary. If there was one thing that Jaws had said to her that had given her a cold crawling feeling of dread, it was 'I might be tempted to take advantage of you, too'.

26

Katharine was still so shaken that Vicky gave her two of her Unisom and helped her back up to bed. Rob had suggested that both of them should call for a taxi and go to spend the night at the Tavistock House Hotel, but Katharine didn't want to leave Allhallows Hall in case Martin made some kind of reappearance, and Vicky wanted to stay because she was convinced now that Timmy was still somewhere in the house.

'She's fasters,' said Vicky, when she came back downstairs. Rob and Grace and Portia were sitting around the fire. They had left the television on, but mute. Seeing a Sky newsreader's face helped them to feel less isolated, and that there was still an ordinary world out there, with ordinary people in it.

'We still haven't heard from Francis,' said Rob. 'I was hoping he might be able to find out what in the name of hell is going on here.'

Vicky sat down next to him. 'I couldn't help thinking while I was upstairs... what if we never see Timmy again, ever? How are we going to go on living? How are we going to forgive ourselves for bringing him here? And what if we never see Martin again, either?'

'I'm not allowing myself to think like that yet. If Katharine heard Martin whispering to her, then he must still be here. And if Martin's still here, there's every chance that Timmy's still here. *And* Ada. I'm beginning to believe that John was right about a parallel dimension, if that's what you want to call it. And if you can go into a parallel dimension, surely you can come back out of it.'

'I was reading about that the other day,' put in Portia. 'Quite a lot of scientists think that there's an infinite number of parallel dimensions, and that they're all just like this one, except they all have very subtle differences. Like, we'll all be in them, all of us, but dressed a little differently, and talking a little differently, and maybe the colour of our eyes will be different. And when we go outside, the grass will be a different shade of green, if it's green at all, and there'll be different birds and trees.'

'It sounds like *Alice In Wonderland*,' said Vicky.

'Well, perhaps that's where Lewis Carroll got the idea from. He used to visit Alice in her family's big house in Oxford, didn't he? Perhaps *that* house had presences, too, just like this one.'

'I feel as if I'm dreaming this,' said Grace. 'I hope and pray I don't hear any of that whispering tonight. I'm not sure I can take any more of it. I don't care who it is.'

Portia reached across the sofa and held Grace's hand. At the same moment, there was a knock at the front door. They all looked at each other. It was dark outside now.

Was it good news or bad news, or no news at all? Was it better to keep on hoping, or to be told that the volunteers had found a body?

Rob went to open the door and found DI Holley standing outside, with DC Cutland.

'What's this?' he asked, and held out both of his hands as if he were expecting to be handcuffed. 'Come to arrest me, have you?'

'Not this evening, Mr Russell, no,' said DI Holley. 'We won't receive the final DNA analysis until tomorrow at the earliest. But we've made some interesting progress with all that luggage you found in the attic here. May we come in?'

'Of course, yes. Come through to the library.'

The two detectives took off their raincoats and then they followed Rob into the library and sat down. DI Holley was carrying a black plastic file, which he placed on the table in front of him and opened up. Rob could see that the first sheet of paper in it bore the letterhead of Dartmoor Prison.

'We paid a visit to the prison this afternoon and I must say the governor was most cooperative. She gave us access to all the inmate records going back more than forty years. Who was locked up there, who was released and who was transferred.'

'And did you find out who all these suitcases belonged to, and why they were stored in the attic?'

'We found out who they belonged to, yes. Every one of them belonged to an inmate who was serving a sentence during the time that your father, Herbert Russell, was governor. There were thirteen of them altogether, and every one of them had been convicted of corruption or fraud. As you know, Dartmoor is only a C-category prison, so that's where they send white-collar criminals, although "white-collar" is stretching it a bit with some of them.'

DC Cutland leaned over and read a name from the list in DI Holley's file.

'Here's one. Jeremy Porter, more commonly known as Jez the Jeweller. He made a fortune out of faking diamond certificates and selling inferior gemstones in Hatton Garden for a huge mark-up. Anybody who complained or threatened to squeal on him would have their fingers crushed in a taxi door, and be told in no uncertain terms why it had happened. Except nobody could prove that Jez was behind it, which was why he was only category C.'

'The list goes on,' said DI Holley. 'And during the nineteen years that your father was governor, every one of these inmates was transferred from Dartmoor to HMP Ford, which is an open prison in Sussex. The records show that he'd assessed every one of them as suitable candidates for a special rehabilitation programme called Social Conscience, and that this programme could see them being granted a much earlier release. Some of them might have as much as four or five years knocked off their sentences.

'Every one of their transfers to Ford was signed off by your father and the head of the Offender Management Unit.'

'But if they were being transferred to this open prison, what the hell were their suitcases doing in his attic?'

'That, I'm afraid, we don't yet know. We've tried contacting HMP Ford but the governor is away at a conference until Monday and the staff who deal with inmate records won't be available until tomorrow.'

'All right. I suppose you'll be able to tell me tomorrow when you come here to arrest me. I don't know why you bothered to come here tonight, to be honest with you. I already knew that those suitcases all belonged to prisoners, from the labels.'

'I wanted to see your reaction, Mr Russell.'

'And what has that told you?'

'It's told me that your father's death is a lot more complicated than a straightforward quarrel over the ownership of this property. There's something iffy going on here, in my estimation, something extremely iffy, and it goes deeper than you've been letting on.'

'You still don't seriously believe I killed my father? Have you contacted any of my witnesses yet?'

'Surrey police are doing that for us. We should have heard by tomorrow. Once they've been in touch I'll be wanting to have a word with your missus, too.'

'"Tomorrow and tomorrow and tomorrow",' Rob quoted. 'And now you might as well know, my brother, Martin, went missing last night and still hasn't turned up yet, and so has a young woman called Ada Grey who came to visit us.'

DI Holley stared at him as if he couldn't believe what he had just heard. DC Cutland looked at DI Holley as if to say, *Is this a wind-up?*

'I think you need to tell us a bit more, don't you, Mr Russell?' said DI Holley. 'When you say "went missing", what exactly do you mean?'

Rob's head slumped down. He felt infinitely tired.

'I wish I knew. I wish I knew but I don't. "Missing" as in "not here any more", that's all I can tell you.'

DI Holley was thoughtfully tapping his middle finger on the table.

'"*Missing as in not here any more*"?' he repeated. 'That's not very helpful, now is it? That's not very helpful at all.'

Before they left, DI Holley and DC Cutland went into the drawing room to speak to Vicky and Grace and Portia.

'When exactly was the last time you ladies saw these two missing persons?' asked DI Holley.

'The last time we saw Martin was early yesterday evening,' Vicky told him. 'He and his wife, Katharine, went into Tavistock for something to eat. We heard them come back but it was late and we didn't see them. We heard Katharine go up to bed but we didn't hear Martin.' She didn't add that they had both sounded drunk, and how fiercely they had been arguing.

Rob said, 'In the morning his coat was on the sofa but he was gone, and we haven't heard from him since.'

'Where's his missus now?'

'Asleep at the moment,' said Vicky. 'She's extremely upset.'

'You'll be able to talk to her when you come back tomorrow,' said Rob. None of them mentioned that Katharine thought she had heard Martin whispering to her in her bedroom.

'And this Ada Grey? When and how did she go missing?'

'She came here early this afternoon because she was interested in seeing this house.'

'Any particular reason?'

'Well, it's supposed to be haunted, and she's a medium.'

'Oh, talks to your dead granny, all that kind of malarkey? Crystal balls and Ouija boards?'

'That's about it, yes.'

'So when did she disappear?'

'We're not sure. About half past one. One minute she was looking around the house and then she wasn't. We looked everywhere for her, but we couldn't find her.'

'Does she live locally?'

'Yes, Rundlestone.'

'You're sure she didn't just get fed up or bored and leave the house without telling you?'

'Or shit-scared, if it really is haunted,' put in DC Cutland, without even the hint of a smile.

Rob didn't answer that. He was tempted to tell these two detectives everything about the whispering and the witching room and the way that Ada had been dragged into the wall, but he was desperately worried that if the police came barging into the house, knocking holes in walls and lifting up floorboards, the reaction from the whisperers would be even more hostile than it was already. If there was the slightest chance that they could bring Timmy and Martin and Ada back from whatever parallel existence they had been taken to, he didn't want to jeopardise it.

'Is there any reason you can think of why either of them would have gone missing? Any disagreements? Any personal problems? Depression? Mental illness?'

Rob shook his head.

'You've tried to contact them, I imagine.'

'Martin left his phone here, so we haven't been able to – and no, we haven't yet tried to get in touch with Ada.'

'Any reason for that?'

Yes – she disappeared into a solid wall. How the hell do you think we were going to get in touch with her?

'No – well, we were waiting for her to get in touch with us. She's what you might call a free spirit. A very independent young woman.'

DI Holley gave DC Cutland a look that clearly meant: *Independent young women, nothing but trouble.* Then he said, 'Very well. I'll report both of them as mispers even though neither of them have yet been gone for twenty-four hours and they're both responsible adults. You'll let us know immediately, won't you, if either or both of them turn up?'

Rob showed the detectives to the door. While he was buttoning up his raincoat, DI Holley looked around the hallway and said, 'There's definitely something iffy going on here. I can feel it in my water.'

As he said that, a fork of lightning flickered over Pew Tor, only half a mile away, and it was followed almost immediately by a colossal rumble of thunder, like a hundred barrels rolling down a flight of stairs. Somewhere in the darkness, a black kite screamed in panic.

27

Ada opened her eyes. She had the most extraordinary sensation that she was weightless, and that she was sliding up the wall behind her. She found that she was standing up, and even though the witching room was dark, she could vaguely see the wavering outlines of at least eight or nine men, like the reflected ripples at the bottom of a well.

'She's up,' whispered one of them, and the rest of them whispered in what sounded like excitement. At first Ada couldn't make out what they were saying, but then she heard a voice say, quite clearly, '*There… I told you she wouldn't be able to hold off the weary much longer. None of us did, the first time we were chanted.*'

There was more whispering, and then she heard a swishing sound as somebody approached her. Chilly fingers took hold of her hand, and she tried to wrench herself away, but the fingers clutched her even tighter.

'Don't be frightened. It's me, Thomas. I'll take care of you.' He was so close that she could smell the stale incense on his cassock, and his musty breath.

'What's happening to me? I feel… I feel like a ghost.'

'You're having a weary. Your physical body is resting, to recover from the shock of your chanting. But your essence is still awake, as it always will be.'

'I don't understand.'

'This is you. Your essence. This is who you are. This is what people mistakenly believe is your soul.'

'You're a priest. Don't you believe that people have souls?'

Ada could almost feel him smiling in the dark. 'I used to, before I was incarcerated here. Now I know what I really am, and what everybody really is. Our souls are not supernatural. They are not granted to us by God. Our souls, if you want to call them that, are manifestations of the same energy that makes the stars shine and the wind blow and the clouds stream over our heads. That is why you can leave your weary physical presence for a while, as you are doing now.'

'I want to wake up.'

'You will, when your brain and your body have recovered.'

'Thomas – I want to wake up. I want to get out of this room. I want my life back.'

'What is your name?'

'What difference does that make? Ada, if you must know.'

'Ada! That is a beautiful name, Ada. It is one of the first women's names mentioned in the Book of Genesis. It means "bright", or an "adornment", and you are certainly both.'

'I don't care if it means "miserable bitch". I just want to

get back to the way I was, before you pulled me through that wall.'

Thomas was silent for a long time, although he didn't release his chilly grip on her hand. Eventually he said, 'I'm afraid you underestimate the force that commands this room, and the whole of this house.'

'What are you talking about? What force?'

'I cannot speak its name, Ada, and neither can any of the men confined here.'

'Just tell me what it is. If you think I'm going to stay stuck here for ever and ever amen you have another think coming.'

She felt somebody else approach, and it was only because she could smell Old Spice that she recognised who it was.

'Father Thomas ain't giving you no grief, is he, love?'

'No. But he won't tell me what it is that's keeping us all here, or how I can get out.'

'That's because you can't, darling, I've told you that. The best you can do is survive. Come on – come with us, we'll show you how you can make the best of both worlds.'

'I don't want to. All I want to do is get back to the way I was.'

'Ada,' Thomas coaxed her. 'One day we may be able to find a way, and if we do, we can *all* find our freedom. I can't tell you how desperately we all long to open the door and walk out of this house, into the daylight. But for now, we have to accept that we are where we are, both in time and in space, and thank the Lord that we are still conscious, and able to talk, and that for all of our suffering, death has not yet been able to claim us.'

'You've been stuck here in this house for four hundred years,' Ada retorted. 'Four hundred years! Haven't you had enough? Don't you *want* to die?'

Again, Thomas was silent for a while. Then he said, 'Death will be much the same as this. One dark day after another. So what's the difference?'

'Come on,' said Jaws. He put his arm around Ada's shoulders and gently pushed her towards the wall.

The sensation of passing through the wall was like walking naked through a shower of ice-cold sparkling water. It lasted only a split second, but Ada felt as if her entire personality had been disassembled into atoms so that they could flow between the atoms of the wall, only to be reassembled on the other side. Here she was, standing in the end bedroom, next to the stack of chairs and the table crowded with cobwebby candlesticks.

Enough light filtered along the corridor from the hallway downstairs for Ada to see that Jaws was already here beside her, next to the stack of chairs, although he was semi-transparent, so that she could see the outline of the window frame behind him. There was a soft shushing sound, and then Thomas appeared right through the wall behind her.

'All right, darling?' Jaws whispered. 'You'll get used to it. Just keep in mind that this is the actual you, but your body's still sitting in the room back there.'

'Why do we have to whisper?' Ada asked him. 'Why can't we talk in our normal voices, or shout? What difference would it make? The people who are staying here, the Russells, they've already heard you whispering. Why do you think we came looking for you?'

'It's not *them* we're worried about.'

'Then who?'

'Never mind that. Let's show you what we do while we're having a weary.'

'Don't give me "never mind that"!' Ada hissed at him. 'If you're whispering for some reason, I want to know why! You don't want to wake somebody up, is that it?'

Thomas laid his hand on Ada's shoulder. 'Please, Ada. We can't answer you, not without jeopardising our lives. We don't want to live like this, but we don't want to die.'

Ada could have let out a hysterical laugh. 'We don't want to live like this, but we don't want to die' was a line from a song by the rock band Vampire Weekend. The same bleak words, she thought – the same hopeless sentiment – spoken by a man from four hundred years ago.

Jaws laid his hand on her shoulder and gently propelled her out of the end bedroom, past the stained-glass window of Old Dewer and along the corridor to the landing. She could see other presences climbing up and down the stairs, whispering to each other, even though they were no more substantial than the images in a black-and-white photographic negative – just like Jaws and Thomas and herself.

When she turned the corner, she saw even more of them. Three or four were gathered outside the master bedroom, their heads close together as if they were furtively discussing what they were going to do next.

Jaws stopped outside the door of the first bedroom, where Grace and Portia were sleeping.

He leaned close to Ada's right ear and whispered, 'What we need more than anything else, love, is *breath*. Even when it's second-hand.'

'What?'

'You wait till you've been breathing your last breath a thousand times over, day in and day out. You'll start to feel like somebody's trying to smother you with a stinky old pillow and won't take it away. You ain't got to that stage yet, but give it a month or two and you'll be gasping, I promise you.'

'Why can't we just go outside, and breathe some fresh air there?'

'Because we can't, love. We can walk through all these indoor walls when we're having a weary, but the outside walls – no. They're as solid to us as they are to them what hasn't been chanted. Believe me, I've tried enough times.'

'So what are we going to do now?' Ada whispered.

'Here, I'll show you. Thomas, mate – are you joining us?'

Thomas shook his head and pointed down the corridor towards the master bedroom. '*She* is the one whose breath I wish to savour.'

'Her?' said Ada. 'That's the wife of Rob Russell's older brother.'

'I don't care whose brother he is. I want to go back and tell him how much I relished the taste of her.' With that, his tongue darted out and licked his scabby lips.

'Why? What's he ever done to you?'

'He told me when he first set eyes on me that I was a disgrace in the eyes of God. A walking blasphemy, that's what he called me. Why do you think I chanted him?'

'You chanted *him*, too?' asked Ada. 'You've trapped him, the same as me?'

'He deserved it. Nobody should take the name of the Lord our God in vain. Nobody should denigrate somebody who gave his own mother solace. And above all, nobody should question the integrity of a man whose devotion to the Almighty has kept him imprisoned in the moment of his sacrifice for century after wearisome century, and for countless wearisome centuries to come.'

Thomas was whispering as he spoke, but intensely, almost hatefully, and he pronounced 'quessstion' with an extra snake-like hiss.

'Martin, that's his name, isn't it?' asked Ada. 'I don't know what he looks like, but none of the men I saw in the priest's hole looked as if they could have been him.'

'He was having himself a weary, I expect,' said Jaws.

'Martin?' whispered Thomas. 'I never asked his name. One never speaks the names of demons or those possessed by demons – not when one is chanting them. He is among *us* now, yes, and thanks to me the world at large is purged of his presence for all eternity. For that, I think I deserve to be lauded, don't you?'

Ada didn't know what to say. When Thomas had first approached her, she had thought that he was sympathetic and friendly, and that he might be able to help her to find a way to escape from this nightmare. Now she began to see that his four-century confinement in Allhallows

Hall had unhinged him, and made him vengeful – even if he hadn't already been deranged on the day when he was first trapped here.

Without saying another word, Thomas grinned and turned and went off along the corridor to join the other whispering men outside the master bedroom.

Jaws gave a dismissive grunt. 'Don't let the holy father get to you, darling. He's a dirty beast, so what do you expect? All dirty beasts are funny in the head. They have to be. All that walking on water and feeding the five thousand and raising the dead. You've got to have a fucking screw loose to believe in all that cobblers.'

He pressed his hand between her shoulders again and said, 'Come on. Let's snag ourselves some of that breath.'

Ada still couldn't believe that she would be able to pass through the bedroom wall as if it had no substance at all, and when Jaws pushed her towards it, she turned her face to one side and tried to shy away. But with that same sharp, effervescent tingle, she found herself standing in the gloom of Grace and Portia's bedroom. It was lit only by the red numbers on the digital clock that Portia had borrowed from the kitchen, although both she and Jaws seemed to have a faint luminosity of their own.

It was 3:11, and then 3:12. Both Grace and Portia were deeply asleep, back to back, with the quilt drawn up under their arms. Portia's mouth was open and she was softly snoring.

'Here, love,' whispered Jaws, 'this is what you do.'

He made his way around the end of the bed and carefully laid himself down next to Portia. He made no impression on the covers at all, as if he weighed nothing, but he was able to fold back the corner of the quilt to give himself unobstructed access to Portia's face. He stared at her for a moment, so close that the tips of their noses were almost touching, and then he opened his mouth and pressed his lips against hers.

She murmured and jerked her head, but Jaws kept their lips stuck together. Every time she breathed out, he breathed in. They passed the same breath between them over and over, until his eyelids began to droop with the sensation that she was giving him, and gradually they starved the oxygen out of the air that they were sharing.

At last he sat up. She found it hard to read the expression on his face. The last time she had seen a man looking like that was after her boyfriend, Will, had made love to her but had gasped out another girl's name when he climaxed. *Ferna!* She had never found out who Ferna was, but that had been the beginning of the end of her relationship with Will.

Portia was snoring again. Her hand lay on the pillow with her fingers twitching slightly.

'She hasn't woken up,' Ada whispered.

'No. She won't. Even if she did, she wouldn't be able to see us. Now it's your turn.'

'What do you mean?'

Jaws nodded towards Grace. 'Go on. Don't tell me you're not feeling a little breathless.'

He was right. Ada's lungs did feel constricted. Ever since she was little she had suffered from asthma, and although this tightness didn't feel exactly the same as an asthma attack, she still felt as if she needed an inhaler. Or Grace.

'I can't,' she whispered, but all the same she sat down on the side of the bed, next to Grace. 'Suppose she wakes up?'

'She won't, I promise you. But even if she did, I don't think she'd mind, do you? Tutti-frutti like you.'

Ada lay down beside Grace and looked at her closely, and even though the radiance that she was giving off was only dim, it was enough to illuminate Grace's face. Her eyelashes were almost transparent and she had a spatter of freckles across the bridge of her nose. Her pink lips were bow-shaped and slightly parted and now that she was this close, Ada could hear her quietly breathing in and out.

'Kiss her,' Jaws urged her. 'But keep your mouth open. Take her breath in, and then give it back. In and out, in and out, until you start to go dizzy.'

Ada kissed Grace, lightly at first, but when she breathed out, she kissed her harder, so that their lips would be sealed tightly together and none of her precious exhaled air could escape. Once she had taken it into her lungs, she breathed it out again, back into Grace's mouth. Grace made a muffled sound, and tried to twist her face to one side, but Ada took hold of her head in both hands, burying her fingers in her gingery hair, and held her fast.

She couldn't believe that she was so greedy for this exhaled breath, even though it was so depleted in oxygen. It made her feel light-headed and it aroused an excitement in her – not so much erotic as the kind of helpless thrill she had felt on a roller-coaster. She sucked again and again at Grace's lips, drawing out the last remaining gasp of breath from her lungs, until at last she sat up, panting, and now she knew why Jaws had looked so post-coital. It was nothing like anything she had experienced in the whole of her life – the fear of suffocation but exhilaration, too, and the sensation that she was sharing so much more than another woman's breath; she was sharing her mortality.

'What now?' she whispered.

'That's it. We can take a tour of the house if you like. But you'll have plenty of time to do that in the future. You'll have years and years and years, until you know every floorboard and every windowpane and every knothole and every curtain hook by heart, same as I do.'

Ada looked down and saw to her surprise that Grace's green eyes were open, and were staring up at her. For a moment, she forgot that Grace was unable to see her, and she promptly stood up, and raised both hands, as if to apologise for having kissed her and stolen her breath.

Grace raised her head off the pillow, still staring, but *through* her, rather than at her.

'Is there somebody there?' she said quietly, obviously not wanting to wake Portia.

Ada looked across the bed at Jaws, who shook his head, warning her not to answer. But she was desperate for Grace to know that she was still alive, and still in the house.

She leaned forward and whispered, '*Yes, Grace, there is somebody here! It's me, Ada! Ada Grey! Please, Grace! I'm in the priest's room! Please find a way to get me out of it. Please!*'

Jaws came storming around the bed and seized her arm.

'What the fuck do you think you're doing?' he demanded, his whisper blasting directly into her right ear.

'Get off me!' she snapped back. 'Do you really believe I'm prepared to stay like this? If you think I have any intention of living with you and all those other leches for the next thousand years you must be out of your brain, if you even have one! I'd rather kill myself!'

'Keep your fucking voice down!' Jaws whispered at her.

Grace sat up in bed now and waved her arms around, trying to feel Ada, even if she couldn't see her. '*Ada? Ada! And who else is here? Ada!*'

Now Portia sat up, too, rubbing her eyes. 'Grace! What's going on?'

'Ada's in here! Ada's in here! And some – some *man!*'

Jaws twisted Ada's thick glossy hair twice around the knuckles of his left hand and hooked his right arm around her waist. He was almost invisible, but he was twice as powerful as she was, and he was able to force her towards the door. She kicked and struggled as furiously as she had kicked and struggled when she had first been pulled through the wall in the witching room, but he was far too strong for her.

'*Grace!*' she screamed. '*Grace, save me! Call Francis! Tell him that I'm here! Save me!*'

Jaws pushed her through the bedroom door in what felt like an explosion of millions of atoms. She found herself out in the corridor, still struggling to get free. Jaws unwound his grip on her hair and stepped back, shaking his hand as if in disgust, with a grim expression on his face.

'You don't have a clue what you've fucking done, do

you? I *told* you not to talk out loud, didn't I – let alone scream your fucking head off! Don't you understand what you are? You're something and nothing, but most of all you're nothing, because you're not sitting in that room tonight, you're sitting in that room yesterday, and tomorrow you'll be sitting in it the day before yesterday, and so on and so on and so on.'

He was still whispering when Ada heard a deep rumbling sound, accompanied by a high-pitched buzzing like dozens of wasps trying to get out of a window. The floor began to vibrate, and the floorboards squeaked against each other. It felt as if Allhallows Hall were being shaken right down to its foundations. One of the oil paintings of the Wilmington family dropped off the wall next to the landing and fell flat on its face, chipping off a corner of its frame.

The rumbling and creaking went on for nearly half a minute, and then it subsided, and the house was silent again. The door to Rob and Vicky's bedroom opened, and Rob appeared and switched on the light. He stood there for a while, listening; and then the door to Grace and Portia's bedroom opened, too, and Grace appeared, clutching her dressing gown around her like a survivor from an earthquake.

Grace said, 'Rob – you're not going to believe this.'

Jaws tapped Ada on the shoulder and when she turned around he beckoned to her and silently mouthed the words, '*Come on. Time for us to go back.*'

Ada was tempted to run along the corridor to Rob and tell him, too, that she was still here, and still alive, but the huge tremor that had shaken the house had seriously frightened her. Had she set it off herself by screaming like that? And if she had, what force was it that she had disturbed? She had felt hostile vibrations in houses before, when she was holding séances. She had heard eerie whistling and malevolent humming, but nothing like this, ever.

Jaws had warned her to keep her voice to a whisper, hadn't he, and Thomas had said that if she spoke too loudly she would be jeopardising their lives.

'*We don't want to live like this, but we don't want to die.*'

28

None of them could sleep for the rest of the night, except for Katharine, who was still deeply sedated with Unisom, and hadn't stirred even when the house had started shaking. They sat around the kitchen table drinking coffee and talking quietly to each other, while the fire in the range crackled.

Outside, a pearly-grey dawn gradually appeared behind the gnarled veteran trees that surrounded Allhallows Hall. Some of those trees were more than a hundred years old and Rob always thought they looked like elderly women with their hair sticking up in fright.

'I'll call Francis as soon as I'm pretty sure that he's awake,' said Rob. 'I can't think what else we can do. Whatever's happening in this house, the police won't be able to deal with it, any more than we can.'

Portia ran her fingertips lightly and thoughtfully across her lips. 'I had the strangest dream just before Grace woke me up. I dreamed that some man was kissing me. And I don't mean a peck on the cheek. A proper full-on snog. But I've never been kissed by a man like that, not once.

Not ever. Grace said she heard a man in our bedroom, but I didn't.'

'I'm sure I heard a man, as well as Ada,' said Grace. 'I couldn't see him, but then I couldn't see Ada, either. When Ada was shouting at me, it sounded like he was telling her not to. I'm not sure. He was whispering, so I couldn't really hear what he was saying.'

Vicky spooned more sugar into her coffee and stirred it. 'They all sound so *panicky*, these whisperers. You know, as if they're terrified of something. Perhaps if we can find out what it is, we'll be able to set them all free. Or give them some kind of peace, anyway.'

'Well, perhaps,' said Rob. 'But even supposing we can find a way to bring them back into the real world, what's going to happen to them then?'

'What do you mean?'

'We don't have any idea how long they've been stuck here, do we? What if some of them have been there ever since the Wilmingtons first converted that priest's hole into a witching room? I mean, they must have done it for a reason, mustn't they? Maybe they had some enemy they wanted to trap. Why else would they have had it put in? And that same person could still be there now, that enemy. Or enemies, plural.'

'You don't know,' said Portia. 'Perhaps they didn't have it installed to *trap* anybody. Perhaps one of the family was dying of pneumonia or something, and they wanted to make sure that he or she lived for ever.'

'That's a possibility, I suppose. But unlikely, don't

you think? The Wilmingtons were all fervent Catholics. They would have been quite certain that when they died they were going to Paradise – in which case, surely they wouldn't have thought that dying would be anything to worry about. If they hadn't been so pious, they wouldn't have risked having a priest hole built, would they? Like John Kipling said, it was a fantastic risk in those days.'

'Were they all that pious?' Portia asked him. 'They denied knowing that poor Jesuit they'd been hiding, didn't they, when the priest hunters caught him. I don't call that being very pious.'

'Perhaps they didn't fancy being hung up from the ceiling and having their stomachs cut open, like Nicholas Owen.'

'Oh, *Rob*,' Grace protested. 'I think we're all feeling queasy enough as it is.'

'That's what they used to do to Catholics, though, if they refused to renounce their faith. And much worse. You ask John.'

They were still talking when Rob's phone rang. It was Francis.

'Rob? I was going to call you last night, but then I looked at the time and realised you'd probably be asleep.'

'As it happens, we had what you might call a disturbed night, and I was going to call you anyway. How's it going with your research?'

'Pretty well, on the whole. I've dug up some really obscure stuff about witching rooms, and about Sampford Spiney, too. I'll come round a bit later and give you all the gory details. First of all I need to run over to Tavistock and have a chat with Father Salter. He's the parish priest at Our Lady of the Assumption.'

'Really? Is he an exorcist? I thought you didn't believe in exorcisms.'

'I don't. Not in the conventional sense, anyway. But some exorcisms have been successful in helping people who appear to be possessed by evil spirits, even if that possession has nothing to do with Satan. There might be something in them that can help us to clear all those spooks out of Allhallows Hall.'

'What time can we expect you?'

'It depends what response I get from Father Salter. I've only met him a couple of times, but he seems quite modern in his outlook. He believes that priests should be able to marry, that kind of thing. On the one hand, that could be good. On the other hand, it might mean that he's a bit too sceptical when it comes to "malevolent presences". Might think it's all too medieval, if you know what I mean. But I need to sound him out about a particular type of spiritual decontamination, and if he's prepared to do it himself, or if he knows of some other priest who might be persuaded to.'

'"Spiritual decontamination"? What's that when it's at home?'

'It's a very specific kind of Roman Catholic ritual, and as far as I can find out it hasn't been used since an incident in a village called Hathersage in the Peak District near Sheffield in October of nineteen forty-nine. It's a form of exorcism, if you like, but it's not recognised by the Vatican and it's not the usual "begone, foul spirit, the

Lord commands thee" kind of a job. No floating in the air or vomiting or heads turning three hundred and sixty degrees. In some ways it's scarier than that.'

'Scarier than that? What could be scarier than that?' Rob looked across at Vicky, whose eyebrows were raised. 'It's okay,' he mouthed, and gave her a quick wave of his hand.

'I'll try to get to you by midday,' said Francis. 'When you say you had a disturbed night...?'

'More whispering. Grace heard Ada in her bedroom, not just whispering but screaming at her. And we had something that I can only describe as a mini-earthquake. The whole house shook.'

'Really? Now, *really*? That fits in with what I've been researching. I think I'm beginning to understand what we could be dealing with here, although I'd rather it was something else, to be honest with you. Much rather.'

'Can you give me some idea?'

'Let me talk to Father Salter first. Meanwhile, I'd advise you to stay well away from that witching room, and if you *do* hear any more whispering – or screaming, for that matter – try to turn a deaf ear to it. If I'm right, we're up against a force that takes a very dim view of being interfered with.'

Francis hung up, leaving Rob staring at his phone as if he couldn't think what it was.

'That was Francis?' asked Vicky. 'What did he have to say that was so scary?'

'I don't know exactly. He's an atheist, but he wants to

perform some sort of an exorcism. He's going to Tavistock to see if he can persuade a priest to do it.'

Grace was about to say something when, very indistinctly, they heard a child crying.

'*Shh!*' said Vicky. She stood up, went over to the kitchen door and opened it wider. There was a long silence, punctuated only by the ticking of the longcase clock, and then they heard the cry again. It sounded like a small boy – a very miserable small boy.

'That's Timmy! I'm sure that's Timmy!'

'Vicks – Francis said if we heard anything, we should ignore it.'

'But why? We can't ignore it, if it's Timmy—'

'He seems to think that we're in some kind of danger.'

'I don't care – that's Timmy – I'm sure that's Timmy! *Timmy!* Can you hear me? *Timmy!* It's Mummy!'

Vicky ran across the hallway and started to mount the stairs. Rob followed her, and Grace and Portia came out of the kitchen, too.

'Vicks!' Rob shouted. 'Vicks, for Christ's sake, be careful!'

Vicky reached the landing at the top of the stairs and Rob caught up with her. They hesitated for a moment, listening, and then they heard the boy wailing. He sounded as if he were down at the far end of the corridor, in the bedroom that led to the witching room – the same as the last time Vicky had thought she heard him, and had been so violently pushed over.

'It *is* Timmy,' she said, clasping Rob's hand. 'I know it is.'

'It does sound like him, doesn't it? Timmy! Is that you, Timmy?'

They waited, but there was silence, punctuated only by the ticking of the longcase clock. It suddenly struck a single *bong!* to mark the half-hour, which made Vicky jump.

'Timmy, it's Daddy here… can you try to stay where you are? We're coming to find you.'

Rob started to walk slowly along the corridor, with Vicky close behind him, her left hand placed nervously on his shoulder.

'Timmy? Are you still there? Say something, Timmy, even if it's only "I'm here"!'

They were less than a third of the way along the corridor, passing the first of the three bedroom doors, when they heard a sharp crackling sound, like somebody treading on a sheet of glass, and breaking it. The black hooded figure in the middle of the stained-glass window suddenly shot both of its arms upwards and whirled around, so that they could see its face.

Rob stopped where he was, in utter shock. Not only had the figure of Old Dewer moved, but his face was terrifying. His eyes shone blindingly white, as intense as two halogen headlights, and his chin was stretched downwards as if he were screaming at them, except that he was totally silent. His tongue was split like a snake's, and it was glistening grey.

'Oh God!' Vicky gasped. 'Oh God, Rob, what's happening? It can't be real! *It can't be!*'

The hooded figure flapped both of his arms, and before Rob and Vicky could turn around, the five bristling black hounds that surrounded him sprang out of the window and landed on the wooden floor of the corridor with a scrabbling of claws. Their eyes, too, were shining, and their red tongues were flapping out over their teeth. They came running towards Rob and Vicky, all five of them panting hungrily.

Rob snatched at Vicky's sleeve and pulled her back along the corridor to the landing. They had nearly reached the top of the stairs when Vicky stumbled and fell onto her knees. One of the hounds leaped on top of her and started ripping at her sweater, and when Rob swung his arm around and hit its head, another hound sprang on him and bit right through his jacket into his elbow.

They felt hairy and coarse, these hounds, and they were heavy, too, and smelled strongly of sulphur and wet grass and faeces. Rob punched and pushed and kicked at them, but he couldn't stop them from snapping at his hands and tearing his jacket, and all the time their eyes were flickering and dazzling him like strobe lights.

He kicked one of them hard in the belly and then again in the ribs, so that it toppled back against the two behind it. That gave him a split second's respite to thrust his hands under Vicky's armpits and heave her up off the floor. One of the hounds jumped onto his back and tried to bite the back of his neck, but he lurched himself sharply to the left and it rolled off him. With his arm tightly around Vicky's waist, he reached the top of the stairs, and together they started to stagger down them. After three or four steps, though, they both lost their footing and tumbled, all arms and legs, down the first flight of stairs and collided with the panelling.

Grace and Portia had come out into the hallway. 'Rob! Vicky! What's going on up there? What's all that noise? Jesus, what's happened?'

Rob had hit his head hard against the skirting board. He blinked, stunned, and looked up towards the landing. The five hounds had gathered at the top stair, and were staring down at him and Vicky with those piercing white eyes. Their tongues were still hanging out and they were still panting as if they would have given anything to come bounding downstairs and rip their lungs out. After a few seconds, though, the light in their eyes died out, and they turned away, and Rob could hear them trotting back down the corridor.

Grace and Portia came up the stairs and helped them onto their feet.

'Your *clothes* are all torn! Rob – you're bleeding! What on earth's happened to you?'

Vicky was so upset that she could hardly speak. Portia put her arm around her and guided her gently down to the hallway. Rob was about to follow her, but then he climbed cautiously up the stairs to the landing again, and peered down the corridor to the stained-glass window. There was enough daylight gleaming through it now for him to see that it was unbroken, and exactly as it had been before Old Dewer had turned himself around and the hounds had come chasing after them.

Grace stood watching him. When he came back down, wordless, still frowning in disbelief, she said, 'Rob?'

He shook his head, but said nothing.

'Come on, Rob. Tell me what happened. After

everything we've seen in the past two days, nothing's going to surprise me.'

Rob followed her downstairs, glancing back just once to make sure that the hounds had stayed in the window, and weren't coming after him.

When they reached the hallway, he said, 'Francis was right, Gracey. There's something in this house that really doesn't want to be interfered with.'

29

Back in the kitchen, Grace cleaned and bandaged the bites on Rob's elbow. There were five purple teeth-marks, in a semicircle, but his tweed jacket had been thick enough to prevent the hound from biting right down to the bone.

Portia was standing with her back to them, looking out at the overgrown garden. 'This house... It's a different kind of world altogether. It's like none of the laws of nature apply here.'

'You're right,' said Rob. He winced as Grace knotted a clean tea towel tightly around his arm. 'I mean, how in the name of God can dogs jump out of a stained-glass window and attack us? If I hadn't been bitten and Vicky's sweater hadn't been torn, I could have convinced myself that we were high on something.'

'It was that Devil... that Old Dewer, or whatever they call him,' said Vicky quietly. 'It was him who set the dogs on us. And I thought that window was supposed to keep him away.'

'With any luck, Francis has discovered what's causing all this weirdness, and he's found a way to get rid of it. "Spiritual decontamination", that's what he called it.'

Grace stood up. 'I'd better go and check on Katharine. She's been sleeping for ages now.'

She didn't add '*I hope she's still there, and that* she *hasn't disappeared*', but all of them thought it.

Rob stood up too. 'I'll come with you. Just in case those bloody dogs come jumping out again.'

They didn't need to go up to Katharine's bedroom. As they left the kitchen, she was coming downstairs, still looking a little unsteady but with her hair brushed, and wearing eye make-up, and blusher on her cheeks.

'I'm *starving*,' she said. 'I feel as if I haven't eaten in days.'

'Come into the kitchen and Portia will make you a sandwich if you like,' said Grace. 'Or there's some muesli if you fancy some. Or yogurt.'

'Anything. What was all that noise upstairs? I thought I heard a window breaking.'

'You did and you didn't,' Rob told her. 'Come and sit down and I'll tell you all about it. You haven't heard from Martin again, have you?'

'No, nothing. But those pills really knocked me out. What's happened to your arm?'

Katharine sat at the kitchen table with a mug of coffee while Portia made her a cheese and tomato sandwich and Rob and Vicky told her about the stained-glass window and Old Dewer's hounds. She listened and nodded but said nothing. All of them had now come to the point where they were prepared to accept and believe almost anything, no matter how strange and frightening it was – whisperers who they couldn't see, but who could push and kick them;

247

Ada disappearing through a solid wall; Timmy and Martin vanishing yet their voices still being heard; the whole of Allhallows Hall shaking as violently as Herbert Russell used to, in one of his rages.

'If we had a choice, we'd be out of here in five seconds flat and you wouldn't see us for dust,' said Rob, and then realised how ironic his words were. 'Unlike the rest of the people who live here.'

Soon after eleven o'clock, DI Holley arrived with DC Cutland, but without any uniformed officers.

DI Holley smelled as if he had just put out a cigarette and he had a tight, vexed expression on his face. He looked like a hawk that had managed to pick up a particularly plump mouse in his beak but had accidentally dropped it from fifty feet up in the air.

The detectives kept their coats on, and DI Holley said, 'We won't keep you long, Mr Russell. A quick word in private, if we may.'

Rob took them through to the library and closed the door, but they didn't sit down.

'No handcuffs?' Rob asked them.

DI Holley gave him a small, sour smile. 'No, Mr Russell. Not today, anyway. We've had the final results of the DNA tests from the murder weapon this morning and – not to keep you in suspense – you're in the clear.'

'Really? I thought the DNA matched mine.'

'It does. At least, it shows that you're related on the male side to whoever wielded that hammer, although the mitochondrial DNA doesn't tally. That's the female DNA. The perpetrator who killed your father didn't have the same mother as you.'

'This is confusing me. I realise that Herbert Russell wasn't my father, and that my mother must have had an affair at some time with somebody else.'

'It doesn't really matter too much, Mr Russell, because the lab carried out a carbon-14 test on the DNA, too, and that can pinpoint an individual's birth date to within two years. In this case they calculated that the perpetrator was born between nineteen forty-nine and nineteen fifty-one, which is more than thirty-five years before you were.'

'So whoever killed my stepfather... you've proved that it wasn't me... but they were related to me?'

'Related? There's no question he was related. He was your father.'

'My real father killed my stepfather? Is that what you're saying?'

'It certainly looks like it. And I think we can reasonably conjecture that some rivalry between them regarding your mother could have been all or part of his motive.'

Rob pulled out one of the chairs and sat down. He was beginning to feel as if he were going mad.

'Are you going to be able to find him?' he asked.

'Your real father? Of course we made enquiries around Sampford Spiney in case anybody noticed any suspicious vehicles in the area on the day of your father's death. So far, though, no luck. Hardly surprising, with a population of only a hundred and seventeen and nothing in the way of what you'd call nightlife. I reckon the locals are all in bed after *News at Ten*. But we haven't given up.'

'I see.'

'I can reassure you, though, that you're completely out of the frame. We've also heard from Surrey police and they confirm your witness reports. You weren't here on the evening Herbert Russell was murdered and the DNA found on the murder weapon wasn't yours.'

'And that's conclusive, is it?'

'Yes, Mr Russell. The lab technicians told us that the DNA was much better preserved than they would have expected if the hammer had been lying outside in the garden for any length of time. I think we can assume that after it was used to kill Herbert Russell it was either taken immediately out of the house to be hidden in the flower bed or, more likely, thrown out of an upstairs window.'

DI Holley paused, and then he nodded towards Rob's bandaged elbow. 'Had a bit of an accident, did you?'

Yes. I was attacked by a ravening hound that leaped at me out of a stained-glass window, what do you think?

'It's nothing. Tripped over, that's all. Only a scratch.'

'Right, then, we'll leave you in peace. Of course, if you do think of anything that might assist us in our investigation... or if by chance your real father should make an appearance...'

'Of course,' said Rob. He showed both detectives to the front door and watched them walk away as if it were the end of a film.

Vicky came up to him. 'They're not going to arrest you?'

'No. They've seen sense. Which is more than we have.'

*

After about an hour, Rob considered going upstairs again to take another look at the stained-glass window, and also to check the end bedroom.

'Don't,' said Vicky. 'Let's wait until Francis gets here. He did warn us to keep away from the witching room, after all.'

'I only want to make sure that I'm not going insane. If my real father was psychopathic enough to murder my stepfather with a hammer, who knows what genes I might have inherited?'

'Rob, I was attacked by those dogs, too, and you couldn't meet anybody saner than my father.'

'I don't know. How sane do you have to be, to be a rewards manager?'

'Very sane. If you weren't, you'd go mad.'

It wasn't until the clock struck four that Francis knocked at the front door. He was carrying a black leather doctor's bag and a walking stick with a silver knob on the top of it. He was accompanied by a balding, fiftyish man with ruddy cheeks and rimless spectacles. When this man took off his raincoat, Rob saw that he was wearing a dark grey tweed jacket, a black shirt, and a dog collar.

'Rob, this is Father Salter, from Our Lady of the Assumption in Tavistock. He kindly agreed to come over and do a bit of a spiritual recce.'

'Thank you, father, we appreciate it,' Rob told him. 'This is my wife, Victoria, and this is my sister, Grace, and her partner, Portia. And this is my brother's wife, Katharine.'

'Francis has explained to me in broad terms what seems to have been happening here in this house,' said Father Salter. He spoke in a quiet, clipped voice, as if he were trying to explain to a particularly slow parishioner the meaning of transubstantiation.

'We've had another incident since I spoke to you,' said Rob, and lifted his elbow to show Francis the tea towel wrapped around it.

Father Salter took three or four steps into the middle of the hallway and circled around. Then he stopped, and closed his eyes, one hand raised for silence.

'There *is* an atmosphere here, no question about it.'

'You can definitely feel it?'

Father Salter crossed himself. 'Oh, yes. An atmosphere. A highly febrile atmosphere. And its excitement seems to be rising, as if the house itself is aware that a messenger of God has entered into it.'

'What happened to your elbow?' Francis asked Rob.

'It was that stained-glass window upstairs. You know, the one with Old Dewer and his dogs. We heard what we thought was Timmy crying, so despite what you'd said we went up to see if he was there.'

Father Salter was listening to him now, and very intently. Rob hesitated, because he knew what he was going to say was totally bizarre, but then he thought that if Father Salter had been able to sense the tension in Allhallows Hall as soon as he had walked in, he would probably accept that he was telling the truth. He must have heard stories in the confessional that were equally weird.

Haltingly, trying to sound as rational as possible, Rob

described how the hounds had sprung out of the window and attacked them.

Vicky came and stood close to him and took hold of his hand. 'It's true, father. I swear it. Look – one of the dogs tore my sweater.'

Father Salter crossed himself again. 'I believe you, my dear. I believe you. Why would I not? The Devil has so many extraordinary ways of manifesting his presence. Less so, these days, because we live in much more sceptical times. But this house was built in a time when the Devil was known to roam freely over the moors, and in *this* house, as in every house, the stones of its construction are imbued with the beliefs of those who built it.'

He paused, and frowned, and turned around to look at the bricked-up door of the cellar. Then he said, 'This window... may I see it?'

'Well, yes,' said Rob. 'Francis – will that be okay?'

'Of course. I was going to take Father Salter up to see the witching room in any case.'

'I think we'll stay down here, if that's all right with you,' said Grace. 'I'll light the fire in the drawing room and put the kettle on for some tea.'

'That sounds most welcome,' said Father Salter.

Rob led the way upstairs. When they reached the landing, Francis said, 'Father Salter went to the Vatican last year and took its course in exorcism.'

'It's comparatively new, this course,' said Father Salter. 'But there has been an increasing demand for it, not only from Catholic priests but from priests of other denominations, and the Pontifical University has opened its doors to them, too.'

'This "spiritual decontamination" that you were talking about, Francis…'

'That was a fifteenth-century ritual that is very rarely used these days,' Father Salter told him. '*Mala omnia expurget*, they call it in Rome. Today's exorcisms are much more relevant to modern life, and much more specific. Most are designed to rid people of the evil influences that can enter their soul when they are feeling exhausted by their jobs, or stressed by an unhappy personal relationship, or have doubts about their gender.

'The very last exorcism I carried out was to dismiss a demon that had possessed a transgender woman in her moment of greatest indecision, and was tempting her into having homicidal thoughts about her family and her friends.'

Rob pointed along the corridor to the stained-glass window. 'There it is. It's completely intact now, but I swear to you that figure of Old Dewer turned right around and glared at us, and then the glass shattered and the dogs jumped out.'

Father Salter strained his eyes to focus on it.

'Rather blurry,' he said. He tugged a handkerchief out of his breast pocket, took off his spectacles and wiped them. Then he peered at it again.

'Come and take a closer look,' said Rob, and started to walk along the corridor. 'The way into the witching room's down here, too.'

Father Salter followed him, with Francis close behind, but then Father Salter abruptly stopped, so that Francis almost bumped into him.

'What's the matter, father?' Francis asked him.

'I can't – I can't go any further.'

'Are you feeling okay?'

'No, no I'm not. I can't go any further. I'm sorry.'

'Father, you're shaking,' said Francis, and took hold of his arm. 'Rob – Father Salter's having a bit of a turn – help me get him back downstairs.'

Rob came up and held on to Father Salter's other arm. The priest was shaking even more now, so that he could barely stand up. All the rosiness had drained out of his cheeks and his teeth were chattering like a typewriter. As Rob and Francis slowly helped him to drag his feet back to the top of the stairs, his spectacles dropped off and his knees suddenly sagged. It took all of their strength to keep him upright.

'I can't,' he blurted out, turning to Rob as if he were appealing to an executioner to spare his life. 'Please, get me out of here. *Please!*'

'It's all right, we will. Try and hold up. Francis – I think we need to call for an ambulance. It's like he's having a fit or a cardiac arrest or something.'

'*Get me out of here!*' Father Salter screamed at him. '*Get me out of here before the Devil does for me!*'

Clutching at the banister rails to support themselves, Rob and Francis manhandled Father Salter down the stairs, his shoes clumping and bumping against every step.

'*Vicks!*' Rob shouted. 'Call nine-nine-nine for an ambulance, can you! Father Salter's having some kind of attack!'

'No!' said Father Salter. 'I don't need – I don't need an ambulance – please! I need to get out of here, that's all!'

They reached the hallway, and Father Salter managed to stand up on his own, holding on to the newel post. He was still shaking, but not so dramatically.

'I'm sorry,' he said. 'It's this house. Please, I don't need an ambulance. I'll be all right once I leave. It's quietening down, it's quietening down, now it knows that I'm going.'

Vicky and Grace and Portia had all come out to see what was going on. Vicky draped Father Salter's raincoat around his shoulders, while Rob quickly ran back upstairs to pick up his spectacles. When he reached the landing, he looked along the corridor but could see nothing that might have frightened Father Salter. The black hooded figure of Old Dewer was still standing in the middle of the stained-glass window with his back turned and his hounds around him. The window was intact, and neither Old Dewer nor his hounds showed any signs of movement.

He went back down, handed Father Salter his spectacles and guided him to the front door. It was utterly black outside because there were no street lights around Sampford Spiney. The wind had risen and was whistling softly through the leafless trees.

'Don't you worry, father,' said Francis. 'I'll run you straight home to Tavistock. Rob, I'll come back here after I've dropped Father Salter off, if that's okay. I'll leave my bag here. I shouldn't be longer than half an hour.'

'I'm so desperately sorry,' said Father Salter. 'I feel so weak, and so powerless. I wanted to help you, but this force that possesses your house – it recognised me at once for what I was.'

'It's not your fault, father,' Rob told him. 'I'm just

glad that you haven't suffered a heart attack or something like that.'

'The house – it knew what I was. It *knew* that I was a priest. When I saw that image of Old Dewer in that stained-glass window, I appealed to God at once to give me strength, but the house shut me off. It *blocked* me, in the same way that you might jam a radio signal. Usually I can feel my prayers reaching the Almighty, but not this time. For the first time ever, I could see and hear nothing in my mind but a blur of white noise.'

'Come on, father,' said Francis, laying a hand on his shoulder. 'The sooner and the further we get you away from here, the better.'

'I will pray for you all tonight,' Father Salter told them. 'And I will say a prayer for you now, too, before I go, for your safekeeping. Some parting words of defiance, in the face of immeasurable wickedness.'

He turned around in the open doorway so that he was facing the hall, and made the sign of the cross, with his little finger and his fourth finger curled inward. '*Princeps militiae caelestis*,' he recited. '*Satanam aliosque spiritus malignos, qui ad perditionem animarum pervagantur in mundo, divina virtute in infernum detrude. Amen.*'

He turned back to Rob and Francis. 'That's a prayer to the archangel Saint Michael, the head of the Church Militant. Roughly translated, that means Satan and all your demons, go to hell.'

30

It was almost an hour before Francis returned from Tavistock. When he had taken Father Salter into the living room of his parish house, the priest had suffered another momentary fit of the shudders.

'It was almost like his own house could sense where he had been – as if it could *smell* Allhallows Hall on him, the way your pet dog can smell another dog on you, and it was reacting against it. There was a crucifix over his fireplace and it dropped off the wall. He kept insisting that it was nothing supernatural and that it had dropped off before, but I think he was in denial. I reckon that he was embarrassed because he had been so frightened, too.'

'He was sure that there was something seriously bad about this house, though, wasn't he?' said Rob. 'He wouldn't have had that fit of the shakes, otherwise, and want to go shooting off so quickly.'

They were all sitting in the drawing room. Rob had piled half a dozen ash logs onto the fire to make it seem warm and welcoming. They were drinking coffee and Jail Ale, and Grace and Portia were heating up pasties in the kitchen. Francis had stressed the importance of keeping their evening as normal as possible, and not allowing the house to frighten them.

He opened his doctor's bag with a click and took out a blue manila folder. 'The force that's here – and we know now for certain that there *is* one – the force that's here is the kind of force that will do everything within its power to make you feel uneasy, and then to terrify you, and if it can it will drive you hysterical. It feeds off fear and hysteria… that's what gives it its strength.'

'Do you have any idea what it is, this force? Or *where* it is?' asked Vicky. 'Is it in the walls, or the woodwork, or the foundations? And where did it come from?'

Francis looked serious. 'I do have some idea, yes. At least, I'm fairly sure that I do. But I'm not going to say out loud what I think it might be. What's that old slogan they used to use in wartime? "Even walls have ears."'

'So how much have you found out?'

'From the research that we've done between us – John Kipling and me – we can say for certain that the Wilmington family arranged for Nicholas Owen to install a priest's hide here. It was in or around the year 1588. John came across an entry in an old ledger for "repair work" undertaken here by a carpenter called "Little Michael", which was one of the aliases that Nicholas Owen used to avoid detection by the authorities. "Draper" was another one.

'The Jesuit priest who was hidden here by the Wilmingtons was called Father Ambrose. He had been sent over from Rome as a missionary, to restore the Catholic faith here in England. Of course, it was treason in those days not to swear the oath of allegiance to Queen Elizabeth as head of the Church. The Wilmingtons hid him here on and off for nearly six months before he was discovered and taken to London to be tortured and executed.'

'The Wilmingtons denied that they knew him, though, didn't they?' said Grace.

'Yes, they did, and that saved them from being arrested as traitors, although it's possible that in the years to come they hid other priests here, too.'

Rob lifted his hand and said, 'Hold on. Is that somebody out there?'

He was sure he had heard a creaking sound, the sound that they made whenever they started to climb the staircase. He crossed the drawing room and opened the door wider, but when he looked out into the hallway there was nobody there. Nobody that he could see, anyway.

He went to the foot of the staircase and looked up. For a fleeting moment, he thought he saw a curl of smoke or a gauzy fragment of fabric floating across the diamond-patterned window, but then it had vanished. All the same, he stayed there for a few seconds, watching and listening. He had the distinct feeling that somebody had been eavesdropping on them, but had now crept off upstairs.

When he returned to the drawing room, Francis said, 'Anything?'

'I don't know. Something and nothing. Like you said, we mustn't let this house get to us.'

'Do you want me to take a look?'

'No, you're all right. Like I said, it was something and nothing. Just a squeak.'

'It was John who found the clincher,' Francis went on.

'He has a friend who volunteers at the Tavistock Museum, so they allow him access to some of the archives that the public generally don't get to see. He found an antique order book that had been kept by a local apothecary back in the late seventeenth century, and it included an entry that refers to Allhallows Hall. Here – he scanned it for me.'

Francis opened the manila folder and took out two sheets of paper. One had the image of an old handwritten page on it. The writing on this page was slanting and crowded, and almost illegible, but John had deciphered it and sent Francis a typewritten version.

'"*June 16th, 1687, To the order of Jeremy Wilmington Esq. at Allhalloes Hall, Sampford Spiney, the following in the quantities of three and one half pounds each: Quicksilver, Salt of Hartshorn, Plumbago, Stibnite, Spiritus Fumans, Philosopher's Wool and Fulminating Gold.*"

'Those are old names for chemicals like mercury and antimony and zinc oxide. But this list wouldn't mean much if you didn't know that they're the main ingredients for mixing with plaster and creating a witching room.'

'These chemicals,' asked Rob. 'Would they be all that you need?'

'As far as I can make out, they're just the basics. I could find hardly any information at all about witching rooms, even on Google, but from the little that I *have* been able to discover, these chemicals were used to make the room receptive to whatever force you decide to summon up. Once that force has permeated the walls, though, and if it's triggered with the right incantation, you can hold anybody who enters the witching room in suspended animation. Or "time-durance", as one of the seventeenth-century wizards calls it.'

'When you say "force"—' asked Vicky, 'what exactly are you talking about?'

'I can't be sure yet, not specifically, and like I said, I think it would be safer for all of us if I didn't say its name just yet. It might not be the right name, but I wouldn't want to take the risk, especially since it seems to be growing increasingly active – like setting those hounds on you.'

'I know it sounds loony, but are you talking about a demon of some sort?'

'You know I don't believe in Satan and all the traditional demons. But I do believe in invisible forces that can affect our lives – forces that we don't yet have the science to be able to identify. Think about it – it wasn't until 1931 that we were able to see viruses for the first time, even though we'd suspected their existence for at least forty years.'

'So how are we going to get rid of this force?'

'Well, I was hoping that Father Salter was going to help me by trying to exorcise it. I didn't think that exorcism would really do the job, but it might have helped us to narrow down exactly what we're dealing with. If we said its name out loud, for instance, and it lashed out against us, then we'd know that we had struck a nerve, and we'd have a much clearer idea what to do when it came to spiritual decontamination.'

'But now we don't have Father Salter. What are you going to do – see if you can find another exorcist?'

'That won't be easy... especially if it gets around that Father Salter got cold feet about doing it. The Catholic

Church still believe that exorcism works, which is why they've opened up their exorcism classes. But they don't want to be seen to be defeated by some evil spirit, especially if it gets out on social media. You can imagine some of the trolls they'd get.'

'Francis, I don't give a toss about the Pope's public image. I want our son back, and Katharine here wants her husband back, and I'm sure you're just as desperate to rescue Ada. Right now, that's all that matters.'

'I know, Rob, I know. Which is why I'm prepared to give it a go myself.'

'You know how to carry out an exorcism?'

'I know how to carry out a spiritual decontamination. I have the full text, which was first written down by a Jesuit priest called Raphael Hix. He was a real oddball and apart from being a priest he was a gleaner, like me – or a wizard, if you want to call me that. In the early eighteenth century he was paid by Baron Robert Petre to decontaminate Old Thorndon Hall, the Petre family seat in Essex.'

'The Petres? Who were they?'

'They were hereditary peers, the Petres of Writtle, in Essex. They'd always been staunch Roman Catholics. Twelve of the family were Jesuits and two of them were bishops. It was Bishop Francis Petre who decided to call in Raphael Hix, because he had tried to exorcise Old Thorndon Hall himself, but he had failed, and he didn't want the Pope to find out that he had failed. As it was, the Pope did eventually find out, and because of that he refused to make him a cardinal.'

'So what was it in this Old Thorndon Hall that needed to be exorcised?' asked Rob.

'It was a spirit that had plagued the Essex salt marshes for decades, known as the Lamper. It was rather like the Jack O'Lantern that was supposed to haunt the Suffolk marshes. If you were out walking or gathering oysters on the marshes, a dense sea fog could roll in quite unexpectedly and it was easy to find yourself lost. But after you'd been wandering about a bit you'd see this lamp waving in the distance, or what looked like a lamp, and you'd walk towards it, thinking that somebody was guiding you. The next morning your dead body would be found in a creek, naked and lacerated all over as if you had been whipped with barbed wire, with your eyes missing.'

'Urghhh!' said Portia, with a shudder. 'Remind me not to go looking for oysters on the Essex marshes, won't you?'

'Oh, the Lamper doesn't haunt the marshes any more, because Raphael took care of him – or her, or it, or whatever sex it was. Mind you, more than half the marshes have gone, too, because the sea's washed them away.'

'How did the Lamper get into Old Thorndon Hall?' asked Vicky. 'I mean, what was he doing there?'

'Pretty much the same as the force that's here in this house. Robert Petre and members of his family had been attacked time and time again by Protestants – physically as well as verbally. His wife had horse dung flung over her when she was stepping down from her carriage in Westminster, and gangs used to creep into the estate at night and smash all the downstairs windows.

'Robert Petre had no doubt at all who was behind these

attacks – the suffragan bishop of Bradwell, the Anglican diocese that borders the Catholic diocese of Brentwood. His name was Leonard Montague and according to several historical records he had an almost incandescent hatred of Catholics. Nobody quite knows why, but he made no secret of it. He called them the "Lice of Rome".'

'Charming,' said Vicky.

'Well, that's exactly what Robert Petre did. He brought in a charmer like Ada, a witch whose name unfortunately we shall never know, and she created a witching room for him. She did that by luring the Lamper to the Thorndon estate with the promise of a safe dark hiding place in the wine cellar. From there he could come out at night, or whenever it was foggy, and roam around the local area, snatching any passers-by whose eyes he took a fancy to. He would also be free to drink as much of Baron Petre's wine as he wanted.'

'Now that my hangover's gone, I think even I would be tempted by that,' said Katharine. 'The wine, not the eyes.'

Francis opened his folder again and showed them a seventeenth-century plan of Old Thorndon Hall. 'The witching room was installed on the first floor here, right at the back, overlooking the three-hundred-acre park. Once it was ready, Robert Petre invited Bishop Montague to visit him, so that they could discuss some kind of a truce between them. He also hinted that he might donate a considerable amount of money to the Bradwell diocese, as a gesture of reconciliation.'

'But he trapped him?' asked Rob.

'Exactly. He showed Bishop Montague around the

house, ending up in the witching room, where the charmer was waiting for him. She recited the incantation that catalysed the Lamper's force in the walls, and *bam!* there your bishop was, stuck for all eternity in that moment that he'd walked in there. Even if there was a God, not even He could have rescued him.'

'But if Robert Petre's problem with Bishop Montague had been sorted out, why did he want to have the place decontaminated?'

'That wasn't until three or four years later. The Lamper was growing restless. Local people avoided the estate like the plague because too many of them had been found dead with their eyes missing, so there were fewer victims for the Lamper to go after, and it had drunk most of Robert Petre's wine. Its force started to appear around the house, with flickering lights and strange noises, and Bishop Montague could be heard all night whispering prayers. Several of the servants left because they were too frightened to stay there, and Baroness Petre went up to their house in Scotland and refused to return to Old Thorndon Hall until the Lamper was exorcised.'

'So that was why they called in this Raphael Hix?'

'That's right. Because Raphael Hix was the only priest they knew who had actually practised this spiritual decontamination. It was known about by the Catholic Church and it was known to be highly effective when it came to curing people who were thought to be possessed by demons and cleansing houses that had been taken over by dark forces. But it was officially disapproved of, because it was a combination of Christian exorcism and

Druidic chants, with some rituals thrown in that you could only describe as witchcraft. Sticking scores of cloves into slugs, for instance, until they resembled hedgehogs, and having them crawl up the walls. In Druidic culture, cloves are supposed to be spiritually cleansing.'

'You're not going to do that, are you?'

'I'm going to have to, and a few other gruesome things besides.'

'You haven't brought the slugs in your bag, have you?' Grace asked him, leaning over to look inside it and wrinkling up her nose.

'No, no. I won't be carrying out the decontamination until tomorrow. It'll be a good time to do it, because Raphael Hix recommends carrying out the ritual during the three days when the moon's energy is at its strongest. "Full moon magick" he calls it, with a "k".

'If it's all right with you, though, I'd like to look around the house one more time and carry out one or two preparatory tests – things I was hoping to do with Father Salter.'

He stood and picked up the walking stick he had brought with him. They could see now that the silver knob on the top was in the shape of an old woman's head, with her eyes closed.

'This is a wand, rather than a walking stick,' he told them. 'The woman is Cailleach Bheur, the Druidic goddess of air and darkness. Her name means "the veiled one with the shrill voice". She detested sunlight and warm weather. In the summer she would turn into a grey rock, and lie there waiting for the darkness and the cold days to come.

She used a wand like this to strike against walls to find out if anybody was hiding inside them, and if there was, she would strike the wall again and turn them into ice.'

He smacked the wand in the palm of his hand. 'I don't think I'm capable of doing that, but it might help me to locate where the force in this house is hiding.'

'I'll come with you, if you like,' said Rob. 'You never know what might jump out at you.'

31

They went upstairs first, and along the corridor to the stained-glass window of Old Dewer. Francis tapped the glass gently with the silver head on the top of his wand and then held the wand up straight.

'Yes,' he said. 'There's some energy there. Here – hold it. You can feel the force for yourself.'

Rob took hold of the wand just below Francis's hand. It was faintly humming, like a tuning fork. The vibration lasted only a few seconds before it died away, but he had distinctly felt it.

'Maybe we should smash this window,' said Rob. 'That would get rid of some of its power, wouldn't it?'

'No, no – we don't want to do that. This window has been put here for a reason, and I don't think it's the reason that you've always believed.'

'We were told that it was to keep Old Dewer from coming into the house and stealing our souls. If he saw that we respected him, he'd stay away.'

'Nice story, but not very likely. I'd say it was put here so that he could continue to keep an eye on the outside world, even though his real force is hidden somewhere else. At the moment he's looking outward, isn't he, so that he can see the garden and the moor beyond it. But you said that you saw him turn around, so he's obviously capable of keeping watch on what goes on in the house, too.

'His force possesses this house, Rob. It completely possesses it. It's *his* energy that gives the witching room its capability of trapping people in time, and it's *his* energy that allows them to walk around at night, whispering. The same as the Lamper in Old Thorndon Hall.'

'You said that we shouldn't say his name out loud, but we have, and nothing's happened.'

'I know. And do you know what that tells me? This isn't Old Dewer at all. It might be the same presence that Dartmoor folks came to call Old Dewer, but they were wrong. This isn't the Devil we're dealing with here. This is something totally different.'

'So you really think you know what it is?'

'As I said, I have a good idea. But I won't want to speak its name until I've found it. I've dabbled in some strange and dangerous things since I've been a gleaner, but I'm not suicidal.'

They went into the end bedroom, and Francis knocked three times on the dado with his wand. When he had done that, he handed the wand to Rob, and Rob could feel a prickle running down it, as if it had become charged with electricity.

'The force in these walls is really strong, as I would have expected, but let's see what it's like in the other bedrooms.'

They went into one bedroom after another, with Francis tapping at the walls. He tapped at the walls as he walked along the corridors, too, and ended up in the bathroom.

'It's much weaker in all of these other rooms. Feel it now, Rob... there's hardly any buzz at all. Let's try downstairs.'

As he followed Francis down the stairs, Rob noticed that several strands of his long white hair had fallen out and had been caught on the shoulders of his purple herringbone jacket. At first he was reluctant to say anything, but when they reached the hallway where the light was brighter he could see that even more were falling out.

'Francis... you're losing your hair.'

Francis looked down at his jacket. 'Bloody hell. So I am.' He brushed the strands off his shoulders and then he propped his wand against the panelling and ran both hands through the wings of hair on either side of his head. When he took his hands away, he was holding clumps of white hair in both of them, and there were bald patches around his ears.

'*A-barth an Jowl!*' he exclaimed in his thin, rasping voice. In desperation, he started to pull at his hair and more and more of it came out, until the left side of his head was almost completely bald.

'It's *him* that's doing this! Him – or it! He knows that I'm a gleaner and that I'm looking for him and he's trying to stop me!'

'Then maybe you *should* stop,' said Rob. 'He might do something worse to you than make your hair fall out.'

'No! I'm going to find him! I'm going to find him and I'm going to decontaminate him! He might be able to scare off a Catholic priest but he's not going to frighten me away! I'm a Cornishman and Cornishmen are frightened of nothing, especially devils!'

He picked up his wand again and walked stiff-legged around the hallway, knocking loudly at the panelling. 'Where are you, you *bylen*? Where are you hiding yourself? Show me where you are, you coward, and I'll show you what I'm made of!'

Vicky and Grace and Portia came out into the hallway to see what the shouting and the banging was all about. Rob waved his hand to indicate that they should just let Francis continue to circle around, knocking at the walls, and not interrupt him. Vicky pointed to her own head to show him that she could see how much of Francis's hair had fallen out, and mouthed the words *What's happened to him?* But all Rob could do was shrug.

Francis stopped knocking the panelling at last, and stood in the centre of the hallway, breathing hard. He tugged in anger and frustration at the remaining hair on the right side of his head, and most of that came out too. There were tufts of white hair all over the hallway floor, as if two furious albino cats had been fighting each other.

Rob went up to him. He didn't know what to say.

'He's here all right,' Francis panted. 'He's here, he's close, and he's fully awake now. Hell on earth, my heart's beating like a hammer and I'll bet it's him that's causing it.'

'What are you going to do?'

'I'm going to do what I set out to do. I'm even more certain of what's needed, now that I'm pretty damn sure what he is.'

He coughed again, and wheezed like a pair of old bellows, and then he took hold of Rob's arm, made his way unsteadily across the hallway and sat down on the chair.

'Are you sure you're up to it?' Rob asked him.

Francis nodded, and kept on nodding. 'I have to be up to it, because nobody else is going to do it, are they? Nobody else is capable. Who's going to rescue Ada and your brother and your little boy if I don't?'

He coughed again. 'I'll have to collect quite a few things. I'll need water from the Druid's Bowl, which is like the Druidic equivalent of holy water, but I've a bottle of that already, so that will save me a trip up to Cosdon. Candles, plenty of candles, and a turfing iron, as well as sheep shears. I'll have to have wolfsbane. And cloves. And slugs, of course. My friend Dorothy will have plenty of those in her garden.'

He stayed seated for a while, his chest rising and falling. Vicky came up to them and said, 'Are you all right, Francis? You've lost nearly all of your hair.'

'I'm sorry. I've made a mess of your floor.'

'I'm not worried about that. I'm worried about *you*. You look terrible.'

'I'll be all right. I've had to deal with hostile forces before. None quite as hostile as this one, I'll admit. But I'll survive. Once I've cleared it out of here, I'm sure my hair will grow back. If not, I'll just have to buy myself a toupee, won't I?'

Rob said, 'Don't make light of this, Francis. Are you really sure you're going to be able to manage it?'

Francis stared up at them, unblinking, with his colourless eyes. His expression was even more biblical than when Rob had first seen him.

'I have to, Rob. It's my destiny. Sometimes you're confronted with things in your life and you realise that you *have* to deal with them. You don't have a choice, because that's what you were born for. I could leave here now and drive home and try to forget that I ever discovered the force that's holding this house in its grip. But how could I ever forget it? If I don't decontaminate Allhallows Hall tomorrow, I'd be guilty of criminal negligence – manslaughter, even – because I could have saved Ada and your brother and your little lad, but I would have been too much of a *meregyon* to try. *Meregyon*, that's Cornish for sniveller.'

He stood up, leaning on his wand for support, and cautiously patted the side of his head to see if any more hair was going to fall out.

'I may look weak but I have plenty of strength in me,' he assured them. 'I knew what I was getting into when I became a gleaner. There's nothing Harry Potterish about wizardry, believe me. The dark forces you're up against, and the things you have to do to send them back where they belong, like strangling a badger or turning a live hare inside out.'

'All right,' said Rob. 'We'll see you tomorrow then. But if you need any help in the meantime, or if you change your mind about doing this, you've got my number.'

'I won't change my mind, Rob. I can't. When I'm able to tell you what we're up against – *who* we're up against – you'll understand why.'

'You can't even give us a clue?'

Francis shook his head. 'If I gave you a clue, and you worked out what his name was, and spoke it out loud – even if you *thought* it – that *would* amount to my committing manslaughter. Worse than manslaughter – murder.'

Rob helped him into his raincoat and together he and Vicky showed him to the front door. They watched him walk slowly across the courtyard to the driveway, where he had parked his car. Halfway across the courtyard, next to the headless cherub, he turned around and looked back at Allhallows Hall like a general surveying a fortress that he would have to assault at dawn.

Behind the trees, a full moon was rising, bleak and pale.

'We should try and have an early night tonight,' said Rob. 'From what Francis was saying, this spiritual decontamination is going to be like all hell let loose.'

'You really think that any of us are going to be able to sleep?'

Rob closed the front door and the draught made the tufts of Francis's white hair blow across the floor like dandelion puffs.

They didn't go to bed early, but stayed up until midnight, talking. They agreed that with all of his knocking on the walls, Francis seemed to have provoked even more tension in the house, even tauter than the silent, suspenseful atmosphere that Father Salter had sensed in it.

'I know it sounds insane, but I can't help thinking that the house has started *listening* to us,' said Grace. 'I don't just mean this force that Francis kept on talking about, whatever it is – this force that we're not allowed to mention – but the whole house. The floors, the curtains, the walls, even the pictures on the walls, all of them listening to every word we say. Especially the pictures on the walls.

'That portrait at the top of the stairs – I don't know which Wilmington it is, but his eyes don't just follow you across the landing, they feel as if they're following you all the way down the corridor and then spying on you through your bedroom keyhole while you're getting undressed.'

'I agree with you, the house does feel alive,' said Vicky. 'But in a way that makes me feel a little more hopeful about Timmy. If it does have life in it, then wherever it's keeping him hidden, perhaps he's still alive – and Martin, too, and Ada.'

The clock in the hallway struck twelve, very slowly, because it needed winding, and they agreed that it was time to call it a night. Katharine went upstairs first, and when Grace and Portia had finished their drinks they followed her. Rob damped the fire down while Vicky cleared up their glasses and mugs.

'His eyes are still following me!' called Grace, from the landing.

'Turn his face to the wall!' Rob called back. 'Or hang a towel over him!'

Vicky returned from the kitchen, and Rob wrapped his arms around her and kissed her. She felt cold, and so he held her close until she had warmed up a little. Even her flowery perfume smelled cold.

'I can't wait for tomorrow, Rob,' she told him. 'I can't wait for it, but I can't tell you how much I'm dreading it.'

32

'It's a full moon tonight, love,' said Jaws, easing himself down on the floor close to Ada and whispering in her ear. 'Not too many clouds, neither, so it's nice and bright and shiny.'

Ada shifted herself away from him. 'What does that mean?'

'It's the *fulness*, that's what it means. The fulness. That's what we call them three nights when the moon's supposed to turn people into lunatics and werewolves. I don't know about that, but that's when all of its energy comes beaming down to us – you and me and all the other poor sods that are trapped with us here.'

'So what does that do?'

Jaws reached out and playfully flicked the tip of Ada's nose with his fingertip. She flinched, and shifted even further away from him.

'I'll tell you what the full moon can do, darling. It can give us a fucking break. While it's up there high in the sky, it can set us free from the moment when we was trapped in here, like being let out of our cells for a bit of exercise. It's only for one night a month, but for that one night it can fetch us forward from *then* into *now*. It can make us feel real again. Do you know what I mean? Hearts beating, lungs going in and out, like we're living the way we used to.'

'Only while it's up there? Then what?'

'Then it's all over. Then we go back to being stuck in the second we was chanted, just like we are now. Don't ask me why, or how, because I don't have the first fucking idea. But all you have to do is go out and stand in front of that window with the devil and the dogs in it, with the moonlight shining through it. "Unlocking", that's what we call it. Well, you can understand why.'

'Is that all you have to do? Stand in front of that window?'

'That's right. You stand there and you let the moonlight shine into your eyes, and you cast your mind back to what you was like the second before you got trapped. Before you can say holy forking shirtholes you'll be as solid as you was at that very moment. I'm not kidding you. Even your watch will start working again.'

Ada narrowed her eyes and looked at him suspiciously.

'You don't believe me, do you?' said Jaws.

'I don't know *what* to believe any more.'

'Why would I tell you a porky about something like that? What would be the point? Go out there and stand in front of that window, and see what happens. If fuck all happens, then what have you lost?'

'But how can I? I can't get out of here, can I?'

'Your *energy* can, love, the same like we did before, when we went out for a quick breather from them two girls. All you have to do is close your eyes like you do when you're having a weary, leave your body behind and walk through that wall. Once you go up to that window and stand in the moonlight and get yourself unlocked, your body won't be here in this room any more. That's because you won't be stuck in the day before yesterday any more, you'll be right where you are *now.*'

He inched himself closer, and caressed her hair with his knuckles, and again she shifted herself away. The smell of Old Spice was making her feel nauseous.

'You'll be able to walk around the house the same as your friends. Go downstairs and help yourself to a glass of plonk, watch some telly, do whatever you want. Me – I'm going to do it. I always do, every full moon. I'll be doing it tonight, if you do.'

'But my friends are going to hear us, aren't they, and come out to see what's going on?'

'They won't, love. Usually, there's nobody here in the house when there's a fulness. But before I go and stand in front of the window, I'm going to go sneaking around to your mates' bedrooms, lock their doors, and take out the keys.'

'Supposing they break the doors down?'

'Come on, you've seen those doors. Solid oak. You'd need a fucking tank to break those down. We could even put on some music and have a dance. As soon as the moon goes down I'll put the keys back, but if they come to look for us, we'll be gone, back in here, and they'll be none the wiser.'

Ada was silent for a long time. She could see from the

small stained-glass windows in the witching room that the moon was shining brightly outside. It made Jaws look as if he were wearing a multicoloured Pierrot costume. Even his face was triangulated in red and green and yellow.

At last, she said, 'All right. But if the moonlight can set me free, what's to stop me walking out of the house and never coming back?'

'Sorry, darling. You can't. I don't know what's holding us all here, but you simply fucking can't. I tell you something, it's more secure than Dartmoor. I've tried it more than once, and some of other blokes have tried it. Oh yes, you can open the door, but you can't walk through it. I've stood right there with the door wide open and I've seen outside. I've heard the birds twittering and I've felt the rain on me mush. But it was like I was paralysed. Couldn't move a muscle. Three times I've tried it, at least, and it's always the same.'

'Perhaps it'll be different for me.'

Jaws pulled a face. 'Might be, might not. You won't know unless you give it a whirl, will you?'

'If it gives me any chance of getting out of this room, then I'll do it. But what about all the other men here? How many did you say? Seventeen of them? Don't all of them want to be free for a while, even if they can't escape from the house? Even if it's only till the moon goes down?'

'A few of them do. Maybe five or six. The rest of them – nah. All it does is piss them off even more than they are already, so they don't want to do it any more. You think of Father Thomas. Nearly four hundred years he's been here in this room. And Bartram, he's been here more than two hundred and eighty. They don't want to be reminded of what they used to be like, when they was able to do something different every day apart from sitting here feeling sorry for themselves – when they was able to grow up, and grow older, and then snuff it, the same as the pilgrims, as Father Thomas calls them. We can't even commit suicide. Bartram tried it once, during a fulness. He took a carving knife out of the kitchen, fetched it up here and cut his throat. He's still got the cut and that's why he whistles when he talks. He's had to accept the fact that we're all going to be here forever, until the end of the world, and even beyond.'

'Still – I'll try it,' said Ada. 'When do you want to do it? Now?'

'There's five other blokes unlocking along with us. I'll go and tell them to make themselves ready, and then I'll be back. All you have to do is close your eyes, relax, and get yourself into a weary.'

He stood up and padded silently on the horsehair carpeting back down to the other end of the witching room, where seven or eight men were gathered, whispering to each other. She saw him talking to them, and occasionally looking over at her.

It could be that he was right. Maybe she would never be able to return to the life that she had been leading before she had been chanted. As a charmer, though, she knew at least half a dozen incantations for breaking spells and reversing conjurations. She had been reciting them over and over under her breath since she had been trapped here in this room, without any success. But perhaps they had failed to work because she was trapped in the moment when she had been dragged through the wall. If she were unlocked and living normally again, if only for the few hours while the moon was up in the sky, she might be able to undo the chant that had trapped her here and escape.

She looked across at Jaws and the other men. Five of them were sitting down now, with their eyes closed, so that they would fall into a weary. Only Jaws still had his eyes open, and when he saw that she was looking in his direction, he winked. Then he closed his eyes, too.

She did the same, but first she whispered a small prayer to the Druidic goddess Druantia, asking for her protection. Druantia was not only the guardian of women, but the goddess of sexual passion, and the creator of phases of the moon. If any spiritual being could take care of her now, she couldn't think of a better one.

33

Ada's energy rose out of her body in the same way that she had risen before. She still found that it made her feel unbalanced, and swimmy, and she wondered if this was what it was like to be a spirit, after you had died. The most disturbing thing was to look down and see herself still sitting propped up against the wall, her eyes closed and her lips slightly parted, breathing her last breath over and over again. *That's me. That's what I look like to other people.*

Down at the far end of the room, Jaws and the other men were rising out of their bodies too. Once they had all taken shape, Jaws approached her and the other men followed him. She had never seen such a hard-looking collection of men in her life. They were stretching and jiggling and sniffing like footballers preparing to run out onto the pitch for a match. Jaws was giving her his usual enigmatic grin but not one of the others was smiling.

'Ready, love?' Jaws asked her.

'I suppose so. What are all these fellows going to be doing?'

'Them? Oh, I think they've got something in mind, haven't you, lads? Ricky here, he's been stuck in this room two years longer than what I have. I'm sure he knows what he needs to cheer him up.'

A young man with a blond crew cut and a white T-shirt bulging with steroid-swollen muscles gave Ada a sideways twitch of his head, as if to say 'awright?', but he still didn't smile.

'Go on, you go first,' said Jaws, and guided Ada towards the wall that would take her through to the end bedroom.

She turned around to look at the men following them, and she began to feel that something was badly wrong.

'I'm not sure,' she said. 'Maybe I won't do it.'

'If you don't do it now, love, you won't get another chance until the next full moon.'

'Yes, I realise that. But I don't know. If we can't leave the house, and we're still going to be trapped when the moon goes down, what's the point of it?'

'What's the point of it? Don't you want to feel your heart beating again? Don't you want to breathe some fresh air, in and out? I know it's only for a few hours, but don't you want to feel like you're a real human being again, instead of a fucking spook?'

'Go on, darling,' said the young man in the white T-shirt. 'We ain't got all fucking night.'

Ada hesitated. But then she thought: whatever my misgivings, this could be the only way to escape from Allhallows Hall. I think I know an incantation that could free me – the same incantation that was used by Alice Kyteler, the first woman to be sentenced to die for witchcraft in Ireland. The night before she was due to be burned at the stake, she had disappeared and was never seen again.

'*Glaoim ar na taibhsí gach doras a oscailt*,' Alice Kyteler's incantation had begun. 'I call on the ghosts of every door to open.' It had been found, written down, in her abandoned cottage, and after she had read a feature about it on the *Irish Examiner* website, Ada had memorised it.

Jaws placed his hand against the small of Ada's back and gently pushed her towards the wall. She didn't resist him. As she penetrated the plaster, she felt the same frosty tingling that she had before, the same sensation of having all her millions of atoms disassembled and mingled with the atoms in the wall before she was reassembled in the bedroom on the other side. All the lights in the house had been switched off, but the door was half open, and she could see the moonlight falling on the floor of the corridor.

Jaws appeared behind her out of the wall, and then the other men, one at a time, until the room was crowded.

'Right,' said Jaws. 'I'll nip along and lock all them bedroom doors so your mates can't come out and give us bother. *You*, my love – you go first and stand in front of the window. Do like I said and stare right into the moonlight. Try not to blink too much, and think hard about what you was like before you was chanted. Once you're done, all these other geezers will do it, too, me included, and then we'll all be unlocked.'

He went off along the corridor and Ada found herself standing in front of the stained-glass window with the other five men gathered in a semicircle around her.

'Get your skates on, darling,' said a middle-aged man who bore a striking resemblance to Charles Bronson

– weathered, baggy-eyed, with a tangled fringe and sideburns. 'The quicker you get yourself sorted, the longer we got.'

The men were standing so close behind her that Ada could smell them. Stale cigarettes and body odour, and another smell, too, strangely metallic, like chicken that was past its sell-by date. She took a step closer to the window and there right in front of her was the hooded black figure with his black slavering hounds all around him.

Ada could see the full moon shining through a squarish panel in the window that was stained dark blue to represent the night sky. She looked quickly behind her to make sure that the men hadn't shuffled any closer, and then she concentrated all of her attention on it. Occasionally a cloud passed across it, and its light dimmed and brightened again, but even when it was obscured she could feel the penetrating chill of its negative energy, gradually numbing the spell that was keeping her trapped in time. It was like standing close to the open door of a freezer, giving her goosebumps and making her shiver.

She tried to think back to what she had felt like before she had been chanted. What it had been like to laugh, and eat, and breathe, and walk freely over the moors wherever she wanted. She thought about going out into the garden at the back of her cottage, on a morning when all her herbs and vegetables were still wet and sparkling from the previous night's rain, and picking bitter nightshade for a potion that would help to heal a broken heart.

Staring at the moon gave her the revelation that none of us want time to pass, and to grow older, and that time will eventually take away from us everything that we hold dear. Yet without time we would never have the chance to find love, or happiness, or excitement. Whatever fulfilment we find in life, time brings it to us, even if the day will inevitably come when it drains it all away again, like an ebbing tide sliding away across the sand.

Ada understood then that living for ever, suspended for all eternity in the same second, was a far worse punishment than death.

At that instant, she felt as if warm syrup had been poured all over her, from her head right down to her feet. With a distinctive thump, she felt her heart start to beat, and when she took in a breath she could smell not only the sweaty men around her, but the musty oak smell of Allhallows Hall. The moon had brought her forward out of the day before yesterday into the present time.

She turned around, holding up both her hands so the men could see that she was unlocked. Just then, Jaws came briskly along the corridor, smiling and rubbing his hands together.

'Right, that's them all banged up! Stand back, lads, and let the lovely young lady come through. Ray – your turn next. Then you, Phil.'

One by one, the men stood in front of the stained-glass window and let the moonlight shine on them. One by one, they stepped away from it, unlocked, and Ada was struck by the difference in their appearance. Even after she had been chanted, and she had been able to see the whisperers who had been roaming invisibly around the house in the form of energy, they had still appeared to be translucent.

Now they were solid, and real, and she could tell that they even had weight, because the floorboards creaked as they walked along the corridor and gathered on the landing.

Jaws was the last to stand shining in the moonlight. When he came walking towards them along the corridor Ada noticed that he had a slight limp, and that his left foot turned inwards.

'Okay, lads,' he whispered. 'We've got about four hours max before the moon goes down. Let's hope there's still plenty of booze left downstairs. Before that, though, we've got to celebrate the good Lord smiling on us, and sending us this angel.'

He gave Ada a mischievous grin, and for the first time the other men smiled at her, too, and two of them gave her the thumbs up.

'What are you talking about?' she demanded.

'Shh! You don't want to wake them friends of yours up. They'll be knocking on their bedroom doors and putting us off our stroke!'

'Yeah – the only ones doing any knocking should be us!' whispered the man who looked like Charles Bronson, and he gave a lewd chuckle.

Jaws took hold of Ada's arm, but she immediately twisted herself away. 'If you think what I think you're thinking, then you can all go to hell!'

'We've all been in hell for years, love, don't you worry about that. That don't bother us.'

'Just stay away from me. I had a bad feeling about this, and I was right, wasn't I?'

'Depends what you mean by a bad feeling, darling,' said

the young man called Phil. 'I can give you the best feeling you've ever had in your life, I can promise you that. Phil the Firework, that's what my girl used to call me, 'cause I always made her go off with a bang, every time.'

'I want to go back to the priest's hide, right now,' said Ada. 'How do I get back?'

'You're not going to be a spoilsport, are you?' asked Jaws. 'After all, I think you owe us one, don't you, or maybe even two or three? Waltzing in there with your friends and chucking that dust all over us, trying to flush us out. That's what you was up to, wasn't it? Trying to flush us out? Now Old Semtex is gone, they'll be wanting the house to themselves, won't they? Won't give a shit what happens to us.'

'Old Semtex? Who's Old Semtex?'

'Governor Russell. Ex-governor of Dartmoor nick. They called him Old Semtex because he was always liable to blow up without any warning.'

'I'm going back,' said Ada. It occurred to her that since she was real, and here in present time, she could lift up the window seat and open the dado to get back into the priest's hide.

She tried to push her way past Jaws, but two of the men grabbed her arms from behind and held her tight. She ducked and struggled and kicked at their legs, but they were far too strong for her.

'Let go of me, you pigs!'

'You don't mean them two? Stevey and Mandeep? That's an insult to pigs, that is!'

'I'm a witch! How do you think I managed to throw

that dust on you and show you up? You lay one finger on me and I swear that I'll make your life a misery once we're back in that hide!'

'You're a witch? *What?* Do me a favour! Witches are butters, ain't they, with long noses and black cats and ride around on broomsticks! They ain't peng like you, with whopping big bristols. Besides, even if you was a witch, there's no way that you can make our lives any more of a misery than they are already!'

The young man in the white T-shirt opened the door of the bedroom right behind him, and switched on the light, even though the heavy brocade curtains were open and the moonlight was shining in. Inside, there was a large tester bed, with dusty embroidered drapes and a damp-looking green satin quilt with brown stains scattered across it. It looked as if nobody had slept in it in years.

Stevey and Mandeep forced Ada down onto the quilt, face down, and then rolled her over. The other men crowded into the bedroom as Stevey held her pinned to the bed while Mandeep crammed all her necklaces and talismans down into the neck of her black sweater and then started to pull it off.

'*Get off me!*' she screamed at them, but as soon as Mandeep had dragged her sweater over her head, Stevey clamped his hand over her mouth. She kicked and bucked up and down as Mandeep unfastened her jeans and wrenched them off, too, inch by inch. Once he had wrestled them over her ankles, he pulled down her black lace knickers, spun them around his finger, and tossed them across the bedroom. All the men let out a soft, hissing cheer.

'How about that, she's shaved it in a heart shape!' whispered Ray. 'Must be to show us how much she loves us!'

Between them, Stevey and Mandeep lifted Ada into a sitting position, so that Mandeep could unfasten her bra. Stevey's hand slipped from her mouth and she threw her head from side to side and was able to scream out, *'Get off me! Let go of me!'* before he muffled her again.

'I never could get the hang of these things!' whispered Mandeep, still struggling with the catch of her bra. Eventually, though, he managed to open it, take off her bra and throw it across the bedroom after her knickers.

'Now *that's* what I call a great pair of melons,' growled Charles Bronson, under his breath.

'I'm first in the queue,' whispered Jaws. 'The rest of you can fight it out between you.'

Ada could only stare at him as he lifted his grey T-shirt over his head. His snake tattoo wound its way up from underneath his waistband, sliding through the dark hair on his narrow white chest until it licked with its forked tongue at his neck. When he reached down to loosen the cord of his baggy grey sweatpants, she could see that he was already aroused.

He dropped his pants to the floor and climbed up naked onto the end of the bed, his purple-headed penis so stiff that it was parallel to his stomach, and almost touching his navel. Ada closed her eyes tight so that she wouldn't have to look at him, and she bounced even more furiously on top of the quilt.

Jaws whispered, 'Come on, lads, give us a bit of a hand

here, will you, and hold down this fucking bucking bronco for me!'

While Stevey and Mandeep kept Ada's arms spread wide as if she were being crucified, two more men took hold of her ankles and parted her legs. Ada opened her eyes again and saw Jaws leaning over her, holding his penis in one hand as he guided it between the lips of her vulva. He looked down and saw that her eyes were open and that she was staring up at him, and he gave her that warm, mocking smile.

'You're going to love this, darling,' he told her. 'It's getting on for forty years since I last had a shag, so believe me, this is going to blow your brains out. Phil the Firework? This is Ron the fucking Apollo Rocket.'

Ada jerked her head up and bit Stevey's fingers, so that he whipped his hand away from her mouth, flapping it and saying, '*Shit!*'

'I hate you,' she spat at Jaws. 'I'm going to put a spell on you that makes your ridiculous little dick drop off! And that goes for the rest of you – *mmfff!*'

Stevey had pressed his hand even harder over her mouth, digging his thumb and his fingernails into her cheekbones.

Jaws pushed himself into her, but almost as soon as he did he was whipped right out again. He jumped backwards off the end of the bed like a skydiver jumping backwards out of a plane, and he hit the wooden floor so hard that Ada heard his head banging against it. She lifted her head and saw a man standing over him, and then stamping on him.

Jaws shouted out, '*Jesus!*' and then, '*Jesus!*' as the man stamped on him a second time.

Ada could see that the man was tall, and well built, and it appeared that he was wearing a blazer and a loosely knotted tie. Unlike Jaws and the rest of the men in the bedroom, though, he didn't appear to be solid. He had that fluid, wavering, semi-translucent appearance that all of the whisperers shared, herself included, when they were wandering around Allhallows Hall as nothing but energy, with their physical bodies left behind.

Jaws snatched at the end of the quilt and tried to pull himself up, but the man smacked him full in the face with the back of his hand, and he tumbled back onto the floor.

The man turned around to Stevey and Mandeep, and to Phil and Ray, who were holding Ada's ankles.

'You'll be letting her go now, won't you?' he told them. The tone of his voice made it clear that it wasn't a question, it was an order. They hesitated for a second, and then they released their grip on her and backed away from the bed.

'Now bugger off, the lot of you. Do you hear me? And don't let me catch you trying to attack this young woman again, or it'll be the worse for you.'

Even though he was at least six inches shorter, Charles Bronson went up close to the man, his chest inflated, his fists clenched and his jaw jutting out.

'Oh, yeah?' he whispered defiantly. 'And how do you think you're going to do that, exactly?'

The man looked down at him with a tired, indulgent expression. 'I overheard you chaps talking, back in the priest's hole. As I understand it, you're solid so long as the full moon's up, as solid as you were before you were trapped. That's all well and good, I would have thought, but what happens if you're seriously injured while you're solid? Correct me if I'm wrong, but I imagine you'd be stuck with that injury for ever and ever amen.'

The man jabbed Charles Bronson in the chest with his finger. 'Maybe *I'm* not solid at the moment, my friend, but I'm still perfectly capable of breaking your nose, or poking your eyes out, and logic tells me that you'll have to stay that way for all eternity. So… do you want risk it?'

Jaws climbed to his feet, holding his sweatpants. His penis was flaccid now, as if it were hanging its purple head in shame and disappointment.

'You'll fucking regret this, I warn you. One day, mate, when you're having a weary…'

'I'll worry about that when the time comes,' the man replied. 'Meanwhile, off you all go.'

34

There was a moment of extreme tension. From the fierce looks on their faces, Ada thought that the men were going to jump on her saviour, beat him up, and then go back to raping her. But Jaws pulled up his baggy sweatpants, tugged on his T-shirt and said, 'Fuck this for a game of soldiers. Let's go down and see how much of Old Semtex's booze there is still knocking around. She's not just a witch, anyway. She's a slag, and we don't want to be catching the knob rot off of her, do we?'

The men shuffled out of the bedroom, and after the last one had left, Ada climbed off the bed and picked up her jeans and her sweater. The man stood by the door with his back to her while she quickly pulled them on. She found her bra and her knickers lying in the corner and stuffed them into her pockets.

Further along the corridor, she could hear Rob rattling the handle of his bedroom door and calling out, 'What's going on out there? Who's locked this door?'

She went up to the man and stood close behind him.

'I can't thank you enough. They were going to take it in turns to rape me. All of them.'

He turned around, looking serious. 'You must be Ada Grey, the witch that Rob was talking about.'

'Yes,' she told him. 'Well… a charmer is what I call myself, rather than a witch.'

'I've overheard those men talking about you, too, but I'm afraid I haven't been too *compos mentis* since they trapped me. Being *chanted*, that's the word they use for it, isn't it? I managed to leave that priest's hole last night and talk to my wife briefly, but that's about all. The rest of the time… it's all been a bit of a blur, to tell you the truth. Rather like being totally sozzled.'

'Who are you? Are you one of the family?'

'That's right. You wouldn't think it, because we don't look at all alike, but I'm Rob's brother. His older brother, Martin.'

They heard Rob knocking at his bedroom door again, and furiously rattling the handle.

'Who the *hell* has locked this door? Come and open it! Grace? *Grace!* Is your door locked as well? Katharine?'

'That fellow you pulled off me,' said Ada. 'The one who calls himself Jaws. Before he became solid, he locked all your family into their bedrooms.'

'Perhaps we ought to see if we can find a way to let them out.'

'No… best not. Not yet, anyway. Not till the moon's gone down. If your brother goes downstairs and finds them, who knows what they might do to him. They're not what you might call happy at the moment, are they? I'm right amazed they didn't attack you.'

'I think I guessed right and they were afraid I might do

them an injury, whereas there was nothing they could do to me. I'm not solid at the moment, am I? I'm only my energy, or my spirit, or the ghost of me, or whatever. I have the power to hurt *them*, but I have no physical substance, have I, so they can't hurt me in return. It's rather like being a gale-force wind. A gale-force wind can blow you over, can't it, but there's nothing that you can do to retaliate. You can punch the wind like Tyson Fury, but of course it won't feel it.'

He paused, and then he said, 'What are you going to do now? I don't know how long you have left before the moon sets.'

'There's something I want to try, now that I'm solid. I want to see if I can get out of here. There's an incantation I know, if I can remember all of it. I need to go down to the front door, if you don't mind coming with me. You know – just in case they try to attack me again.'

'Of course.'

Rob was pummelling on his bedroom door even harder, and now it sounded as if he were using both fists.

'I feel really bad just leaving them there,' said Martin.

Ada looked back along the corridor. Rob had switched on the lamp inside his bedroom and the light was shining under the door. She could see then that the key was lying on the floor right outside. On the other side of the corridor, the key to the master bedroom was also lying on the floor. Jaws must have entered the bedrooms by walking through their doors, even though they were closed. After he had locked them, he would have had to kick the keys through the gap underneath, because that would have been the only way for him to get them out. Since he himself had been only a collection of energised atoms, he had been able to pass through the inch-thick oak panelling as if it were no more substantial than smoke, but the keys couldn't.

Ada pointed towards the keys and said, 'There, look. We'll be able to let them out later, when it's safe.'

She went along to the landing, leaned over the banister rail, and listened. It sounded as if Jaws and the other men were in the kitchen. She heard bottles clinking together, so they must be helping themselves to Herbert Russell's Jail Ale, and toasting each other. A kitchen chair scraped on the floor, and she heard Phil laughing. She shivered when she thought how close she had come to being raped by every one of them.

Martin was standing close behind her. 'I don't think they'll bother us, even if they hear us.'

'Let's hope you're right.'

Ada crept down the staircase and crossed the hallway, and Martin followed her. She opened the front door and peered outside. The full moon was illuminating the courtyard, with its headless cherub and the two granite barns behind, as brightly as a film set. The night was achingly cold, and she could see stars winking over the leafless trees, the same stars she consulted when she made astrological predictions. Rigel, and Aldebaran, and Sirius the brightest of all.

She tried to step through the door, but her legs simply wouldn't work. Her brain refused to make them move, or even to recognise that she had legs at all.

'Are you all right?' Martin asked her quietly.

'No! I'm stuck!'

'What do you mean, stuck?'

'I've lost all feeling in my legs! That Jaws fellow told me about this. He said that he tried to leave the house at least three times when the moon was full, but he couldn't. I can't, neither. It's so strange. It's almost like my legs have been amputated.'

'How about that incantation you were talking about?'

'I'm going to try it. I don't know if it'll work, because it's Irish, and this is England, but it's worth a try.'

She reached up under her sweater and fumbled through her necklaces and pendants until she felt the circular bronze talisman embossed with the face of Arianrhod, the Druid goddess not only of beauty but of reincarnation. She wanted to be reborn. She desperately needed her life back, the way it had been before she was chanted.

She pressed the talisman tightly between finger and thumb, closed her eyes and recited the words that Alice Kyteler had written.

'*Glaoim ar na taibhsí gach doras a oscailt* – I call on the ghosts of every door to open. *Iarraim ar bhiotáille na hoíche mé a scaoileadh saor* – I ask the spirits of the night to release me. *In ainm Danu, lig dom siúl faoi shaoirse ar fud an domhain arís*. In the name of Danu, let me walk freely in the world again.'

She waited. At last, from the direction of St Mary's church, she heard the harsh, abrasive call of a nightjar, like a football rattle. She took that as a signal that the incantation may have worked, and she tried again to take a step forward. Nothing happened. Her legs still refused to move.

She turned around to Martin and he was looking at her so sympathetically that her eyes brimmed with tears.

'It's no good. I've been trapped here for ever.' Her throat constricted as she pointed to the courtyard outside and said, 'That's my whole life out there. That's my cottage and my family and my friends and my future. They've all been taken away from me, and for *why*, and for what?'

'Don't give up hope, Ada. There must be some way that we can get out of here. Rob and his wife, Vicky – they're both convinced that their little son, Timmy, is still trapped in this house somewhere, aren't they, and they're trying everything they can think of to find him. Well – they called *you* in, didn't they? And didn't they say something about a wizard?'

'Yes. Francis Coade his name is. He's brilliant. If anybody can find out how to set us free, he can. I haven't seen any sign of Timmy, though, have you?'

They heard raucous laughter from the kitchen, and one of the men shouting out, 'Here's to the next full moon!' followed by more laughter and beer bottles being clanked together.

Martin said, 'Timmy? No. I've not seen him. Vicky was sure that she'd heard him, faintly, but who knows? In this old house, it could have been anything. It could have been the draught blowing down one of the chimneys. Or an owl, outside.'

Ada quietly closed the front door, and for a moment she pressed her head against it, in despair.

'Why don't we go into the library?' Martin suggested. 'We can stay there until the moon goes down.'

Ada nodded, and followed him into the library. She sat down in the red leather armchair by the empty fireplace, while Martin stood by the window. They couldn't see the moon from in here, but they could see the shadows lengthening, and the garden gradually filling up with darkness, like an inkwell.

After a while, Martin said, 'Being trapped like this, Ada, it's certainly made me look at things from a very different point of view.'

'Such as?'

'Life, for a start. There's every possibility that you and I are never going to grow any older, and that we're never going to die, so what's the point of it?'

'I don't know. We can always go on hoping that one day we're going to be free.'

'I suppose so. But you've heard those men talking. None of them seem to have any hope left at all. That bloody priest, what's his name, Thomas. He's been here for literally hundreds of years, hasn't he? I'm surprised he still believes in God.'

'His faith – it's probably all he's got left.'

'But being stuck in time like this, for ever, it's taken all the meaning and all the purpose out of our lives. If you know you're going to die, every second is more valuable than anything else you can think of. That's what I understand now. Every second is more valuable than money, or property, or half a dozen Rembrandts hanging in your hall. Tonight, I can tell you, I'd happily give up everything I own, even my big fat pension fund, just to be up in that bedroom lying next to my Katharine and to be able to put my arm around her and hear her breathing and feel that everything was normal again.

'That priest, that Thomas... he might have given me all the time in the world, but he's stolen my life.'

'It was *Thomas* who trapped you? Why?'

'I don't know. I wish I could remember, but I can't. I've told you how much of a pig's dinner my mind's been in, since he chanted me. I took Katharine to Tavistock for something to eat and I drank too much. Actually, we both did. I know we had an argument and I stayed downstairs, in the drawing room, while Katharine went to bed.'

The moon had set now, and there would be half an hour of absolute darkness before dawn began to lighten the sky. The library window was as black and shiny as Ada's obsidian scrying mirror had been, and she could see herself reflected in it, but not Martin.

Martin thumped his fist against his forehead, as if that would help him to remember what had happened.

'I can vaguely recall shouting at Thomas for some reason and I know I was very angry but I can't think why. The next thing I remember is him standing over me in his black habit and his dog collar and laying a hand on my shoulder and chanting. It felt like the whole world was sliding sideways and the floor was opening up and I was being tipped into hell.'

They sat in silence, each with their own feeling of helplessness. As the moon sank further below the moors, Ada had the strange feeling of being pinned more and more forcefully against the back of the leather armchair. It reminded her of being pinned by centrifugal force against the wall of the Gravitron fairground ride on Barry Island.

'*Martin*—' she gasped, reaching out both hands and trying to rise up out of her seat, but for a few seconds she felt as if she were glued there. Then – just as suddenly as it had started – the tension relaxed and then died away completely.

When she looked at her uplifted hands, she could see that she was now in the same state as Martin, still visible but translucent, and that she was no longer reflected in the window. Through her bare feet, she could dimly make out the pattern of the red Kendra rug that lay under the library table.

'It's over,' she whispered.

'What?'

'It's over. I'm trapped again. I'm not real any more.'

Martin went to the door and listened. There was no more laughing and clanking of beer bottles from the kitchen. Jaws and the other men must have been taken back up to the witching room too, and it would be a month before there was another full moon – the wolf moon, in January.

Ada stood up. 'We can go and slide those keys back under their doors now, so that your family can all let themselves out.'

She took hold of Martin's hand. It was the strangest feeling – more like the feeling of cold air blowing from a hand dryer than a human hand.

'You know that I'll never be able to thank you enough for saving me tonight,' she told him.

He leaned forward and gave her a kiss on her fringe.

'You're not the only one who was saved, Ada. I found something inside myself that I never knew was there.'

They were about to leave the library when they saw the shadowy figures of Jaws and his companions crossing the hallway and mounting the stairs, whispering to each other. Martin held Ada back in the doorway until they were gone, and then the two of them went up too.

When they were only halfway up, Ada heard a long, low groan, and she was sure that she felt the staircase moving under her feet, one oak joint creaking uncomfortably against another, as if the house were having a bad dream, and stirring in its sleep.

35

Only five minutes after Rob had climbed back into bed and switched off the bedside lamp, Vicky said, 'Honestly, darling, I need to go to the toilet.'

He switched the lamp back on. 'Oh God. Are you sure?'

'Of course I'm sure. I've been trying to hold it for the past half hour, but I can't.'

'You'd think an old house like this would have chamber pots, wouldn't you? Maybe you could use a pillow to soak it up.'

He swung his legs out of bed and went across to the door, gripping the handle in both hands and wrenching it as hard as he could, trying to break the deadbolt out of the strike plate. He yanked it three or four times, without budging it, but as he stepped back to pull it again, he stepped on the key. He looked down at it, baffled, and then he bent over and picked it up.

'I don't believe this,' he said, showing it to Vicky. 'I'm sure it wasn't here before. It must have just dropped out of the lock.'

Vicky climbed out of bed, too. 'I don't care if it fell from heaven, Rob. Just open the door so that I can go to the loo!'

After Vicky had hurried out to the bathroom, Rob walked down the corridor to Grace and Portia's bedroom, listened for a moment, and then knocked.

'Who is it?' called Grace.

'It's only me. I'm just making sure that you're okay. Is your door locked?'

'Hang on.'

Rob waited while Grace came to the door and tried the handle. 'Yes, it is locked. I locked it myself last night before we went to bed, in case anybody else tried to get in. But where's the key?'

'Look down on the floor.'

'Yes... it's here. How did you know that? Have you got X-ray vision or something?'

'No, the same thing happened to us. Didn't you hear me? I was shouting and banging for ages.'

'We were dead to the world, Rob. We were both exhausted and we'd had a bit of a smoke, to be truthful.'

She opened the door. Behind her, Portia was sitting up in bed with the quilt pulled up to her neck. The bedroom smelled of Chanel No 5 and stale skunk.

'This house,' she said. 'I think we'll have to leave today. We don't want to abandon you, Rob, but I'm not sure that we can take any more.'

'Can't you at least wait until Francis has done his decontamination thing? He should be here about eleven. If it works... well, maybe this house won't be haunted any more. Maybe we'll get Timmy and Martin back, and Ada.'

'You really think so?'

'Yes. No. Who knows? But Francis seems to be sure that he's worked out what's possessing Allhallows, doesn't he – this force or whatever it is, and how he's going to get rid of it.'

'All right, Rob,' said Grace. 'We'll stay until then. But if he *can't* get rid of it, we'll have to go.' She lowered her voice and added, 'Portia might come across as tough, but she's practically having a nervous breakdown. Especially since she had that nightmare about a man kissing her.'

'I understand,' said Rob, and looked over Grace's shoulder to give Portia a wave and a smile, as if to reassure her that they weren't talking about her. Portia gave him a half-hearted wave back.

When Francis arrived, lightning flickered over the distant village of Buckland Monachorum as if it had been specially arranged by God, or by the director of some Gothic horror film. It was five miles away to the south-west, although Rob counted at least ten before he heard the first bumbling of thunder.

Underneath the hood of his raincoat, Francis was wearing a beige woollen beanie. As he came in through the front door, he pointed at it and said, wryly, 'Can you believe it, practically all of my hair had dropped out by the time I got home. I looked like a moulting guinea pig. What was left of it I shaved off. Now you wouldn't be able to tell me apart from what's-his-name from *Star Trek*, Captain Picard.'

He humped a large grey hard-shelled suitcase over the front step, and then wheeled it into the centre of the hallway, lining it up with the library door.

'I have everything I need in there. Three dead cats, for a start.'

'You what?' said Rob. 'Three dead cats? You're joking, aren't you?'

'I'm afraid not. They're an essential part of the ritual. But don't worry – I didn't kill them myself. They were strays given to me by my friend the vet in Launceston, and they'd already been put down. It was either here or the crematorium, so they wouldn't have known the difference.'

'I see. What else have you brought?'

'Druidic chanting beads, made of obsidian and moss agate and gold. An antique Celtic shield, with a pentagram embossed on it, and a sword to go with it, of about the same age. When I bought the sword, I was told that it had been used to decapitate baby dragons as soon as their heads appeared out of their mothers' wombs. As you can imagine, I took that with a large pinch of salt, but all the same it carries a solar cross on its handle. That means that when it was forged it was invested with great natural power.'

He laid his suitcase down flat on the floor, and Rob could hear something clanking inside it.

'I also have a copy of *The Great Book of Lyre*. Jonathan Lyre was a great twelfth-century wizard. His main claim to fame was exorcising Buckfast Abbey. It was haunted by scores of malevolent misty spirits that the Cistercian monks had been unable to exorcise themselves. His book contains the recitation that Raphael Hix adapted for Old Thorndon Hall. And of course I have herbs.'

'And slugs?' asked Grace, from halfway down the stairs.

Francis smiled and shucked off his raincoat, and Vicky hung it up for him. 'I'm afraid so,' he said. 'Quite a few slugs. With cloves stuck into them.'

It was then that Rob realised that the blanket he had taken from the witching room was no longer lying on the floor behind the umbrella stand.

'Grace? Vicky? Did either of you move that blanket?' he asked.

'Not me,' said Vicky, and Grace shivered and shook her head. 'I wouldn't have touched that with a bargepole.'

'Well, someone's taken it. I couldn't persuade any of the police dogs to come anywhere near it, so I was going to ask Sergeant Billings if he could send it to their forensic laboratory in Exeter.'

Francis crouched down and clicked his suitcase open.

'It wouldn't surprise me at all if your presences came down here and took that blanket back to their witching room. They may be invisible but they have enough energy to knock you over and kick you, so they must have more than enough strength to carry a blanket upstairs. I've come across several instances of unseen presences throwing pots and pans around the kitchen and tipping chairs over. Folks generally call them "poltergeists", although that's not what they really are.'

He lifted the circular iron shield out of the suitcase, and it was so heavy that he had to use both hands. It was battered and tarnished and Rob guessed it must be hundreds of years old.

'Would you mind shifting that chair over here?' Francis asked him. 'Then I can set up my altar.'

Rob dragged the mahogany chair into the middle of the hallway. It was too heavy to lift and it made a scraping sound on the floorboards that set all their teeth on edge.

Francis took out a compass and then he scraped the chair a few centimetres from side to side to make sure it was angled in the right direction. 'Forgive me the noise, but I have to make sure it's facing *exactly* due north.'

As soon as he was satisfied that it was positioned correctly, he reached into his suitcase again and brought out a large grey sheepskin. It was unwashed and greasy-looking, with thistles still tangled in it. He gave it a hard shake, and then draped it over the back and the seat of the chair.

'See this? This is supposed to have been cut from one of the five grey wethers over at Sittaford Tor. One of the early gods turned them into granite to punish a shepherd who stole one of his neighbours' sheep, but for one night only every spring they turn back into living sheep. If you're lucky enough to catch them while they're alive, you can shear off their wool. That's the story, anyway.'

He placed the shield on top of the sheepskin, face down. Then he unscrewed the top of a glass bottle of water and splashed it into the shield as if it were a bowl. Into the water he emptied three white china jars of dried herbs – yarrow and camomile and wild tobacco. After he had done that, he picked up a turfing iron and stirred it thirteen times, murmuring to himself as he did so, '*Tubu fis fri ibu, fis ibu anfis, fris brua uatha, ibu lithu,*' over and over.

Next he took out a Tupperware box and prised open the lid. It was crammed with slippery white ghost slugs, all writhing on top of each other. He had already pierced each one of them with at least ten cloves, and one by one he picked them out and stuck them to the oak panelling around the hallway, about a yard apart, just above the skirting board. They all started to creep vertically upwards, leaving silvery trails of slime up the walls.

Grace covered her eyes with her hand and said, 'Oh my Lord. They're disgusting. I've never seen white slugs before.'

'Well, white ghost slugs are comparatively rare, so that doesn't surprise me,' said Francis. 'They don't have eyes, because they live so deep underground that they don't need to be able to see, and their heads and their breathing holes are both at the same end of their bodies. They're carnivorous, too, unlike most other slugs. They feed on earthworms mainly, biting them with a single tooth. But if you stud them with cloves, they can disinfect a room of almost any pre-Christian demon you care to mention.'

Grace peered at them through her parted fingers. 'They're *horrible*. They make me feel sick. And aren't they in pain, with all those cloves stuck in them?'

'I don't know. They may be. But I don't know of any other way to isolate the force that we're up against here, and if we don't isolate it, we won't have any realistic chance of dismissing it.'

Now Francis took out *The Great Book of Lyre*, a thick

leather-bound volume with roughly trimmed pages. He opened it to a page that he had already bookmarked, and laid it flat on the floor in front of the chair. Then he bent over the suitcase and lifted out a large brindled cat.

Even Rob said, 'Bloody hell, Francis!' The cat not only had a heavy, drooping body, with its legs dangling down, but it had three heads crowded together on its neck, all with their yellow eyes staring sightlessly at nothing at all.

'My friend the vet did this fancy bit of needlework for me,' said Francis. 'He took some persuading, I have to admit, but he owed me a considerable favour. These cats, they're the very core of this ritual. You can call it a spell, if you like, the legendary rule of three, rather than a ritual, because it goes way back to the days when Dartmoor was Druid, and probably way before that.

'It's even mentioned in Shakespeare, would you believe? It's in *Macbeth*, when the witches are stirring up their brew. "*Thrice the brinded cat hath mew'd...*" What many scholars today don't realise is that Shakespeare wasn't saying the cat had let out one mew after another. He was saying that it had mewed three times all at once, simultaneous-like, and it could do that because it had three heads.'

'My God,' said Katharine. 'My friends are never going to believe this, when I tell them. If I ever do have the nerve to tell them.'

'Is there anything you want us to do?' asked Vicky.

'No, my dear, nothing – except to stand behind me and give me your moral support. Hopefully, once I've started reciting the ritual, you'll be able to feel the force rising out of the house. Once you can feel that, try to concentrate your minds on expelling it – out of the floors, out of the walls, out of the door and away across the moor. Your mental hostility to it will be a great help to me in hurrying its dismissal.'

Francis took nine large tallow candles out of his suitcase, fixed them into silver candleholders and arranged them in a circle around his makeshift altar. He lit them all and let them burn for a while, holding the sword in his right hand and the Druidic chanting beads in his left. Rob and Vicky and Grace and Portia gathered close behind him, although Katharine kept herself well back in the drawing-room doorway, her arms protectively crossed over her chest, almost hugging herself. She was frowning as if she were sure that something catastrophic was going to happen.

'I'm making sure that the candles burn down a little – not like that match I lit up there in the witching room,' said Francis.

'What if they don't burn down?' asked Portia.

'If they *don't* burn down, that would tell me that the force has somehow managed to suspend time here in this hallway, too, and that it's probably done that because it's aware that I've entered the house – just like it was the last time – and that it's guessed what I've come here to do. And *this* time it might try to do me a great deal more mischief than simply pulling my hair out.'

He waited a little while longer, while the candle flames swivelled and dipped, but then he said, 'No… it looks as if it's fine, and it hasn't yet twigged that I'm here. After all, I haven't spoken its name yet. That'll be the test, believe me. That'll be the test.'

He bent down and picked up the three-headed cat, holding it so that its heads were resting on his left shoulder. He stroked it, over and over, and while he stroked it he leaned forward so that he could read the words from *The Great Book of Lyre*.

'Hear me, o sleeping malevolence... awake from thy slumbers and hear my commands. Awake from thy slumbers and rise up, I adjure thee. Rise up and quit this domain, for today and for all eternity, and never seek to return. I command thee to leave in the name of Arawn, and in the name of Manannán, and with the power of Cailleach the veiled one, whose three spirits rest here now on my shoulder. It is daytime now, when the full moon is blinded and trusts in the guidance of saintly men and women, and when thou cannot divert its innocent strength for thine evil intentions.'

Rob could feel a humming under the floor, as if a huge electrical generator had started up somewhere beneath them. The frames of some of the paintings around the hallway started to rattle softly against the panelling, and from the kitchen he could hear the sound of plates jingling together on the dresser.

'Hear me, o sleeping malevolence!' Francis repeated, much louder this time. 'Awake and take heed of my commands! Awake and quit this domain instanter! Quit this domain and release it from thy corrupted influence! Thy days and nights of dominance here are over forever!'

The humming grew louder and louder, until the whole house felt as if it were vibrating, and the circular gilt-framed mirror hanging next to the umbrella stand dropped off the wall, its frame chipping and its glass cracking in half. Vicky reached out and gripped Rob's hand, and Grace put her arm around Portia. Even Katharine left the drawing-room doorway to come and stand close beside them.

'I know thou canst hear my voice, o malevolence!' Francis shouted. 'I know that thou canst hear my voice and recognise the influence that I carry on my shoulder! Rise up and take thy leave, I command thee, by the sacred rule of three! Thou art banished from this domain until time turns in upon itself, and the heavens are swallowed up by darkness for all eternity!'

The humming grew louder still, and the vibration intensified, and now an oil painting of one of the Wilmingtons' racehorses fell off the wall.

Abruptly, Francis stood up straight, still holding the cat on his shoulder, and roared out, *'Esus! I know thee! I recognise thy presence here! Esus, I command thee to rise up, and quit this domain for ever!'*

Outside, lightning flashed and crackled. Through the window by the front door Rob saw a dazzling bolt of lightning strike the headless cherub on its severed neck, so that lumps of broken marble tumbled across the courtyard. The lightning was followed almost at once by a bellowing roll of thunder, so loud that he couldn't hear what Francis screamed out next. Even when the thunder had grumbled away, the vibration in the hallway continued.

Francis was standing still now, his eyes closed and his teeth gritted as if he were battling with some demon inside his head. He grunted with effort, lifting the three-headed cat an inch or two off his shoulder and then letting it drop back again.

'Francis?' said Rob. 'Francis, what's—?'

But Francis ignored him. Instead, he stepped sideways, away from the chair that he had made into a makeshift altar. He hesitated for a few seconds, stamping his left foot again and again, like an impatient horse. Then he flung the cat all the way across the hallway so that it thumped against the library door.

As soon as the cat dropped to the floor, all the candles blew out, one after the other, so that the altar was surrounded by drifting ribbons of smoke. Francis reached over, picked up the Celtic shield and tossed all the water in it over the sheepskin. Then he hurled the shield to one side so that it bowled along the hallway into the drawing room and then fell over with a reverberating clank.

'Francis – what's wrong?' Rob asked him, but again Francis didn't seem to hear him. He turned and stared back at Rob with those colourless eyes, but the expression on his face was unreadable. It wasn't helplessness. It wasn't fear. It wasn't hatred, either. He looked as if he couldn't understand who or even *what* Rob was, and as if he couldn't understand who or what *he* was, either.

'Francis, this is all going tits up, isn't it? Let's stop.'

'Francis, Rob's right,' said Grace, taking a step towards him and holding out her hand. 'We'll have to try something else. Perhaps your friend Father Salter can get in touch with that school of exorcism in Rome.'

Lightning flashed again, and again, as if a jostling crowd

of paparazzi were taking pictures of them through the window.

Francis lifted one hand to his ear. He appeared to be listening to somebody who was whispering to him. He nodded, and nodded again, and then said, '*Esus.*'

'Esus... is that the name of this force?' Rob asked him.

But Francis didn't answer. Instead, he turned around and walked towards the sealed-up cellar door, his arms by his sides, as if he expected to be able to walk right through it. He collided with it, and then he turned around again, so that he was facing outward, back into the hallway.

'Francis—' said Rob.

Francis still had that bewildered look on his face, but then suddenly he stretched his mouth open wide and let out a harsh, horrifying shriek. The upper plate of his dentures dropped down onto his lower teeth, so that for a split second it looked as if he had two mouths. He flung up his arms and galloped with his legs and it was only then that Rob realised what was happening to him. The back of his beige beanie was rapidly being soaked in dark crimson blood and his shoulders seemed to be clamped hard against the wall.

'*Esus! Stop!*' he screamed. '*Esus! I beg you!*' But with a complicated series of snaps and cracks like twigs breaking, his skull was pulled into the plaster, followed by his ribcage and his arms and his pelvis and his legs. Only his bones disappeared. His face was flattened into a grotesque, rubbery mask with two eyes bulging out of their sockets, and his entire skin slithered down like a flaccid sack into his tattered Aran sweater and his ripped-open corduroy trousers – a sack bulging with his lungs and his liver and his stomach and heaps of slippery intestines.

His body slid slowly to the floor and fell sideways, staring up at the ceiling with one boneless sleeve flopped across his chest like a bloody parody of a fallen scarecrow. All around the hallway, the white ghost slugs dropped off the wall and lay squirming.

The vibration drummed louder through the floorboards, and then died. There was another flash of lightning, but it was dim and more distant this time, and they didn't hear an echoing boom of thunder for at least eleven seconds. After that, Allhallows Hall was deathly silent.

Katharine, mewling softly with shock, crept back into the drawing room, where she climbed onto the sofa and pressed a cushion against her face. Vicky and Grace and Portia stood staring at each other in terror and disbelief. They were too stunned to speak.

Rob approached Francis's body. He felt numb, and he had no idea what to do next. There was no point in calling for an ambulance. But should he call the police? If he did, would they believe him? If he hadn't seen Francis's skeleton being pulled through that wall in front of his eyes, he wouldn't have believed it himself. Yet the police would have no choice – they would have to believe it. No human being could conceivably have pulled all of Francis's bones out of his body, including his skull. He had left a bloody silhouette on the plaster, both hands outstretched, like the rayograph of somebody caught in the flash of an A-bomb.

No, thought Rob, *I have to call Detective Inspector*

Holley. Francis has been killed and enough of us have witnessed how it happened.

He stepped back from the bricked-up doorway. The force must be somewhere down there – down in the cellar – and that was presumably why it had been sealed. Although the vibrations had completely died away now, he was sure he could still feel some tangible energy emanating from behind that wall. It was the same scalp-prickling sensation he had when he was convinced that he was being watched, even though he couldn't see anybody watching him.

Francis had spoken its name out loud, *Esus*, and that had woken it up. If nothing else, it had proved that he had correctly guessed which demonic force they were dealing with. But it had also proved that the spiritual decontamination that he had borrowed from Raphael Hix was nowhere near powerful enough to exorcise it – despite the clove-studded slugs and the holy water from the Druid's Bowl and the herbs and the sword and the nine candles. Not even the three-headed cat had been enough to dismiss it.

Rob tried not to think the name *Esus*, in case the force could read his mind. He couldn't imagine the agony that Francis must have suffered, having his skeleton ripped out of his body.

It was impossible to tell from his face, which had now collapsed so that his forehead sagged down over his nose with his eyeballs peering out from underneath it like a furtive animal.

Rob was about to turn around and say that he was going to call the police when he heard a thick, coarse, churning sound. Right in front of his eyes, the sleeve of

Francis's sweater was being dragged into the wall. It was simply disappearing, inch by inch, followed by his beanie and the empty skin that had once been his face and his neck. His intestines bulged up inside his sweater as if they were being slowly cranked into a mangle, but then with a sharp squishing noise they disappeared, too, followed by his trousers. One of his Oxford shoes tipped up, but it took only a few seconds before that vanished, and then there was nothing left of Francis at all.

Rob went slowly back to rejoin Vicky and Grace and Portia. Portia was nearly hysterical, shivering and biting her thumbnail. Vicky looked up at Rob in fear and bewilderment and said, 'Now what? Now what are we going to do? How are we ever going to get Timmy back now?'

36

They all made their way into the drawing room, where Portia sat down on the sofa next to Katharine and hugged her, trying to calm both of them down. Vicky took a seat on Herbert's throne while Grace went over to the painting of the hooded figures and stared at it as if she might be able to pick out which one of them had pulled Francis into the bricked-up cellar.

Rob paced up and down in front of the slowly collapsing fire, frantically trying to think what to do next. Eventually he stopped and said to Vicky, 'What you suggested before... getting in touch with Father Salter. I think that was a good idea. In fact, I don't see what else we can do. We could call the police but there's no trace of Francis to prove he was here, except for his suitcase and all his paraphernalia, and do you seriously think they're going to believe us? We've got candles and a sheepskin and a dead cat with three heads lying on the floor, apart from all those slugs. They're going to think we're some kind of weird sect.'

'There's a demon in that cellar, isn't there?' said Portia, looking up at Rob with her mascara all smudged. 'A real, actual, genuine demon. It's like something out of *The Exorcist*, only worse.'

'Francis didn't actually call it a demon. He said it was a "malevolent force", but I suppose that could mean anything, including a demon. He shouted out its name, though. You heard him. And he addressed it as if it could hear him. So I don't think you're entirely wrong. And if it *is* a demon, maybe that's how Father Salter can help us. He's a trained exorcist, after all, and he told us that he'd recently exorcised a woman who was possessed.'

Grace said, 'Yes, but when he came here he was so frightened he almost had a heart attack.'

'Who else are we going to turn to, Gracey? I'll just have to persuade him that he's the only person who can help us to get rid of this thing. Maybe he can pray to God to give him a bit more bottle.'

Rob suddenly caught sight of himself in the tall, narrow mirror next to the drawing-room door. His dark curly hair was unkempt and his face was white, with plum-coloured circles under his eyes. Vicky had always said that he looked like Lord Byron, but this morning he thought he looked like Lord Byron when the poet was suffering from the fever that had eventually killed him.

Right, he thought, *I can't go on like this*, and he took out his phone. He found the number for Our Lady of the Assumption in Tavistock and tapped it out. Father Salter answered almost at once, as if he had been holding his phone in his hand and waiting for Rob to call.

'Hello. Maurice Salter speaking. How can I help you?'

'Father Salter, this is Rob Russell. We met when you came to Sampford Spiney to visit Allhallows Hall.'

There was a lengthy pause. Then Father Salter said, 'Yes... Allhallows Hall. Have things settled down there now? Francis called me last night and told me he was coming to carry out his decontamination this morning. Has it been successful?'

'He came to do it this morning, father. But there's no easy way to tell you this. He's dead.'

'He's passed away? Oh dear Lord, I'm totally shocked. How did he die? I had no idea that he was ill.'

'He wasn't ill. He was halfway through his ritual when he woke up the force that's possessing this house and it killed him. You may not believe this, but it pulled him through the wall. All his bones first and then the rest of him.'

Another long silence. Then Father Salter said, 'Sorry. I'm still here. I was saying a small prayer for Francis. Commending his soul to the Lord, that he may be eternally happy in heaven.'

'We need more than that, father. We're in desperate trouble here. We still believe that our son, Timmy, is trapped here somewhere, as well as my brother, Martin, and Ada Grey. Francis brought along everything he needed for the ritual, but this force – this demon, if you want to call it that – it didn't seem to be deterred in the slightest by anything he said or anything he did. In fact, he only made it even more violent.'

'I don't know what I can say to you, Rob, except to offer you my deepest condolences.'

'Father – it's not your condolences we're asking for. It's your help. We need you to come here and exorcise this demon for us. We even know its name, or at least we're pretty sure that we do. I won't say it out loud. That's what seemed to rouse it into killing Francis.'

Yet another silence. Then, 'I know its name, too, Rob. Francis told me. I know *exactly* what it is, and it is not the Devil. I sensed that when I came to visit Allhallows Hall, and that is why I was so reluctant to confront it... and why I am exceedingly hesitant to confront it now.'

'I understand that, father. I fully understand. But we can't think of anybody else who can get rid of it for us. At some point we'll have to report Francis's death to the police, but the police don't carry out exorcisms. Neither will the local rector. He's an Anglican, and Anglicans don't do exorcisms, do they?'

'It's not unheard of. There have been a few occasions when an Anglican clergyman has been given the authority to cleanse a home of suspected demons. First of all, though, he must be given permission by his diocesan bishop, and the possession will be thoroughly investigated by the deliverance ministry. They usually send along a qualified psychiatrist to interview the people concerned, and also a medical doctor.'

Rob looked across at Vicky, and then at Portia and Katharine. Grace still had her back turned, staring at the painting.

'We can't wait to go through all that rigmarole, father. This is urgent. As far as Francis explained it to us, Timmy and Martin and Ada are trapped in the very second when they disappeared, which means that with every minute that passes they're further and further behind us in time. It's like we've dropped them off by the side of the road somewhere and driven away and left them there. If we delay it any longer, I'm really worried that it'll be too late to get them back. It may be too late already.'

Father Salter said, 'In this case, I may not need to apply to the bishop for permission before attempting an exorcism. I most certainly would do, if we were talking about the Devil – Old Dewer – or any one of his pantheon of demons from the *Lesser Key of Solomon*. And, like the Anglicans, I would probably have to call in a psychiatrist, too. I would have to purge Allhallows Hall of anything that could harbour evil spirits – paintings, drawings, horror and fantasy novels, mirrors and stained-glass windows. If you had a Ouija board, that would have to be thrown out and burned.'

'But we're not talking about the Devil or any of his demons, are we?'

'No, Rob. We're talking about something that walked this earth long before Satan was first given a name. Something far more powerful than Satanic demons, although like all demons it obviously had its weak spot, its Achilles heel. That must have been how it was caught and incarcerated in Allhallows Hall in the first place.'

'So what do we have to do to get rid of it?'

'We have to *release* it, do you see? Not exorcise it so much as set it free. I have to warn you, though, that the danger involved in doing that is almost incalculable. It will be like a lion let out of its cage, which has no gratitude for the keeper who unlocked it, but sees only one of the men who kept it imprisoned for so long, and on whom it wants to take its bloody revenge.'

'Well, you say you know this demon's name, so presumably you know what it's capable of.'

'Yes, I do. And this morning you have sadly witnessed some of its appalling supernatural power for yourself. One of its many alternative names is Bonebiter. Sometimes it was known as the Fluter, because it was said to make flutes out of the shin bones of its victims so that it could whistle for its pack of dogs when it took them out hunting at night. That's why the locals call them Whist Hounds.'

'So you know what it is. What I'm asking you is, do you think you're capable of setting it free? And if you are, *will* you?'

Rob's question was followed by the longest pause yet. It was so long that Rob eventually said, 'Father Salter? Are you still there?'

'Yes, Rob. I'm still here. But my car's in for a service. You'll have to come to Tavistock to fetch me.'

'You mean you'll do it? The exorcism?'

'As a minister of Jesus, who sacrificed His life to save those who begged for salvation, I can hardly refuse, can I?'

'Thank you, father. Thank you. I'll be there in about twenty minutes.'

Father Salter was waiting for Rob on the steps outside Our Lady of the Assumption when he came driving up the hill. It had started to rain again, so the priest was holding up a large black umbrella. In his other hand he was carrying a flat black leather briefcase. Obviously the exorcism that he intended to carry out didn't call for three-headed cats or Celtic shields and swords, or Tupperware boxes full of white ghost slugs.

Rob climbed out so that Father Salter could stow his umbrella in the boot.

'I can understand how much you don't want to do this,' he said. 'Believe me – if I could have found anybody else to ask, I would have.'

Father Salter eased himself into the passenger seat and fastened his seat belt. 'There are times in our lives, Rob, when all of us have to face up to what we fear the most. I have no fear of Satan and his demons, because I have been fighting against them all my life, and I know their many tricks and deceits, but I also know how much they fear God, despite all their mockery and their bravado.'

Rob turned the Honda around and started to drive back across the Tavistock Canal to Sampford Spiney. 'But this malevolent force? Now we're so far away, can I mention its name?'

'It would be safer if you didn't. Dartmoor and all its surrounding area was the land in which he was dominant since time immemorial, and it's quite possible that even in his captivity he can hear every whisper and every branch break from miles around. He was known by that name in the days of the Druids, and the Druids' human sacrifices were made to appease him. I call him a "him" in the same way that I call Satan a "him", but they are both abstract forces of pure evil that have no human identity.'

'But he's not Satan – or Old Dewer, as they call him round here?'

'Ah, but that's exactly who he is. When Christianity took over from Druidism and all the beliefs that had gone before Druidism, the clergy taught the local people that this malevolent force that rode around the moors with his pack of hounds must be the Devil as he was recognised by the Christian Church. But of course he wasn't. He was still the demon whose name we are being cautious enough not to speak out loud.'

'And did he really ride around the moors, hunting for unbaptised babies?'

'Well, something or somebody did, and this continued until the late seventeenth century. The parish records show that, over the years, scores of mutilated children were discovered on the moors – bodies that appeared to have been brutally cut open and then savaged by feral dogs. The way they had been killed was consistent with Druid sacrifices. And as it happened, very few of the babies were unbaptised. That was an embellishment added by the clergy in order to encourage the local people to have their children christened. Although I say it myself, the clergy can be notorious liars when it suits them.'

They were driving past the Moortown junction now, and it was raining so hard that Rob could barely see the lane in front of them.

'But *when* did you say the killings stopped? The late seventeenth century?'

'That's right. Quite abruptly, from what I've read about it, and the demon and his hounds were never heard around

Dartmoor again, although of course he continued to live in legend. Even his original name survived among the few locals who still practised Druid magic. And this is an interesting fact: when he visited Plymouth, William Blake, the poet and artist, was told the legend by an old fellow from Tavistock, but probably because of the old fellow's thick Devon accent he misheard the name as "Jesus".

'Blake mistakenly assumed that Jesus had walked around Dartmoor, seeking out unbaptised babies, and that was when he wrote "And did those feet in ancient times, walk upon England's mountains green?" What he didn't realise was that his poem was inspired not by the Son of God but by one of the most malevolent forces in all human history.'

They reached Sampford Spiney and turned into the driveway of Allhallows Hall. Rob switched off the engine and sat quiet for a moment before he opened the door.

'You're sure that you're up to this?' he asked Father Salter.

Father Salter laid a hand on his arm and said gently, 'Probably not. But if I can chase out *this* demon, I shall know that I can beat any other evil spirit that ever comes my way, and that includes the Lord of the Flies himself.'

37

Vicky opened the front door for them and pressed her hand to her chest in relief.

'Thank you so much for coming, father. I was petrified that you wouldn't.'

'As I was telling Rob, my dear, we don't call ourselves "Christian soldiers" for nothing. There are times when we have to gird our loins and face our enemy, no matter how fearful we are.'

Rob led Father Salter into the middle of the hallway. 'We've left everything just as it was when Francis was killed.'

Before he looked around at anything else, Father Salter went across and stood in front of the silhouette of Francis on the bricked-up cellar doorway. The blood was beginning to soak into the plaster and it was already turning brown. He reached out and touched it with his fingertips and then he made the sign of the cross and murmured a benediction. *'In nomine Patris, et Filii, et Spiritus Sancti...'*

After that, he turned away from the wall and surveyed

the scattered remains of Francis's attempt at spiritual decontamination.

'I can see that Francis was trying to carry out the ritual we call *Mala omnia expurget*, but with the addition of some strong Druidic symbolism, such as this cat with three heads, and this horrible grey sheepskin. He told me that he would be. I'm extremely surprised that it wasn't effective.'

'After he had shouted out its name, the whole house started shaking,' Vicky told him.

Father Salter unclipped his briefcase and took out a white fringed stole, which he kissed, draped around his neck, and then again made the sign of the cross.

'From the way in which poor Francis was pulled through the wall here, there's no doubt at all in my mind that the force is located here, behind this blocked-off doorway. But even though it's confined down in the cellar, its evil influence is clearly strong enough to have permeated the foundations and the very stones of the walls themselves, all the way up to the tiles on the roof. Its great supernatural strength was obviously the reason that it was hunted down and caught and brought here. Its presence here in the house gave the Wilmingtons the power that was needed to convert the priest's hide that Nicholas Owen had crafted for them into a witching room.'

'Who do you think caught it? And how?' asked Rob. 'I mean, how the hell do you go about catching a thing like that and bricking it up in your cellar?'

'As I said before, Rob, every demon has its weak spot,

just as the purest among us are susceptible now and again to temptation. Whoever caught it must have had an intimate knowledge of the moors around here, and of the stories associated with every tor and every leat. You said that you'd met John Kipling. He'll be the man to ask about it. He's likely to know the date when dead children stopped being found on the moors, and he may even have a census of who was living in Sampford Spiney at the time, and who was acquainted with the Wilmingtons.'

He approached the cellar doorway again, and stood there silently for a few seconds with his head bowed. 'Do you know,' he said, 'I can actually *hear* it. At the Pontifical University in Rome they teach you how to listen for the malevolence that sometimes radiates from demonic possession. I have heard it several times before, but I have never come across anything like this – *never*. This has a completely different pitch to it, if you follow me. Satan's demons almost always sing sweetly and seductively, to cajole us into doing wrong, but this is so jarring and discordant. It's like some wind instrument being played in all the wrong keys. The Fluter.'

Rob came and stood next to him. 'I could sense something myself. I don't know... I couldn't hear anything, not like you, but I could certainly *feel* something. It was like static electricity, like when you rub a balloon and it makes your hair all stand on end.'

'Then we must get to work, Rob, without delay, and exorcise it. But before we begin the ritual of exorcism, we should go up to the witching room and offer prayers and words of encouragement to those who are trapped there. We may not be able to see them, but they will be able to hear us, I'm sure, and if any souls are going to give us moral and spiritual support, they will.'

'If you do manage to exorcise it, will they all be set free?' asked Vicky.

'I would be lying to you if I said that I knew,' said Father Salter. 'I am hopeful, though, and I am placing my trust in the Lord.'

'But some of them have been trapped in that room for decades, or even longer,' Portia put in. 'If we manage to set them free... won't they be incredibly old?'

'Again, I don't know. This is completely unknown territory for me, spiritually speaking. As I say, I am familiar with the ways of Satan and his legions, and the modern ways of dealing with them. They made several fundamental errors in that film of *The Exorcist*. If I had been there, instead of Father Karras, I would have dismissed that petty demon in a matter of minutes. I certainly wouldn't have allowed him to screw that poor girl's head around in a circle like that.

'*This* force, though, *this* presence... he's a different kettle of fish altogether. If he predates the Druids and the Romans, he may not have a grasp either of English or of Latin. It is no good trying to dismiss a demon who can't understand a word you're saying to him.'

Vicky held on to Rob's arm and said, 'I'm frightened.'

Father Salter gave her a wry smile. 'So am I, my dear. More than you can imagine.'

*

They climbed the stairs and walked along the corridor to the stained-glass window. Rob now knew that the figure in the black cloak with his back turned wasn't Old Dewer, but he tried hard not to think of his real name, or even the fact that William Blake had misheard it as 'Jesus'. Instead, he tried to recite Jerusalem in his head: *Bring me my bow of burning gold, Bring me my arrows of desire.*

He lifted the window seat and pulled up the crucifix. Father Salter watched apprehensively as the pulleys beneath the floor clicked and whirred and the dado panel swung slowly inwards.

'This is remarkable,' he said, bending sideways so that he could peer underneath the dado rail into the witching room. 'I have never seen a priest's hide as enormous as this. Forget about a single Jesuit, you could fit half the diocese in here!'

Rob glanced at him, and realised by his expression that he was only trying to sound light-hearted to hide his fear.

Rob ducked down and went in first, followed by Father Salter and then Katharine and Vicky. Grace came in, too, to stand by Rob and Vicky.

Portia held back. 'My heart's pounding like a hammer,' she said. 'I'll go and lie down for ten minutes and give myself ten minutes of intensive vipassana meditation.'

The witching room appeared to be empty, although the blankets were still lying in untidy heaps on the horsehair flooring. Rob couldn't be sure if the blanket that he had taken downstairs was back here now, because they were all the same colour and equally filthy.

Father Salter walked slowly down to the end of the room and back again, his hands pressed together in a gesture of prayer. Now and again he hesitated, as if he had bumped into somebody, and once he stopped dead and looked around, as if somebody had called him by name.

'My goodness,' he said under his breath, when he came back to join the rest of them. 'It's *crowded* in here. Crowded with souls! I can't even guess how many. They're *here*, of course, but they're not *now*.'

'You can actually feel them, can't you?' said Vicky.

'Only faintly, but yes… and I can sense so many different feelings among them. Some of them seemed to be resigned to their fate, and have accepted that they could be here for as long as this house remains standing. There are some others, though, who are still filled with pent-up rage because they've been imprisoned. Perhaps the more recent captives.'

He frowned, and closed his eyes, and lifted his fingertips to the lobes of both ears, and when Grace started to say something he said, '*Shh!* Quiet, please, for just a moment!'

They waited, and then Rob asked him, 'What? What can you hear?'

'I believe that I can hear a child crying. It's very indistinct, and I can't tell for sure if it's a boy or a girl. But, yes… it is a child, and it sounds as if it's crying in its sleep – as if it's having a nightmare from which it can't wake up.'

'Oh my God, it's Timmy!' Vicky gasped. 'It's Timmy and he's here and he's still alive! I knew it, Rob, I knew it, I knew it!'

She clasped her hand over her mouth and started to sob.

Father Salter touched her shoulder and said, 'Have faith,

my dear. Have courage. When they lifted Our Lord down from the cross you can imagine what Mary felt, and how she must have wept. But her son rose again, did he not? And if God is willing, your son, Timmy, will reappear to you in just the same way.'

For the first time since Timmy had disappeared, Rob had a blasphemous thought. *If God is willing? He'd better be fucking willing. I'll never forgive Him if we don't get our son back.*

Father Salter went over and stood between the two stained-glass windows that overlooked the garden. It was still raining and the rain tipped and tapped against the windowpanes. Rob thought the rain sounded as if there were beggars outside, persistently trying to catch their attention, beggars walking on stilts so that they could reach the first floor. He didn't know what had conjured up such a bizarre and disturbing image in his mind, and he kept glancing at the windows to reassure himself that it wasn't real.

Father Salter raised both hands and said loudly, 'All of you souls in this accursed room, I implore you to listen to me. We cannot see you, because you have each been imprisoned in a moment that has now long passed, some of you for very many years. We know, however, that you can see us, and hear us. And we wish you with all of our hearts to understand that we are doing everything we can, my friends here and I, to release you at last from your imprisonment.'

As he spoke, the witching room began to be filled with a soft, barely audible whispering. It sounded like, *what, what, what, who is this and what does he want?*

'My name is Father Maurice Salter, from the Catholic church of Our Lady of the Assumption in Tavistock. I am newly trained by the Vatican in the dismissal of malevolent presences, and I am aware that it is the power of a malevolent presence that first trapped you here and which continues to keep you trapped.

'I have come here today with the intention of exorcising it. I have no illusions that it will be an easy exorcism, because this presence, too, has been incarcerated in this house against its will, and it will undeniably be simmering with as much rage and resentment as you.'

The whispering grew louder, and more excitable, although Rob thought that he could hear protesting voices too. *What, what, what, who does he think he is, he's a fraud, he's a fake, he's only going to make things worse for us. Trouble, he's going to cause trouble.*

Rob and Vicky and Grace and Katharine moved closer together, because they could all feel the whisperers jostling around them, even though they couldn't see them. It was like standing in a chilly, blustery breeze.

Father Salter lifted up his hands again, and declared loudly, 'Whoever you are – whatever the reason for your having been trapped here – whether you welcome my intervention or whether you resent it – I am first going to pray for you. I am going to petition the Lord for your freedom and for your survival outside this unhallowed room.

'In return, I ask you to direct all of your energy, all of your goodwill, every atom of your humanity towards supporting my ritual here today. I am not going to pretend to you that dismissing this presence is not the most challenging exorcism that I have ever faced, or by far the most frightening, or that I am at all certain of success. But every ounce of passion that you can muster against the malevolent presence that has been holding you captive for so long will weaken it just a little more, and strengthen my hand.

'*Oro Deum ut eriperet de tenebris vos aquam desperandum.* I pray to God to rescue you from the dark waters of your despair. Amen.'

The whispering grew louder and more flustered, until it sounded as if the witching room were filled up with the flapping wings of a whole flock of panicking birds. Then, suddenly, it fell silent. Rob felt as if somebody had brushed close past him, as he had before, but that was the only indication that there was anybody there.

Vicky looked up at him and said, 'Do we have to go? Do we have to leave Timmy here?'

'I don't know, darling. Father? Can we stay?'

'I'm afraid that would be very unwise,' said Father Salter. 'Not until I have completed my dismissal, anyway. As I understand it, these walls are imbued with an occult power beyond anything that we can imagine, and the Lord alone knows what may happen when we start to leach it out. There's even a risk that the whole house might collapse. But if my exorcism turns out to be successful, we can come back up here and open the door again, and release all those souls who are able to leave. Including, I pray, your Timmy, and your brother Martin, and Ada.'

'Right, then,' said Rob. 'I suppose we'd better get on with it.'

*

They closed the panel in the dado and silently went back downstairs. Father Salter went around the hallway picking up the three-headed cat and the candles and Vicky found him a dustpan and brush in the scullery so that he could sweep up the white ghost slugs. Rob brought back the shield that had rolled into the drawing room.

Father Salter wrapped everything up in the sheepskin, bundled it back into Francis's suitcase, and locked it.

'I can fully understand why Francis thought that these Druidic artefacts might give him more power to dismiss a pre-Christian malevolence. But it's possible, even *likely*, I would say, that this demon predates even the Druids. Dartmoor is two hundred and eighty million years old, after all, and it used to be forested and well populated in the Bronze Age, when the climate was warmer.

'This cat and these slugs and the sheepskin and the shield, they may have had the reverse effect, and aroused the demon's ire even more. After all, if somebody came at me with that atomic whirl that atheists display as their symbol of disbelief, shouting that God didn't exist and that I should quit my church and never come back, I think I should find it difficult not to lose my temper, too.'

'Do you need our support?' asked Rob. 'I mean, do you want us to stay here with you?'

'Definitely not, no. Thank you for your offer, but this is going to be a one-to-one contest between the presence and me. I will need total concentration – *total* – and I don't want to be worrying about you and your welfare. It's quite possible that the presence could threaten your lives in order to divert my attention away from completing my ritual. He may well realise that it is my sworn commitment to protect those in danger, and take advantage of it.'

'Well – if we retreat to the drawing room... is that far enough?'

'I should hope so. But don't be surprised or upset if I suddenly tell you to leave the house altogether. It may become necessary, depending on how violently the presence reacts. We're not talking about some petty little troublemaker like Pazuzu here.'

Rob said, 'Okay... but if it all starts getting out of hand... just yell.'

Father Salter raised his hand in acknowledgement, but from the way he was standing alone in the middle of the hallway, with his shoulders hunched and the red blotches of his cheeks looking more pronounced than ever, as if he had been made up for a part in a pantomime, Rob thought that he looked as if he were waving goodbye.

He left him and went to join the others in the drawing room, but he lifted one of the Jacobean chairs nearer the door, so that he could sit there and watch him. Father Salter would never have come here to carry out this exorcism, after all, if he hadn't persuaded him, and if anything happened to him – if he was dragged into the wall in the same way as Francis – Rob knew he would never be able to forgive himself.

Father Salter stood in front of the cellar doorway and made the sign of the cross. After the Latin benediction, he began to speak clearly and slowly, at a pitch slightly higher and more expressive than his normal voice. Usually, he sounded as if he were patiently explaining something to somebody who was having difficulty in grasping it. Now he sounded as if he had stepped onto a stage in front of an audience.

'Hear me, Esus! I have come here today in the name of the Lord to release you from your captivity. I come in the spirit of reconciliation, and of forgiveness, and in the understanding that all beings are equal, substantial or insubstantial, whether they recognise the supremacy of the Holy Trinity or not.'

He repeated the sign of the cross, three times, and then he said, 'Esus! I free you from whatever spell or ritual is holding you here in this house, no matter how complex, no matter how ancient. It is the Lord who created every fibre of this world, and the Lord can untangle any knot of mischievous magic made by men.

'*Surge Esugenus et vade in via! Vacat vobis, liberum!* Rise up, rise up, Esus and be on your way! You are free!'

The house remained silent except for the soft crackling of the drawing-room fire and the rain-beggars still tapping at the windows.

Father Salter went up to the cellar doorway, his chest rising and falling with stress. He waited for nearly a quarter of a minute, and then he called out, 'Esus! You cannot ignore me, because I speak with the voice of God! Rise up, Esus and return to the moors! Rise up!'

Rob felt that deep vibration starting up again. The floor began to tremble, and the paintings on the walls began to rattle against the panelling. This time, the vibration was even more violent, and they could hear the ladles and

341

colanders and saucepans that were hanging in the kitchen jangling like some frantic fire alarm. A kitchen chair tipped over onto the tiled floor with a loud clatter.

'Esus! It is the Lord God who releases you! Acknowledge his supremacy, acknowledge that He alone has the power and the divine authority to free you! Accept that He is the master of the world, and the custodian of the moors over which you used to pursue your quarry! He will allow you to return there, and to ride with your hounds at night! All you have to say is, Lord, I accept your pre-eminence! Lord, let me go!'

The vibration was deafening now. It felt as if everything in the house was juddering and groaning and squeaking. From the library came the thumping of books as they tumbled off the shelves, one after the other, and from halfway up the staircase they heard one of the leaded windows crack from side to side.

Vicky came up and stood beside Rob's chair. Her voice was watery with fear, and he could scarcely hear her. 'It doesn't sound as if it wants to acknowledge God, does it? Oh, *please*! Why doesn't it just give in and go free?'

Father Salter stepped back into the centre of the hallway. He grasped both ends of his stole and said, 'Esus, o evil one, I order you now to rise up and leave this house. In the name of God, and in the name of the one who commands you, Arawn, king of the underworld, lord of darkness, who also has to kneel to the Lord.'

There was a bang so loud that Vicky screamed. Out in the hallway, Father Salter stood up straight and rigid, quivering, his arms pressed down by his sides. Then the top of his head exploded like a watermelon and his skull flew up into the air, still attached to his spine. Next his shoulders burst apart, followed by his chest. His shoulder blades and his ribcage followed his skull up into the air, and all the rest of his bones came rattling up after them, some connected but some disconnected, flying up in a high arc over the hallway and into the cellar doorway, where they hit the bloodied silhouette that Francis had left behind, and vanished.

All that was left of Father Salter after his skeleton had been wrenched out of him was a pile of clothes, sodden with blood. His jacket and his trousers and his underwear were all torn into shreds, and among the tatters lay lumps of flesh held together with translucent stretches of skin, as well as his liver, which lay on top of his glistening pink intestines like a basking brown seal.

His white fringed stole had been spread out on top of his remains and his blood-spattered dog collar perched on top of that, as if they had been carefully laid there by a respectful mourner.

Gradually, the vibrations died away. There was a high ringing noise from the kitchen as one metal spatula dropped off its hook, but then there was silence again. Rob stood up. He took a step towards the doorway but Vicky snatched at his sleeve and said, 'No, Rob. Wait.'

'I've *killed* him, Vicks. I should never have persuaded him to come here. He didn't want to come but I made him. I might just as well have murdered him myself.'

'It's too late. Stay here. Wait.'

Rob stayed where he was, staring at the small ragged

heap that was all that was left of Father Salter. He was trembling with anger and guilt, but he accepted Vicky's intuition. She had sensed several times before when something bad was about to happen to them, or that somebody they had met was not to be trusted.

Portia and Katharine were sitting on the sofa together, wide-eyed, silent and shocked. Grace said, 'What are we going to do now, Rob? It looks like nothing is going to get rid of it. I mean – if even *God* can't get rid of it—'

It was then that they saw Father Salter's remains stirring as if they still had life in them – his shredded clothes and his ripped-up lumps of flesh and his piles of intestines. They began to slide across the polished oak floorboards, heading towards the cellar doorway. To begin with they left behind them a shining slug-like trail of blood and mucus, but as they neared the wall this trail rapidly dried up, leaving no trace.

When his remains reached the wall, they slid straight into the plaster, and disappeared, exactly in the same way that Francis had been absorbed. Apart from his open briefcase, there was nothing in the hallway now to show that Father Salter had ever been there.

'This is a nightmare,' said Grace. 'We'll have to call the police now, won't we?'

'What's the point?' said Rob. 'If two exorcists can't get rid of this demon, what can the police possibly do? Arrest it?'

'But that's two people *dead*, Rob.'

'Yes, and if this demon didn't have our Timmy trapped I *would* call the police. Then I'd walk out of this house and

I'd never come back. But we're almost one hundred per cent certain that Timmy's here, and we're equally sure that Martin's here, too, and Ada.'

'So what are we going to do?'

'Somebody has to clear him out of this house, somehow, and it looks like the only person left to do that is me.'

38

Rob poured himself a glass of his father's Jameson's whiskey and phoned John Kipling.

He stood by the library window with books scattered on the floor all around him, looking out over the kitchen garden. It was still raining, but in curtains of fine drizzle.

Vicky sat at the table listening to him. She had tied up her hair and in her ankle-length coffee-coloured dress she looked more like the Lady of Shalott than ever.

'John? It's Rob. Rob Russell. I've got some really bad news, I'm afraid.'

Haltingly, Rob told John how Father Salter had attempted to dismiss the force that they believed to be secreted in the cellar, and how it had ripped him into a fountain of bones.

John said, 'Oh, Jesus. That's terrible. That's just terrible. What are you going to do now?'

'I don't see that I have any choice, John. I'll have to try and get rid of the damned thing myself. What other chance do I have of getting our little Timmy back? And our Martin? And Ada?'

'Rob – do you have *any* idea what you're up against?

He may be walled up in your cellar but he's still on his home ground, and that makes him more powerful around here than any other presence you could think of, and that includes Old Dewer.'

'John, Vicky and I have been hit and kicked and bitten by dogs that jumped out of a stained-glass window. Of course I know what I'm up against, and that's the whole reason I'm calling you. Father Salter told me that he'd talked to you about this presence, whatever you call it. I'm wondering if you know anything at all about it that could help me. Anything.'

'I'm not entirely sure, but I might. Yesterday I was searching through some old parish records from Sampford Spiney, going right back to the late sixteenth century. They're all stored online these days, which makes it a whole lot easier. It seems that in June 1695 the parish priest of St Mary's was visited by one Matthew Carver from London, who said that he was – here, I've noted this down – "a remover by royal appointment of sundrie supernatural abominations".'

'What's that? A jobbing exorcist?'

'It sounds like it, doesn't it? Apparently he had been paid by the Crown to purge some of the navy's ships in Plymouth harbour of evil spirits. Their crews had been going down "with all manners of the foulest pox" and suffering any number of fatal accidents, like falling out of the rigging or getting themselves impaled by anchors. The suspicion was that they had been infected with these evil spirits by the French, sometime during the Nine Years' War.'

'So what was he doing in Sampford Spiney, this "remover of abominations"?'

'The parish priest recorded that Matthew Carver was a guest of the Wilmingtons at Allhallows Hall. He said that they had hired him to track down and remove the malevolent spirit called Old Dewer by some locals, but known also by other names, such as the Flute Player or the Fluter. He said that the Wilmingtons wanted this spirit exorcised because he had been randomly slaughtering their sheep and blighting their crops.'

Rob said, 'Wait a minute – Matthew Carver – that name rings a bell. There's a gravestone with that name on it in St Mary's churchyard. There's a Latin inscription on it, too, something about time standing still.'

'Listen, Rob, I don't want to jump to any erroneous conclusions,' John told him. 'What you're proposing to do – it's mind-blowingly dangerous, I mean it, and you could get yourself killed, like poor old Francis and Father Salter. But my first thought when I read about Matthew Carver was that the Wilmingtons didn't call him in to chase the Fluter away. Instead they'd asked him to catch him, or it, so that they could use its power to turn Nicholas Owen's priest's hide into a witching room – although God alone knows why they wanted to do that.'

'Don't talk to me about God, John. He's not exactly my favourite person at the moment – not that He ever was. But you reckon Matthew Carver could have been the one who caught this presence and bricked him up in the cellar?'

'Everything points to it, doesn't it? Although I may be wildly off beam.'

'But if this presence is so powerful – even more powerful than Satan – how did Matthew Carver catch him? That's what I need to know. Father Salter said something about every demon having an Achilles heel.'

'He mentioned that to me, too. He said that some demons couldn't stand the sound of bells, and some other demons you could chase off with smoke from particular herbs, or incense. There's one demon who's terrified of two-pronged forks, because he believes you're going to stick them into his eyes.'

'But this one?'

'He wasn't sure, and neither am I, to be honest, although I did look him up in *Catesby's Compendium of Pre-Druidic Demons*. It says in there that he was possessed with "the madness of dogs", and that he was never seen out when it was raining. That may suggest that he's infected with rabies, and because of that he suffers from hydrophobia. On the other hand, it may simply mean that he's a psychopath who doesn't like getting wet.'

Rob looked out of the window. The knobbly stalks of Brussels sprouts were glittering like pale green sceptres, and the overgrown rhubarb leaves were repeatedly nodding and nodding as the raindrops fell on them.

'It's raining now. Maybe this is the right time for me to chance it.'

'I don't know what to say, Rob. I know how desperate you are to rescue Timmy and your brother and Ada, but maybe we need to find out more about this Fluter before you try anything.'

'If I hold off any longer, it may be too late. And in any case, how *can* we find out more? This thing is a myth. It's a legend. It's a supernatural demon. How do we know if the stories that people have been telling about it are true? Just because nobody's ever seen it in the rain, that doesn't mean that it's *never* been out in the rain, or that it has some kind of aversion to water.'

'Why don't I come over and help you?'

'Because Francis and Father Salter have both been killed and I don't want to risk any more people dying because of me.'

John was silent for a few seconds. Then he said, 'All right, Rob. I can't stop you. But don't do anything rash, okay? You might have lost your Timmy, but as far as you know he's still alive. Ada and your brother too. Even if you never get them back, they'll still be there. Maybe they're not living a happy life, but it's better than no life at all.'

Rob ended the call and put down his phone. Vicky said, 'Well?'

'John says it may not like rain.'

'Is that all?'

'He's not even sure about that. But there's only one way to find out.'

Rob and Vicky went back into the drawing room, where Grace and Portia and Katharine were sitting around the fire.

Rob said, 'I'm going to have a crack at getting rid of this demon. I won't be trying any prayers or ritual chants or appeals to the Lord because I don't know any. I'm hoping that if I don't say anything religious to it then it won't get riled up the way it did with Francis and Father Salter. But if it *does* get angry—'

'What then?' asked Grace. 'What if it kills you, too? What are we supposed to do?'

'You'll have to decide that for yourselves. But if Francis and Father Salter couldn't get rid of it, and I can't, either, then I'd say that your only option would be to leave this bloody house and lock it up and never think of coming back. John Kipling said that Timmy and Martin and Ada Grey are probably still alive, and if Francis was right they'll probably live for ever.'

They sat looking at each other in silence. A draught whistled softly down the chimney, sending up a flurry of sparks and blowing a ghostly wraith of smoke between them.

'It's like Father Salter said to me, when I was driving him here from Tavistock. Sometimes you can be faced with something that frightens the living shit out of you, but life doesn't give you any other choice except to confront it head-on. Timmy's our son. I'm his father and I have to save him or die trying.'

'Rob—'

'No. Stay in here. Keep the door closed and no matter what you hear, don't come out until I call you, or until it goes totally quiet.'

He hugged Grace and gave her a kiss, and then he gave

Portia and Katharine a quick hug too. He held Vicky tightly and kissed her and then he gently stroked her cheek and said, 'Listen. I love you.'

Vicky nodded, unable to speak, with tears running down her cheeks. Rob kissed her again and then he walked out of the drawing room and closed the door behind him.

He passed the sealed-up cellar. The silhouette that Francis had left behind had almost completely faded now. He felt strangely buoyant and unafraid, as if he had always been destined to do this. It occurred to him that he had felt more fearful on the day he had given in his notice at the design studio where he had been working for four and a half years and started working as a freelance animator. He had been deeply in debt, with all his credit cards maxed out, and Vicky had been seven months pregnant with Timmy.

There was a narrow oak cupboard beside the front door, in which Herbert Russell always hung his house keys. He also used to keep a rubber-covered flashlight in there, in case he heard what he thought might be prowlers outside the house. Rob opened the cupboard and found to his relief that the flashlight was still there, and when he clicked it on, it worked. He pushed it into his inside pocket.

He opened the front door and crossed the courtyard to the larger of the granite barns, kicking aside a lump of stone from the shattered cherub. The rain was little more than a fine mist now, and he hoped that it would be enough to put the Fluter into a panic. That was always supposing that he really *was* hydrophobic, and that his fear of water wasn't just an old dummons' tale.

Forcing open the collapsed barn door, he went inside and crossed over to the gardening tools that he had seen when he was looking for Timmy. There was a shovel, a pitchfork, a pair of shears, two rakes and a sorry-looking broom with hardly any bristles, but what he was after was the pick. He walked back to the house with it, hefting it from one hand to the other, like a Viking warrior pumping himself up to meet his enemy with his battleaxe.

Back in the hallway, he stood in front of the sealed-up cellar, his eyes closed, his head bowed, trying to detect any vibration or any sensation that the force was aware he was there, and what he had in mind. After all, hadn't Father Salter said that it was so sensitive to its surroundings that it could hear a twig snap, even while it was imprisoned here in the cellar of Allhallows Hall?

The drawing-room door opened a few inches and Vicky called out softly, 'Rob?'

'I'm okay. Close the door, darling. Please.'

'No. Here, look. Take this. Just in case.'

He walked back to the door and saw that she was holding out a ten-inch carving knife from the kitchen. He hesitated, but then he took it, and said, 'Thanks. With any luck, I won't need it.'

She gave him a sad smile and then closed the door. He tucked the carving knife into his belt and went back to the sealed-up cellar.

He paused, took a deep breath, and then he almost ran towards the wall, holding the pickaxe high over his head. Using the silhouette of Francis's head as a target, he smashed it into the plaster. A lump the size of a breadboard clumped onto the floor, exposing the rough yellowish bricks underneath.

From inside the cellar, he heard a hoarse, grating groan, more like the cry of an agonised sea creature than the cry he would have expected from a malevolent spirit. The floorboards began to shudder underneath his trainers and a prickly wave of static came flying out of the wall. He felt as if he were facing into a blizzard of very fine sand.

He narrowed his eyes. *You're in there, you bastard, and no matter what you do, I'm coming in to get you.*

He struck the wall again and again until his shoulder muscles began to hurt. Most of the plaster dropped off easily, because it was mixed with horsehair, and the mortar between the bricks was not only old and crumbled but had clearly been slapped on by somebody in a hurry.

He knocked out two bricks, and then another three, and once their support had gone, almost all of the bricks underneath the header collapsed. He knocked them into the darkness with the point of his pickaxe, and he could hear them rattling and bouncing down the cellar steps. The remaining bricks stood knee-high and he kicked at them three or four times until they fell over.

The groaning had stopped, but the vibration and the prickly feeling of static in the air continued. He tugged the flashlight out of his inside pocket and pointed it into the cellar. He could see dusty brown cobwebs drooping down from the ceiling and he wondered how long they had been there. How had spiders managed to crawl in here, once it had been bricked up? Maybe those cobwebs were hundreds of years old.

He climbed over the broken bricks and started to make his way down the cellar steps, kicking aside more bricks as he went. When he breathed in, the air in the cellar smelled stale and dusty, but he could smell something else, too, something deeply unpleasant, like a chicken breast turned green.

The floor beneath his feet was littered with human bones, scores of them, and tattered clothes, and the clothes were stuck together with putrescent black slime. He saw at least five skulls, so Francis and Father Salter had not been the first to be pulled through the wall.

He pointed the flashlight upwards, and he could see the huge oak joists that supported the floor above him. They were all thick with woolly spiderwebs, and in some of the webs he could see the transparent skeletons of long-dead spiders.

The left wall of the cellar was lined to the ceiling with shelves. They were crowded with a collection of old wine bottles, all of them empty. Presumably the Wilmingtons had taken all their wine upstairs before the cellar was bricked up, and stored it in the larder.

Seven or eight large picture frames of tarnished gilt were leaning against the right wall, and standing guard beside them was a mangy stuffed fox with green glass eyes and a semicircular cobweb connecting its nose to its front feet.

Most of the cellar, though, was taken up with a massive tent-like structure of brown tarpaulin. This was suspended from the ceiling with an elaborate array of iron hooks and a cat's cradle of greasy ropes, and pinned to the floor with rusted iron stakes driven at yard-wide intervals into the hem all around it.

Rob carefully picked his way between the bones and shone his flashlight at the tarpaulin. It was completely opaque, and so he could see nothing inside it, although the rotten-chicken smell grew even more pungent as he approached it. The smell clung to his sinuses and he could taste it on his tongue. He shivered as if he were about to wet himself. His initial confidence had suddenly drained away, and he was seized with the urge to go bounding back up the cellar steps and shout at Vicky and Grace and Portia and Katharine to collect up their belongings and get out of the house right now – *now!* – and then to put as many miles between them and Sampford Spiney as they could before nightfall.

By now, the vibration had built up into a loud, nagging drone, so that sawdust was drifting from the ceiling and the hooks holding the tent to the joists above it were jiggling and clinking, and the empty wine bottles on the shelves were tinkling as if they found it amusing that he was so frightened.

With his heart palpitating, he circled around the tent, shining the flashlight this way and that. On the far side of the tent, he found where the tarpaulin was joined together. Both sides had been pierced by metal grommets and knotted together with cords.

There was another groan from inside the tent, followed by a long slurring sound, like somebody trying to breathe with congested lungs, and then a rustling noise.

Oh shit. I can't do this. I need to get out of here. How is this going to bring Timmy back? I've lost him, just like so many grieving parents lose their children. I've lost him for ever and I'll have to accept it. Martin, too. And Ada Grey. I simply can't do this.

Strangely, though, as if it didn't belong to him, his left hand drew the kitchen knife out of his belt and started to slice evenly and deliberately at the knots that were holding the two sides of the tarpaulin together. The rope was hemp, tarred black like liquorice, and tightly twisted.

From inside the tent came yet another groan, and then a voice said, '*Art thee?*' At least, that was what Rob thought it said, because it was gurgling and clogged-up and it had such a strong accent.

He didn't answer, but kept on slicing. He cut through three, four, five knots, and gradually the two sides of the tarpaulin started to sag apart.

'What art thee?' the voice repeated – still gurgling, still thickly accented, but much clearer this time. 'Not *grove,* art thou? Not conventus? And not holy Papist, neither.'

'I've come to release you, that's all,' Rob said, in a voice far less steady than he had intended. 'I've come to let you out of here.'

'Thy coming... it was foretold! The rule of three! A sacrificer, then a priest, and then a kiffy man of no faith!'

Rob cut through the last knot but he kept his knife in his hand. Using only his forearms, he pushed the tarpaulin flaps wide open and shone his flashlight into the tent. The smell was so sweet and so foul that he couldn't stop himself from retching. Two grey reflective eyes looked up at him.

'So... thou hast come to release me at last, as it was spoken in the stars a hundred and twenty thousand and sixteen days ago – a hundred and twenty thousand and sixteen days ago to the very day. Here, then, sever my bonds, o man of no faith. Thee and me, we shall ride the moors and be faithless together. My name is Esus, and thou may call me Esus, and consider thyself my servant from this day forth.'

39

Inside the tent stood a long wooden trestle, draped over with layer upon layer of filthy grey blankets. The figure that was lying on the blankets appeared to be a man, but he was at least a foot taller than most men. He was dressed in a jerkin and breeches of rough black suede, criss-crossed with thin leather straps, with leather gauntlets on his hands and heavy black riding boots with bucket tops. His wrists and ankles were bolted to the trestle with thick iron hoops. The stench he gave off was almost unbearable, as if he had soiled himself again and again, for every one of those a hundred and twenty thousand and sixteen days.

Rob shone the flashlight into his face. It was long and narrow, with sharp triangular cheekbones, a long curved nose with white hair sprouting out of his nostrils and a chisel-like chin. His hair was white and long and wild, shoulder-length at least. His lips were white, too, as white as the ghost slugs that Francis had stuck on the wall, and drawn back across his pointed irregular teeth in a condescending snarl.

It was his eyes that disturbed Rob the most. They were plain silver, with no pupils or irises, and slightly wolf-like in shape, but even though they had no pupils or irises they still seemed to be staring at him directly, with an expression that was partly pleased and partly mocking, as if he were thinking, *You don't know what you've let yourself in for, do you?*

Rob stood beside him, the back of his left hand pressed against his nose and mouth, trying to suppress his breathing so that he wouldn't retch a second time.

'Was it Matthew Carver who brought you here?'

Esus tossed his white hair contemptuously. 'Carver, that dawcock! Thought he could best me. Locked me down here right enough, but I dragged the raymes right out of him before he could walk half a chain.'

'Do you know *why* he wanted to lock you up?'

''Course I do. It's 'cause of my power to hold back time, should anyone call on me to do it, and should anyone chant the right chant.'

'You know that there are people in this house who are trapped in time, because of you.'

'I have no say in it. If the chant is chanted, my power is drawn from me, if'n I will it or if'n not.'

'But when you leave here, when I set you free, those people will be set free too?'

Esus looked at Rob slyly. 'Why dursn't thou release me, burd, and discover that consequence out for thyself?'

'That's all very well. But if *they* won't be set free, there's no point in my setting *you* free, is there?'

'Ah, but if thou decideth *narrrt* to release me, I'll juggle the bones right out of thee as soon as blink. Thy leg would make for a gurt fine flute.'

Esus raised his head from the trestle and grinned at him, and Rob thought, *I can't believe this. I must be going out of my mind. I'm down in the cellar of Allhallows Hall trying to bargain with a demon.*

With horns and a tail and a forked tongue like Satan, Esus would have been scary enough, but it was his down-to-earth rustic clothes and his slurry Devon accent and his creepy insinuating threats that Rob found so terrifying. Even locked up here he had the power to drag the skeletons out of living people, and pull them through walls, so who could guess what he might do if Rob were to set him free. He might simply disappear and cause no more trouble, but even if he did, Rob had no way of knowing for certain that they would ever get Timmy or Martin or Ada back.

'Well?' Esus croaked, and his throat cackled with phlegm. 'What's it to be? Wilt thou release me, kiffy man, or watch thy raymes jump out of thy skin for a dance on its own? I'd play it a right merry jig if my hands was free.'

'You're so powerful, I'm surprised you couldn't pull off those shackles yourself.'

'Oh, *zurrprized*, art thou? That tells me thou knowest naught about magic and spells. These irons, they was forged with a curse that not even God Himself could unweave.'

Rob said nothing, but lifted up the pickaxe, turned it upside down, and forced one pointed end into the space between Esus's left wrist and the iron hoop that was holding it there. He pushed the handle sideways, leaning against it with his whole weight, and gradually the bolts that were holding the hoop came squeaking out of the trestle. The hoop dropped to the floor with a clank and Esus lifted his arm and flapped it three times to shake off his gauntlet. His bare hand was white and finely wrinkled and claw-like, with liver spots and long curved nails.

'Arrh,' he said, and reached up to claw at his withered neck. 'To scratch again, what a boon that is, and when I'm free I'll scratch every crevice of me, between my toes, and my ballsack too.'

Rob pushed his way under the tarpaulin to the other side of the trestle, and started to prise off the iron hoop from Esus's right wrist. This one was fixed more firmly, and he had to pump down on the pickaxe handle again and again before the hoop finally dropped off and clanged onto the floor. Esus shook the gauntlet off this hand, too, and then lifted himself up into a sitting position. His stench was so strong and his jerkin was so rough and greasy when it rubbed against Rob's hand that Rob retched again, and his mouth filled with bile, which he was forced to swallow.

'Come on, now, kiffy man, let's be having my feet free! If I'm not walking the moors again before ten minutes is up, I'll be carving a curvy whistle out of thy rib, I promise thee that. *The Kiffy Man's Lament*, that's what I'll be after playing thee, except that thou'll be naught but bones and natlins by then, and deaf to even the prettiest tune.'

Rob wrenched the iron hoops from around Esus's bucket boots. Then, half-stifled, he pushed the heavy tarpaulin aside and struggled his way out of the tent. He realised then that the vibration that had been shaking the house had abruptly stopped.

'There,' he told Esus. 'You can go now. You can leave this house and never come back.'

Esus slowly eased his legs off the trestle. He sat there for a while, tugging on his gauntlets again and staring at Rob with his silvery eyes.

'Tell me, kiffy man, what is the world like now?'

'I don't think you'll recognise it, although the moors haven't changed that much. Not nearly so many trees.'

'One hundred and twenty thousand and sixteen days have passed, and I have aged not. I'll need thee to stay with me, to be my servant and my guide.'

'I've set you free. I'm not doing any more.'

'Thou believest that thou hast a choice, thou bag of whistles?'

'The moors are out there. There's plenty of places where you can hide yourself.'

'I will need *hounds*! Thou willst have to acquire hounds for me.'

'Esus, those days are gone – long gone. You can't go hunting for babies any more.'

'There must still be chrisemores. Don't tell me that the world has become more devotional to that skyfool.'

Rob held up the pickaxe in his left hand, and shook it, to show that he meant business. His chest was heaving and his throat was so constricted with stress that he could barely speak. 'Listen – I've released you so that my son and all the other people trapped in this house can go free. But that's all I'm doing for you. I'm going now, and you can get yourself out of here as soon as you like.'

He backed away from the tent, still holding up the pickaxe, and kicking aside some of the bones on the floor with his heels. Esus stood up, and he was so tall that his fraying white hair touched the joist above his head. He took one unsteady step towards Rob, and then another, but it was obvious that centuries of being shackled to that trestle had atrophied his muscles and tightened his tendons. He was a supernatural creature, but he still needed a physical presence so that he could walk the earth. As Rob's divinity teacher had once told him, 'Even Satan has to have a heart.'

Rob reached the cellar steps. Esus was still coming towards him, but very slowly, his bucket boots shuffling through the bones and the slimy rags.

'I'll leave the front door open for you,' Rob told him. 'Once you're gone, though, I never want to see your face again.'

Esus didn't answer him. He kept on coming, stiffly and painfully, but relentlessly, gritting his sharp crowded teeth with every step that he took. Rob mounted the steps and climbed up to the top, stepping out through the broken hole in the wall and back into the hallway.

Because the vibration had stopped, Vicky opened the drawing-room door and looked out.

'Rob? Rob! You're all right! Have you done it? Has it gone?'

'Don't come out yet, Vicks. He's still down there.'

Rob went across to the front door and opened it wide. Although the courtyard outside was wet and puddly, it had stopped raining now. *Please let it be wet enough to weaken him, even if it doesn't do for him completely.*

He stood at the foot of the staircase, holding up the pickaxe in both hands now, breathing hard, waiting for Esus to appear in the cellar doorway. He could hear Esus groaning and his boots scraping with every step that he took, but he couldn't yet see him in the darkness.

He was still waiting when he heard whispering coming from upstairs. To begin with, only two or three whisperers, but then more. Soon it sounded as if the landing was crowded with whisperers, all speaking quickly and excitedly. He looked up, and saw five tough-looking men peering over the balustrade. Four of them were shaven-headed, but one had black hair greased up like a shark's fin. These men were whispering to each other, too, with great intensity.

'Hey – you!' Rob called up to them. 'Who are you?'

They carried on whispering to each other, but didn't answer him. The one with the shark's-fin hair turned away, though, and Rob saw him beckoning, and after a few moments a thin-faced priest appeared, wearing a dog collar. He made the sign of the cross, and said, 'Is it you, my brother, who has released the malevolence that has been holding us here?'

'Esus. Yes. He's coming out of the cellar right now.'

'We are whole again, may God bless you. All of us are whole again.'

'Is my son there? Little Timmy?'

'We dare not come down until the malevolence has quit this house completely.'

'I said, is my son there? Timmy? He's only five. Timmy! Are you up there? Timmy! It's Daddy! Can you hear me? Martin – are you there?'

The priest turned away, and Rob started to climb the stairs. At that moment, though, Esus stepped out from the cellar doorway, so tall that he had to stoop down under the header, his white hair wild, dusty cobwebs flying from his shoulders. He saw Rob on the opposite side of the hallway and screamed, '*Here! 'Tis thee I want with me now!*'

He came hobbling across to the staircase, but Rob swung the pickaxe at him, right and left, and although he didn't hit him, Esus took a staggering step back, and then another.

Rob ran for the open front door. If he could get Esus out of the house, maybe Timmy and all the rest of the whisperers would be free of his curse at last. He crossed the courtyard, splashing in the puddles. When he reached the gateway, he looked over his shoulder and saw that Esus was already out of the front door and coming after him – limping, as if one knee had seized up, but so long-legged that he was gaining on him fast.

He pushed his hand into his jacket pocket and pulled out his car keys. Running towards his Honda, he pressed the key fob and tugged open the driver's door. He was about to climb in when he realised that Esus had almost caught up with him, so he turned around and slung the pickaxe at him as hard as he could. It hit Esus on his upraised arm, and he stumbled down onto the shingle on one knee, which gave Rob just enough time to scramble into the driver's seat, jab the key into the ignition and start the engine. The door was still half open, though, and Esus picked himself up and made a grab for the handle.

'*Thou cans't escape Esus!*' he screamed. '*No man can't never escape Esus!*'

Rob jammed his foot on the accelerator pedal and the Honda's rear wheels showered up shingle before it slewed along the driveway towards the road. Esus was still hanging on to the handle and his boots were dragging along the ground, so Rob opened the door wider and then slammed it.

He looked quickly in his mirror, expecting to see Esus lying on the ground behind him, but instead he heard a loud thumping and a scrambling sound on the Honda's roof. Then he heard something scrabbling at his side window, and when he glanced to his right he saw that Esus's curved fingernails were clawing at the glass. Somehow he had managed to climb on top of the car and was clinging on to the window frames.

Rob felt a sickening surge of helplessness. Esus had the body of a man, or a body that resembled a man, but he was a malevolent spirit, not a man, with powers that could only be guessed at. If he had been able to kill Francis and Father Salter so easily, he must be able to kill *him*, too – drag the skeleton out of his body like boning a turkey. He could only guess that he hadn't killed him already because he wanted him to be his servant and to familiarise him with a world he hadn't seen since the late seventeenth century.

Esus drummed his fist on the roof. '*Stop!*' he roared. '*Stop or I shall kill thee!*'

Rob swerved the Honda from one side of the lane to the other, trying to shake Esus off. He could see the toes of his bucket boots in the top of the back window, so he must be spread-eagled on the roof. He swerved again, and again, and deliberately drove up the grassy bank on either side, so that the car jolted and bounced, but Esus clung on as tightly as if he were magnetic.

Water, Rob thought. *I need to find water. A leat, a river. A ford.*

He sped south on the Dousland Road at over seventy miles an hour, through Yelverton, swerving as violently as he could. Several other drivers blew their horns at him and as he weaved his way through the middle of the town he came close to colliding with a bus. Still Esus held on, and started hammering even harder on the roof. As Rob turned down Meavy Lane, with the Honda's tyres shrieking operatically, Esus smashed his windscreen into a milky jigsaw, and suddenly he was blinded.

He hit the high banking on the side of the road and there was a loud crunch as his nearside mudguard struck a tree stump. He managed to steer back into the middle of the lane and then he punched at the windscreen with his fist. His first punch only made the shattered glass bulge outwards, but then he punched it again, even harder, and he succeeded in knocking a jagged hole in it that allowed him to see enough of the lane up ahead.

'*Stop! I give thee but one more chance!*' roared Esus. But Rob was surging with adrenaline now and his confidence was beginning to grow. *He* needs *me,* he thought: *he really needs me, or else he would have killed me already. He's found himself in a world that he doesn't understand at all, speeding along unfamiliar roads, desperately clinging on to a vehicle that can travel faster than anything he has ever seen, a vehicle without any horses.*

After he had driven through Hoo Meavy, he saw that he was approaching the Dewerstone car park. *Water,* he thought. *The River Plym.* He slewed into the car park in a shower of grit, and as he did so an attendant in a high-vis jerkin strode forward, waving at him frantically to slow down and stop.

'Hi! Stop, there! You've someone on your roof!'

Rob ignored him and circled around the parked cars until he reached the wooden footbridge at the far side of the car park. The bridge rattled loudly as he drove over it, and onto the rough granite track that had once been a tramway for iron miners. He knew where he was going: the tramway wound a steep and tortuous path up through the woods, all the way to the summit known as the Devil's Rock, two hundred metres above sea level. The Honda lurched and bumped and its suspension clonked but Rob kept his foot down. One of Esus's talon-like hands appeared in the hole that he had punched in the windscreen and started to tear away the broken glass, piece by piece, furiously pulling it free from its polyvinyl interlayer.

Rob drove higher and higher through the woods. The sun had come out and the light flickered through the trees like a stroboscope. He scattered a group of hikers, who shouted obscenities at him and shook their fists, and as he spun the wheel to avoid another elderly walker with a backpack he struck a glancing blow against a fir tree, denting his offside wing and cracking his headlight.

'*Stop!*' screamed Esus. He had now torn away so much of the windscreen that he was able to lean over from the roof and stare in at Rob, his face upside down, his white hair flailing wildly and his silver eyes even more wolf-like with anger. '*Stop, or I will pull thy raymes out now!*'

He reached into the car with one hand and seized the top of the steering wheel, twisting it violently from side to side. The Honda collided with one tree after another, with a series of loud, hollow bangs, but Rob slammed his foot down even harder on the accelerator, half-lifting himself off the seat so that he was pressing down on the pedal with his full weight.

With its tyres squittering on the granite, the car shot forward, straight towards the brink of the Dewerstone. Beyond that was nothing but a two-hundred-foot drop to the River Plym below. At the last moment, Rob kicked down on the brake pedal and yanked up the handbrake. The car tilted, nose down, and for a split second he was sure that he was too late, and that the car was going to go flying off the precipice and into the air.

In that same split second, a picture flashed into his mind of Vicky bringing up Timmy without him, but he thought, *At least I've saved Timmy from Allhallows Hall.*

The Honda's front wheels went over the edge, but then it lurched to an abrupt stop, its back wheels jammed into a deep crevice in the rocks. At the same time, Esus lost his grip on the roof and slid forward, head first, and fell. As he plummeted down, he let out a scream like no scream that Rob had ever heard before. It sounded like a choir of demons, twenty demons rather than one, each voice shrieking louder than the other. It grew fainter and fainter and then, except for the softly fluffing wind, there was silence.

Rob gingerly eased open his door and stepped out onto the rocks. Several people were running towards him, but he went to the very edge and looked over.

He was in time to see that, far below him, Esus had plunged into the river, which was fast-flowing with foaming rapids. At first it looked as if he had miraculously survived the fall from the top of the Dewerstone, because he was thrashing his arms and legs. But then Rob saw that a dark streak was bleeding away from him and flowing away downstream. The streak grew darker and blacker and wider, and after a minute Rob realised what he was looking at.

'Here, bloody hell – did I just see what I thought I just saw?' said a grey-haired hiker, hurrying up to stand beside him.

'No,' said Rob, without looking at him. 'You didn't.'

'I saw a fellow falling right off of the top of your motor there, I'm sure of it.'

'No,' said Rob. 'There was nobody.'

'Well, my eyes must have deceived me, then, because I swear blind that's what I saw.'

'Yes,' said Rob. 'They must. Deceived you, I mean.'

The black streak in the River Plym gradually thinned out, like an oil slick, and soon it had slithered off between the rocks altogether. So John Kipling had been right that Esus was afraid of water, and now Rob had seen why. It could dissolve him.

Esus, sometimes known as the Bonebiter, or the Fluter, the demon mistaken by Dartmoor folk for the Devil, or Old Dewer as they called him, had melted away in the water that he had always dreaded.

A woman in a woolly hat and a bulky red sweater came up to Rob and said, 'Are you all right, love?'

'I don't know yet,' he said. 'It's still too early to say. But thank you for asking.'

40

It was three hours before he could return to Allhallows Hall. Two police officers came from Crownhill to question him and give him a breathalyser test, and a tow truck had to be called in from Tavistock to haul his damaged Honda down off the Dewerstone.

'There's witnesses here that say they saw a man hanging on to the roof of your car as it come up through the woods, and that he went toppling off when you come to a sudden stop at the edge here.'

Rob shook his head. 'No. It wasn't a man. It was only a black rubbish bag full of old clothes that I was taking to the Cancer Research charity shop in Plymouth.'

'Those two climbers over there, they're dead sure that it was a man.'

'You haven't found a body in the river, have you?'

'No, we haven't. But we haven't found no rubbish sack full of old clothes, neither.'

'Maybe the bag burst open and they just got washed away.'

The police officers looked at each other and shrugged. Without a body they had to accept what Rob had told them, and even though he had taken a glass of his father's whiskey, he was well under the limit for alcohol. They cautioned him and said that they would be considering a charge of dangerous driving, but that he was free to go. In fact, they would give him a lift back to Sampford Spiney.

While he waited for the police officers to make notes and take photographs, he borrowed a phone from one of them so that he could call Vicky to tell her he was safe. He didn't mention Esus because the police were in earshot.

All he said was, 'It's all over, Vicks. He's gone, and he's never coming back. Is Timmy there? And Martin?'

'I don't *know*, Rob. I just don't know. The whisperers won't come downstairs and they won't let any of us go up. One of them's a priest and he says they're still afraid. "Mortally fearful", that's what he said.'

'What are they afraid of? He's *gone*.'

'They say they need proof that he's never coming back. They still think he's going to take his revenge on them because they were the only reason he was kept shut up in the cellar for so many hundreds of years. They're absolutely terrified that he's going to trap them in time all over again, or else he's going to kill them.'

'Have you asked this priest if Timmy's there?'

'Yes, but he wouldn't say.'

'Listen, darling. Try to stay calm. I'll be back as soon as I can. But you can tell that priest, you can tell all those whisperers, they're free now.'

He looked across at his dented and damaged Honda, and saw that one of Esus's gauntlets was still caught in the handle of the driver's door.

'Tell them I can bring them proof.'

The police drove him back to Allhallows Hall. Both officers were friendly and chatty, although one of them kept shaking his head and laughing and saying, 'I've seen motocross before, but I've never yet seen nobody try to drive up to the top of the Dewerstone. I can't think for the life of me what must have been going through your head to do that.'

Rob smiled tightly but didn't answer. He couldn't stop thinking of Esus staring through the shattered windscreen at him, upside down, his silver eyes shining with hatred.

When they turned into the driveway of Allhallows Hall, he saw that there were two other police cars there already, as well as DI Holley's car, and John Kipling's, too.

'Hello,' said one of the officers. 'Looks like the dicks is here, for some reason.'

As soon as he climbed out of the police car, Vicky came out of the front door and ran up to meet him. He hugged her and kissed her, and then he held up the gauntlet.

'Proof,' he said.

DI Holley and DC Cutland were standing outside in the courtyard, talking to John Kipling. Five uniformed officers were standing around, looking impatient.

'I gather you've been doing some rather adventurous cross-country motoring, Mr Russell,' said DI Holley.

'Yes,' said Rob. 'I've already been cautioned.'

'Anything to do with what's going on here, by any chance?'

'You know what's going on here?'

'Your lady wife has given us a pretty comprehensive picture of the situation, which is why we've refrained up until now from entering the premises. To be frank with you, it's all extremely hard to believe. But – incredible as they are – the facts do appear to tally, and she's begged us not to go barging into the house with undue haste, and so we haven't.'

'What has she told you?'

'She's said that the house has been covertly occupied for some time by a number of males who appear to be criminals. She explained that there's a particular room in which they've been concealing themselves, and that this room has some highly unusual properties. She said that she hesitated to use the term "supernatural" but that's what these properties appeared to be.'

'What are these facts that you mentioned?'

DC Cutland passed DI Holley a thick plastic folder and DI Holley held it up. 'All I actually came here today to tell you was that we've completed our investigation into all those prisoners whose suitcases were found in the attic of this house. We certainly didn't anticipate this stand-off situation.'

'You've found out who those prisoners were?'

'Oh, yes. The present governor at Dartmoor was extremely cooperative. The records show that every one of them was approached by your father, the late Mr Herbert Russell, when he was governor. Each of them was offered a transfer to Ford Open Prison in Sussex to take part in the Social Conscience programme, which carried with it a strong possibility of early release.'

Rob glanced towards the open front door. Vicky was there now, waiting for him, and he could see that she was growing increasingly distressed. He lifted his hand to show her that he wouldn't be talking to DI Holley much longer.

'What I came to tell you was that none of those prisoners ever arrived at Ford,' DI Holley went on. 'Not one of them. They were collected from Princetown by a private security company called Headlock and driven away and that was the last that anybody saw of them. When their relatives came to visit them at Dartmoor, they were informed that they had absconded.

'There is not and never has been a private security company called Headlock. And when our forensic accountants ran checks on the bank accounts and other liquid assets of the missing prisoners, we found that shortly before their disappearance all of them had made substantial transfers of funds to a company based in Tavistock called Florence Holdings.'

'Florence,' said Rob. 'That was my mother's name.'

DI Holley raised both eyebrows. 'I'm afraid to say that all the evidence now points to your late father, Herbert Russell, having extorted payments from those inmates at Dartmoor who he knew or suspected still to be harbouring substantial criminal assets after their convictions. We also managed to gain partial access to the accounts of Florence Holdings and it appears that in the last ten years of his tenure as governor of Dartmoor Prison, Herbert Russell was paid well over seven and a half million pounds by those inmates to whom he had offered the chance of early release. Very little of it is left. Florence Holdings now has assets of less than fifteen hundred pounds.'

'He must have spent *all* of it on gambling,' said Rob. 'He never made it a secret that he bet on the horses, and he liked to play blackjack and roulette at Genting's Casino in

Plymouth whenever he could. But we never had any idea that he was betting on that scale.'

'In the coming weeks we'll be looking into your late father's accounts even more comprehensively,' said DI Holley. 'But from what we've discovered so far, I don't think there's any doubt about what he was up to. The crucial question that's facing us today is – what happened to all those prisoners who disappeared, and are the individuals who are now on your property those very same men? Did your late father keep them in hiding here for all these years? And if so, how?

'We've been talking to Mr Kipling here and he's explained his theory to us. As I've said, it seems unbelievable, but it coincides in a great many respects with what your lady wife has just told us, and so far there seems to be no alternative explanation that makes any sense.'

'He's told you about the witching room? And the way that the people in there come out at night and whisper? He's told you that our son, Timmy, was probably taken that way, too? And my brother, Martin? And Ada Grey?'

John said, 'Yes, Rob. I've told them everything. There didn't seem any reason not to, not now.'

'The *force* – the presence that was keeping them all here – it's gone for good,' said Rob. 'You can believe it or not, but it was a demon of sorts, called Esus. It was imprisoned in the cellar and I let it out. It fell into the Plym, John. Well, I gave it some help to fall into the Plym. It just – *dissolved*. I saw it, and that's the only word I can think of. It dissolved.'

'Is that what you were up to, with your reckless driving?' asked DI Holley. 'You almost drove off the edge of the Dewerstone, from what I was told.'

'It's gone, that's all I need to tell you at the moment, detective inspector. It's gone, and it's never going to come back.'

John said, 'I've found out why the Wilmingtons asked Matthew Carver to install a witching room in Allhallows Hall. It's explained in a letter that Matthew Carver wrote to his cousin, who was a lieutenant in the navy, when the Wilmingtons first asked him if he could do it.

'They were being persistently threatened by a Jesuit priest called Father Thomas Blakely. He had discovered that, years before, the Wilmingtons had refused to acknowledge to the priest hunters that they had hidden a priest called Father Ambrose in Allhallows Hall, or that they even knew who he was. They were an influential family, and even if they had forfeited some of their property as a punishment, Father Ambrose would never have been tortured and executed. At worst, he might have been exiled.

'Father Thomas was the great-nephew of Father Ambrose, and the good work that Father Ambrose had done in healing the sick and taking care of the poor was legendary in his family. So Father Thomas threatened to get his revenge on the Wilmingtons by reporting them to the Crown authorities. The Wilmingtons decided it would be too risky to have him murdered, and so they arranged for Matthew Carver to trap him in the witching room, for ever. There's an implication in his letter that the Wilmingtons had other enemies, too. Perhaps they believed that having a witching room in Allhallows Hall would be an effective way of disposing of anybody who crossed them, if and when they needed to.

'There's no written evidence to prove it, Rob, but I can only assume that your father found out somehow about the witching room and the chant that could trap people in it, and decided it would be an effective way to make himself some money.'

Rob looked over at Vicky again. She was beckoning him to hurry up.

'It's over now, detective inspector,' Rob told him. 'It's really over. Whatever year or month or day these men have been trapped in, they're free to go.' He held up the gauntlet and said, 'Apparently they're only waiting for proof that Esus has gone for good.'

'And that's it? That glove? Let's go and tell them, then. But you realise that if they are who we're guessing they are – inmates unlawfully released by your late father from Dartmoor Prison – we'll have to arrest all of those who have yet to complete their sentences. It won't make any difference how long they've been banged up in that so-called witching room of yours.'

DC Cutland showed him a clipboard. 'We have the complete list of their names here. All those who were promised by Governor Russell that they would be eligible for the Social Conscience programme. And there's a van on its way from Crownhill.'

They crossed the courtyard and entered the house. As they approached the foot of the staircase, they could hear frenzied whispering from up on the landing. Rob thought: they could have spoken in their normal voices

380

now, but they must have been whispering for so long that they were afraid to talk out loud.

Vicky was already there, next to the dark broken-open doorway to the cellar, and as Rob and John and the police officers came in, Grace and Portia and Katharine came out of the drawing room, too.

DI Holley went to the bottom stair and looked up. At least seven whisperers were looking back down at him, including the one with the shark's-fin hair.

'Right,' he said to Rob. 'You'd better tell those fellows that the boogie man's gone and they can come down.' He paused, and thoughtfully cracked his knuckles, one by one. 'If they don't, though, we'll have to go up and fetch them. By force, if necessary. Two of the officers outside are equipped. This whole situation has already gone far beyond the bounds of what you might describe as reasonable.'

Rob climbed up the first three stairs, and they creaked loudly as always. The whispering died down, although more of the whisperers came to the balustrade and leaned over.

'The presence that was keeping you trapped in time here has gone for ever,' Rob announced. 'I drove Esus to the River Plym and he fell in, and that's the last the world will ever see of him. You can feel now how real you are, can't you? You can come down, and you can walk out of this house, and you need never come back here again.'

He held up the gauntlet and waved it from side to side. 'You see this? This is his glove – Esus or the Fluter or Old Dewer or whatever you want to call him. He's gone, I promise you.'

There was yet another flurry of whispering. Then,

slowly and cautiously, the whisperers began to descend the staircase. The priest was first. Rob took him to be the Father Thomas that John had told him about – the vengeful priest for whom the witching room had been installed in the first place. He was followed by three thuggish-looking men with shaven heads and tattoos, and then, to Rob's relief, by Martin, looking dazed. If Martin had been freed, then surely Timmy must have been, too, although he didn't want to tempt fate by shouting out his name.

As the men came down, they gathered in the hallway, and DC Cutland and two other officers went up to them, one after the other, asking their names. Father Thomas stood on his own in the corner, his head bowed as if he were praying. When Martin came down, he stared at Rob as if he couldn't believe his eyes, and then said, 'Rob. Thank God.' Katharine ran up to him and threw her arms around him, sobbing.

Two or three of the men in old-fashioned dress appeared to be utterly bewildered. Bartram stumbled on the stairs and had to make a grab for the banister rail to stop himself from falling over.

Ada Grey came down, looking shocked. John took hold of her hand and led her into the drawing room, where she could sit down. He asked her again and again how she felt, but she was speechless. All she could do was open and close her mouth and shake her head.

Last of all, Jaws descended the stairs, and in his arms he was carrying Timmy, although Timmy's arms and legs were floppy and he looked as if he were sleeping.

Vicky let out a cry of sheer joy, and ran up the stairs to

meet him. Rob felt his eyes fill with tears, and he couldn't help thinking: *That God that I don't believe in, maybe I do now.*

Although Vicky held out her arms for Timmy, Jaws wouldn't hand him to her. He came right down to the hallway, still holding him, and stood there for a moment like a sportsman who has just been awarded a trophy.

DI Holley went up to him and said, 'You – what's your name?'

'Shearing, if you must know. Ron Shearing, Usually known as Jaws.'

'Well, now, Mr Shearing. Why don't you hand this young lad back to his mother so that this can all end happily ever after?'

Jaws looked down at Timmy and smiled. 'He ain't asleep. He's hypnotised. We had to do it to stop him from crying all the time. Lenny over there, he done it. Used to be a wossname – hypnotherapist.'

'That's enough, whatever. Hand him over.'

'But we've got a connection, this little fellow and me. We're bonded, flesh and blood. You don't know how much I love him.'

'What the blazes are you burbling on about? I said, hand him over.'

Jaws looked across at Rob and winked at him. 'I love this little fellow because he's my grandson – and that bloke standing right next to you, that's my son.'

'*What?* You're mental, you are.'

'No, I'm not,' said Jaws. He bent his head down and kissed Timmy on the forehead, and then he carefully lifted him up and passed him over to Vicky. Vicky took him and immediately hurried him out of the hallway and into the drawing room.

Rob stayed where he was, staring at Jaws in disbelief. 'I'm not your son, whoever the hell you are.'

'Oh yes, you are, mate. Do you want to take a DNA test? I was one of the first ones that fucking Herbert Russell trapped in this house, pardon my French, but at first he didn't catch on that when the moon was full, we always had a few hours of being real. We couldn't leave the house but we was *real*. Solid.

'One day during the fulness he had a row with his missus like you wouldn't believe. Yelling at her, whacking her. He was a right fucking bastard. She come running upstairs and into one of the bedrooms to get away from him, and so I went in after her to give her some comfort. Well, she fucking deserved it, I can tell you. She was a lovely woman, lovely. We got talking and I calmed her down and after that we spent the night together.'

'You made my mother pregnant?'

'Not on purpose, mate, but I didn't have a johnny, did I?'

'But how do you know that I'm yours?'

'Because your mum and your dad never slept together for nearly six months after that. I know, because I used to come out at night and stand there for hours and watch her sleeping. I used to watch you, too, when you was growing up. Sometimes I used to kip under your bed, just to hear you breathing. So don't try and tell me that I wasn't a good father to you, as much as I could be.'

Rob didn't know what else to ask him, or what else to say. The conversation that he had overheard between his father and his mother now made perfect sense, and so did the fact that he bore no resemblance to his father at all.

It was DC Cutland, though, who came to the most damning conclusion of all.

'The DNA on that hammer that was used to kill Herbert Russell... that must have been yours, Shearing. Did you kill Herbert Russell?'

Jaws did nothing but give him one of his condescending smiles. 'What do you reckon, Mr Dick?'

It took a little over half an hour for all the whisperers to be identified. Thirteen prisoners from Dartmoor who still had unfinished sentences were taken to one side and handcuffed, including Jaws. Five more police officers arrived from Crownhill so that they could all be boarded into a van and driven back to prison.

The whisperer called Wellie was first out of the front door, but he had taken only two steps before he pitched sideways onto the granite paving stones and lay there shuddering. DC Cutland knelt down beside him to see if he could give him CPR, but when he turned him over onto his back he was shocked to see that he had aged at least twenty years. His moustache was white, most of his hair had fallen out, and his face was puckered and wrinkled. His heart had stopped beating and it was clear that he was dead.

'Guv,' said DC Cutland. 'Come and look at this. He's only snuffed it.'

DI Holley bent down beside him. Wellie was staring up at them with pearl-white eyes and his mouth hanging open.

'Christ. Maybe we should—' DI Holley began, but it was too late. The remaining twelve prisoners had already been led in a straggling line out of the front door, and as they came outside they all showed instant and dramatic signs of aging. Professor Corkscrew dropped to his knees, coughing. Yet another prisoner staggered and fell over sideways, hitting his head on the paving stones. After less than half a minute, only eight of them were left standing, and the rest were lying on the ground, either gasping for breath or dead.

Bartram appeared in the doorway, almost blocking it.

'No!' shouted DC Cutland. 'Stay inside!'

But Bartram took two steps forward and immediately thumped face first into the porch. His long leather jerkin fell flat, and by the time DC Cutland reached him his russet curls were iron-grey and there was nothing inside his jerkin but bones and dust.

The last to come out was Father Thomas. DC Cutland made no attempt to stop him. He could see now that what was happening to all the whisperers was nothing more than their real age catching up with them. They had remained suspended for decades, some of them, while the ones they called pilgrims had lived out their lives and grown older and died. Now it was their turn.

It looked as if Father Thomas knew what was going to happen to him. He stepped over Bartram's jerkin with his eyes lifted to heaven and his hands pressed together in prayer. He cried out, '*Lord! Turn back the clock!*' but he managed to take only three steps before his head dropped down into the neck of his cassock and he collapsed like a demolished chimney.

Rob had heard the shouting. He left Vicky in the drawing room and hurried to the front door to see what was happening.

DI Holley said, 'Don't come out, Mr Russell. It looks like time has taken its toll.'

Rob looked across the courtyard, where the eight remaining prisoners were waiting for the police van to be reversed up to the gateway. He saw Jaws staring at him, and smiling. He was no longer an orphan, but finding out who his real father was made him feel as if he were standing naked in an icy wind, at night, with no shelter – a wind that would never stop blowing until the day he died.

He went back to the drawing room. Vicky was tearfully cradling Timmy in Herbert's throne, but Timmy's eyes were fluttering open as he came out of his hypnotised state and he was clinging tightly to his mother.

Martin and Katharine were standing beside them. Martin was smiling and shaking his head with relief.

'That priest, Thomas... has he gone now?' he asked Rob.

'He's totally gone, Mart. He just fell apart. There's nothing of him left but bones and dust.'

'That's all he deserved. It was *him* who trapped me. When I was stuck in that room, my mind was like a bloody kaleidoscope and I couldn't remember why. Now I can. I was dozing off down here on the sofa after we'd come back from Tavistock, and he came into the room. Father Bloody Thomas. And guess who he was holding by his hand. Timmy. And Timmy was sobbing his heart out. I told him to let Timmy go and when he said he wouldn't, I told him that he was a disgrace to the cloth. That was when he put out his hand and he chanted me.'

'What are we going to do now?' asked Katharine. 'Are we allowed to leave?'

'Are you joking?' said Rob. 'You'd have to nail my feet to the floor to keep me here. But there's just one thing.'

He went over to the fireplace and picked up the poker. He left the drawing room, crossed the hallway and mounted the stairs.

'Mr Russell?' called DI Holley, but Rob took no notice. He reached the landing and strode along the corridor to the stained-glass window of Old Dewey – or Esus, as he now knew him to be.

Gripping the poker in both hands, he smashed it into the black figure with its back turned. Then he smashed the hounds, one after the other, and the sky, and the trees, and the moorlands, until the window frame was empty.

When he returned to the drawing room, Ada looked up at him and she must have guessed what he had just done. She stood up, and came over, and took hold of his hand. She didn't have to say thank you – the expression in her eyes was enough.

She leaned close to him and whispered,
*'Thar be piskies up to Dartymoor
An' tidden gude yew zay there bain't.'*

41

Rob switched off his computer and sat back, lacing his hands behind his head.

'Is he asleep now?' he asked Vicky, as she came into the dining room.

'No, but he's very dozy. I read him that story about Chris Cross in Snappyland. He loves that.'

'Maybe we should learn how to hypnotise him.'

'Oh, don't say that. At least Doctor Ferris said that it hadn't affected him.'

'He doesn't seem to have too much of a memory of being stuck like that. All I can say is thank God for that.'

'I think we can thank God for a lot of things, Rob.'

Rob stood up and pushed in his chair. 'I just want to be shot of that house, that's all. DI Holley said it was going to be at least three weeks before they finish their forensic examination. He's keeping an open mind about what happened to Francis and Father Salter. At least he said he was.'

Vicky came up and rested her hands on his shoulders. 'It's all over, Rob. And it's all over because of you. You were so brave.'

Rob looked away to see his face reflected in his computer screen. He didn't want to think about Esus staring at him hatefully, upside down.

They left the dining room and went through to the living room. They were crossing the hall when they heard a high, piping noise from upstairs.

Rob stopped and said, 'What's that? Is that Timmy?'

They stood still and listened, and the piping went on – a thin, plaintive, repetitive tune, like a breeze whistling through bracken on the ridge of some desolate moor.

'That *can't* be Timmy,' said Vicky, but all the same she mounted the stairs and Rob followed her.

They eased open Timmy's bedroom door. He was sitting cross-legged on his bed in his Marvel pyjamas, in the dark. He was holding a stick-like instrument to his lips and playing it.

Rob switched on his light. 'Timmy – what are you doing? What's that you've got there?'

Timmy said nothing, but held it up so that Rob could see it.

It was a chicken-bone, which he had made into a flute.

Devon words interpreted

angletwitch – fidgety or disobedient child
brimmel – brambles
chrisemores – unbaptised babies
crocky down – crouch down
dawcock – stupid fool
dimpsey – dusk or twilight
dreckly – immediately or as soon as possible
dummon – 'dumb one' affectionate term for wife
gurt – big, but also 'very' as in 'gurt lush'
kiffy – left-handed
shag – friend or mate
raymes – skeleton

About the author

Graham Masterton is mainly recognized for his horror novels but he has also been a prolific writer of thrillers, disaster novels and historical epics, as well as one of the world's most influential series of sex instruction books. He became a newspaper reporter at the age of 17 and was appointed editor of *Penthouse* magazine at only 24. His first horror novel *The Manitou* was filmed with Tony Curtis playing the lead, and three of his short horror stories were filmed by Tony Scott for *The Hunger* TV series. Ten years ago Graham turned his hand to crime novels and *White Bones*, set in Ireland, was a Kindle phenomenon, selling over 100,000 copies in a month. This has been followed by ten more bestselling crime novels featuring Detective Superintendent Katie Maguire, the latest of which is *The Last Drop of Blood*. In 2019 Graham was given a Lifetime Achievement Award by the Horror Writers Association. The Prix Graham Masterton for the best horror fiction in French has been awarded annually for the past ten years, and four years ago he established an annual award for short stories written by inmates in Polish prisons, *Nagroda Grahama Mastertona "W Więzieniu Pisane."* He is currently working on new horror and crime novels.

Visit www.grahammasterton.co.uk.